BLACK RANDALL

Black Randall

JOANNE BRAITHWAITE

Jo Anne Braithwaite

Dedication: To John Randall

I call upon the last reserves of my imagination. I am standing outside a public toilet, a concrete block at the foot of Bethel Steps in Circular Quay, Sydney. I remove that building and the cruise ship terminal, and I plant a forest of giant trees in their place. I block out the noise of jack hammers and cars and hear instead cockatoos, screeching at each other and the intruders to their land. They are joined by kookaburras, and butcher birds, by magpies and crows and currawongs. I take a breath but don't smell exhaust fumes or the bacon from a nearby café. The clean smell of eucalypt trees fills my lungs. Harbour ferries scuttle across the bay like small green beetles. With a flick of the wand of my mind, they become a fleet of eleven wooden ships, some barely bigger than my living room. The sails are down. Their masts are bare. A young Asian girl jostles me. She apologises energetically. The twangs of an American. Two Chinese men in sombre dark suits and sombre dark attitudes break into a smile for the camera. I send them away. Governor Phillip paces around the bay. He holds a stick and draws a line in the sand, the perimeter of the new colony. No one may cross the line, he instructs. I wait. He comes at last. John Randall wades to land. He glances up. Does he see me? Standing next to the flagpole? The Union Jack, though not identical to the one we know today, flutters in the breeze. It is intended to tell us that this land now belongs to England. It is planted where the toilet now stands.

I nod at John, just in case. My hand reaches towards him. I wish I could hold his face.

Prologue

John trudged the rutted lane on reluctant legs, his body weak and barely recovered from its injuries. He would have preferred to stay in the hospital, on his trolley with the sheet pulled over his head, hiding from the world. Instead, he'd gone to re-join his regiment. His foot slipped on the scree and he fell to his knees. He paused, gathering his will before pulling himself to his feet and continuing the journey. A hot wind whipped grit into his face and he raised a hand to protect his eyes.

He found the sergeant on the parade ground, about to make an announcement. The soldiers huddled close, for the wind threatened to steal his words.

'John. John is back.' Rough men greeted him, fumbling for kindness. 'Yer lookin' grand, John.'

'Did they stretch you, up there at the hospital? You're taller than ever.'

'Listen up. I have news,' the sergeant interrupted. 'Talk to John later,' and he pulled the men to attention with an icy glare, though he did not meet John's eyes. 'York Town is gone.' Blank looks met his words. 'Cornwallis surrendered. The rebels have won the town,' he continued.

'There were 8,000 men stationed there.'

'What does this mean for us?'

'We're done for, is what it means.'

'The war is over then?'

'We're going home?'

'Nothing known for sure. But I wager we can't win. Not now. They'll be suing for peace to be sure.' The sergeant still failed to look at John. His glance lingered on the other men and in the spaces around him.

It was too early to celebrate. But on the beaten ground before the barracks in the rubble of a battered town, in the windy heat that made every breath an effort, and amid the stink of decay and the buzz of flies, tired soldiers stretched and shrugged and seemed to settle into more comfortable shapes, as though already retiring to their arm chairs at home. That place they called home across the sea.

Slouched against the trunk of a tree, all but lost in its shade, John called out. His words cut through their thoughts and they were surprised. His voice had changed. It no longer held the soft roundness of childhood. Nor the uncertain down of youth. Not even the muscle of a man. It prickled like a porcupine, sharp and protective of the soft belly hidden within. Nor had he thought to put on his smile. The life had fled from his eyes, leaving only smudges in the dull black of his face.

'What of the captured soldiers? Our men? What have they done with them?'

'Taken to camps. Exchanged.' The sergeant paused. 'Except for the blacks.' He took a long breath as if dragging in courage for his next words. 'Washington has demanded the return of all former slaves.'

'You promised us,' John said. 'You said that if we fought for you, we'd be free.'

The sergeant could not look at the man, a former slave. A ripple seemed to pass through the group, a barely perceived shuffling. In a circle of men, John stood alone. No, not alone, for his master seemed to stand before him, a sneer upon his face, eyes lit with triumph. He dangled a whip in one hand, a collar and shackles in the other. 'Got you now, Boy.'

Chapter One

North Stonington, Connecticut. 1769

A hand clasped Boy's, trapping him within its grip. A fledgling chick in a nest. Calloused skin against soft. Bony fingers wrapped around his own, guiding them into the earth.

'Like this,' Ol' Ma encouraged. 'Pull from the root. Else you're just making more work for yourself.'

They crawled in the furrows of the field, pulling weeds from around newly planted maize. One of them was too old, the other too young, to drive a plough or wield a hoe. The spring sun hung above the horizon and behind clouds, too timid to show itself. The soil held the cold and damp of winter and clung to his hands and knees and feet. And the breeze that ruffled his hair and blew up his shirt had also failed to note the change of season. The child crept forward, but a stone dug into his knee and he winced. His lower lip quivered.

'Can we rest soon?'

'A little longer.'

He tore his hand from her grasp, sat back on his haunches, and sucked at his fingers to warm them. His eyes followed the straight lines of young shoots. Their green spears marched like warriors in formation until they blurred into a single point and ran into a wall of trees. The forest surrounded them on all sides, making a prison of the farm.

Ma told him that Indians had lived there, and their gods lived there still. *Not powerful, not like the African ones. Else, why they go let the Indians die?*

Elijah worked down there at the edge of the forest, burning roots, clearing more land. Smoke billowed into the sky, mingling with the clouds, reflecting the fire in violent reds and purples, soft pinks, grey and mauve. He will return home tonight, black with soot, eyes red and swollen from the smoke, rubbing the small of his back with one hand. 'Stand on my back. Walk out the aches,' he will ask Boy and lie himself down on the dirt floor of the hut with a groan.

But Ol' Ma will shuffle him out the door with her broomstick, 'Not till the chile has eaten an' you has washed yerself.'

And though Elijah could pick up the old woman with one hand and toss her over his shoulder, he would do as he was told.

Boy's gaze sought his mother. She pushed a plough behind two cows at the far end of the field, close to Elijah. A smoky haze hid her lower body and to Boy's eye, it seemed she did not walk upon the earth. He dreaded the icy silence she would carry home with her tonight. She always complained about working in the kitchen, but sure as god is in his heaven, she didn't take to field work.

'Better not let the Master see you dreamin' your time away. He'll whip your hide.' Ol' Ma's voice broke into his thoughts.

Boy knew Master Randall wouldn't lash him. Master said it was an ungodly thing to do to ignorant savages.

But, the child reflected, *ain't ungodly to lock me in the shed all night, let me near freeze to death.* 'Why's I have to do this? Why can't I feed the chickens?' he whined, kneeling back to his task. The mistress had given him a chick of his own. He had grown real big. Hand-fed Beaker followed him around the yard as Boy swept, pecking at his toes, attacking the twigs of the broom.

'Master says you're a big boy now. Gotta earn your feed.'

Boy paused, digesting the idea. The child dreamed of the day he was growed and a warrior like his father. He would fight Indians and kill bears. And when he came home at night his mother would smile and tell him he was a brave boy.

'Master says you've been spoilt too long, getting too big for ya britches.'

Ol' Ma rarely made mistakes with him, but at this, his little body tensed, and he turned to her, hands on hips and bottom lip out. She hustled to recover the advantage. 'Master says, if it be true you're the son of warriors, then you're strong enough now.'

'When did I start wheedling the boy,' Ol' Ma wondered. 'I ain't doing him no favours, building him up like this. He sure get to thinking he's above his station.'

She yanked at a stubborn root. *Should give the little whelp a hiding. Thinks his six years on this earth gives him all the answers. Talk back to Our Blessed Jesus he would.* She glanced over at him. He wore a sulk upon his face but kept pace with her.

Ah, my little mite. She moved to tousle his head, but he jerked away. She shook her head and smiled.

'Stop laughing at me. I'm not funny.'

He can huff all he likes but I know by tonight, he'll have forgotten, and he'll heat up the water and rub my feet till I think I died and gone to heaven. Sure as I don't know where that boy got all his loving from.

She gave him a sideways glance. He held up a hand. An ant had left an angry swelling and he rubbed it dramatically, moaning loudly but avoiding her gaze.

The injured warrior.

The truth is, Ol' Ma had sworn never again to smack a black child, not if her life depended. Thirty, maybe forty years ago, she had clouted her own two boys. A smack on the mouth for a word badly spoken. A tap to the head for a sullen look. Then she saw how others in this world did the job more thoroughly than she could. She had been in the south then. They sold her youngest – 'Buck: 200 pounds' – but he was her baby, just fourteen. She watched him stumbling behind a cart, his wrists bound, twisting to catch a last sight of her. She watched till he was gone. Then she had watched her eldest, a humble boy of not yet 16 years, strung up by his feet to a tree and left to hang. It took him three days to die. She had kneeled on the ground below him, holding his gaze for every second. She poured so much love into him she thought she'd be all dried up and have no more for anyone else. The master and the mistress strolled by to observe the progress of his death. Then they sold her. She thought it a blessing to arrive in the north.

¬

Boy and Ol' Ma pulled weeds together all morning. The sun climbed higher. The furrows slipped away beneath their knees. Their sacks filled with weeds. They emptied them on a growing pile at the far end of the field. Back and forth.

'You want to sing some?' she asked. 'Pass the time?'

He shook his head. 'You got a voice like a coon.' But he looked sideways at her and giggled at the face she made.

She laughed. 'I sees a flower this morning. You're still snoring away in the hut. But this flower. Prettiest thing you ever did see, peeping up from the slush. First of the season, I reckon. Covered in dew. It sparkled like it were wearing jewels. Diamonds, maybe. I put it in my box.' She picked up a pebble, wiped it clean with her spit and held it to the sun. 'This is pretty, ain't it?'

'What box? You ain't got no box. I knows what you got and you ain't got no box.'

'I got a box. A memory box. Put all the things that make me happy in that box. Take them out when I'm down and need cheering.'

'What's in your box?' He picked up a stone, held it to the light and tossed it aside.

'So many things. You in my box. When you asleep. Not when you awake and giving cheek.'

He laughed at that.

'Tell me a story.'

'Did I tell you the one about the chief and his best friend? They were close alright. Couldn't tear them apart. The best friend, his name was Adisa. He had this habit, see. Anything that happened, didn't matter what it was, he would say, "That is good." Then one day, they's out fighting, in a big war, and the chief loses his thumb. Cut right off! "Well," says the friend, "that is good." This makes the chief real mad, and he sends Adisa away. "Don't ever come back," says the chief. Well, the months go by. The chief, he out hunting and gets caught by another tribe. Those fellas, they were gonna eat the chief. Have him for supper.'

'Nooool' Boy interrupted. 'You can't eat people!'

'This is my story and they were going to eat the chief. Anyway, just before they stuck him in the frypan, they see the chief's thumb was missing. "Can't eat this fella," they says, "he ain't pure." And they let the chief free. *Well*, thinks the chief, *Sure is a good thing I lost my thumb*. And he feels real sorry for sending away his friend and goes looking for him.'

'Does he find him?' Boy had stopped picking weeds.

'You get back to weeding and I might tell you. Yes. And you know what the friend says?'

Boy shook his head.

'He says, "Well, that is good. Sure is a good thing you sent me away." The chief was mighty puzzled about that. He couldn't think why it was a good thing. Nope, not at all. Can you?'

Boy shrugged.

'See. Thing is. That friend not been sent away, he would have been with the chief when he was captured. And he would be the one cooked up and fried in a pan.'

They continued working. They filled their sacks again. They emptied them again. The pile at the far end of the field grew bigger.

When Ol' Ma felt sure that the master was sitting at table, enjoying a glass of wine, some cold ham and apples maybe, or the beef pie she had seen cooling on the windowsill, she sent Boy off to Elijah, to rest and nibble on the corn cobs she had boiled for their lunch.

Beaker clucked, pecking in dirt for the grain Boy dropped. Ol' Ma had told the child to sweep the yard. And he would. In a moment. But Beaker had found him and demanded attention. The sun caught in her feathers; glistening russet and orange fell like a cloak over her green chest. *I will put you in MY box*, Boy decided. If Ol' Ma could keep a box, he would too. And his box would have MORE beautiful things in it. He crouched to pick up the chicken, nestling her to his chest and under his cheek. She stretched her head to the side that he might scratch under her chin.

I could eat you up, you are so beautiful. He buried his face in her soft down. *You even smell nice. I would never eat you.*

She complained, fluttering her wings, before settling down with her head on his shoulder. He stood, nursing her like a baby, his fingers fondling her soft underbelly, her body warm against his in the chill morning.

'Boy!' The lad's head shot up. The master stood over him. In the early light, his shadow stretched the length of the yard.

Boy stared. His throat restricted as if it would say something, but words wouldn't come. He clutched Beaker tighter, earning a squawk for his efforts.

'Fetch a chicken to your mother. We need it for lunch.' The master looked at Boy as if for the first time. 'What are you doing with that one? It will do.' He turned toward the house.

'Master, sir. This one here's mine. The mistress...' He dropped Beaker to the ground. The bird poked in the dirt around Boy's feet, ignoring the kicks that urged it to run.

The master spun on his heels. He towered above Boy, blocking the light. The child could not see the expression on the man's face. He stared up, frozen, unable to breathe. He would like to say he would get another one ... there were lots of other chickens. But his tongue refused to move. Only his heart pumped, ready to burst.

No sounds came from the house, or the barn, or the slave hut yonder. Even Beaker had ceased her pecking and looked up at them, black eyes alert.

The master broke the moment. He bent. He lifted the bird. He twisted its neck. He thrust the chicken into Boy's arms. 'Take it to your mother.'

Ol' Ma startled when the boy stumbled through the door and into the hut. He ignored her questions. Instead he fell upon his bedding. He lay curled tight, and he rocked. Back and forth. She picked him up and held him in her arms, holding him as close to her heart as she could, willing him to cry. He didn't. He held his pain tight. He stared into the distance, beyond the hut. Only when his mother returned did the old woman find out what had happened.

'Remember Adisa, Boy. It is good. It is all good.'

He turned towards her. His chin jutted forward. Eyes wild. Fists clenched. He threw himself at her, pummelling her as hard as his six-year-old strength would allow.

'It is NOT good! It is not, you stupid old woman.'

Chapter Two

His body ached, and he threw back his head and shoulders to ease it, earning a pinch from Ol' Ma. She sat squeezed next to him on the narrow wooden bench in the rear of the church. He glared and jerked his hand from her grasp. His bum ached too, and he glanced toward the door. *How long before this is over?* It was the first week of summer and he wore new clothes. Ol' Ma had tied a rope around his waist to stop the trousers from falling. Then she had taken the sleeves of his shirt, folding and folding them back above his wrists, releasing his hands again. 'You'll grow into them,' she had promised.

The coarse material scratched his skin, but he raised his arm to bury his nose in their clean smell. He bent over to see if the trousers also smelt new. Ol' Ma pinched him again.

He looked around for somewhere to settle his thoughts. He couldn't understand why the Lord Jesus Our Almighty Saviour lived here. The black walls and low ceiling of the church smothered the light. The shutters had been thrown open and fingers of sunshine descended through them into the darkness. They lingered on the shoulders of some in glorious blessing. They threw others into deeper shadow. He counted the rows of light and dark. One, two. Good, bad. Happy, sad.

He sat beyond the light from the shutters.

Next to him, his mother held her hands folded on her lap. She didn't flow into his space like Ol' Ma but kept a distance between them. Nor did she fidget like those around her. She held her head high and still. She did not look like him, with her almond eyes – half closed – high cheek bones and a long straight nose.

She is so beautiful. He thought of her as an eagle, soaring the skies. But never coming to ground. Ol' Ma said that eagles throw their young from their nests and hope they learn to fly before they hit the ground. He inched his fingers towards her, so slowly she might not notice he slid them into her lap. She didn't wrap hers around his. She didn't pull away. His fingers sat upon hers until he retrieved them.

He caught sight of his friend Calvin scratching at lice so hard he might scour the hair right off his head. Calvin was like that. After church when the adults caught up with the gossip, he and Calvin would chase each other around the grounds. Though smaller and slighter, Calvin could outrun Boy, turning to taunt and pull a face. But Boy didn't give up. He would tackle him, sit on him and make him plead for mercy. Suddenly aware of his own itchy scalp, Boy dug in his nails and rubbed.

Calvin turned and grinned. Boy pulled a face to make him laugh and get in trouble. He did laugh, and his mother growled at him. Boy snorted and received another pinch.

With a sigh, he shuffled around on the bench and counted the scabs on his feet. The thunderous voice of the Reverend Mitchel interrupted him. The preacher stood at the front of the church, his black suit disappearing into the wall behind him. Only his face and hands, blessed by a ray of light from the shutters, gleamed white. To Boy's eyes, they floated like the Holy Ghost. The child squinted through the darkness, waiting for the man to move. He and Calvin had decided that he must have a stone in his shoe, he was so aggravated with the world. But they had studied his every step and never seen him limp. Boy watched now as the preacher threw his arms around, thumping the pulpit. Thwack! Then he paused. With a gesture, the reverend pulled the congregation towards him, holding them still and quiet, like small and timid birds. Boy held his breath and gripped the bench he sat upon, lest he be sucked off his perch and into those arms. That man knew who sinned against the Lord Jesus Our Almighty Saviour. He would know if a boy cursed his master or dreamt of hitting him with a stick. Boy slunk lower on the bench in the shadows.

Peering between the bodies in front of him, he saw the preacher step forward into the light and stand with his arm raised, like an avenging angel come out of the darkness. 'We must stand as one! We will demand our freedom. We will not bend beneath the yoke of British injustice.'

Boy mouthed the words along with the preacher. He heard them every week.

After the service, while the white folks ate sandwiches and argued about the king and parliament, and the black folks passed the secrets of one farm to another, two small warriors hunted for Indians and bears in the woods behind the church.

'Hey, lookie here!' Boy stood up, a fledgling bird in his hand, no more than a pile of bones and loose skin and a squawking red beak.

'Is it sick?'

'Dunno, Ol' Ma will know.' He stroked its complaining mouth and muttered in its ear, 'Don't worry. I'll care for you. You'll make it.' He held it up and looked directly into its eyes. 'You are going to fly! To be free!'

With the bird cupped in his hands and held close to his chest, Boy went in search of Ol' Ma.

Folks were shaking hands and waving farewells, and some had started on the long walk home.

'Ol' Ma?' Boy found his mother.

She jerked her head toward the lane way. 'Gone on ahead. What you got there in your hands?'

He stepped back out of reach, but opened his palms, barely enough for a red beak to poke out.

'Get rid of it.'

'It ain't got no mama. I have to look after it.'

'You're too soft.' She gave it another glance. 'Bad things happen when you love too much. It's gonna die. Get rid of it.'

Focused on the treasure clasped to his heart, Boy did not see the master approach. He sensed his mother stiffen.

'Laisa. You're to go to the Wheelers. They are moving to Boston and have need of a girl.' He frowned. 'And wipe that look from your face.'

For Boy, the world stalled. The hum of conversation stopped and a great roar filled his head. The forests, the church, the people blurred as if in a storm. He saw only his mother, who stood still, impervious as a statue to the winds that raged around her. 'My son?' she asked.

'He stays. You'll have your hands full with their new babe.'

For the briefest moment Boy thought that he felt her hand graze his head. Then she turned to leave.

'Nooo!' He threw himself at her, scrabbling at her skirts, dragging in the dirt as she moved away. He grabbed her ankle, near causing her to trip, but the master caught him by the shoulders and threw him back. She did not slow her step or turn toward him.

Boy sprawled in the church grounds, his arm still stretched out to the place his mother had been. His throat ached from unspoken screams and his heart beat so fast he thought it might burst right out of his chest. He couldn't get up. The fledgling chick lay dead beside him, dropped and trampled.

'Miserable cub. Should sell you south before your mother comes back.' The master turned away.

It was the Mistress Randall who found him. She detached herself from a group of chattering women wrapped in shawls and big bonnets and strolled over. Boy loved this daughter of the household with her pretty face and happy smile and her big, embroidered bag which held a mystery of things. But now, he could only watch wordlessly as she crouched down.

'My goodness, Boy, don't take it so hard. You know how the master is. He could not live without his Laisa. He hasn't sold her. Your mother will be back.' She pulled a boiled lolly from her bag. 'Now, give me a big smile and get yourself up.' The words echoed as if down a funnel and did not lodge in his brain. But she pulled at his arm and he grasped what she wanted.

Each limb required a conscious effort to move. They weighed too heavy for his six -year -old body, but he dragged himself to his knees, arranged his face into the form she required and found himself clasping a lolly. He regarded it, before letting it fall from his hand.

Ol' Ma and Boy sat together on the steps of the cabin. She held him close to her and stroked his head while he explained to her that he couldn't love her anymore.

'Bad things happen when you love too much,' he repeated the words his mother had said. 'I loved the little bird. An' I killed it.' He looked earnestly into Ol' Ma's eyes. 'I don't wanna kill you.'

'I ain't goin' nowhere. And you ain't gonna stop loving me. Oh, my boy. Don't you know that your lovin' is the best of you?'

The wind had picked up and it howled through the forest. They could hear the hiss and crackle of their evening fire, burning down for the night. Clouds hid the moon.

'Ol' Ma?'

She cocked her head, eyebrows raised.

'When the white folks are free from the yoke of injustice,' he articulated those last words with care, 'we gonna be free too?'

Ol' Ma drew in a breath and took her time to answer. Only the clenching and unclenching of her fist betrayed her. Boy waited.

'I can't tell you that, Boy. I jes' don't know. But I can tell you this. Freedom's a funny thing. Some folk, they free to roam the world and cross the seven seas but they still wear chains.' She placed a finger to his heart. 'But no one can own this.' She placed a finger to his head. 'Or this, lest you let 'em.'

Chapter Three

January 1770

'Why won't you help?' Boy turned to his mother, his face tear stained.

He didn't expect an answer. She had tired of his pleas and accusations. 'Just sit with her. There is naught else. The fever will decide,' she had said earlier.

She squatted by the fire, poking at the embers, but the wood had burned itself out and her jabs failed to taunt them back to life. Though she had returned from Boston, she seemed more distant than ever before. He could barely see her, a shadow in the glow from the ashes.

The shutters had been secured against the storm that had raged all week. They rattled in their struts while the wind shrieked through gaps in the planking of the wall. Boy wondered how the shack could withstand the beating. Maybe the storm would blow them all away. Outside, snow whipped against the building so that drifts banked against the door. Inside, no one slept. They sat in heavy, smoky, thunderous darkness.

Boy hunkered on the lumpy hessian mattress he shared with Ol' Ma. He folded a sweat-soaked rag, seeking a dry patch, and wiped the old woman's forehead. He pushed a lock of hair from her eyes. They quivered but did not open. Though his own fingers felt stiff and numb with cold, she burned to his touch. She heaved herself up. A cough rattled from deep in her chest, shaking her so hard he thought she might break free of the body that held her to this earth. Then she slumped back onto the bedding.

Like a broken baby bird. He shuddered at the memory of the fledgling.

He tried to feed gruel to Ol' Ma, forcing the spoon between her lips, but it dribbled uselessly down her chin. Not knowing what else to do with his hands, he once again smoothed the thin blanket around her chest. Straw had spilled from a torn seam in the wadding and scattered on the dirt floor of the cabin. He gathered it and pushed it back, but it escaped again. With a sigh, he lay down, wrapping his own thin little arms around the old woman. He could feel her heartbeat, fluttering like the wings of a dying moth.

'You're strong, Ol' Ma. You can make it.' He squeezed her tight. 'I won't let you go.' Then, so only she could hear, 'Please don't leave me.' He glanced in the direction of his mother.

With his head buried against Ol' Ma's chest, the raspy crackle of her breathing filled his ears, louder and more frightening than any storm.

He didn't hear it at first, a rippling of soft chords that ventured across the hut. Amid the whistling and rattling of the room, the notes sought him out. Gentle as they were, they pressed back the terrors that gripped him. Elijah offered his solace. Elijah with the aching back and gentle eyes who talked to people with his music and to animals with his hands.

'He has magic in his hands,' Boy had told Ol' Ma. He had seen those hands calm a frightened horse. And when they held a flute, they put stars in a dark sky. They brought courage to a little boy.

'Mayhap we should go get Mistress Randall?' he asked. Again.

'She'll not come out in the dark. Not in this weather.'

'But Ol' Ma – She may –' The words choked him.

'Mistress Randall won't care. Ma is no use to them. She's old.'

Sobs escaped through his fingers.

¬

Dim light poked through the slits of the shutters. Boy forced open eyes swollen from crying and tiredness, watching as dark forms crept into light and took on their familiar, more comfortable shapes. Ol' Ma still breathed beside him.

Elijah rose, stamping his feet on the floor. Boy heard the tread of his boots as he crossed the room, knelt to cover them with his blanket and then stooped to take hold of Ol' Ma's hands and put them to his lips. He listened as the man threw his body against the door. It didn't budge the first time. On the third try, he cracked it open enough to squeeze out. The wind sliced in, biting at hands and faces. Boy squashed closer to Ol' Ma, protecting her. He heard the scraping of the spade as Elijah scooped snow and cleared the path and finally left to hazard the track to the stables.

In the gloom, his mother fumbled with her shawl, wrapping it around her head and shoulders.

'You need to raise yourself. Master will expect you to clear his path.'

She heaved against the door and left. He pictured her racing to the house, head bowed into the wind, clutching the faded red shawl to her body. At the big house she would light the fire and heat the water and bake the bread for the master and mistress before they woke, as she did every day.

'I have to leave you, Ol' Ma,' Boy whispered. 'I'll get the mistress for you. She'll make you better.' He bent and kissed the old woman's cheek. 'Promise me you'll stay here.' He walked toward the door, turning back before he left, 'On your oath.'

¬

Mistress Randall stayed inside the walls of the big house. Boy cleared snow from the veranda and the path to the front door, raising a sweat that chilled him to the bone once he stopped. He fed the chickens, his fingers red and numb in their cut-off gloves so that they spilled the grain. He looked for what else he could do to keep watch over the house. The mistress must notice him sometime. He saw his mother open the kitchen door and rushed to help her carry wood.

'Why won't you ask the mistress to fix Ol' Ma?'

'There's naught they can do. Go help Elijah in the stables. It's warm there.'

Why don't you tell her!

He stared at the door, as if by the force of will alone he could make the mistress appear. The door remained shut.

Elijah made his way down the path, hauling wood to the shack. As a thin line of smoke curled out through the chimney, Boy pulled his jacket tighter and smacked his frozen hands together and thought of the relief a fire would bring. He waited.

He stamped his feet and jammed his hands under his armpits and hummed songs, the words leaving his mouth in puffs of smoke. He waited.

So hard was he staring at the door that he did not see the horse trot up the carriageway until it was nearly upon him. Master Wade, the youngest, and, to Boy's mind, the best of the Hewitt boys dismounted.

'Why are you standing there, boy? Go find refuge.' Wade fumbled at a package bound to his saddle. 'But first'—he turned his smile on Boy, tousling his hair— 'be a good man and stable my horse.'

Boy took the reins and made to tell him about Ol' Ma, but the door opened and received Wade before he could respond. He hastened to the barn before returning to his vigil. Within minutes Master Randall strode out, holding the parcel.

'Boy, take this to Elijah. A blanket for Zeus, straight from New London. Tell Elijah to make speed and put it upon him. It's damnably cold in those stables.'

'Master. Master Randall. Ol' Ma is sick.' The words stumbled over each other.

The man shrugged. 'She's old.'

'But – some tonic, Master?'

'God's oath, Boy. Just do what you are told!'

Boy was left staring at the empty wooden porch, swept and mopped by Ma every day that he could remember. The door still flaunted a Christmas bouquet, tired and sad with its withered blooms and faded red ribbons.

He struggled with the heavy blanket, not to the stables but to the quarters. The wrapping had torn open and was only loosely retied. The blanket came alive in his arms, unfolding and wrapping itself around his legs, tripping him as he went. He fell through the door, spilling it to the floor. It brought the blue of summer skies into the hut. He lifted it and wrapped it around himself. The smell of sheep lingered in the wool. His frozen, shaken limbs relaxed, and his heartbeat slowed.

'It's for you, Ol' Ma.'

Chapter Four

With Ol' Ma warm, Boy went to help Elijah in the stables, but the animals had been fed and the stalls cleaned, leaving no work to do. Boy climbed the gate to peer into Zeus's stall.

'I'm sorry, ol' fella. I hope you're not cold. But Ol' Ma needs that blanket more than you just now. I'll bring it back.'

Elijah pulled out his flute. Boy nestled into his lap and the man put his arms around him, guiding the child's fingers along the smooth wood to make a tune. His whiskers scratched Boy's face and his breath smelt of warm tea. He sat back allowing Boy's fingers to find the rhythm on their own, nodding approval at the tune they stumbled upon.

'Elijah!' A gust of cold air and the creaking of the barn door interrupted them. Master Randall stood aside to allow the mistress to enter, before striding into the barn.

'How does Zeus like his blanket?'

Boy jumped up, spinning around. Elijah looked at him. A frown slid across his face. He rested his arms on the boy's shoulders.

Master Randall peered over the stall at the naked horse.

'Where's the blanket I sent?'

'Master?' Boy had not told Elijah of the blanket.

'The blanket.' The master turned his attention to Boy. 'What did you do with it?' The child stared at his feet. His right foot jigged.

Elijah's fingers tightened on his shoulder as the Master moved towards the boy. He raised his arm.

'You little thief! You miserable cub.'

Boy's legs wouldn't move. He stared at the figure towering above him. Time slowed and he cringed at the raging eyes, the spittle that flew from the lips. When the blow fell, it threw him from Elijah's grasp and off his feet and he flew backwards, smashing against the wooden gate of Zeus's stall before tumbling to the ground. He floundered there, struggling to make sense of the spinning room. From a long way away, he could hear the mistress.

'Papa, he's just a child.'

Boy's fingers grasped a handful of straw, something solid to steady the world. He tried to crawl to his knees.

'A child who'll be a man.' Boy heard a gasp as the master thrust his sobbing daughter away from him. He cried out as the kick landed, knocking him flat again. He lay in the straw. All strength flown from his limbs. His leg pounded where the blow had landed, but he didn't have the strength to rub it. Blood from a wound to his brow dripped into his eyes. He thought he should wipe it away, but his arm wouldn't work. He felt more than saw the man hovering above him.

'Please, Papa. Please.' He had never heard the mistress cry. Her skirts brushed his face. *She'll get blood on her gown.*

She must have placed herself between him and her father for he could see nothing but her white petticoats and the blue overskirt. *The same blue as the blanket.*

The master's voice came from a long way off. He had moved towards the door. Slow, clear words. 'Elijah! Lock him in the woodshed.'

'Papa, please. He'll freeze.'

'Your soft heart does him no favours. Upon my word you will see him hanging by a noose from a tree. Discipline is kindness to a lad like him.'

'I'm sorry, Boy.' Elijah shoved the door shut.

Boy heard the latch fall and listened to the crunching of snow as Elijah left him in darkness. With his hands stretched before him he felt along the side of the wall, looking for some sacking or someplace to sit. But the familiar shed had become a different place. Unknown beings scuttled between the logs of the woodpile. A web brushed his face and he screamed as he stumbled over a bucket and fell to the ground. There he sat, arms wrapped around his chest, whimpering.

'Ol' Ma. Ol' Ma.'

He sat like that until the notes of Elijah's flute found him and the icy dampness of the floor forced him to his feet. His arms felt too heavy and cold to move and he wanted only to lie down. He would close his eyes and imagine Ol' Ma beside him, telling her stories, her voice hoarse in his ear and her hands gentle on his cheek. He pulled down some blocks of wood to build a pallet, wincing as a splinter pierced his skin. But his bruised back and legs complained at the hard bed and his mind held too many horrors. Hadn't Calvin told him just last week how a rat had nibbled at a baby's eyes, and eaten its fingers and toes? In the end, he resigned himself to trudging the length of the shed. Around and around, until his head swam, and his eyelids drooped; he moved as in a dream.

He did not hear the small boy enter. Did not see him until he near tripped over him. Boy fell back, pushing himself against the walls of the shed.

'Oh dearie, dearie me!' The newcomer waved his arm around the prison. He snorted, as if trying not to laugh. 'What a fine mess you are in.'

Despite the cold, he wore only shorts, striped in black and red and around his neck hung a necklace, beaded black and red. His skin was black, and his hair fell in tight curls around his face.

Boy knew his name. He recognised him from the stories Old Ma had told him. He pushed back into the wall of the shed, the planks rough and cold against his back.

'You are Elegua?'

Elegua started a small bow but could not help himself, and launched neatly into a somersault, before landing in splits on the ground. He grinned.

'Clever, huh?'

'You're the god of mischief!'

'And decisions. Some call me the Lord of the Crossroads.' He fingered his beads. Boy knew them for what they were. Life and death, beginnings and ends, good and evil.

'You made me take that blanket!' Boy's fingers had curled into fists. His misery glad of a target.

'Oh no! No! You can't blame that on me. That was all your doing. Though indeed I did find it amusing.' Elegua beamed.

'Why are you here?' Boy feared the mischief maker. His appearance meant the start of a journey and one could not tell where it might end.

'I have come to tell you a story. You will like that, won't you?' He did not wait for an answer. 'Do you know the story of Yizum and Nkinki?'

Boy did. Old Ma had told him the story of the two mice.

'Nkinki and Yizum were the best of friends,' Elegua started, but stopped as he spied a mouse, scampering in the corner. He seized it by the tail, dangled it in Boy's face, laughed and tossed it away. 'Nkinki lived in a village, a big village, much bigger than here.' He looked around, with the smallest of sneers, as if they sat in the church square of Stonington. 'Yizum lived in a field. You work in a field, don't you? A friend of yours perhaps?'

Boy scowled, not caring to be likened to a mouse.

'One day, Yizum invited Nkinki to his home for a meal. Oh Lordie, he worked hard that day. He sought out the best of seeds, he collected roots, he found fruit and beans and he laid out a fine feast before his friend.'

With a sweep of his hand, a feast appeared on the hard ground of the shed. He gestured to Boy who lunged at the food, grabbing handfuls of seeds and nuts and thrusting them in his mouth.

'But Nkinki was not impressed. Indeed, I would almost say he was quite rude. For he said to Yizum, "Is this all you have? You must come to my home, and I will show you what we eat in my village." So, the next evening the two friends travelled to the village where Nkinki lived. And Yizum gazed around in wonder. Food lay on the ground wherever he looked. Mush and meat, corn and yams and fruit like you never have seen. And Yizum thought, with a twitch of his whiskers and a blink of bright eyes, that maybe Nkinki was right, and he should consider moving to the village. But as the thought formed in his mind, Nkinki screamed, "Run, Yizum, run!" And Yizum did. He ran till he thought his feet would fall off and his lungs would burst but still the cat followed him and he ran around corners, across roads and up pipes and the cat followed him still until finally, he saw a hole and dived down into it. He lay there panting. Well, he thought, if it is a choice between these dangers and my safe and simple life, I know what I choose. Elegua finished. His eyes danced, and Boy thought he might leap into another somersault.

'Yes,' he fiddled with his beads. 'I do believe you are at a crossroad. A very important point in your life. Who will you be? Yizum or Nkinki? One day you must choose.'

'I'm not a mouse!' But his voice came out high and squeaky sending a blush to his face and doubling Elegua into a fit of laughing.

'Oh? Then what?'

'A warrior. I'm going to be a warrior.'

'Ah, a warrior who works the fields and says, "Yes, Massah?"'

'I will not say that. He'll not tell me what to do! I'll tell him what to do. Everyone will do what I tell them.'

'Ah, indeed? I will watch with interest. Now, some more seeds before I go?'

That night, soothed by the soft sounds of Elijah's flute, Boy pondered on the story of Yizum and Nkinki.

I will leave here. And no one will tell me what to do. I'll be the master.

Outside a mantle of snow lay on the ground, hiding its secrets and its seeds.

⌐

He slept wedged between the wall and the wood pile, his head resting on his arm. He didn't hear the crunch of Elijah's steps in the snow or the scraping of the latch. He woke only when Elijah picked him up and cradled him in his arms.

They did not talk much on the trail back to the quarters. Boy clung to Elijah, his head buried in the man's chest, comforted by the smells of sweat and smoke and hay. When Boy raised his head to ask about Ol' Ma, Elijah replied, 'It's too early yet. But her fever is passed.'

Boy moved to snuggle back again, then paused. 'Thank you for the music.'

When Elijah kicked the door open and carried him to the bed where Ol' Ma lay, Boy could see little more than a pair of bright eyes peering at him from under the blanket. He threw himself against her, unable to stop the sobs. A scrawny hand reached out to tousle his hair and pinch his cheek.

'Why would you do such a foolish thing? You dear, loving child. Don't ever do something like that again. Oh, my blessed Boy.'

Chapter Five

'I will not love her!' Boy told Ol' Ma one night. Since his beating, he had avoided the Mistress. Her eyes - so full of pity - shamed him for reasons he could not understand.

Ol' Ma lay propped against the wall. Boy crouched beside her, spooning gruel into her mouth.

'You don't have to. But don't keep your smiles from her. You'll need them back one day. Here, I can do that.'

He dodged her efforts to take the bowl.

'You'll spill it. Your fingers are too wobbly.'

When she pushed the bowl away, refusing another mouthful, he ran his tongue around the sides to catch what was left, then nestled down with his head in her lap. Her bony fingers scratched through his hair, picking at lice. He heard her grunt of satisfaction as she pierced one with her nail and bit it between her teeth. Elijah and his mother sat on the front steps, enjoying the light of a full moon. The notes of Elijah's flute drifted through the evening.

'Is Elijah my father?' The question popped out more abruptly than he intended.

The fingers stopped their hunt.

'No! No, Boy, no! Such a notion! Foolish chil'l'

'Then who? Who is my father?'

Boy looked sideways up at her, his one eye studying her reaction. She opened her mouth as if to speak but shut it again. He knew the stubborn old woman would not be pushed, so he held his breath and pretended an interest in the threads of his shirt.

'Oh Boy. My sweet chil'.' He tensed, kept every muscle still, less he distract her. Any movement might frighten her off and she would change the subject and launch into some story about Africa he had heard a thousand times. She did that when she wanted to avoid a question. Her hands stroked his head as she wandered about in her thoughts.

Talk to me, Ol' Ma. Tell me.

She bent to kiss his forehead.

'Your mother weren't always like the way she is now. Oh, my lordie, that gal had fire. And she had a laugh and a swish in her tail that could set a body spinning. Ooh, and that mouth? That mouth could give sass. And she weren't afraid of the master. No, she had him tied right tight around her finger. Sometimes I even went to thinking he loved her but was too proper a gentleman to take 'vantage. It was just after the passin' of his wife, and he sure were lonely.'

Boy didn't move. He struggled to settle her words into his picture of his mother, but it was two different people he saw.

'And then came this boy. Jordan were his name, like the river that freed the slaves. And he was a free man. Had papers and everything. He born free. His daddy before him been made free and worked as a carpenter. They say his daddy were good at his work, but Jordan were the better. I would watch him. He sit and study an old piece of wood, just any old log, and lo, with a whish and a chip, it would be a horse or a chicken or a duck and you could all but hear it quack. The master git him come over and work on the barn. It falling down and need fixing. Mind you, it were an insult to his talents, just repairing an ol' barn. But if you look, you'll see. Every piece of wood planed smooth and fit tight. And your mam? Well, she set her sights on him and that poor boy was lost. I watched them once, she teasing him, "That barn sure is taking its time to git built."

He blushed so much, I thought he might catch fire. "Well," he says, "I am somewhat distracted." "Indeed, you are," your mam said, "and by the look in your eyes, you are no gentleman." Aw, that girl had sass alright. Poor Jordan. He were no match for her. "Maybe were you to take yourself off to someplace else, I might get to my work," he said to her. "Maybe," she said, "or maybe you just lay yourself down pining."'

Lying in the dark, with his head on Ol' Ma's lap, Boy ached to see it for himself. His mother. Happy.

'Was she beautiful?'

'Most beautiful girl I ever knowed. She lit by something deep inside. She glowed. Oh, I watched those two,' Ma continued, 'And over the weeks and the months, I could see them gettin' right close. Your mam used to sneak out at nights, go meet him I know not where. But she met him alright. I'm sure of that. One night she could not keep herself still. Jiggering all over the place like a rat in the woodpile. "What is it?" I asked. "Keep yourself steady, gal." Your mam was meant to be skinning a rabbit. Jordan had brought it for our meal. "Sha girl," I said to her, "You waiting for that rabbit to cook itself?" And your mam, she turned to me. "Ma, he is going to buy me. I'm going to be a free woman. Ma, we going away and build us a home by a river, far away where no one knows us. And we will have a son." I will never forget the look in her eyes, so full of love and joy. "Our son will be a free man. He gonna run through the forests and swim in the lake. And he'll shape wood, like his pa, crafting things to his will." She stopped and looked at me full in the eyes. "And he know that his life is his to shape for himself."

'Oh, your mother. She never looked so beautiful,' said Ol' Ma. 'And I realised then that she was already with child. With you. When that barn was finished, we thought Jordan was good to his word. We watched him climb those steps to the big house. We watched as he came out again. He were meant to meet your mother that night.' Ol' Ma paused, shaking her head, the pain of it still true. 'He never came. He didn't come that night nor the one after. Every night your mother waited. She waited for a week, and then a month. And I watched the light go from her eyes. I think she still waiting.' Ol' Ma shook her head. Her voice had sunk low and Boy thought she might not go on.

'When you born,' she continued, 'she carry on like a panicked deer. "I can't protect him," she told me.'

Boy could feel Ol' Ma shaking her head. He thought she had finished. But she surprised him.

'You see that trinket your mam wears?'

He nodded. A carving of a bird in flight hung from his mother's neck on a loop of leather. He had fondled it since he was a baby, teethed on it, gripped it in infant fists. Sometimes, he thought he could feel the air in its wings, could feel it soar, wild and free.

'It came to here in a package for her. Jordan's father brought it. He said it had come, hand from hand all the way from down south. Made there by a slave and smuggled out with the prayer that it find her. He was a broken man, that man was. He held on to that package like it were his child but handed it to her nonetheless.'

'Jordan?'

Ma nodded. 'So's we suspect.'

'How can that be?'

She sighed. 'Traders hereabouts round that time. Saw the master talkin' to them. They don't worry about no papers. A black man's a black man.'

She stopped. Sometime later she mumbled to herself, 'Could be just a co-incidence.'

'Is he still alive?'

She shrugged.

'I'll find him.' And Boy wondered what it would be like to feel the arms of a father around him. And his mother would smile again. And then the three of them – five of them, for Ol' Ma and Elijah would come too – would go and find that place where he could run in the forest and swim in the river.

Chapter Six

December 1773

Boy perched on the bench at the front of the wagon, making every effort to replicate the solemn expression Elijah wore, but an unruly grin ruined the effect.

He had never been permitted to drive the mistress into Stonington. Alone. But the master had needed to go into town ahead of them, and Elijah had to help with a pregnant cow. And the mistress had begged her father until he'd agreed, although with little grace and a stern warning to the child to go carefully. Now Boy held the reins and had charge of the carriage.

'My, you look as proud as the king of England.' The mistress laughed.

He gave the reins a click. Snake-like sinews of leather, dark with age and supple with wear, rested between his hands. He controlled Zeus through them. He pulled himself higher in his seat and clicked the reins again, setting them to a jig, enjoying the rhythm, the coil and recoil of their weight.

'Easy, Boy,' the mistress called from her place in the back.

She and her friend Mistress Tilly chatted in the tray of the cart. Their voices came to him softly, the mistress's gentle tones interrupted by snorts of laughter from her friend.

'I only need to mention womanly matters to him,' the mistress said, 'and he blushes bright red, agrees to anything, and runs away.'

Boy returned to his own thoughts, enjoying the steady clop of hooves in mud and the patter of raindrops falling from the foliage above.

Zeus trod the track with no need of guiding. They travelled through the forest. Large trees grew on either side of the path, their limbs reaching to the sky. Light slanted through the canopy and caught in the swirling mist. The forms of ghosts and demons shapeshifted before Boy's eyes. Nothing seemed solid and everything possible.

He wondered if Indians still roamed the forest, sheltered in the shadows. Perhaps even now they held him in their sights. He shivered as an imaginary arrow pierced his back and could not help but look behind. But the Indian Wars were over, and the Indians defeated by muskets and disease. Now just deer and bears, squirrels and bush turkeys sought shelter in these woods. The bears rested, hidden in hollows, waiting for summer.

A breeze tousled his hair, bringing with it the damp smell of earth and decay. An eagle circled above the trees and, as always, Boy thought of his mother. He pulled himself straighter, wishing she could see him. He clicked the reins again. Zeus obeyed and jolted into a trot.

'Boy, I told you to take it steady,' the mistress admonished from the back.

They rode down Willow Street, past the few houses that lined it, their shutters closed against the cold and smoke drifting from the chimneys, past the general store where the mistress brought her thread and the master brought his tobacco, and past the shed where the stagecoach stopped on its way to Norwich.

Boy pulled up outside the wooden structure that served as the church and town hall, meeting place and courthouse. Some called it the new church though it were near fifty years old. Others called it the black church, for its board walls had darkened to a dead black. It caused the hairs to stand up on his arms.

He jumped down to help the mistresses and took the elbow of Mistress Tilly, so she would not fall. Holding her long skirts out of the mud with his other hand, he deposited her on the pavement and returned to support Mistress Randall. But he stopped, something having caught his eye. He exploded in a howl of laughter.

'Boy. What's the matter with you! Pay heed.' From the wagon, the mistress rebuked him, but as she followed the direction of his mirth, she too joined in.

'Oh, no!'

Calvin stood, stiff and still, beside his wagon. He looked straight ahead, his face blank, giving no indication of having seen them. Boy's friend shimmered in a uniform of purple. Baggy, shiny, purple trousers stopped at his knees, giving way to long white stockings. A white froth of lace secured his head to his neck, and again secured his wrists to his arms. The waistcoat was yellow, the yellow of sunflowers, and large silver buttons marched down the front. A purple coat completed the outfit, hanging to his ankles. Yellow tassels ran the side of his arm, seeming to twirl with every small breath.

The mistress had shown Boy a book once. She liked to settle him on her knee and read to him or show him pictures of far-away places. 'Here, this is London,' she had said. 'And this is a barrel man. Can you see his monkey? See his shiny clothes? The barrel man plays his music and the monkey dances for him.'

Calvin looked like that monkey, but he wasn't dancing.

'Shush boy.' The mistress pulled herself up, attempting a serious face. 'We mustn't laugh. It's the fashion, I'm sure. I do believe that Mr Duncan has just returned from London.

He would be following the fashion.' Beside her, Mistress Tilly snorted into her handkerchief.

The two women strolled into the church. Echoes of their laughter lingered behind.

Boy sat himself on the ground, leant against the wagon and wiggled to get comfortable. He would take note of every detail so that he might report back to Ol' Ma. He pictured her on the porch beside him, her shoulders heaving, her eyes screwed tight and the tears running down her face. 'Tell me again,' she would say.

Further up the road, the master was engaged in earnest conversation, blocking the path so that those hurrying to the church stepped off the sidewalk to move around; even old man Swan with his walking stick shuffled into the muddy and rutted street. None dared to move the master on.

As the master strolled towards the church, where he halted to finish his conversation, Boy put his head down, focused on a pebble and strained to hear.

'Fair exchange, then.' The master offered his hand in a shake, apparently pleased with his deal, his companion less so.

Bet he done him the dirty, Boy thought, for he often over-heard the master boasting of the bargains he had won at another's expense and knew he was not averse to taking advantage of another's misfortune.

He watched as his owner turned to move into the church and predicted his next moves. He saw him smooth back his hair with his fingers, flick imaginary pieces of dust from his shoulders and pull his waistcoat tight around him. He would make his entrance, assured that everyone would be looking at him.

Boy mimicked him with exaggerated gestures, a sneer on his face.

He turned to share the moment with Calvin, expecting a laugh, but his friend still stood as if held by strings, no doubt under the threat of a beating should he get dirt on his clothes. A pulse in his neck and a flush to his cheeks belied his indifference.

'Um... sorry I laughed.' Boy said.

Unsure whether Calvin had heard him, Boy opened his mouth to repeat himself. Then closed it again. His friend would need some time. *He ain't never hurt me. Ain't right what I did, laughing like that. Ain't his fault. He don't need no shame.*

Master and Mistress Main, new to the village, approached the meeting hall, the master holding his dignity like a shield across his chest and the mistress peeking this way and that as if to see who noticed their arrival. 'Mind yourself, woman.' Master Main pulled her by her arm, hustling her in the doorway.

Boy laughed and hazarded another look at Calvin. His friend still stood mute and solid as stone. The pulse still ticked in his neck. Boy fought the urge to wrap his arms around him for there was something naked and vulnerable about that beating pulse.

The Deanes, the family Swan with all six sons, and the Hewitts came clattering down the road, racing each other into town, cheering wildly and sending up a shower of mud. Horses nickered; wheels creaked. Women shouted admonishments to their husbands.

'Do hurry, my love, we'll be late'.

'Oh, mind my dress, please, sir!'

Boy rushed to help Mistress Hewitt, a portly woman and not so nimble on her feet but regretted it the instant she leant on him. He stumbled and heard Calvin's gasp. Wade, the younger of her sons, caught them both.

'We need be careful, Mother. What would Mistress Randall say were you to flatten her pet?' He winked at Boy.

To Boy's mind, Wade could do little wrong. His smile softened harsh truths. Boy had seen it turn an argument on its head. Men who one moment cursed the other instead threw an arm around a shoulder and clapped a back and agreed they'd acted like fools. That smile was a handy tool and Boy thought to practise it.

But now he squirmed at the words.

Ain't nobody's pet.

He thought of his mistress and her small dog, a tumble of tail and tongue. She would pull it onto her lap and turn it on its tummy for a cuddle. And when she was tired of it, she tied it to a pole and let it lie in the sun to snap at flies. It was of no account. A dog on a lead.

Boy shook his head to rid himself of the image. *Ain't no good collecting bad thoughts.* He heard Ol' Ma's voice in his head. *World sure got a ton of them. Just weigh you down so you can't move about your work, they will.*

But the day had lost its sparkle.

He sat back down. His hand fretted with the dirt, making small mounds and smoothing them away. He picked up pebbles to let drop through his fingers. He tossed one at the church but started at the solid thwack it made against the timber.

'Those white folks sure have themselves worked up.' He shot Calvin a questioning look. 'What interest could there be in that ol' hall?'

Calvin relented. 'Heard talk about Boston. Somebody's been poking a hornet's nest down there.'

'It's a long ways away.'

'Not so far. Heard the English are right mad at them, those folks in Boston.'

'Thought white folks were English.'

'Seems not. They co-lo-ni-als.'

Boy hadn't heard the word before.

'And here? Is that English king mad at the mistress and master?'

'Dunno. Figure that's what the meeting's about.'

'Oh, my! Now there's a fancy nigger if ever I saw one.'

'Do you dance, nigger? Come on, give us a dance.'

Boy jumped up as two youths sauntered up to Calvin.

The smaller of the two, and to Boy's eye, the meaner, pranced around him, tugging at the tassels and pulling at his buttons. Calvin stood leaden. Staring into the space ahead of him.

'I said dance, nigger. You hear me?' The voice sounded louder. Meaner. Tugs had become jabs.

Calvin remained rigid, held by invisible arms. A small distance away and not by his side, Boy felt as though spikes held his feet to the ground. His hands balled into fists and his chest grew so tight he thought it might squeeze the life right out of him. He prepared to throw himself at the smaller one, tackling him around the knees. If he took the small one down, the larger would run.

That boy will hang by a noose from a tree.

Just a pet dog and a dancing monkey.

'Dance. Dance.' The plump fellow squealed, in sycophantic mimicry.

Calvin made as if to move one foot. It didn't budge.

A voice called out from across the road, 'Hey, you lads. Burton, isn't it? Move on there. I'll be having words with your mother.'

Hooting with the fun of it, one stooped to scoop a ball of mud and hurled it at Calvin's shiny purple coat with the dancing yellow tassels. Then they tore away. Their jibes splintered the air.

Calvin did not move. Only his fists, clenched tight, held him upright. His face a bruise of shame and red from tears he would not allow.

Boy did cry. But he swallowed the tears in small grunts, so they ran down into the pit of his stomach and stirred up the bile in his belly. He leant forward and retched up an acid mess, his body shivering.

From inside the church the sounds of a hymn could be heard.

Christ, the Lord, is risen today, Alleluia!
Sons of men and angels say, Alleluia!
Raise your joys and triumphs high, Alleluia!
We shall overcome, Alleluia!

The white folks had finished their meeting.

'Boy, we must go past the Wheeler homestead. Mr Wheeler has hurt his elbow and cannot drive. They walked all the way here.'

Mistress Randall, Mistress Tilly, Master and Mistress Wheeler all mounted themselves into the wagon. Each talked over the other, none listening.

'I have the pamphlet right here. They say the messenger rode from Boston to deliver them to every church and meeting hall on the way.'

'Can you believe it. They hurled the tea right off that boat.'

'The captain stood aside. Did nothing to stop them.'

'They were painted as red Indians. He was in fear of his life no doubt.'

'Oh tosh, of course he knew they were not red Indians.'

'They say the crowd just rose up. As one. They say it was magnificent to see the people come together in common cause. I would that I could have been there,' the mistress said, her voice dreamy.

'This brings trouble. The King will not stand by and see his laws thwarted. I fear for those responsible.' For once, Mistress Tilly was not laughing.

'I think it would have been fun. A proper party!'

'A tea party?'

They all laughed at this.

'It's been coming. Ever since the Stamp Tax. The Grenville Tax. The Customs Massacre. And mark my words, it won't stop here.' Master Wheeler's words rung across the forest like a call to arms. The women stopped their commentary to listen to him.

'The British want to tax us. Taxation without representation? That's tyranny. They will take everything, and we will have no say in it. We will be slaves on our own land. We must fight. We cannot bow.'

'Please, Master Wheeler, take care with your words. We needs have faith in His Majesty. We are His loyal subjects.' Boy thought Mistress Tilly might break into sobs. 'We must explain ourselves to him. He will listen.'

'His Majesty has lost faith in *us*!' Mr Wheeler spat. 'He views us as ignorant savages. No better than that boy up there.' He pointed to Boy, who hunched his shoulders and tucked his head down.

'He would grind us under his boot. How many times have we sent our petitions and pleas? They have fallen on deaf ears. Worse, he sends his Redcoats here, to stalk the streets of Boston, to abuse us of our laws, to mistreat those good citizens with their demands and arrogance. No, it's time.' He paused. 'There comes a time when a man must stand straight. We must be masters of our own fate. We will not be slaves. We will be free.'

Boy repeated the words to himself, each one slowly, just to be sure. *A man must stand straight. Masters of our own fate. We will be free.* Then he repeated them again. A shiver ran down his spine. He lifted his head.

The light breeze he had so enjoyed this morning had gathered strength. A gust of wind shook the cart. A flurry of leaves stung his eyes. Branches groaned and creaked. Zeus tossed his head and broke the steady rhythm of his gait.

Boy pulled his jacket tighter around his neck and took a stronger grip on the reins. But he could no longer eavesdrop on the conversation. He thought, *The wind wants to steal the words from me.*

No. Too late. They are mine. I won't let them go.

'Boy, be careful,' the mistress cried from the back as a storm tore through the trees and the forest shook with the crackling and rustling and swooshing of limbs and leaves. *Warriors shaking their spears and stamping their feet. Ready for war.* The passengers covered their faces with their shawls as debris hurled into their eyes. Boy leaned his body into the wind that tore through his hair and ripped at his shirt and threatened to hurl him off the carriage. But he was a man now, and he would keep control.

⌐

When finally they turned into the carriageway of the homestead, he let out a sigh of relief. He recognised the tall, thin shape of Elijah pacing the lane, his jacket clutched to his body, and watched as his sharp lines relaxed in a sigh of relief.

Elijah rushed to help the mistress from the wagon and into the house, but his eyes held those of Boy. He nodded at him.

Boy clambered down from the wagon, his back and legs stiff. He stretched, reaching his arms into the air while the wind whistled around him.

⌐

That night he shared his words with Ol' Ma.

'A man must stand straight,' he told her, looking her in the eyes, nodding his head for emphasis.

He slept with those words.

He dreamt them.

Chapter Seven

Old man Swan hobbled through the doors of the hall, his stick in one hand and a granddaughter supporting the other. The youngest of the Deane boys pushed past him, receiving a clip around the ear and a reprimand from his mother, 'Mind your manners, son!' The people from Stonington gathered to hear the news. Women with large bonnets, the serving girls from the tavern, labourers, shopkeepers and farmers crowded into the meeting hall. They squeezed along benches, shuffling together to make room for newcomers, calling out to friends, chatting in loud voices and whispering in anxious ones. A mother petted a squealing baby, anxious less she be asked to leave.

A messenger, weary beyond measure and grey with dried mud and dust, slumbered in a corner, drawing cautious looks. He had ridden into the Hewitt property that lay on the northern side, leading to Boston. Nearly falling from his horse, he had conveyed his news. The three Hewitt boys had relieved him of his mission and raced to call the meeting. Then they'd ridden still further, each in a different direction. The thud of horses' hooves, like the pounding of war drums, sounded on tracks and trails, through woods and meadows and vales as riders had relayed their pamphlets to every hamlet and holding across the country. Small bits of paper scattered like seeds.

From his position at the back of the hall, Boy studied Master Randall who stood behind a podium at the front. He stood with his shoulders back, his head held high, scanning the room as if he owned it and all who sat within it, even the white folks. Most would not have noticed that the pamphlet he held trembled between his fingers, or that he tapped his foot in agitation.

Mistress Randall had seated herself in the front pew with Mistress Tilly beside her, laughing and talking with greater vigour than usual. The mistress had pleaded with her father to share with her the contents of the pamphlet. Boy had watched with some interest as she had peeked at the Master from lowered eyes, smiling so that her dimples might show.

'Please, Papa. I won't tell anyone.'

That look will win for her, Boy had thought.

But the master had been adamant. 'Be patient, daughter. This is not some piece of gossip to be carelessly tossed your way.'

On her other side sat Master and Mistress Main. Mistress Main peeked around and gave little waves to those whose eye she caught. Boy noticed she had a new bonnet, for she kept touching the ribbons and posing her head. He hoped Calvin might come soon but when Master Duncan arrived without his mistress, he concluded that he had ridden alone on his horse.

Master Randall gave a small cough to clear his throat. He smoothed back his hair with shaking fingers, flicked imaginary pieces of dust from his shoulders and pulled his waistcoat tight around him. He took a deep breath. The crowd silenced. A loose shutter tapped against the wall like a drum, or a gavel. He began to read.

Boy struggled to understand the unfamiliar words and wished again for Calvin. Between them they would sort out the meaning. But as the master's voice settled into a slow, steady rhythm, so the language became clear.

'We hold these truths to be self-evident, that *all men are created equal*, that they are endowed by their Creator with certain unalienable rights, that among these are *life, liberty and the pursuit of happiness.'*

Boy frowned. *All men?* The white congregation cheered. The Wheeler boys jumped to their feet and pounded their fists in the air. Old man Swan stamped his walking stick. At the back of the church, only blank faces returned Boy's questioning look.

'But when a long train of abuses and usurpations...evinces a design to reduce them under absolute despotism, it is their right, it is their duty, to throw off such government,' the master continued in the same steady tone.

The authority of the words silenced the crowd. Boy watched as Mistress Tilly took her friend's hand. Master Main drew his wife closer.

'A prince, whose character is thus marked by every act which may define a tyrant, is unfit to be the ruler of a free people.'

Heads nodded. Murmurs of 'Amen' echoed throughout the hall.

'We, therefore ... solemnly publish and declare... absolved from all allegiance to the British Crown ... have full power to levy war ...We mutually pledge to each other our lives, our fortunes, and our sacred honour. My friends, we are at war with England.'

Master Randall stopped speaking. He put the paper down and gazed at neighbours he had known all his life. He was crying. Someone stamped their feet, and everyone joined in. The shutter banged against the wall, adding to the rhythmic pounding and stomping that gathered into a storm.

Boy stumbled from the building. Something had happened that he didn't fully understand. Only those first words meant anything. *All men are created equal.* Everyone had heard them. They had cheered.

That means me, he vowed to himself, injustice burning red in his belly. *Even if those white folks don't like it.*

After the darkness of the hall, the sunlight blinded him. It had rained, a gentle summer rain that washed the dust from the leaves so that as he regained his vision, the world seemed to shimmer. A breeze had blown the skies clear and carried with it a hint of smoke from where Master Duncan had been clearing land.

When the mistress finally determined to leave, her eyes red and cheeks aglow from the smiling and sobbing and cheering and stamping, Boy helped her as she clambered into the wagon. He waited as she organised her skirts and settled among the cushions and pulled her shawl close, but before he took his seat he gave her a nod, as if to encourage her. He knew she wouldn't say the words he wanted to hear, but he thought it only fair to give her this chance. *So, Boy. You too have the right to liberty. Take your mother and Ol' Ma and Elijah and pursue your own happiness. You are free.*

'Boy, what are you waiting for? Hurry along now,' she said.

He gave her his smile, the one that reassured her that everything was right in the world, but even as he turned away it had fallen from his face. He wondered at its flimsiness in the face of burning resentment. He wondered how long before it burst into flames.

On their journey home they passed the land Master Duncan had cleared. Enormous oak trees had been felled. Boy had thought this part of the forest would exist forever. Yet the trees lay broken and shattered. The breeze carried the scent of bruised and beaten leaves, and sap leaked like blood from the ruined branches.

Walking in the door of the shack he saw his mother. A mouse had snuck into the shelter of the shack, and she was chasing it with her broom.

Run, little mouse, thought Boy. *This is no place for you.*

Ma lay on the mattress with Elijah's head in her lap. She hunted for nits. She spied one, pinning it to Elijah's scalp before deftly sliding it up a hair and pinching it between her fingers. Boy witnessed this scene every night. Nothing changed. Yet everything had. The world had turned and thrown him off balance. He couldn't understand how the pounding and the stomping did not set the earth to trembling and create such a rippling and a rocking that this hut of slaves did not fall and lie broken like the oak trees.

Chapter Eight

July 1779:

The war lapped at Stonington. That small world heaved as rumours raced from one homestead to another, feeding on fears and growing fat with speculation.

'The British demolished our troops at Redding. Burned the town down. Everything. Barns. Stores. Meeting Houses.'

'Our men had no chance. No supplies. That was the problem. Out of ammo.'

'Heard we were walloped at Horse Neck, too.'

'They say Lobster-backs bin crawlin' in the woods down roun' New Haven.'

'Only a short ride from here.'

'Had those Hessians with 'em. Half bear, half man.'

Boy gazed across the fields to the forest and queried every shadow, every movement of the wind. He couldn't decide whether he feared the arrival of the English troops or longed for it. And while he trudged through his days as he always had – fed the animals and harvested the fields, swept the grounds and went to church and prayed on Sundays – while he did that, he fought the Hessians with his hoe, and bashed the brutes with his broom.

But when he could sneak away and find a quiet place, it was Cecilia he took with him in his dreams. It was she who lay beside him as he fell onto his sleeping mat, his desire so strong he could not catch his breath and would need to creep from the hut to find some relief. She belonged to the Swan family and worked as their house girl and Boy had seen her in church every week of his life as she sung her hymns, made her prayers and signed her cross, sitting with her family on the bench ahead of him. One tousled black head among many. Lately, he and Calvin had found themselves glancing too long as she sauntered by, her worn grey dress stretched tightly across her breasts, her buttocks swaying in a most unholy way. Their eyes moved to her rhythm until they would catch sight of the other and laugh. A nudge, a tap, and the next moment they wrestled on the ground, two stags rutting.

'You watch out for that there gal,' Ol' Ma had warned him. 'She looks at you boys like she looking for chickens to pluck.'

Maybe, Ol' Ma, I wanna be plucked.

And so, he spent his days lost in a dream. When not fighting the Redcoats, he would be exploring Cecilia's body. He put his head between those breasts, clutched that round arse to him, lost himself in her soft curves. 'I'll be gentle,' he thought. 'I'll treat her like the highest lady in the land. And when we have children...'

You ain't having no children with that girl. It was his mother's voice he heard in his dreams. *I see how the master looks at you. You just a big black stallion he goin' to sire out. You be mated with who he tells you and no one else.*

And the moment would be lost and he would thump the ground, fists clenched, a silent scream splitting the universe.

But he had a plan. He would join the army, fight the British and win his freedom.

He chopped wood behind the barn. A quiet hung over the farm. Birds and animals had sought shade from the midday sun, and the only sound was the steady strike of his axe and his own hoarse breathing. But in his mind, the noise was deafening. He pictured the moment he staggered into camp. *Colonel Washington rises to meet him and stretches out an arm in greeting, 'A slave has come to join us, but a free man will fight beside us.'* The rhythm of his swing against the block mingled with the cheers of the crowd. He paused to smile and stand tall as men gathered around to clap him on his back. He relaxed his grip on the axe and it fell to the ground.

'Miserable cub. Put a mind to your task!' The master stood behind him.

Boy stooped to retrieve the axe, his grip so tight he thought it might break.

'And lose that complaint in your eyes.' Master Randall looked around at the clatter of hooves up the drive. Recognising the visitor, he stood straight to greet him, pulled a hand through his hair, flicked dust from his shoulders, straightened his waistcoat and turned to greet his guest.

Wade Hewitt swung off his horse, tossing the reins to Boy. Wade had run to the war the moment General Washington had called the colonies to fight at Bunker Hill. He and his big brother Cade had fought at New York when it fell to the English. Cade had been born the elder, a shy and finicky person, always picking the fluff off his shirts and rarely looking straight into the world. He had disappeared into one of the British prison ships. No one had seen him since. And though Boy had felt no special bond with Cade, it worried him to think of the man sitting in a smelly dark cell, with no way to keep clean and no doubt missing the peach pies his ma made and which Boy had once tasted.

Wade returned to Stonington when he could to rally recruits and procure provisions for the army. He kept the community in news. He still owned his smile, but as Boy studied him, it seemed to be slower now. *Seems like it need do battle with his eyes before it can lay claim upon his face.* A tracing of scars from the smallpox pitted his skin, craters on a battleground.

'S'alright, Boy,' Wade said, catching sight of Boy's look. ''least I'm alive. Others aren't. That pox blew right through the camp. Took everyone before it. Randall!' Wade held out his hand in greeting to the master. 'You going to release this lad to come fight with us? We need good men.'

'You think the army has chickens to feed? Is all he's good for.'

Boy watched as the two men walked into the house. Wade turned, and though it took only an instant to assume a mask of indifference, Boy feared he had surprised the hatred that had shown clear on his face.

'I'm sorry. Boy. He does wrong to jibe you. For one, I'd be proud to have you at my back.'

Boy smiled and with a nod, bent to retrieve his axe and returned to his task. He hoped that Wade had not noticed the trembling of his fingers, could not guess how they itched to hold the weight of that axe, or to feel the release of swinging it down – his master's head upon the block. His rage scared him.

Not until he put his head in Ol' Ma's lap on her mattress in the cabin, and felt her bony fingers prowl through his hair, hunting lice, did he relax. A parting of the roots, a barely perceivable intake of breath and a quickening of her hands across his skull signalled a catch.

'Ow,' he complained.

'Got it.'

Doors and shutters hung wide-open and moonlight cast shadows into the room. The clean smell of wood and leaf mingled with smoke from the evening fire. A bobcat screamed in the distance. *Mating*, thought Boy. He wondered what other life stalked through the night, deep in the forest. He wondered what Cecilia was doing.

'They found Jack.' From her spot near the fire, Boy's mother gave the news. Those few words, short and blunt, sounded like the knoll of a bell. Jack was Mr Wheeler's man. He had run off to join the Redcoats. He had wanted to be free. The black community had talked of little else for the three days he had been gone, for in some way he stood for them all. Boy had pictured him loping through the woods to a new life. 'Dogs got him. Wheeler said it were a mistake. Just one of those things! They didn't get there in time to call 'em off.'

Ol' Ma made another stab at Boy's scalp.

'Left him, bits of him, on his mother's doorstep. Master said it were fair exchange. Said she were to blame, putting thoughts in his mind.'

'Always fair exchange for him. S'long as he gets what he wants.' Ol' Ma pulled at his hair.

Boy's head shot up, ready to complain.

'You stay right there.' Ol' Ma pushed it back into her lap.

That night, Boy dreamt of Eligua and the story he had told and of a small mouse in a big town, being chased by a cat.

Spring ripened into summer. Sundays rolled from one to the other. Birds feasted on the berries that hung heavy on bushes, ready to drop. The air smelt thick, pregnant with rain, but the skies remained a solid blue. Boy sprawled in the grass under the trees beyond the church, watching a bee as it crawled up his arm, wary of its sting. He swatted a fly that tickled his nose, but otherwise lay content to breathe in the dusky scent of damp earth and fresh grass and allow a ray of sunshine that had snuck though the branches to soothe his belly. Calvin had been sent on some errand after church. He could not see his mother and Ol' Ma but knew they gossiped on the lawn with those from other homesteads, as they did every Sunday once the service was over. He returned his thoughts to Cecilia.

A body flopped beside him. Thinking Calvin had returned he opened one lazy eye in greeting but flinched when he saw the girl. He blinked in an effort to clear his thoughts, then sat up and made as if to move, as if it were him in the wrong space, and she laughed.

'Stay, Boy.' She might have been addressing a bumbling puppy.

Boy looked around. He was indeed awake. In the woods behind the church. Not dreaming. Not knowing what to do with his arms or feet, he attempted a careless posture. He lay back. Arms were arranged into position behind his head. Feet were crossed. He studied the sky, his every sense alert to the movement of air between them. Time slowed. Each second stretched into a year.

'You've grown,' Cecilia said eventually.

'Yes.'

'You must work hard. You look very strong.' A hand unbuttoned his shirt and laid itself on his chest.

'Yes.' Boy swallowed. He fought the temptation to look down at himself to see what she saw. He felt a single finger stray across his nipple and its path could be felt deep in his groin.

'Have you ever been kissed, Boy? Here?' Celia moved her hand and traced the lines of his mouth with a small plump finger. Boy swallowed again as he tried to follow its course with his eyes. That same mouth she touched fell open. He groaned when she undid his belt and pulled his trousers free, submitting, aching for more, afraid that a breath or gesture might wake him or send her away. Nor did he move as she pulled her own dress over her head, though he could barely breathe and his member strained and threatened to burst. But when she lay upon him, her breasts warm on his chest, and when she took his fingers and used them to stroke between her legs, and when she rubbed herself against him, he lost all restraint. With a cry he rolled her around and threw himself upon her, thrusting into that warm, wet place. He thought he heard her caution, 'Slow down,' but could not be sure. It was over in a moment. He rolled off her and lay on the grass, panting, moving an arm to pull her against his body but she was not pleased. Within minutes, she climbed upon him, 'Now, we try again. This time, do as I say.'

When Celia had gone to re-join her family, he hung back to bask in the moment, drained and feeling at peace. Triumph had replaced festering rage. He felt capable of anything. She had wanted him. She had screamed for him. She had begged him, 'Harder. Harder.' And he had delivered, leaving her soft and limp and glowing, stroking his skin, caressing his face. No one had ever touched him like that. It soothed those aching, abandoned parts of his heart. Her smell lingered on his fingers. He stowed it in his memory box. Catching sight of Calvin, he grinned and swaggered off to boast.

Calvin sat with his back against a tree, sucking a stem of grass between his teeth. He nodded as Boy approached.

'She says I'm graceful as a deer, with long, long legs.' Boy stretched out a long, deer-like leg in demonstration, near toppling in his efforts.

Calvin seemed more interested in the grass than his friend.

'And my skin. My skin is burnished wood. See. See how smooth it is.' Boy made to grab Calvin's arm, but his friend wanted nothing to do with his smooth skin and butted him away.

'And my eyes. Ah! The finest eyes she ever has seen. Such long lashes.' Boy leered at Calvin with his fine eyes and batted his long lashes. Only then did he notice that Calvin was not playing the game. 'You alright? What's the matter anyways?'

'Not a deer.' Calvin spoke through the grass in his mouth.

'Huh?'

'I said, "Not a deer." You don't look like a deer.'

'What are you talking about?'

'I seen you, when you think no one's looking. You prowl like a cat, a puma, caged and collared and ready to strike. Sometimes I whisper to myself, "Not now, Boy. Not yet."'

Boy flopped to the grass beside his friend. His mood gone and replaced with the angry restlessness he lived with.

'Wade Hewitt is back.' Calvin flicked his stem of grass into the bushes.

'He been up the house, yesterday. Come to get the master. Take him away to Washington's army. They riding out together.'

'You going with them?'

A cardinal caught Boy's attention. Its piping song disturbed the bushes behind them. Two of them, brilliant red plumage, high red crests, black faces, foraged for fallen berries. Boy studied them. 'Nope!' He used a stick to stab a leaf.

Storm clouds crawled up from the horizon, casting shadows over the day. From where they lay, the two boys could see the long table set in the shade of the church, around which the white congregation gathered to eat their sandwiches and chew over the sermon. Fractured phrases of conversation drifted to their ears, 'Our men must rally soon. They can't take another winter.' 'With no ships from England, I no longer know the fashion.' On the far side, the black community gathered under the trees, and shared the crumbs of news garnered from dinner tables and wagons. Boy's eyes sought out Ol' Ma. Standing near the church gate, she pulled her shawl closer as a wind came through.

Calvin turned to sprawl on his front. He plucked another piece of grass and chewed it. Boy poked at ants. One. Two. Three. A solitary drop of rain, fully laden, exploded in the dirt between them.

'Master Duncan looking to sell me. Me pa heard talk of it.' Calvin also stabbed at an ant.

Boy swung around to look at Calvin, his head shaking in denial, and then he let out a breath, long and slow. He turned his eye to the congregation. He watched as Cecilia prepared to leave with her family on the long walk home. She looked around for him, a smile playing on her lips. He picked up the leaf and crushed it in his hand, letting the pieces fall through his fingers. He whispered her a soft farewell.

'Then we gotta go,' was all he said.

Calvin's eyes searched Boy's face. 'To Washington?'

Boy shook his head. 'The Redcoats.'

Even as the words slipped from his mouth, he realised that they had only been waiting for their moment. The decision had been made a long time ago. He and Calvin just needed to stroll over to those English soldiers and be free. That's what they promised. He pictured the master's face when he discovered him gone. He saw himself running through the woods, dogs baying behind him, leaping at him, tearing his body limb from limb. He pictured an old woman holding his broken body in her lap. With a shudder, Boy searched for Ol' Ma. She had already left for the long walk back to the slave hut. He resisted the urge to run after her.

Instead he returned his gaze to Calvin. The two boys looked at each other, their futures held in balance. The cardinal had stopped his piping. Seemed like he was listening. The voices of their families, the congregation, the masters and mistresses retreated. Scarcely even a hum.

'When we going?' whispered Calvin.

Chapter Nine

He broke from cover, sprinting across open ground with the grace and speed of a deer and into the shadows of the forest. Warrior trees stomped their feet and shook their spears as he darted beneath them. Stumbling, slipping, tripping, he thrashed through the undergrowth, until his arm caught something soft and warm.

'Ol' Ma?'

'Boy. You promised to look after me,' Ol' Ma whimpered. She was propped beneath a tree. A bayonet had pierced her chest. Blood streamed from her mouth. Her eyes reproached him. Beside her the master reared up on Zeus. Moonlight gleamed off the steel of the bayonet he held above him. He caught Boy's eye and then he impaled her again. 'Fair exchange!' he laughed.

'Noooo!'

'Boy! Wake up, child.' Ol' Ma shook him.

He buried himself against her chest. Thin arms held him. He didn't need light to see the hut, the dirt floor, trodden hard by bare feet, the worn mattress that bore the restless form of his mother. She grumbled in her dreams at the coming day. Elijah snuffled in his corner, making more sound in his sleep than when awake. A single loon wailed in the distance, crying for his loved one. Inside, Boy lay safe with all that he knew. Tonight, he would talk to his mother. First, he must survive another day, holding his secret close, keeping his face bland, his smile in place.

¬

The master and Wade were leaving this day. Boy walked up the path towards the yard. Though the sun had risen, the moon still hung heavy, diminished but resistant as if reluctant to cede this new morning. As was Boy's custom he released the fowl from their nightly habitat, stopping to observe their break into the yard. Old Earl, the rooster, recognised his foot-steps and stood ready at the door. At first crack, he hurled himself out of his cage and into the yard, near knocking Boy over in the process. His feathered lady friends, Biddy, Siddy and Miss Liddy, flustered after him, jamming themselves at the threshold in their haste to be out and about and pecking in the lawn. Only Old Jane hung back, content with her small space and knowing it offered safety from the foxes that lurked beyond the borders. She was a safe, but not a happy hen, all huddled up in her fear. He thought of Beaker with her black, inquisitive eyes. *She would never have stayed caged.*

Wade waited by the porch for Master Randall. Boy decided to sweep the front yard, in the hope of catching a word with him.

The heavy clunk of footsteps announced Master Randall's arrival. He appeared in the doorway, shoulders thrust back in a show of military form. He smoothed back his hair and dusted imaginary flecks from the shoulders of his jacket, scanning the yard as if it held a throng of admirers and not merely his slave hand. Boy recognised his shirt as the one the mistress had been working on all these weeks. He had watched as she worked in her chair on the veranda and dreamt of wearing one like it. Sewn in the style popular among fighting men, worn lose with rows of fringe around the edges. It made the master look to be a better marksman than Boy knew he was. His breeches hung to his knees where they found stockings of virgin white and new black, shiny leather shoes. Wade had warned him, 'You'll need good shoes. The army has left a trail from the blood of their feet'.

Mistress Randall stood on the porch, achingly erect. She held a handkerchief between her hands, twisting it between her fingers. Boy had watched her sew that handkerchief, occasionally stabbing herself instead of the cloth and letting out an oath. She had laughed at his expression and placed a finger to her mouth. A secret shared. She had been proud when she had finished it, the yellow flowers growing around its hem and the birds singing in the corner. He thought it a sorry fate to be mangled, as it now were.

The master turned to the mistress, 'You will be alright?'

'Father, I'm not the one who's going to war.' She paused and sought to lighten the mood. 'And I have Boy to protect me.' She smiled. 'Isn't that right, Boy?'

Boy busied himself securing the master's pack onto Zeus: blanket, kettle, water bucket, knife.

Wade mounted his horse. His movements seemed so heavy Boy feared that weariness might drag him off again. 'I'm sorry, Boy,' Wade said, 'you would have made a fine soldier.'

Boy looked away as a thought occurred to him. He prayed to heaven that they would never see each other again. Would he have to kill Wade?

The master turned to the slave, his eyes narrowed. 'You do not wish to fail me, Boy. Be warned.'

Then they turned their horses and trotted down the path towards a war.

The mistress retreated with her mourning into the privacy of her home.

Boy took hold of his broom and swept the yard. He swept away the leaves and twigs. He swept away chicken feathers, horsehair and bits of cloth, and the discarded bones of a forgotten meal. He swept and swept until Ol' Ma called him. But still he didn't think it clean.

¬

'You're too young.' His mother crouched by the fire, stirring the gruel.

Twilight held balance between night and day. The air vibrated with the hum of insects.

'I'm old enough.'

'You're not yet a man.' She gripped the wooden spoon and stirred as if to punch a hole in the pot.

'I'll never be a man if I stay here!'

'You think you can leave? They'll track you. Dogs.' A pause. 'Kill you. Sell you.'

Boy turned away. 'And this is life?' He kicked the mattress that sprawled on the floor. Straw spilled from the stuffing. Her spoon scraped the sides of the pot as she stirred. Round and round. He circled the room. Round and round. He felt the world turning, round and round and thought he might fall off.

'Don't you want more for me?' He recalled a talk with Ol' Ma, long ago. He aimed his words at his mother's heart. 'You can't protect me.'

The spoon knocked against the pot. It stopped its circling. Something had disturbed the insects outside. They ceased their humming. They both gazed at the embers. Smoke hung in the air. Shadows flitted across her face. She jabbed at a log. It cracked. Sparks flickered.

'You are ...' Her head fell into her hands.

He took the spoon from her and ladled the gruel into two mugs. He gave one to her. They ate.

'Take this.' She lifted the eagle from her neck, its wings raised in flight. Wet wood hissed and spat in the fire and a log split, cracking the silence and sending showers of ash, smoke and cinder into the air. The sparks created a halo of light around her head, like dancing faeries ... or demons. A twig caught a flame and her face flickered in its light as she removed the charm from her neck. She passed it into his hands. He had never seen her without it. The fire dimmed and her face collapsed back into the shadows. She looked grey and flat. Grounded.

He left before dawn the next day. He planned to meet Calvin in the woods. His mother didn't look up as he walked away. Ol' Ma didn't look down. Elijah played the flute. The house grew smaller. The woods grew larger. The tunes on Elijah's flute followed him into the darkness. The notes faded. They were gone.

Chapter Ten

July 1779

He found Calvin, hunched in the curve of a tree just off the track that led to the coast, jigging his foot against the trunk, small taps that showed great tension. It disturbed Boy. He wanted Calvin to pretend confidence, to laugh and make a joke, because that was what Calvin did. Instead, the enormity of what they planned settled even more heavily on his shoulders. So, they didn't greet each other. Any word, any shared fear might break the moment and they would flee home like whipped hounds. There was still time to sneak into the shack and pretend nothing had happened and get up and feed the chickens and give the mistress the smile she liked.

Though they followed familiar paths, and a full moon shed light on roots and rivulets that might trip them, they crawled as if pulling against a force that would snap them back. Boy carried a sack filled with some corn and a chicken Ol' Ma had packed, but it felt heavy with the weight of her love and knocked against his hip with every step, urging him to return.

The bark of a dog silenced his doubts. Even as his legs threatened to fall from beneath him, the sweat broke from his body, and as his mind argued, 'It's too soon! They can't know we're gone yet,' Boy dropped his bag and leapt forward. Calvin, always the faster, ran before him, crashing through shrubs and under branches that whipped across Boy's face.

'To the river,' he shouted. His chest heaved and vision blurred. He lost sight of Calvin. Footsteps thrashed through the bush behind him and he arched his back in expectation of the dog's leap, its claws in his skin, its jaws around his neck. Not until he plunged into the river did he realise he had overtaken Calvin and it was he who ran behind him. They sheltered beneath an overhanging branch with just their heads above water, catching their breath. Boy struggled to hear above the pounding of his heart in his ears. 'It was just a dog,' he said at last. A dog on a farm, warning against foxes and protecting its patch.

'Sweet Blessed Jesus.' Calvin let out a sob and sunk back into the waters.

'I thought ...' Boy didn't voice the sensation of having his back ripped to pieces. He too allowed himself to relax in the black water. Holding onto a branch he let his body float in the current, pulling toward the coast.

'Just a farm dog!' Calvin snorted.

'Ssh!' But he chuckled. Washed by the river the two laughed until tears rolled from their eyes and their stomachs cramped. And then they laughed until they cried. 'We need a plan,' said John at last.

Calvin mutely agreed. His head on one side, water dripping from his hair which fell in tails around his face, he waited.

'Alright. We follow the river towards the coast. Then we follow the coast toward New York. And some ways along we find the Redcoats.'

'Good plan,' replied Calvin.

Boy scowled at the sarcasm. 'So? You got something better?'

They travelled through the night. When the red line of a new day was seen on the horizon, they left the track and hauled themselves into a white oak tree. Its wide and low spreading branches made an easy climb and provided a sheltered nook. Settled in a fork like two small bears, the bark rough on their back, they watched the morning wake around them. Across the fields and behind the hills, a cock crowed and carried images of Old Earl bolting from his shed. Cows lowed their discomfort and for a moment Boy longed for the taste of milk, warm and sweet on his tongue, dribbling from his mouth and down his chin. A wagon, early to market, trundled along the trail not far below. It was as ordinary a day as ever had been. Except that somewhere across those fields on a farm in Stonington the mistress was waking and demanding to know where Boy was. Was her kind smile ugly with rage? Had she already organised trackers? Was a posse of men on horses and with dogs already on their path?

Calvin caught the look upon his face. 'It's done!'

They locked eyes and Boy nodded. He tugged at a leaf, green and supple and squashed it between his fingers releasing a fresh and pungent smell.

'Thank you for coming with me,' Calvin said.

John looked at his friend but didn't say anything. How to explain that he couldn't imagine a life without Calvin in it. Only Ol' Ma knew him or understood him better.

'Don't think I could've done it without you.' There was a catch in Calvin's voice.

'I know.' And they both erupted into howls of laughter, each shushing and nudging the other to keep quiet.

'Least I got you away from Cecilia's clutches.' Calvin said, mischief in his eyes.

They sat in the boughs of the old tree, each lost in their thoughts. Calvin finally broke the silence. 'Who will you miss most?'

Boy wished his friend did not stab so directly into his thoughts. 'I'll miss Ol' Ma.' He pictured the old woman's face and how her eyes lost their shadows when they lay upon him. He swallowed a lump in his throat and prayed she would be safe without his care. 'Elijah,' he added. He let the crushed leaf fall from his fingers. *My mother?* His fingers touched the eagle that hung on his neck. She had flown down from the skies and revealed her love for him. And it had left her broken and weak. And he had gone. He covered his mouth with his hands to choke back the sobs, rocking back and forth upon his perch in the tree. His head throbbed with the injustice and he wished it could have been different. He tried to understand how it all had happened, but he couldn't bring the pieces together. He knew only the master was responsible.

For five nights they travelled. For five days they curled up in the branches of a tree or the hollow of a log, well hidden from the road. Calvin still carried his sack and they lived off his few yams and potatoes and the melons they scavenged from the fields.

On the fifth night they hid behind bushes. Though it was neither dusk nor dawn, the sky glowed red and the plop of explosions, though muted by distance, filled their ears. A playful breeze, warm even for a summer night, carried smoke and ash. Militia moved along the road, racing to battle, returning more slowly, fewer in number, heads drooped over sweat-sodden horses.

The two boys froze when the Redcoats passed along the trail. Though this was what they had been waiting for and they needed only to cross a few yards, it seemed like a thousand miles and too large a step. Their feet refused to move. And the body of soldiers trotted by.

'No.' Boy raced onto the trail. 'Wait.'

The soldiers finally heard his hollering and stopped for them.

'We want to join the army,' Boy blurted, looking up into the face of an officer. Seated high on his stallion, his white hair curled above his ears, with his red jacket and gleaming sabre, he seemed god-like. In the scrutiny that followed Boy became aware of his own bare feet, the trousers that hung above his

ankles, his shirtless chest, and his smell but he pulled himself taller and folded his arms in hopes of exaggerating the
muscles. To his side, Calvin did the same. 'We want to join the
army,' he repeated, to break the silence and not knowing what
else to say.

'Best follow us then,' the soldier replied.

Chapter Eleven

The days passed in a blur. They marched behind as the troop of soldiers tracked the coast, plundered villages, villages that looked like Stonington, and left a trail of fire and flames. But nothing they saw rivalled the night when they sat on the shoreline and watched as men in red coats set New Haven alight. They watched as sky and land and ocean dissolved in a swirling, crimson glow of smoke and flame, and shattered in explosions and screams. Beside him, Calvin shivered and echoed his own whimpered prayer, 'Almighty Father in heaven, save us.'

At first, they watched in mesmerised silence as images flashed through the grim, red light, removed from them as in a play. They saw the silhouette of a woman flicker against a blazing building, her skirts alight. A man raced behind, a bundle clasped to his chest. A musket fired. He jerked and flung up his arms. He fell. A baby squealed. A mother begged. Still, they said nothing. But when the flames leapt across to the meeting hall and caught on the huge support beam, Boy stood up and found himself cheering, 'Burn, you bastard, burn.' He cheered as the roof collapsed. It wasn't New Haven he saw, but the hall in Stonington. And it seemed to him that the fires leapt straight from hell to consume the church and stretched their fist to smite an unjust god. And he imagined the congregation, with their smug complacent faces who spoke of Christian kindness but never turned to notice the sorrow of those who knelt behind them, and he willed them to die in the inferno. Smoke choked his throat and burned his eyes and tears streamed down his cheeks, but his voice was hoarse from the cheering and his body felt weak from the rage that coursed through his veins and he collapsed onto the ground, knowing he had glimpsed hell, and wondering if maybe he belonged there.

A different smell assaulted them as they sailed into New York and the sludge of the city nudged the sides of the ship. A body, bloated and festered, floated by, carried by the tide out to sea.

'From the prison ships,' the sergeant who leaned on the rails beside him said. And Boy thought of Cade, Wade's brother who had been captured in battle.

The two boys were given into the care of the sergeant- 'Sergeant Barker, and yes, you will hear my bark'- and advised they were to be musicians with the 63rd Regiment of Foot. *Musicians?* Boy's only experience lay with the groups of musicians who played at village balls and parties, so he stared at the sergeant, debating whether he should explain that he wanted to be a soldier and fight, but he was too shy. Calvin held no such reservations. 'But we want to go into battle. To fire a musket.' The sergeant looked down at the two boys, his eyes twinkling. On first meeting, Boy had stared at the sergeant's nose: a monstrous nose, above which two blue eyes sparkled. That nose and the eyes, they work as a team, he had decided. The one sniffs out trouble and the other freezes it dead.

'Oh, you'll see battle,' the sergeant said. 'Without our drummer boys, there is no army, just a mess of soldiers who don't know what to do. Those drums, they're our heartbeat.'

The boys had little time to digest this information as the fleet docked. They sheltered at the fore of the deck while marines unfurled the sails, lowered anchors and threw down rope ladders and soldiers hauled their kits from below deck and huddled in groups talking of rum and whisky and whores and a long night's sleep, and awaited the flotilla of small boats that came to greet them and take them to shore. And in the midst of this commotion they huddled a little closer, for both felt very small. Boy was glad of Calvin's shoulder, warm and steady against his own, and he worried if he would measure against these bearded, rough-spoken men in a world that was louder and larger than any he had known. The sergeant appeared before them, placing a hand on each. 'Stick close to me. We don't want you getting lost. This town will gobble up two country boys such as yourselves.'

And it seemed not a moment before they were in a dinghy and paddling across the stretch of ocean to New York, a town they had only every heard of, and a place of legend in their small world. Boy trotted after the sergeant as he strode up Fifth Avenue with directions to procure their uniforms, find their barracks and get some food. Crowds parted before that small man. Some shouted greetings or tipped a hat, others clapped him on his back. Boy raced behind, fretting lest he lose sight of him and wondering if he could ever command such presence. But for now, he feared being lost in the crowds, for people jostled him at every step. A whip cracked near his ear and he leapt to the side. A carriage trundled by; a waft of perfume hung in its wake. A movement in an alley startled him, and he turned to gape. A man and woman grappled together. Boy could not tell if she cried out in fervour or pain. He hurried on past black hollows of burned-out houses, past shadows in darkened doorways. Like the gaps and broken teeth of a brutish mouth, they threatened to devour him. He dodged some sewerage thrown from a window above. The crowd growled, but a grinning woman, her hair a flaming red, met their complaint with a finger and a shrug. He only stopped when he stumbled over a man, shuffling along the ground, dragging the stumps of two legs behind. Boy stared in horror, for flies swarmed around the torn and blood-soaked bandages and the man, once tall, received only kicks and curses. A nudge from Calvin moved him along.

He caught up with the sergeant at a corner. The man watched a bear, its claws and teeth ripped from it, its coat shaggy and worn. Chained by the neck, it danced from foot to foot. A youth, his coat torn, lounged against the wall, a cap on the ground to collect the coins. He poked the bear with a sharp-pointed stick and the bear danced faster and turned in a circle. The mark of its tread deep in the ground. Boy had seen bears shot before, but this sickened him. There was something dirty to it.

'I saw a bear like that once. Didn't need a chain. So used to doing as he was told, he didn't know he was free,' the sergeant said.

Boy was thinking on this when they arrived at the office.

'So, what do we call you, son?'

The voice interrupted his thoughts. They stood in the front parlour of what once had been a fine mansion, now assumed by the English. He wondered who had lived there and where they might be now. Army boots had scratched and dented the polished floors. Sunshine streamed into the room, dust motes caught in its light. A fly buzzed at a broken window. The hullabaloo from the streets softened to the hum of that fly. A red-coated officer sat at a desk, a mess of papers before him. He did not look up. The moment held no importance to him. Nor the face that blinked before him. His attention sat on his documents. His script crawled fine and curved across the pages. He collected the pages into a file and assembled the files in piles around the floor.

What happens to them next? thought Boy. Hustled so suddenly out of the streets into this quiet and peaceful room, secluded from the clamour of the town, he felt he had crossed some threshold.

'Your name, son. I asked the name of you.'

'B...' He stopped, his tongue tangled in images of the farm. He pictured the chickens scrabbling in the yard. He heard the voice of the master: 'Boy, if I tell you to wiggle on your belly, you will wiggle on your belly.' He thought that maybe Boy, too, had died in the fire in New Haven.

Startled eyes looked up at him as he opened his mouth to respond. And shut it again. Beside him, his head cocked to one side, his gaze intense, Calvin held his breath. Drawing strength from his friend, Boy replied, 'My name is John. My name is John Randall.'

Calvin released his breath.

The clerk wrote the name on the page and then turned it to John to make his mark. John steadied his hand to stop it trembling. Then he studied the name.

My name. My mark. I wonder who might see it and what importance it might hold.

One, two, three. The clerk counted coins into John's palm. He did the same for Calvin. They shared a look, jiggled them, laughed at their clinking weight. They owned three shillings. John bit into one, although he didn't know what he hoped to find. He had seen others do it. Calvin shuffled from side to side, as if suppressing a dance, a leap, a holler. John laughed again. And for some reason the sergeant and the clerk joined in.

That evening, the boys took themselves off to explore the town and found the Green Dragon, a tavern which John had glimpsed earlier on their journey up Broadway. They loitered outside, drawn by the smells and laughter that drifted from within and an urgent need to spend their shillings but reluctant to enter.

'You!' John jostled Calvin forward.

'No, you!'

'For the love of Christ, show yourself a man.' John ducked behind his friend again.

'You won't get served out here, lads. In you go.' The sergeant had come up behind them. He made an unlikely guardian, but they trailed him in.

'What will it be then?' he asked, having seated them at a corner table.

Neither boy answered.

'A rum it will be.' He put out his hand for their coin. 'And I think maybe some stew, if they can call the mess they serve here a stew. But, if you're not fussy, it's warm and filling. Sit yourselves here.'

They sat and gawked at their surroundings. Beside them, a tankard slammed on a table, sloshing beer, as a heavy man with a walrus moustache made his point. A drunk swayed in the doorway, his pants wet with pee. A small push from behind and he fell to the floor. His companions cheered. One put his hand in the drunk's pocket and pulled out a wallet. Smirking, he called for drinks all round.

John thought of Ol' Ma, and his Mother and Elijah.

Ol' Ma. A man has his hand ... down the bodice of a lady. In public!

She ain't no lady. You stay clear, Boy, and mind my words now. You heed me or I'll whip your butt!

She looks fine to me. I sure would like to make her giggle like that.

He laughed as Ol' Ma turned white.

'Move yourself, darkey. This seat is mine.' A shove landed John off the bench and on the ground. He scuttled away, apologising. Calvin leapt up and they both backed into the shadows of the corner.

'Causing trouble are we, Badgely?' The sergeant returned and very carefully unloaded three glasses onto the table.

'No trouble, Sarge. None at all. Just some niggers need to know their place. Here, share a bench with me.'

Badgely was not to share a bench. With the sweetest of smiles upon his face, the sergeant turned toward him and drove a punch into the other's belly. Badgely doubled over. A second fist followed through, up and under the man's chin, knocking him back. His feet collapsed beneath him. Badgely lay on the floor, shaking his head as if to shake some thought into it.

'Take your seat, lads.' The sergeant beamed a one-toothed smile.

'If it suits you, sir, I'm pleased to stand.' John didn't move from his corner.

'Take your seat, lads.' The sergeant repeated, his eyes steely cold.

They did as they were told.

'So, it's like this'—the sergeant took a healthy swig from his glass, motioning them to follow suit— 'You allow one person to push you around, the rest will think it's a grand idea. You'll find yourself at the end of everyone's boot. Not a good place to be.' He took another swig. 'I won't tell you again, you hear? It's up to you now.'

They nodded.

Stern blue eyes appraised them. 'Not used to standing up for yourselves.'

John squirmed. *A pet dog and a dancing monkey.*

'You've joined the bleedin' army, lads. Going to have to fight. No man going to give you a "how do ya do" out on the field.'

John and Calvin didn't talk that night when they returned to their barracks. They quartered in the western part of the city, on the edge of a section badly burned in a fire. The house had only three walls and had been abandoned when the English occupied New York. As he settled to sleep, John tried to picture it as it might once have been, but drapes and ornaments had been burned or purloined, furniture used for firewood and floorboards scoured by careless boots. The three walls it had were scarred with the names and crude drawings of those who had passed through. A picture of a homely woman with a pleasant smile hung drunkenly off a peg, as if it would flee if it could. *But she has survived*, John thought. *Though trapped, she has survived.* He gazed at that portrait, soothed by the gentle air of the unknown woman. Webs grew across her sweet face. A moth struggled in their snare. A spider, excited by its agitation, crept towards its prey.

That night John dreamt of boots and dancing bears.

Chapter Twelve

Their days held a pattern. The two boys woke and marched and ate and slept to the sound of the sergeant's demands, so that at times they thought the man had taken up space in their very head. They drilled on the parade ground, learning first the simple drum strokes: paradiddle, flamadiddle. *No! I did not say double drag!* and then the patterns of sound that would relay commands across the battlefield and hurl an army of men into the fray or drag them out again. *Assembly! Double quick step advance! We need it now, not at dinner time! You wish us all dead.* John's head pounded: *Drum from your shoulders! Don't stoop!* When they didn't hold their drumsticks, they tapped with a fork, or a stick or their hands. They tapped while waiting in line for food, while lying in their hammocks, and while sitting around the campfire. John woke to find Calvin, his fingers twitching in his sleep. But as the rudiments settled into habit, the drumsticks became extensions to his hands and his hands to his head and his head to the voice of the sergeant. He loved the feel of them between his fingers, smooth and heavy, and welcomed the responsibility that hung from his shoulders.

A month passed. The day neared its end. John and Calvin stood to the fore beside the sergeant, ranks of soldiers lined behind them. Their feet had churned up the dust of the parade ground. Caught in the last beams of sunset, it floated red around their ankles. The unit relaxed while the sergeant consulted a runner. John examined his hands, pleased to see they no longer bled. Blisters had peeled. Callouses grown to protect them. But his shoulder ached and his hip screamed where the heavy drum knocked against it as he marched, leaving a bruise blacker than any he had received at the farm.

'Squad right turn!' Caught off guard, he turned left and tangled with Calvin. His friend laughed, but John frowned at him. He pictured his name in the file on the floor of the clerk's office and feared that a stain would be made against it.

'Can't expect a monkey to know left from right,' Badgely jibed. He drilled among the ranks of soldiers. Others in line laughed and John felt his face glow hot, but he couldn't think of a reply.

As John undressed that night and prepared to crawl into his hammock he stroked the heavy wool of his jacket, marvelling at its jaunty colours. The dark-green coat with scarlet trim and handsome silver braids marked him as a musician and set him aside from the rank and file in their red coats. He wished Ol' Ma could see him in uniform.

So, do I make a fine warrior? He struck a pose, his drum-sticks ready.

Would scare the birds from the trees.

He laughed. Then, like a moth to the flame dared to wonder whether his mother might be proud of him. She didn't answer him.

Perhaps, when he found his father –perhaps then she would be happy.

'Gimme that.' John jumped as Badgely loomed behind him, snatching the jacket from his grip. 'Look boys, scared as a mouse.' He tossed the jacket to where a group gathered around a table. 'Wipe the table, won't you, Jack. Don't want dirt on the cards.'

'No!'

A blow across the face knocked him back. The room spun around and John put out a hand to steady himself. He shook his head to clear it and saw Badgely, drunk as always, stagger to the card table. John clenched his fists and made a step to charge but stopped. He took the coat Calvin had retrieved for him.

'Thanks.' He grimaced at the grease marks on his no-longer jaunty jacket but couldn't face his friend. 'Why does he hate me so much?'

'He hates me, too.' Calvin hesitated. 'But I think he finds you more fun. I mean, look at me! What sport is there in pushing around a squirt of water? But you! John, you could knock him out and you don't. He likes that.'

From the card table, they heard Badgely roar as his card was beaten, and watched as he tipped the table aside and staggered to the door. John picked up a rag to rub at the grease stain. Finally, in a whisper, Calvin asked, 'Why don't you? Knock his brains out?'

Calvin searched the face of his friend. Finally, receiving no answer, he turned to clamber into his hammock.

John continued to rub at the stain, fingers trembling.

¬

'Don't expect to find much. The farms around have been abandoned. The game long gone.'

Calvin refused to acknowledge John's mood and nattered on. He had been assigned to a raiding party outside the city and was falling over himself in eagerness for adventure. John had been allocated to the hospital, where he would scrub the blood off floors and walls, and wash bandages. With a sour look, he settled himself against a corner, picked up his drumsticks and tapped out the familiar rhythms: reveille, advance, retreat. He played the retreat again.

'But we may happen upon some rebels. Have a real battle.' Calvin rocked himself in the hammock.

As they did every night when not drinking in the tavern, the four soldiers who shared the house played cards at the table. Pages torn from a book supported one tipsy leg. 'I win!' The cry of the victor trumped the oaths of those who lost.

John stopped his tapping to watch a mouse scuttle in the shadows, whiskers twitching. *Are you Yizum or Nkinki?* Elegua had come to him often of late, taunting him in his dreams. *So, will you be running back to your country shack? Yes Master. Of course, Master. Immediately, Master. Oh, I forget myself. You are a mighty warrior.* And the boy god would collapse in laughter at his own joke.

From habit John fondled the eagle that dangled from his neck, before, with a shake of his head, he returned to his tapping.

'I swear I done told you. Mum your dugger, you little nigger.' A boot whacked a drumstick from his hand. Badgely towered above him. Spittle flew from his mouth. His belly hung over his belt and from his position on the floor, John could smell sweat and rum and urine. As the boy stared up, Badgely pulled out his spindle to piss.

A hush descended on the room. Calvin stood frozen, the drunken picture of a homely woman, torn from her wall, clutched in his fists above his head. Card players sat fixed as statues, a drink raised, a card not thrown. All eyes on John. He rolled away and scrambled to his feet, fists clenched, glaring at Badgely. No one made a sound and it seemed the whole world held its breath. Waiting. Only Badgely moved, as he swayed back and forth on drunken legs, too slow and clumsy to run. The soft squeak of his shoes on the wooden boards was all that broke the silence. John took a step towards him, his face crumpled in rage, his eyes blind, and an unheard howl from his mouth. He reached out to grab the fat man round the neck and wring the life from him. But then, with a small cry, he flung his arms to his face and bolted for the door.

Laughter broke from across the road. A woman screamed. A curse sounded. The mellow notes of a fife rippled the still night air. The boy ran into the night. He walked around the town. Around and around.

Chapter Thirteen

August 1779.

> *Where is my wife, me noggin, noggin wife?*
> *She's all sold for beer and tobacco,*
> *You see her front, it got worn out and her tail been kicked about,*
> *And I'm sure she's looking out for better weather*

From where he brooded in a corner of the tavern, John glanced sideways at the singers. They made a merry group, arms linked, loud voices. Ale sloshed from their tankards as they rallied to the chorus:

Me noggin, noggin wife

'Sodden boors,' he muttered to himself, annoyed that despite their unsteady gait, they held each other up. He missed Calvin, who was out on the raiding party.

The serving maid brushed past him. She no longer glanced his way to see if he needed a refill. He didn't smile as she tipped a tankard over the head of a drunk whose hand had taken liberties with her bottom. *She has more guts than me.* John's beer sat before him. A disappointment. He enjoyed the anticipation of it, all froth and bubble. And the light caught in its amber glow promised comfort and peace. But the first sip soured him. He could not acquire a taste for it and now he clasped a flat ruin between his hands.

Seated close, a youth of his own age, in the red jacket of a marine and the badge of an officer, teased a pretty woman, dropping morsels of cheese into her mouth. Her tongue flicked out, and she licked her lips in a slow, deliberate tease and leant back, jutting her breasts higher. The lad patted her mouth with a napkin, tracing its lines, taking his time, the smug smile of conquest on his face.

John did not normally frequent this tavern. He had ventured further from his usual haunts in the hopes of avoiding Badgely. But he couldn't escape him. The man filled his head, jeering at him. And when he stopped, John took over. *You are nothing. No one. Go back to the farm.*

He had been so close. An unholy wail of hate and pain had shattered the silence. Fists clenched, face crumpled in rage, he had made to hurl himself at the fat man. But he couldn't. He just couldn't and with a small cry, he had bolted for the door into the night. He had walked around the town. Around and around. A bear shorn of his claws and teeth, chained to his master. Mocking laughter in his ears.

He squeezed the tankard tighter and wished it were his own neck he wrung between his hands.

'You, you cad. Away with you.'

John leapt up as the youth next to him toppled from his bench. An elderly man with a long white beard reared over him, beating him with a cane. 'That's my wife!' The cane slashed down upon the erstwhile suitor who curled on the floor, arms flailing to deflect the blows. The cheated husband raised his cane to strike again and, without thinking, John snatched at it before it fell, giving the youth the opportunity to scramble away and run for the door. As the elderly man turned both wrath and cane upon John, he too raced out to the cheers and claps from the drunken crowd.

In the lane outside, the air felt warm and heavy. No torches lit the darkness. The only sounds came muted from behind the walls of homes and taverns: the sound of laughter and conversation between family and friends. John leaned against a wall to recover his wits but drunken men had pissed against it and their reek mingled with the rank odour of spilt beer, so he wandered on, with nowhere special to go.

'Hey, there you are! I wondered what became of you. But I wasn't heading back to find out. Glad you made it safe enough!' A hand shot out to shake John's. 'Jolly good of you, I must say, stepping in like that. Johnston's my name. Second Lieutenant George Johnston.'

John stood nonplussed while the other pumped his arm up and down, the first time a white man had shaken his hand.

'I thought she was a lady of the night. A strumpet. Felt it in my bones, I did. Was intending to have her. I say, can I shout you a drink? A small thank you? What say you to the Green Lantern?'

John shook his head. 'Err, no. Not there.'

'The Fraunces then. It's just up here.' Without stopping for an answer, George led the way, forcing John to trot. As they climbed the steps of the red brick building, past a huge African who stood watch over the entrance, John paused to look inside. He could feel the eyes of the guard upon him. He understood why as he took in the rugs that lay on the floor and the brocade curtains. *I don't belong here.* But the guard did not challenge him and it wasn't a place that Badgely would frequent.

'Come on then. Claim a bench while I get the drinks.' George urged John forward. With his blond curls and impish grin, he appeared more like a cupid than an officer in the English Navy and seemed fully recovered from his beating. It was John who felt bemused. Things moved too quickly, and out of his control. It didn't seem right to be drinking with an officer in an establishment like this. He wished Calvin were with him.

'So, out with it. What has wound you so tight? Don't think I didn't notice you sitting with the weight of the world upon you.' George set a jug of rum on the bench. 'Direct from the Caribbean! Only the best in this place.'

John shrugged and only sipped at his drink, not knowing the rules with this strange man.

'Is it a girl?' George prodded.

John shook his head.

'A boy?' grinned George.

'What? No!' John pushed his bench back as if to leave.

'Well, you don't tell me, leaves me to conjecture on all sorts of things.' George was having fun, but it was only after several jugs of rum and unrelenting speculation – *You have the pox?* – did George wring the story from him.

'So why don't you just wallop him? Look at you. You're big as an ox.'

John shook his head, unable to explain the abyss that would swallow him should he raise a hand against a white man.

'I'll tell you what I do understand. You won't appease a bully. They only know one language.' George pounded his fist on the table to make his point. 'I say! How about we meet tomorrow and do a few rounds? Get you moving.'

Over the next three days John crept into his barracks late, careful not to disturb Badgely from his drunken stupor. Each morning he snuck out before his nemesis awoke, to work in the hospital and then meet with George in the afternoon. They chose a patch of wasteland, close to the river, sheltered by spruce trees.

On that first day, he hadn't known what to expect. He had headed for the meeting spot, convinced that George wouldn't come – this English officer who had gotten drunk and made promises he had no intention of keeping. *Just playing me for a fool.* And he had swung around to return to the barracks, before spinning on his heel again towards the river. But George had surprised him and greeted him with a handshake and a grin, beckoning him to take off his jacket. Still slightly mystified, John did as directed but while his arms were still bound by the sleeves, George threw an arm around his neck and aimed a kick behind the knees, knocking John's feet from beneath him.

'Lesson one. There are no rules in street fighting.' He stretched out an arm to help John to his feet, but even as the boy turned to take it, George directed a boot to his groin.

'Ahh.' John doubled up.

'Lesson two. The groin and the eyes' – he placed a thumb over John's eyes – 'are the soft spots. Punish them when you can.' He hopped away while John pulled himself to his feet. 'You mad at me? Come on. Attack.'

John lunged, but even as he did, George leapt back, throwing John off balance so that he fell forward. 'Momentum. You don't always meet force with force.' George laughed. John cursed.

'Now come on. Try ag—' But before George could finish, John had charged and tackled him around the knees. 'He— he— hey!' George started to laugh but now struggled on the ground, John's hands around his neck.

John did not notice the arms that slapped at his face and pushed against his chest becoming feebler. He did not hear the pleas, gurgling, becoming fainter. He heard only his own scream of rage as he shook the life from the master. He thought of boots. Boots that had kicked him since he was a boy. He stood to lay in the boot.

'John, stop. Please.' Too weak to move, George had crumpled into a ball.

Mid-kick, John looked down at the body prone on the ground. The master had gone and only George squirmed and groaned.

'Oh, for the love of Christ, forgive me.' John dropped to his knees.

George moaned and shook his head as he raised himself to his elbows. 'I knew you could fight' – he stopped to catch his breath – 'felt it in my bones.' He laughed. 'A little control next time?'

John sprawled beside him, recovering his breath. For as long as he could remember the master had loomed over him, while awake and in his dreams. When John was not rushing to his demands, he was planning revenge. Now and here, among the sharp, needle-like leaves of the spruce tree with their stringent, piney smell, that man belonged to a different world and a different time. John frowned as he tried to recall his image but the lines blurred and faded, dissolving like smoke before he could capture them. Stonington, the burning hall and his simmering rage seemed like a distant memory.

'Thank you,' he said to George.

'My great pleasure,' George groaned. 'I think you may have got the knack of it,' he said wryly, rubbing his leg.

Chapter Fourteen

'My friend, Calvin. Can he join us for training?' John asked as the two youths wended their way to The Fraunces.

As they walked up the steps, the huge African who guarded the door gave John a quizzical look.

'He's with me.' George ushered John past.

'You're young to be an officer.' The question had been puzzling John.

George shrugged. 'Money. Position. Friends. It helps.' He took a swig of rum. 'But I believe I have earnt it now. Acquitted myself well at Bunker Hill. The flag had fallen. I picked it up and charged.' He shook his head. 'We thought this war would be over in a matter of months. Weeks even. But those rebels. Slippery buggers. And brave. They didn't budge an inch.' His hands tightened over his mug. John allowed the silence to stretch. 'My father was wounded that day,' George finally said.

'Is he alright?'

George shook his head. 'Died of his wounds.' He took another swig of rum.

John looked up as the African from the door approached them. Naked to the waist and bulging with muscle, he towered over them. 'May I have a word.'

John shoved his bench back, preparing to stand and leave. George put out a restraining arm. 'I told you. He's with me.'

But the African's attention was on John. 'Your necklace. I noticed your charm.'

John's hand flew to his eagle, but as he looked at the guard he saw a wolf, carved of wood, lying on the man's chest, so finely crafted John thought he could hear it snarl, could see the saliva drool from the teeth.

'Where did you get it?' he asked. His voice remained calm, but his fingers trembled as he reached out to touch the wolf.

'Friend. You?'

Boy had rarely used the words 'my father'. He didn't now. Too unfamiliar for public display, they stuck in his throat. He swallowed. 'Where is he?' he asked, his voice hoarse.

The African shook his head. 'We were down south. Ran off together. Got separated. Sure hope they never caught up with him. You look like him.'

He and George parted early that night. George wanted to get drunk, talk about whores and forget about fathers but John was anxious to see if Calvin had returned. His head was whirling with all that had happened. Calvin would make sense of it with him. Together they would sift things through. He wondered what he would have to say about George. What could the Englishman possibly want with him?

But the barracks were dark and empty. He lit a single candle. It faltered with every breath of air and sent shadows prowling around the room. Then, he sat himself at the table with the tipsy leg, the torn pages from the book too worn to hold it steady. It wobbled under his touch. He fondled his eagle, tracing the lines of each feather, the shrieking beak, the talons that could rip a man apart.

'What's that? Gimme.' From behind John, Badgely lunged for the eagle, pulling it from John's grasp. He held it up to his eyes, squinting to see it more clearly in the dim light. With a sneer he dangled it in front of John, ready to jerk it out of reach should the lad snatch for it, a cat with a mouse. 'C'mon, come and get it. You want it?' The words slurred together and he chuckled, pleased with himself. His shadow wavered huge against the wall as he swayed on woozy legs. He tweaked the eagle again so that it soared upwards, only to be yanked back by the bind that secured it.

Still seated at the table, it seemed to John that the room swirled in a faltering confusion of looming shadows. Seconds passed. And the warnings of a lifetime. He looked at Badgely and saw a drunken bully. He flung himself sideways off the bench and out of the man's reach. He heard an eagle scream and tackled the man around the knees, toppling him to the ground. Was that a thrashing of wings? He kicked him full in the face. Teeth and gristle broke beneath his boot, and blood spurted up his leg. He stamped in the groin. As Badgely writhed on the ground, squealing, John grabbed a handful of the man's hair and jerked back his head.

'Enough.' He spat in the man's face. 'No more.' He retrieved the dropped eagle and secured it around his neck. As he raised his leg for a final kick to Badgely's head, he saw the terror in the man's eyes. Badgely gurgled; blood and a plea bubbled from his mouth. John considered. Then he swung with full force.

Now you are a warrior, Ol' Ma whispered in his ear.

Chapter Fifteen

'I have some news.' Lieutenant George Johnston played a drum roll on the tabletop, calling for John's full attention.

The two men were enjoying a rum at The Fraunces, as had become their custom of a Monday night. John had come to enjoy the tavern's steady rhythm: the hum of conversation, the occasional clatter of glass, the rattle of cutlery, the scrape of a bench on the floor.

Occasionally they went to the river first, sometimes to spar but George had also been schooling John on how to hold and fire a pistol. 'Upon my word, you have the eye of an eagle.' And, at his friend's urging, John had been coaching the British officer in the rudiments of playing a flute, although his student lacked any sense of rhythm and raced through the chords as if desperate only to get to the end.

'So, listen up,' the lieutenant demanded.

John smiled and parodied the pose of a dutiful attendant. *Only George can manage to look scruffy in the full uniform of a British officer.* He took note of the stain on the jacket, a wig that seemed askew. He continued his appraisal. A mouth too big for the fine lines of the face and, he thought, always open. The man was either talking, laughing, drinking or eating. And of course, his chin was marked by a small shaving cut. He would never stand still long enough to take the care that was required.

Eyes gleaming, George attempted a poker face, and in the measured tones of a town crier he announced, 'It is with great...'

'I say! I don't come here to sit next to a nigger. Off with you, boy!'

Caught off guard and hearing only the voice of white authority, John leapt up, sending his bench clattering to the ground. The eyes of the room fell on him, freezing him where he stood, arms thrown slightly back as if to show he held no weapon, mouth caught open in a silent yip of surprise. He glared around, unsure of the direction to take. Opposite, Johnston had raised a restraining arm, his face pale and angry. He too was scrambling to his feet. The owner of the voice, a portly man stood before them, a pair of eyeglasses held to his eye as if to ascertain it really was a black man who had invaded his world. From the corner of his eye, John saw the doorman move in their direction, his face impassive, his steps unhurried.

'And you, my good man, will desist with your attentions immediately. Leave myself and my companion to enjoy our conversation.' Johnston appeared at ease, facing the intruder, and held his voice low, but it carried the disdain of a general rebuking the humblest of privates.

This transformation from mischievous imp to British gentry was one John had seen often in his friend, but it still astounded him.

'And you should seek the acquaintance of your own station and leave your manservant outside.'

'Friend. He is my fri—'

Johnston stuttered into silence. The doorman loomed over the small group and now held the room's attention. He nodded to John and to the lieutenant, bent to pick up the overturned bench, and leant low to whisper something in the ear of the intruder. That portly gentleman put up a hand to straighten his wig, spluttered and reddened and with a loud *hurrumph* marched for the door.

Without a word, the doorman lumbered back to his usual position.

'What did he say?' John hadn't moved, though the room had returned to its former beat.

'I didn't hear, but he may have pointed out that this establishment is in fact owned by a gentleman,' Johnston seemed to hunt for words, 'of colour. Well, at least in part. A mulatto, I believe. Son of a slave woman and a very wealthy man. Well, that's the story, but who would know? Now, I believe I have some news.'

John allowed his eyes to wander the room, resting on the rich brocades, the gleaming, polished wood of the bar, the chandeliers sparkling from the ceiling. 'A black man owns this place?'

'Black Sam, they call him. Oh, my goodness, do sit down. You look stunned. And please close your mouth. It's embarrassing.' Johnston waved John to his seat.

John sat but remained lost in his own thoughts.

'You jumped like a startled rabbit.' Ol' Ma did not accuse John. It was an observation only.

'I know. I...' John thought of the bear he had seen, turning circles at the prod of a smirking boy and groaned. 'It stops tonight. I'll not dance for them. No more. I will break that chain.'

Ol' Ma remained silent, but he could picture the gleam of approval in faded old eyes.

'I say, are you listening?' Johnston's voice cut through his thoughts.

John turned his attention now to the man opposite him. He had been afraid to question their union, delighting in the advantage it brought, before now. *But I will not be his boy either.*

'What on earth are you staring at,' George now demanded, wiping some gravy from his chin and taking another gulp of rum from his mug.

'He was right!' John said, finally. 'We are odd company. I keep expecting you to have your fun, sate your curiosity and disappear, and yet...' John looked around, 'here we are again.' He raised his eyebrows, in an unstated question.

Johnston sat back, for once caught out for an answer. 'Because I...' he shook his head. 'Well, actually...' Again, he appeared to re-think his words. 'No. It is a fair question. And to be truthful, when first we met, I may have had a little too much to drink. My normal strict reserve,' he smiled at that, 'may have been somewhat relaxed. And you fascinated me, sitting there like a bear with a sore head. Felt it in my bones that you had a story to tell...' But John's glare stopped him short. He breathed and started again. 'This society smothers me and I am tired of living within its rules. I was *not* put on this earth merely to follow the paths that others dictate. And if I wish to talk with a man of colour, I will. Ha!' he laughed, 'If our Blessed King can marry his sweet Charlotte, beautiful and intelligent and a little... "dark", surely I may choose to associate with whom I wish.' He cocked his eyebrows and smiled. 'Yes?'

John mused on this. His fingers fiddled with a white napkin, folding and unfolding it, flattening it out and scrunching it up. Finally, he raised his eyes to Johnston and nodded. 'Yes!'

Johnston raised his glass! 'May we each be master of our own fate.'

The words hit John like a hammer blow. His words. Long forgotten. He stared at Johnston and knew without doubt that he and this man were fated to be together. They sat in silence, lost in their deliberations. John rubbed the back of his leg where it had knocked the bench in his haste to respond to a white man's command. 'Master of my own fate,' he repeated to himself.

'Now. I do believe I have some news. Before we were so rudely interrupted,' Johnston made a flamboyant gesture towards the door, 'I was about to fall into a long soliloquy of self-congratulation, interrupted only, I hope, by your own enthusiastic applause.'

John shook his head, smiling.

'You are sitting opposite a bright and sparkling, newly promoted first lieutenant.'

'News indeed.' John grinned, genuinely happy for his friend. *Yes. My friend. A white man.*

'A first lieutenant who is to return henceforth to England. I am to be responsible for recruiting.'

John held his smile firmly in place.

'John. One day, you might come to England.' Johnston shrugged. 'We will find a tavern and recount old adventures.'

John nodded, not trusting himself to use words.

'I do believe we'll meet again. Trust me. The bones...the bones are telling me.' George wiggled his eyebrows, a comic expression on his face.

'Not sure I trust those bones of yours.' John laughed. 'Ah, I'll miss you.' He thought of Ol' Ma. 'But it's good. It's all good.'

'So now, I propose we find some women. Have you ever been with a white woman? I have never been with a black. What say you? Let's mess things up tonight.'

Johnston led the way on a familiar route: past the stately homes of Broadway towards the docks, past the shanty houses of ropemakers and carters, stonemasons and carpenters and into Holy Ground.

John found himself grinning. Narrow streets teemed with shouting, swearing, sweating men. Brazen women signalled them with provocative gestures and lewd remarks. Gin shops and gambling halls and bawdy houses crowded against each other, fighting for attention and the coin of the customer.

When first Johnston had brought him here, John had panicked, overwhelmed by the heaving, pulsating, festering life.

'This ain't no Holy Ground' he had said to Johnston, who had merely laughed.

'Holy, holey!' He made a rude gesture with his fingers and laughed at John's blush. 'Owned by the Church. On my word!'

But now John gloried in it. Here he was no one, and equal to everyone. Landowners and military officers, students and shopkeepers, sailors, labourers, former slaves and even reverends rubbed shoulders in common purpose.

'This way,' Johnston directed. 'I have heard of a new place. The girls are clean. And so are the sheets. A bit of class for our last adventure. Courtesy of me.'

They shoved through the crowds until Johnston veered off the main street into a narrow and quieter laneway. He pointed to a heavy wooden door, lit by a gas lamp. A polished brass bell gleamed a golden invitation. The chords of a piano reached the street with the promise of civility and grace.

John stopped. 'I don't know, George. Don't think this place is for me. You go ahead.' He held out a hand in farewell.

Johnston raised a hand to silence him while he rang the bell.

John took a step back, looking towards where they had come, planning a retreat. 'No, George. You go ahead. I'll catch you before you leave for your beloved England.' He had turned to saunter away when the door opened and a girl stood within its frame, the light pouring from behind her, an aura outlining her slim body.

In the silence of that one moment, John thought of her as a heavenly creature. Her eyes moved from Johnston to him, resting on him, considering. George cleared his throat. She returned her glance to him, gave a slight shrug of her shoulders and a moue of her mouth as if saying it were not her problem, then stood back and beckoned them in.

'See. It's fine.' Johnston grabbed his arm and heaved John up the step and into the brothel. It was like nothing John had ever seen. Gentlemen in smokers' jackets and officers' uniforms lounged in armchairs, glasses of spirits in hand. Barely clad women strolled through the room, pausing to light a cigar or bending to loosen a tie. Despite their immodesty they moved with grace.

John thought that perhaps he would prefer the streets and the open, raucous debauchery that cared only for the coin in his pocket. But he berated himself. *How can I set my own path if I keep only to what I know?*

George nudged him and nodded at a black woman, hair cropped close to her head, long, slender limbs. He waggled his eyebrows and, with a grin, grabbed her hand and led her down a corridor.

Abandoned, John groaned and again considered racing for the door. He caught the glance of an auburn-haired beauty, freckles dotting her pale skin, her body strong. She reminded him of the fields and the fresh outdoors and he felt his body quicken, but she glared at him and moved away, out of his reach.

'You may enjoy a woman of your own kind.' The voice was polite and cold as steel. John turned and recognised the woman who had opened the door.

'I'll take him. He has a pretty face.' Short and plump, a blue-eyed blonde grinned up at him. 'Come with me, my sweet, and don't look so fierce. I won't bite. Well, unless you want me to.' And she laughed, showing dimples and making her ringlets bounce.

'My name is Aurora,' she said as she opened the door to their room and pushed him down on the bed. 'So, let's celebrate. The dawn of a new day.'

Chapter Sixteen

December 1779.

Wet and numb with cold, John shivered in one of hundreds of boats that struggled across the harbour to where a fleet of ships waited to greet them. He wrenched his jacket tight, but he had grown over the last six months, both thicker and taller, and he couldn't fasten it. The wind ripped the ocean, tearing white rags and hurling the shreds at those exposed on the boat. Spray dripped under his collar to run down his back and his feet sat in seawater that had pooled in the bottom of the boat. But he hardly noticed.

The English were leaving New York, setting chase to the rebels in the southern states. He looked around, a sea of red soldiers and, he counted: fourteen warships, ninety transports. He felt tipsy with excitement. He belonged to the proudest army in the world. None could stand before them.

Seated at his side, and groaning with every wave that slammed their small vessel and threatened to throw them all into the snarling, grey sea, sergeant Barker gripped the bench on which they sat, his knuckles white, his blue eyes, faded and dull. On the sergeant's other side, Calvin grinned at John, but John shook his head in warning, for though it amused him to see such terror in one so fearless, he could not bring himself to tease him. Nor could he offer comfort. He would surely receive a tongue lashing. *Ah, but I am very fond of this small man.* The sergeant had a nose for justice and had never asked how Badgely received the injuries that landed him in hospital. Badgely sat at the prow of the boat, an ugly figurehead. A scar pulled down his mouth, a permanent scowl that allowed the filth in him to dribble down his chin. John had learnt that violence prevails, for it was now Badgely who skulked aside while the soldiers hailed John like an old friend. 'You joining us at the tavern tonight, John, lad?' But the man still tormented him, if only by his presence, and he would catch Badgely studying him with malice etched on his lopsided face.

'How many soldiers do you s'pose?' Calvin asked the sergeant.

'Near nine thousand they reckon.'

'All going to Charles Town?'

'So they say.'

'D' you know what it's like? Charles Town?'

'S' not going to be happy.'

'You're quiet.' Calvin addressed John, lost in his own thoughts.

He shrugged. Charles Town. He had talked more with the doorman from The Fraunces. He had mentioned Charles Town. His father might be there.

'It's going to be god almighty hell below decks in this weather,' the sergeant complained as their barge approached the ship and they prepared to scale the netting that had been lowered for them.

'Then we'll find a place on deck,' Calvin suggested.

'Going to be hell there too.'

But while the sergeant hurried below in search of a hammock, the boys chose to brave the wind and spray and watch as New York became smaller, and Stonington more distant. And they shared a look. Surely no one could find them now.

Holding tight to the boat rail, the wood wet and slippery beneath his hands, water dripping down his face in his eyes and off his chin like tears, John tried to recall his childhood, some images of what he was leaving. But just as the fog dropped down to blur the town so his memories of the farm felt clouded. He could not picture the boy who had lived there. *My place is with these men now. And my father. I will find him.*

As night settled upon them, the storm relaxed, allowing men to gather on deck. John and Calvin found sergeant Barker there, leaning against the handrail, watching the sharks that trailed in the wake of the ship. A sailor threw a bucket of bones and gristle from the kitchen over the side and the ocean erupted in a brief flurry as sharks fought over the waste.

'Glad I'm not down there,' remarked John.

'It's the smell of blood what does it. Sends them crazy. Will turn on each other if they smell blood.' The sergeant paused. 'Some men are like that. They sniff out a weakness, they'll rip you apart.'

John considered this. 'Reckon I've already worked that one out,' he said eventually.

The sergeant did not change expression, but his eyes twinkled. 'I believe you have, son.'

John and Calvin pulled out their fife and drum, and the music attracted others to join them. John's thoughts wandered and finally he found the images he had been seeking earlier. He saw himself playing with Elijah under the old oak tree outside their shack. With feet stomping and heads nodding the two of them would send up a tune to tickle the stars and race 'round the moon before it drifted back to be met by Elijah's quiet smile. Recalled to the present, on a ship in the ocean, in a circle of men in red coats, his music and their voices soaring into the night, John hoped that maybe they would meet with Elijah's notes somewhere in those stars.

When most of the soldiers had retired to their hammocks, John, Calvin and the sergeant lounged on the deck scanning the skies for shooting stars. Something had been playing on

John's mind. The sergeant had called him, '*son*'. A figure of speech, he knew, but it had him wondering.

'Sir, do you have a family? A wife? A son?' If he couldn't ask now, he never would.

The sergeant startled and let out a sigh. He seemed to look inwards, past the bounds of the uniform to where the man lived. 'Most beautiful wife you have ever seen. Such pretty blond hair. Rosy cheeks, plump and shiny like apples they are. She waits for me.' He shook his head as if in wonder at that. 'She always waits for me. I can picture her now, outside our cottage, among the roses in the garden.'

Calvin and John shared a glance, wanting more but afraid to intrude on his mood.

'And children?' John ventured.

'I had a son. Fine little chap. We thought it was just a cold. Only two years old he was when he passed.' He shrugged. 'Well, if you will excuse me.'

The boys watched as he pulled himself to his feet, his bearing as erect as always and made his way down the deck to his hammock.

⌐

The English army arrived in South Carolina in February 1780 and set to marching overland towards Charles Town, spreading across the country like a pack – like a thousand packs – of wolves, stalking their prey. For three months, John beat his drum. Behind him, a tail of red wagged to his beat.

Wild men on wild horses wheeled down from hilltops, muskets exploding. He beat his drum. The army snarled and bared its fangs. It sprang and bit deep. Horses screamed, men dropped. John beat his drum. A flash of light from behind a tree. An officer fell. John beat his drum. The red soldiers circled. They fired. John beat his drum. They charged and refired. Musket balls tore and ripped at flesh. He beat his drum. They left the carcasses to rot in the dust behind.

They passed a shack. A worn-out man guarded the entry with a musket. A ragged boy peeped from between his legs. A panicked voice called him away. John beat his drum. The army marched past without incident.

'We must keep the populace on side,' said his sergeant. 'We want them to come across. To fight for us.'

They climbed hills, crossed creeks and waded through marsh. It shined. It rained. It was hot. It was cold. Through that long march he beat his drum. In April, they held Charles Town in their sight. The packs spread out, circling the town. They bayed. They pawed the ground. They waited.

Freed from their drums, John and Calvin had worked all morning to build siege lines, shovelling rocks and stones into sheltering walls and digging trenches. In late afternoon, they were released to scavenge for food to replenish their dwindling supplies. They fashioned themselves slingshots and went to hunt rabbit down at the creek. They returned with one each thrown over their shoulder, arguing over who had the larger, and which shot had been the stronger. Light still lingered in the sky though the shadows were long as they approached their camp site. The sergeant warmed his hands over the ashes of a fire. Weary men, filthy from digging, hunched in quiet groups.

'Wish Ol' Ma were here,' John said. 'She sure knew how to cook rabbit.'

'John.' Calvin pulled John to a halt. 'Look. See there?' Through habit his eyes had sought out Badgely and found him. The man had taken off a shoe and pounded it against the wall, no doubt attempting to shake loose a stone.

John followed his look. 'So?'

'No. Look.'

A snake, its winter pit disturbed by the building works and the pommelling of the shoe, lay coiled, tail raised, ready to strike Badgely.

'Hope it kills him,' said Calvin.

But even as he said it, John had released his slingshot. The stone struck the snake on the head, bouncing to rest beside Badgely's shoeless foot.

'Damn you, you black fucker. You just tried to kill me.' The words spat from Badgely's mouth before he spied the snake dead beside him. 'Oh.' He hopped away, but then, with a shake of the head, his mouth open in shock, he looked at John and then back at the snake. He bent to pick up a stick and poked at the reptile, its silvery grey body banded by brown. 'It's a rattler. I didn't even hear it.' Again, he looked at John, his expression confused, as though he didn't recognise the boy.

'Good shot, John. Though I would have let him die. Why'd you go do that? Save the ugly bastard?' Calvin whispered.

'Yeah. Why'd you do that?' Badgely repeated. He glared at John, as if suspecting a trick.

John shrugged. 'Just didn't think, I guess.' A half-smile played on his lips.

Badgely studied him for a moment, then allowed himself a creaky laugh, rusty from disuse. 'Sure glad you're a slow-witted son of a bitch then,' he said at last.

John bent and yanked a knife from a pouch around his thigh. Badgely stumbled back, arms raised, 'It was a joke, John. I swear. A joke. I thank you, truly I do.'

'For the rabbit,' John rolled his eyes. 'The knife is for the rabbit.'

Charles Town surrendered.

A drumbeat sounded across the wasted space that had been the battleground. Slow. Heavy. To John's ears each stroke held the sound of death, the last sigh of a wounded man, the hammer of a nail in a coffin. A man moved out from behind the barricades that had failed to protect Charles Town. He approached with wooden steps. He held his body as if his every limb needed to be marshalled into place and bullied into obedience. Should he relax his will even for a moment, they would topple to the ground, like a puppet cut of its strings. A small group of aides followed behind. He stopped before Lieutenant General Sir Henry Clinton and proffered him his sword.

The lieutenant general stood arrogant as you please, a sneer on his face. He accepted the sword with a dismissive shrug, tossing it to an aide.

'You notice,' said the sergeant beside John, 'there are no flags. They've been denied the honours of war. It will set many a heart against us.'

'You may order your men to lay down their arms.' John noticed that Clinton did not address the rebel leader by title, Captain Lee.

The order was given. Though John lost count, he heard say that over 2,500 rebel soldiers filed past that day. It troubled him to see them looking so starved and grey, little older than himself and straight from the farms, their clothes in rags, their pride in tatters, herded like animals into pens. But his attention was on the negroes among them, a full brigade. He studied each one intensely, both eager and afraid, wondering how he would recognise a man he had never seen.

Chapter Seventeen

Charles Town, May 1781

Gnarled trees, their branches hanging heavy and dribbling moss, grew out over the water. It seemed that they were crying, so stooped and sad they were. It was dark among the trees. Branches broke what little day was left and cast it away in mottled patches across the muddy ground. Demon shades crept through this swamp of tears. Seen but not seen. There but not there. Waiting.

Silky fingers reached out to stroke John's face. He brushed them away, but the web still clung to him.

A movement in the undergrowth caught his attention. 'Look. There. A pheasant,' he whispered to Calvin and sergeant Barker.

He had been garrisoned at Charles Town for twelve months now. It was said to be an important role, to mind the garrison. But his days did not feel important. They passed in drills and maintenance and routine jobs. And when he had a free moment, he scoured the town, hunting for his father.

'How will we find him?' Calvin had asked.

John fingered his eagle. 'This will find him for me. It found the doorman, didn't it?'

Since the British occupation, runaway slaves had been pouring into Charles Town. They set themselves up in every dead-end lane, every blasted ruin; blacksmiths, shoemakers...and carpenters. John searched the lanes, his eagle flying free on his chest, seeking recognition.

His forays for food were the only other distraction. Some months ago, the sergeant had presented both John and Calvin with muskets of their own and had been skilling them in their use. The three had come down to the swamps to see what they could find.

John raised Brown Bess to his shoulder, pulled the cock back, and sighted down her long brown barrel. His movements were smooth and practised. Sixty yards away a pheasant had found a grasshopper. John admired the copper red of its plumage, the sheen of green and purple, and allowed it the joy of a last meal. He loved this moment, when time paused and the world around him faded and died, leaving only him and his prey. *Take your time, small bird. Death can wait. It finds you beautiful.* John fired.

'Oh, bang on!' Calvin gave a whoop.

'You have a good eye, son. And steady hands. There's not many as could take that shot. Not in this light.'

John looked down, hiding his pride, but not the smile that spread across his face. As always when he held a firearm, he thought of Lieutenant Johnston, the first white man to befriend him, to teach him to fight and to shoot a pistol. He wondered where he were now and if their paths would ever cross again. He had said they would...he felt it in his bones. But would they still be friends?

'We'll be moving out soon. Maybe a day or two,' said the sergeant, interrupting his thoughts.

'Where to?'

'We go to meet Greene at the village of Ninety Six. He has five hundred of our men, Loyalists all, held up in the fort there.'

'Yes.' John pumped his hand in the air eager for action before suddenly realising that it would take him away from

Charles Town and the search for his father. 'How long?' he demanded.

'But a week's march from here.'

'And we'll take our muskets?'

'You'll take your drums. But, on return, we'll see. John' – the sergeant turned to the youth who was brushing away the hordes of flies that swarmed over the dead bird he held – 'They need you in the hospital tomorrow. Be sharp.'

John rose before sunrise, to scurry up the hill to the hospital. There, he worked without a break, washing bodies and serving food, winding bandages and wiping brows and sometimes carrying the dead to the cart, on which they would be wheeled to their grave. Forty men on forty beds crowded into what had been a ballroom. Once, girls in swirling, silk dresses had skipped across the varnished wood floor, had danced a reel, advancing and retreating with flashing eyes and tempting smiles, and tapped a foot as the notes of the violin and piano and flute flew through the room. And men with cigars had followed their movements with acquisitive eyes and cut and thrust for the partner of their choice. Once, the smell of flowers and perfume would have lifted the heart. A different time. John listened for the echoes but could not hear them. Nor could he find a reason to dance. The smell of rotting flesh and disease, of typhoid and diphtheria, filled the air, and the hacking, croaking cough of pneumonia filled his ears, and the only dance was the shuffle and hop of men who had lost a leg or two in battle. He worked now to hold down another victim of the surgeon's saw.

'Hold him. I can't get a grip.' The surgeon rubbed his forehead where the patient had kicked him. Sweat poured from John's brow as he struggled to hold the thrashing man. Ignoring the hand that scratched at his face and the screams for mercy, he shoved the patient back onto the bed, and leant hard on his chest, stilling him. Another wardsman gagged him, silencing his cries. The bloodshot eyes of the young soldier sought John's, pleaded with him and trapped him in their terror, so that the boy felt that he and the man were one, tumbling through a tunnel of fear and pain. The soldier, toughened by battle, had been stoic at first, joking with John that it was worth losing a leg if it meant going home to England and his lady love, but at the touch of the saw to his skin he had kicked out, knocking the surgeon in the face, and seeking to clamber from the trolley on which he lay. The surgeon wielded the saw now, slicing through flesh, and John heaved at the sticky metallic smell of blood. The saw crunched on bone and the man's breath, sour with whisky, came hot and fast on John's face. John wished for a pillow to smother the shrieks; for though muffled by a gag, they pierced him like daggers. And to hide those pleading, pain-filled eyes. Instead he lent harder on the man, whose leg now lay on the ground. 'I'm sorry,' whispered John as he prayed to the gods that it were never him who lay there, for he doubted he could endure such pain.

The shrieks stopped and the man passed out, his head lolling to the side, eyes closed. Released, John stood back from the bed on trembling, twitching legs. The doctor bandaged the stump and motioned for John to retrieve the sawn-off limb and put it in the garbage. John took his time. When it was done, he slumped in a corner, his back to a wall, his body wet with sweat and no longer able to stand. He put his head in his hands and sought to recover the breath he had lost. When time had passed – five, ten, fifteen minutes – he rearranged his face into a smile. And when that was in place, and he felt sure it was well secured and not likely to slip, he patted himself down in search of his saunter. Only when that was carefully compiled did he set out to seek Calvin and join in some banter to let everyone know it was all but nought and nothing to worry a man. 'So, what's for dinner? Eh, this mess smells bad. Rotten leg is it?'

That night, as every night after working in the hospital, those eyes stole into his dreams. Two eyes. Ten. It didn't matter where he looked. They pleaded with him and bore a hole through his brain and into his soul. He tossed on his hammock, sticking first one arm and then the other beneath him to pillow his head, shifting his weight from front to back. He rocked from side to side, gaining speed as his tension grew and receiving a rebuke from Calvin in the hammock beside him. With a groan, he got up and made his way past the ranks of sleeping men, manoeuvred around hammocks, and knocked over a pail of water in the darkness. A soldier cried out in his sleep, but no one stirred. The snuffles and snores continued unabated. He crept through the doors, wide-open to collect the breeze in this sultry summer night, and into what once had been the garden of a grand house. Few plants survived in the rubble of rock and mud. Soldiers, John thought, were not kind to living things.

In the moonlight, he stumbled along the track and up the hill to the hospital. He passed few people. Two drunks staggered back to the barracks, stumbling over each other in the dark and finding it hilarious. A woman, unseen in the night, called out to him, her voice desperate for trade. At the entrance to the ward, a watchman dozed, the brim of his hat pulled low over his eyes, and the collar of his shirt pulled high over his ears. John stood back to allow two wardsmen to pass through. They carried a stretcher. A shroud covered the long body that lay upon it. John checked. The form had two legs and was not his patient. In the far corner a doctor still worked, issuing orders for new bandages. Many in the ward slept. As John tiptoed past the bed of the patients he had washed and fed during the day, he pondered how much their faces changed at night. Sleep had snatched away brave smiles and bawdy jokes, leaving only pain and fear. He returned to the patient who lay in his cot bereft of a leg. In the dark, John couldn't see his eyes, but could tell by his movements he didn't sleep. He dragged a stool close and laid a hand on the man's arm. 'I'm sorry,' he said.

'Had to be done.'

They talked. He heard of the lass with hair like sunlight, eyes blue as the sky, lips red as roses who had promised herself to a man with two legs. Would she lift her chin and turn her back on him, a man who hobbled? From the bed beside them, a soldier who had lost his arm at the shoulder told of his children, three of them, all rosy cheeks, smart as whippets, but dependant on his coin. 'Will it be the poor house for them, my family, now I'm missing a leg?' he asked John as if the youth would know.

'The army will take care of you,' he replied. For that was what he hoped.

Later, when they seemed talked out John pulled out his fife. Its sweet tune drifted through their groans and seemed to settle them some. Their eyes closed. John left the hospital, walked back down the hill and returned to his bed where he found sleep.

'Where did you go last night?' Calvin shook him awake.' Heard you come in, stumbling around like a drunken skunk. Have you got a girl?'

'Don't be fucked. Just couldn't sleep.'

'It's that hospital, isn't it? Messes with ya, I reckon.'

'The army will look after them, won't it?' John asked.

Two days later, they marched under the command of Lord Rawdon to the town of Ninety Six. Three days it took and ninety miles, beneath a mighty and merciless sun. Quick time. John measured the beat and never wavered. Left, right. Left, right. Don't stop. The heavy drum thumped against his leg. Sweat trickled down his face and blurred his sight. Flies crawled over his eyes and into his nose. His throat was parched and if he had used his voice, it would have crackled, dried paper gone to dust. But he did not stop. He kept drumming. The order came to lighten their load and cast off supplies littered the route like the droppings of an ancient beast: woollen jackets, worn out shoes, broken wagons. Left, right. Left, right. He endured, for if he stopped so would an army of men and that could not be. He alone, he and his drum kept them moving along. And though the words did not escape his mouth, two thoughts tossed around in the head of this youth. He feared they would call him nigger and not a man, should he falter. Left, right. Left, right. But every step pulled him further from his father. *I'll come back. I will find you.*

They arrived at the village of Ninety Six in the heat of the day. Twelve sad houses, a courthouse of wood, a jail of brick with a shingled roof. Down the road slumped a fort, battered and beaten, but it had sheltered 500 patriot soldiers loyal to the Crown for twenty-eight days of siege by the rebels, and for that reason it had a right to stand tall. Greene's men had seen the advancing army and slunk away. Only a few stragglers remained, caught and held in chains in the jail with the shingled roof.

Ol' Ma, I would have given them this town. It were not worth the walk. John did not say this aloud. Instead, he searched for Calvin so the two together could find the river and slate their thirst. They had no tents and so, later, they sought a patch of shade and there they slumped, exhausted, to rest on the rock-hard soil. The governors of the town who had hidden themselves well over the last twenty-eight days came out to clasp hands and clap shoulders with Lord Rawdon.

The following morning, weary beyond belief, hungry and weak, John and Calvin and the army of men turned themselves round to march back again. Rawdon gave the order to torch the faithful old fort, for fear it change loyalty and serve Greene and his men. As John picked up his drumsticks to begin his beat, the ash and smoke of the betrayed building filled his nose.

Seems a sorry way to treat a friend, John confided to Ol' Ma.

Hope they treat their soldiers better, she replied.

There is talk this war be over soon. The English will go home. Leave the land to the Rebels.

And you? You will go with them?

That's what they promised. But that was when they thought they would win.

And if they don't take you?

Five days it took to get back to Charleston. Greene's troops harassed them for the length of it, hurtling upon them like a storm of angry hornets, throwing the line into disarray, leaping back, leaving dead bodies in their track. Vultures circled the skies. Jackals followed their trail.

Chapter Eighteen

'Can you make another ... just the same? Same weight an' all?' John handed a splintered drumstick to the carpenter. 'I need it today. Now. We're heading out.' John had no real need for a drumstick. His attention was on the man lounging before him. Calvin stood some steps behind, holding up the flap of dirty leather that served as a door, trying to let in some light. The shop in which they found themselves was full of shadows, the air heavy and still.

They had been sent this way by a butcher, who had found the eagle familiar. It had been John's first lead for several weeks and he had been unable to think of anything other than this meeting. *By the grace of the gods. Let it be him. Let him know me.*

'How do you work in here?' he asked. 'Hard to see.' In fact, as he peered around, he found no sign of tools.

'Workshop's out the back.' The man tossed the drumstick to John. 'Simple enough to make another. Cost ya though. Figure the army'll pay for it. Am I right? No need to skimp, is there?'

John peered at the man. He didn't like him. *Slippery as an eel.* He didn't like the way his eyes slid to the side and he could not look John in the face. He didn't like the way his words slid from the corner of a closed mouth, as if he were too lazy to open it. But he had to find out.

'Have you seen something like this before?' he held the eagle up for the man's inspection.

'Nah. I make me trinkets. That's not mine.' He peered closer. 'Nice enough though. Tell ya what. I'll do ya yer drumstick. You give me the bird. Fair enough?'

John didn't bother to respond. With a nod to Calvin, he turned to make the long walk home.

'No way was he your Pa.' Calvin tried to stay cheerful. 'Don't worry. You'll find him. And you're just gonna know. Just like that.' He clicked his fingers. 'One look it'll take.'

John nodded but wasn't listening. He had scoured the streets for months. His father wasn't here. And if he wasn't here, where was he? He thought of the fields of slaves they had marched past. 'By God's blood. I gotta find him, Calvin. Maybe he needs me.'

They had been back in Charles Town for little more than a month. Relief had turned to routine. Routine had rusted into tedium, but when they returned to their barracks now, the place was in turmoil.

'Where've you two been?' The sergeant demanded as they walked in. 'We're moving out. Get your stuff ready.'

'Hey, John.' Badgely looked up from where he was cleaning his rifle. 'You lose your eagle? Saw one just like it. Near the place they call Rhett's Bridge.'

John froze.

'Go,' Calvin urged. 'I'll get your things ready.'

John stood in a shed, bare of all but a work bench and tools, and piles of wood, but shavings carpeted the floor and the sweet smell of pine and cypress, hickory and birch tugged at his senses. He breathed in deeply. Outside, vendors shouted their wares and haggled with housekeepers. A small boy chased a chicken. His curses would have made a soldier blush. But for a moment John could have been walking in the woods of his home. 'It's nice in here,' he said.

The shopkeeper smiled, his eyes dark and warm, but sad, thought John.

The carpenter had been examining the drumstick. He nodded. 'Come back in...' He raised his eyes as he spoke. And then stopped, his eyes on the eagle around John's neck.

John remained motionless, afraid to breathe, afraid to hope. The carpenter reached out to take hold of the charm.

'Where did you get this?' Both voice and hands trembled. Wide eyes searched John's face.

'It were my mother's.'

The carpenter nodded and took a moment to steady himself, his hands still holding the eagle. Gently, John disentangled them and took a step back, that he might search the face of this man for any similarity to himself.

'Stonington?' the carpenter asked. He paused and swallowed. 'Your mother? She lives?'

And John could have cried for the yearning he heard. His hand trembled as he reached to touch his father's face.

He jumped at a movement behind him, and someone grabbed his elbow.

'John. Forget the stick. Come now. The sergeant has a rage up. He has a musket for you.' A flustered Calvin had raced into the shop. 'But if you don't get back, you'll find yourself in a cell instead.'

'No. Stay.' It was a plea. The man clutched at John's sleeves to hold him.

'Hurry, John. The sergeant is having a fine fit. Now. Come now.'

'I'll come back.' John threw a look over his shoulder as he dashed out. Tears streamed down the man's face. And his own.

A swollen sun sat in a barren sky as two thousand troops marched out of Charles Town. A long red line. They trudged through a dreary landscape of burned-out farms and unloved fields. They saw few people, a surly farmer or a field of slaves who gazed at them with sullen faces. They camped near Eutaw Springs, just fifty miles and two days' march away. They waited. They were to head off Greene's army, for the rebel leader planned to march on Charles Town. Each morning a foraging party set out, looking for yams to supplement the supplies they had brought.

On the third morning, John lay curled on his bed mat, his head buried under his arms, trying to ignore the mutterings of two thousand men, unhappy to face another day. He moaned. He had tossed and turned all night.

'You're detailed to go forage. They're heading out now. Rouse yourself.' Calvin's voice, as bright and sparkling as a river stream, washed over him.

'Cod's wrath! Why are you always so...frisky?'

'Like a little lamb I am,' Calvin laughed. 'Sakes, what's put you in a tangle? And last night - you cried like an old lady.'

Nightmares had tormented John. He had heard the carpenter call to him, 'Don't go,' and seen afresh the sadness in his eyes. Eligua had signalled to him and John had chased him through a grey landscape, a battleground of craters and dead men. A spiderweb had tangled itself around his head, blinding him. He had called for Calvin. But his friend didn't come and he had been left abandoned to struggle helplessly through the world.

Just a dream. The sight of Calvin's face relieved him and he roused himself, shaking his head to clear it. He looked at his friend. 'Give me a moment, will you. Just stop your chattering.'

His cheerful friend studied him for a moment. 'Here's the deal. I find food. You cook it.'

John nodded. With a skip and a jaunty wave, Calvin walked away.

John tried to return to sleep, but it wouldn't come and so he wandered around the camp, hoping to distract himself from his mood. But he had woken to the death of an army of fires: red embers, like demon eyes, blinking out, fading white. Their smoke made a filthy dawn and the air grumbled with the tension of the soldiers afraid of what the day would bring, wishing to have it over. Twice he heard the clack of beads and turned, sure that Eligua were sneaking up behind him but saw nothing. It worried him. Eligua only ever meant trouble. He thought that perhaps he should chase after Calvin, but could not be sure of the direction he had taken and so returned to the ashes of their fire, to sit and wait. He cleaned his rifle. And then he cleaned Calvin's. He thought they should be back by now. He walked to the spring to fill their bottles. As the sun rose and then bridged the hump of the day, he fretted as to what was taking them so long. He jittered and paced.

A group of horsemen saddled up and rode out.

'They will find them and harry them home,' thought John. But it was more a prayer than a belief, for his dream had breached its borders and its bleak, cold tentacles were choking him. *Come back, Calvin. Come home now.* And still Calvin didn't come.

He left the camp to climb a rise from where he could peer across the horizon. A blur of dust signalled the return of the horsemen and John scanned the ground around, looking for some sign of the foragers, praying to see them rounded up and returned home safe. The horsemen grew bigger. The shapes of the riders clearer. The colours of their red jackets brighter. No sign of the men who had wandered out, unarmed to scavenge for food.

'Greene's army is on its way. Not a half days march.' The first horsemen galloped past, shouting their warning.

'They have captured our men. Taken every last one of them.'

'Two thousand and more march down on us.'

John clutched at his belly, feeling as if his very insides had been sucked away. Without the strength to hold himself steady, he slowly sunk to the ground. 'Not Calvin. Please not Calvin.'

The alarm had been sounded. Men raced to pull on their jackets. Fires were doused. Horses whinnied. Orders shouted. Amid the dust and the smoke, John remained fallen. *Frisky as a little lamb I am.* The words played over and over in his brain. 'Calvin! Come back.'

¬

The British gathered towards the west of their camp. John waited, wearing a blood-red jacket filched from a dead soldier. A nest of snakes roiled in his belly and he thought he might puke. He stood shoulder to shoulder with two thousand soldiers. Waiting. Shuffling. He wiped an arm across his forehead. He fondled the eagle on his chest.

I'm afraid, Ol' Ma.

Yes. But you're a warrior. From a line of warriors.

I should be hunting for Calvin.

Fight. Then find Calvin. These men would send you back to slavery. You fight for your life. And Calvin's.

And my father's.

He heard the enemy sound the attack. The first rebel ran from behind the trees. John waited for the single beat of a drum. The birds fell silent. The breeze stilled in the leaves. Only the breath of living men, soon to die, could be heard. A drumroll. He lifted his rifle. He sighted and lined up a grey man. A purple feather in the man's cap lent a festive air as he charged forward, bayonet drawn, ready to plummet it into John's flesh. John's breath came too fast and he worried that he would lose his aim. *Just a pheasant.* He calmed himself. The single beat of a drum. John fired. The grey man fell, his feather trodden under the foot of those who followed. Again: Powder. Cock. Sight. Fire. Fall. And again. Battle lines joined. Bayonet drawn, John shoved forward, making ground, and plunged his blade into a belly, noting the surprise on the freckled face of a boy who fell. He jerked it out and thrust again. Shrieks cut the air. He no longer saw whose lives he cut down. The ground erupted, and mud and stones showered into the air as a cannon exploded and knocked him off his feet. Fragments of flesh and bone splattered his jacket. He pushed himself to his feet, leveraging from a body fallen beside him. Fresh men overwhelmed him. He found himself shoved back. His feet slipped in ground sticky with blood and soft with broken bodies. A drum beat. Advance. He forced his legs forward, though they were shaking with exhaustion and he realised that he was howling. But he couldn't hear himself above the screams and explosions that rocked the world, and he couldn't see for the smoke of cannon and musket. He could only raise his arm and plunge his blade and force himself forward. And when his body felt too weak to move, one thought drove him. *These men would have us in chains.* For three hours the battle surged, men falling in an ocean of mud and blood. He didn't see the blow that knocked him to the ground. He didn't feel the steel that sliced his chest.

Chapter Nineteen

October 1781.

He woke to a throbbing head, a steady drumbeat of pain. He found himself slumped against the trunk of a tree, on the edge of a copse. Men had been there. Some lay there still. An arm, torn from its body had been tossed to fall helpless in a dirty puddle of blood, fingers raised as if seeking its body. A foot lay trodden in the mud. All was broken. Branches hung twisted, like shattered limbs. Grass and bush had surrendered to the trample of feet. Life had flown. Only the vultures circled above. The woods mourned in a silence broken by the distant fire of musket and the occasional moaning of men. A rebel soldier crouched beside him.

I will die before I let him take me. He struggled to stand, but the earth spun and he puked, helpless.

'I've packed the wound. Stopped the flow of blood. You'll live.' The colonial soldier looked at John and smiled. 'But a good thing perhaps, that I found you.' John squinted at him, trying to focus.

Another smile. It fought the pockmarked skin to reach his eyes.

Wade?

'I'm with Greene. Came with him from New York.' Wade smiled again. 'So, you got to join an army!'

John didn't know how to respond.

'And making quite a show of it,' Wade continued. 'I saw you from afar. Standing head and shoulders above the rest and raging like a banshee. Took three men to take you down.'

John gazed at him, allowing Wade's battered smile to steal into places John did not know he'd held open to this man from the village where he had been a slave.

'I have to go, Boy. You'll be fine. Just stay here. Your forces will find you. They're held in the homestead below, but we can't hold them for much longer.'

An urgent thought hit John and he stretched out an arm, entreating Wade to stop. 'Calvin. Your forces have him. They took him prisoner.'

Wade frowned. 'I'll see what I can do.' He bent to clasp John on his shoulder. 'Boy, I must go. I've waited too long. God be with you.' He picked up his musket and turned to leave but paused. 'Boy, Ol' Ma is dead.'

John hesitated as if trying to digest the words and then shook his head, refusing to hear.

'She died the night you left. Simply fell asleep.'

The groans of the dying haunted the air. The rough bark of the stump on which John lent bit into his back. 'Don't say that.' He pushed himself up from the trunk, stumbling towards Wade, intent on silencing the lies. But even as he said the words, his voice cracked.

'I'm sorry, Boy'

'She's not dead.' But it was a plea.

Wade stood steady and held the youth as John collapsed in his arms.

'No.' He allowed Wade to lean him back against the tree. His body hung limp, heavy and lifeless as any corpse. A strangled howl caught in his chest and he thought he might die of the pain.

Wade turned away from the desolation in his eyes. 'I'm so sorry,' he repeated.

A broken boy in a red uniform lay against a broken tree. 'Ol' Ma', he muttered. 'My Ol' Ma.' He looked up at Wade, 'I should never have left. I killed her.'

'No,' Wade shook his head, 'You kept her alive.' He paused, 'I'm sorry, Boy, I must go. Your forces are just yonder.' Again, Wade turned to go.

Wade didn't leave. He fell forward to his knees; a red flower bloomed on his chest, where his heart had been. His smile held a moment and then splintered, exploding like glass and sending a shower of shards into the air where one small sliver found and pierced John's already shattered heart.

Badgely and others from John's battalion rushed forward, pleased to have made it in time, though John barely registered their arrival. He had retired from this dreadful world.

It was many weeks before John could re-join his regiment, finding them gathered on the parade ground. He hid in the shade of a tree, while the sergeant announced the end of the war. His colleagues would return home to England, to that place across the sea. Everyone except him. Former slaves were to be redeemed by their owners. He would be shackled and returned to Stonington. He would live and work according to the will of another, his head bowed. He had thought to be a man and stand straight. Master of his own path. Broken promises, like grit blowing in the wind, stung his eyes and sucked him dry.

Slave traders streamed into Charles Town, a dirty putrid river of them, intent and free to carry away the negroes who had sought refuge there. There was nowhere to run. Words had replaced guns as peace was negotiated, and though the army would not return to their home until the treaty was signed, the contents became known.

'Keep yourself tight in the barracks,' the sergeant warned. 'You hear me, John. Stay away from the town.'

'You can't be here. It's not safe,' his father warned, when John had hobbled into the small joinery. Calvin had shoved his son away in panic.

The days no longer marched to the beat of John's drum. They limped by, wounded, bereft of purpose, disguised as years. He woke to each not knowing how it would end: if it would stand firm or slide away beneath his feet. Warily, the men of his regiment circled his grief. Harsh voices sought softer tones and hardened faces arranged themselves in encouraging lines.

'You'll be fine, John. We'll find a way to sneak you home.'

'The sarge won't let you down, John.'

'Don't worry about Calvin. For sure, he was a fast one. They won't hold him for long.'

'No doubt found himself a brothel, his leg over a whore.'

'Playing his fiddle!'

Their words sank like coppers tossed into an empty well. John did not picture Calvin in a brothel. He hoped he were dead. For then he could fancy him singing songs for the Lord God Almighty and giving cheek to the angels. But he did not think he was dead. He saw him returned to his master at Stonington: he and Calvin both. Their names would be written in the great book that recorded all that belonged to the farm. There would be a column, 'Bucks'. And under that column they would write their names. John wondered if they put that column before or after those they had for horses and cows and chickens and pigs. And some day, they would write the name of his son. And his son. And there were nothing he could do about it. Nothing would be writ about his eye with a rifle, or Calvin's voice, about how it could soar free, and never stopped chatting. *Frisky as a little lamb I am.* A moan escaped John's chest.

They would be punished for running. By law he should be killed. But he was too valuable for that. They would find a way. Flogged? Shackled? Sold south? John had seen a man once with an iron bit in his mouth. His lips had been wrenched back and the metal shoved in, forcing the tongue flat. Only his eyes had run wild, panicked and rearing back like a horse not yet settled to the saddle. The master would teach him his place in the world. He wished he had died, that Wade had not saved him. He wished he could lay his head in Ol' Ma's lap. He would never do that again. John picked at the scabs of his thoughts. He picked till they bled and poisoned his blood.

He spent his days in the wasteland beside the barracks. He lay in the garden of what had once been a grand house. Where roses had bloomed, a maze of tangled brambles now snatched at clothing and scratched at skin, and where jessamine had crawled along trestles in hopeful yellow trails, it now twisted in a snarled mat and smothered the life from other plants. Cannons had turned the house to rubble. Only cats and rats now crossed the threshold of the ruins to make their home in the shadows. *All for naught. Nothing is certain. It all falls down.*

'Here, pussy. Christ Jesus, I won't hurt you!'

He stretched flat on his stomach. His chest was bare, for his jacket lay discarded beneath his hammock, a broken promise. Not even used to support his head at night. He did not want it in his dreams. The gravel on which he rested grazed his belly, raising a rash and a weave of fine lines, like shreds of red silk torn from his skin. They left his flesh burning hot and sore and it pleased him. A distraction from the numbness of his spirit and the chanting in his head. *Ol' Ma! Calvin! Wade! My fault! And my father. I want to see him.* In his hand he dangled a bone nibbled clean of its meat, but not its marrow. He flicked it to entice the attention of the frightened animal within. Not quite a kitten, not quite a cat, it followed the movement with its eye. It had only one eye. Its colours were smudged: blacks, whites, greys. There was nothing sure about it. One paw crept forward, moving into the sunlight, then pulled back again into the gloom.

John could not say why he spent his time with the beast, beguiling it into the light.

Beyond him, the town could be heard struggling through its day. Voices raised in argument as men bickered, each convinced of some absolute truth. *There is no truth. It's a world of lies.* Shovels cleared a straight path through a wall that yesterday had stood tall but had collapsed in the night. The stamp of marching men. They marched every day going nowhere. The unsteady gait of crutches. A slither of gravel. A collapse and a curse. *Humpty Dumpty!* thought John. A popular verse in the mouths of men right now. Dangling bones towards his uncertain cat consumed his days. It was too smart to listen to his promises though.

The fever came early that year. It swept in every August, striking down men with vomit and chills, but this year it was impatient and mean. It came in May. Blood poured from noses, mouths and ears. Blankets were tossed off –'It's too hot' – and then tugged back again to cover the shivers that shook a body from head to toe. It was a teasing disease. Men looked as if to recover, raised their heads and smiled. Some even stood to take turn at duty. But died the next day.

But this morning John woke early. During the night he had uncurled his body and stretched out his limbs. He had snuck from the former ballroom with its snoring men and found a rock upon which he sat in the moonlight. The clogging fist of summer had relaxed its grip and the air felt cool and clean. His cat stalked the hedgerows, for she too found relief in the darkness and ventured outside the rubble. John decided to toss some dice. He would wander those streets and hand his fate to the gods. He was tired of uncertainty. If he were to be taken, so be it. But now, he would go to his father. He was sure he heard Eligua laugh.

The town had changed. Though still first light, groups of soldiers on unsteady feet fell from taverns. One collapsed upon him, 'John. Johnny my boy. Come join us.' Heavy hands wrapped around his shoulders, whether to steady themselves or greet him, he could not be sure. John smiled. And though it was a little rusty, it felt good to have a smile on his face. A gentle shove and the soldier tumbled back onto his friends, toppling them all in a knot of elbows and knees, and a roar of laughs and curses. Men clamoured around the Town Hall; collaborators all, seeking permit and ship to England, afraid of facing old neighbours again. John had seen puppies clambering over themselves like that, seeking their mother's nipples. A clanking turned his head. A line of negroes moved by, chained around the neck. Shackled at the leg. All bore the face of Calvin. Their ankles cut and bleeding, they followed a man of slight build. Thin, greasy hair fell around his face. Another rode at the back, whip in hand, musket balanced across his knees. No one remarked upon the line, for it was common enough. John stepped back into the shadows. He found the shed at the end of the laneway near Rhett's Bridge. It was abandoned.

'Came got him some months ago. Not long after you were here last. He'll be long gone by now.' The neighbour was not unsympathetic.

John felt the last of his strength melt from his body. He leaned against a wall but his legs gave way so he slid down to sit on the ground. The rocks grazed his back, like the sweet flick of a whip.

The morning sun rose. Soft dull light became harsh. Streets jostled. A rat lay swollen and stinking close by. Blood sticky and drying, flies whined over it, fat and heavy. Everyone wanted their prize.

Come get me. I can no longer fight. I am yours to do with as you will.

Raise yourself John. It was the voice of Ol' Ma. *Get out of here.*

I've had enough.

Its good. It will all be good.

For eighteen months the army waited in Charles Town while men in faraway places negotiated the peace that would release them.

'John, will you walk with me? I would have a word.' Sergeant Barker found John seated on a rock outside the barracks and whittling wood, though nothing he crafted turned out as expected. Together they walked towards the river. John carried a musket and his knife, warier of men than alligator or snake. They paused beside a swampy creek, the water black as tea. The sergeant clapped an arm around John's shoulder: a gesture of brotherhood, wondered John, or of support in the face of bad news?

'The battalion leaves next week, John. We're to sail out of this damned place and home to England,' the sergeant said at last. 'Washington has decreed we can't take you. We must leave all their former slaves.'

The boy who had become a man in this army did not respond but looked at his sergeant through sullen and heavy eyes. He had loved this man with his nose for justice, this man who now stood for all who had betrayed him. His fists clenched and he feared he would pummel him into the dirt.

'But Carleton, he told Washington,' the sergeant continued and here he spoke with a plum in his mouth, '"The British Government would never agree to reduce themselves to the necessity of violating their faith to the negroes." Can you not hear him, John? Standing up to the rebels like that! He said that to do so would be a "dishonourable violation of the public faith". Gawds, the man has balls. Don't you think, John? Don't you think the toffee-nosed sod has balls?'

John shrugged. He knew that Sir Guy Carleton commanded the English soldiers remaining in America and been responsible for negotiating peace. *But...*

'And just last week he snuck out five thousand negroes. Right under the nose of the enemy.' The sergeant glowed. One could have thought he'd invented the plan himself. 'Two fleets of British ships sailed down the Hudson River from New York and each carried a belly load of Africans with them. What do you think of that, John?' the sergeant continued.

John held his tongue, recognising but afraid to acknowledge a slight twinge of hope. He watched a duck paddling in the creek. A duck that did not notice the flicker of a gator in the black water behind it.

'But here's the thing, John. Since then, Washington has said that there are to be Americans inspecting the embarkation of every ship, checking that no negroes can escape.'

'And Carleton has agreed to that?' John asked. It had been his last hope, to sneak on board with his comrades.

'Carleton has agreed.' The sergeant nodded.

'And men will inspect these ports?'

'They will.'

'And when you are gone and I lose your protection, they will have me.'

John slumped back against a tree, his legs buckled beneath him.

He had withdrawn his attention from the duck to face the sergeant but turned as he heard a splash in the water behind him. The bird had vanished. The smooth black water held barely a ripple as the gator glided away.

Chapter Twenty

1784

The shoreline blurred under a billowing, black stain of cloud. Lightning streaks and thunder threatened a tropical storm. John watched from the stern of the ship as it ploughed away from the confines of the bay towards the open ocean. Feet planted on the deck, arms resting on the rails, he rolled with the motion of the sea. He pictured Calvin standing beside him and smiled. Arms wrapped around each other's shoulders, they would be laughing and cheering and howling obscenities, congratulating themselves on their freedom and planning a future. But only the wind blew in the place his friend had always stood.

John had not expected to be on the ship. Only last week he had walked with the sergeant on the banks of the river and been told the worst. John had made to turn away.

'But! Hey! Steady, son. I haven't finished yet.' The sergeant had restrained him with a hand to the elbow and then made a gesture, as if he were a magician performing a trick. 'Carleton has said we must issue our black allies with Certificates of Freedom. No man can take another if he has a Certificate of Freedom.' He bowed. A small bow. Pretending modesty. 'You, my son, are a black ally. And here,' with a flourish, 'is your Certificate.'

He had survived. And here he was on a ship to a new land.

But Calvin hadn't. And his father hadn't. And while the wind tore at his clothes and through his hair, John could see no future.

You are free. It is good. It was Ol' Ma's voice he heard and the tears flowed at the memory of her.

It wasn't meant to be like this.

Your life is yours to fashion.

I let everyone down. I should never have let Calvin go foraging for me. I should have dragged my father back to the barracks with me. My mother. I wanted to find him for her.

John leant on the rail, mesmerised by the great and unrelenting ocean swells. He considered how easy it would be to throw himself into their depths. It would take but a moment. The ocean would welcome him. He would sink through shining seams of light into deepest darkest blue. Layers of his life would wash away: hurts and fears and anger drifting off in the currents like layers of dead skin. Layer upon layer, until only the very core of him remained, shining clean and scoured free of pain.

'Thought I might find you here.' Sergeant Barker stood beside him, impossibly erect and steady in the face of the storm. 'Saying farewell to your homeland?'

'It was never my home.'

The sergeant nodded. 'Yes. I see that.'

'If I could, I would tear the place down, every farmhouse and church, every town hall. We didn't burn enough of them.'

'Can't say we didn't try,' the sergeant said wryly.

They stood together in silence before the sergeant spoke again. 'Just twenty-one and your life is ahead of you. What are your plans when we reach England?'

John had no plans. He had always expected Calvin to be with him. They would have worked it out together. The future was a cavernous black hole. No friend to support him. No orders to obey. He shook his head, unable to explain the terror that gripped him.

'I have faith in you, John.' With a tap to John's shoulder, the sergeant turned to leave but stopped. He appeared to consider his next words carefully. They came out slowly, deliberately. 'If my son had lived, I would have been proud had he shown even half your courage; just a little of your loyalty.' He nodded and left to go below decks.

John watched the small man leave, and then he hunched his shoulders into the wind, and struggled toward the bow. There he watched as the boat drove through the ocean, to the place they called England, the place they called home. To his future. The glow of a gibbous moon, shadowed and faint behind the clouds, provided the only light.

When finally, he turned away the moon had slipped behind a cloud. He walked below deck in darkness.

￢

After eighteen months the fleet that carried the 63rd Regiment of Foot made anchor. This day they would dock outside Liverpool and journey to Manchester. Home. The word whispered through the air. It rustled in the sails. It broke from the smiles of men. It crashed on the shores of the sea. It deafened him.

￢

They marched for two days, feet slipping in the marshy soil, as if the earth sought to deter them from that grim city. They were discharged in a blurring of offices and papers. John marked his name with an 'X', as he had many years before. He wondered what the army had done with Calvin's 'X'. Perhaps it still sat in a file, waiting for him. He would have liked to see it and take it with him. Instead, like Judas, he received some coins. But he locked that notion away. For John kept two boxes now. One he opened frequently to breathe in the scent of salt spray, or the warmth of a hug. The other held only death and loss, and he kept it firmly sealed.

Men whom he had stood beside, shoulder to shoulder, had places to go and hurried away. Their line was broken. Only he lingered.

'So, it's farewell, John.' The sergeant remained, no longer a sergeant, just a man in breeches, a jacket, not red, and a knapsack.

John forced a smile as he looked down at the small man with the large nose.

The sergeant fiddled with a knot in his knapsack, his business finished but hesitant to leave.

John forced a laugh. 'Away with you, Sir. Your woman waits.'

Indeed, John had been reminded so many times about the charms of the sergeant's wife, he could easily picture her waiting at the door of the cottage with the rose garden in the village by the river. Sometimes, when he lay alone at night, he built his own little house and planted his own roses and put his arms around his own wife. They bore two children and they would swim in the river and run through the woods.

With a light punch to the chest and a curt nod of his head, the sergeant turned away. John watched the retreating figure until it was lost in the crowds. He would beg to go with him. But he turned towards his own future. Master of his own fate.

¬

The day had escaped and even as he turned this way and that, deciding his movements, it threatened to fade away altogether. Twice he had swung around at a familiar voice, the measured tones of a gentleman, and thought that maybe he had come across Johnston, his old friend from New York. He would find him a job, he was sure. But there were, it seemed, a lot of gentlemen in England. He wondered how he might seek him out.

The colour leached from the sky, leaving only greys and impending darkness. Shopkeepers pulled heavy bars and bolts across their doorways, grim and harried faces relaxing into softer lines at the thought of a hot meal and a warm bed. John yearned to join them.

Beer, a bed, a woman. He willed himself to keep strong, but as he trod the narrow streets under the hostile watch of blank windows in grey unwelcoming houses, he felt himself grow smaller. Manchester is a grey town, he determined. Grey mud sucked at his boots. Grey sky hung low and heavy and people with grey faces scurried by, their backs bent beneath the weight of that sky. Not one had a smile or a hello. They moved with a bothered air that left his own steps slow and out of pace. The blows of hammers, the oaths of men, the rumble of wagons, the crush of stone pressed upon him. His body felt weak, his spirit sapped. A horse pushed unexpectedly past him, and he turned in panic, forgetting his place. A man sneezed. A whistle screamed. If he could, he would huddle in a corner with his hands to his ears.

Stand tall, Ol' Ma hissed at him.

A woman called to him. 'For yer Missus, Sir. I'm sure she'll be pleased.'

He turned to see a slight woman, one hand clutching a shawl to her chest, the other holding a wilted bunch of faded roses.

'The last of the season,' she said. 'You won't be gettin' no more this year. 'Tis a blessing to have these. She will *thank* you, Sir, I'm sure of that.' She tried for a coy smile to match her words.

With a curt shake of his head John made to move on, but as he looked at the woman with her red and weepy eyes, sniffling nose and pale, pinched face, her words grabbed him. *Missus.* He pictured coming home to a lass with love in her blue eyes and a smile on her bonny cheeks.

For luck, he said to himself, pulling at his coin bag, *and if naught else they will cheer me up.* He smiled wryly at the image he now made: a large black man with nowhere to go, carrying a sorry-looking bunch of wilted flowers.

A beer, a bed, and a woman.

Later John would wonder if perhaps the gods looked down on him, holding his roses, and in that perverse way of them, sent him a blessing. For he paused to raise them to his nose and shut his eyes and imagine an arm, pulling him in from the streets, into a warm room. The crowd parted around him as a river might pass a stranded boat. The crushing noise of the town stopped a moment. One small moment: the time it takes to draw a breath. Through the silence came the lilting notes of a flute, high and clear. And once again John sat with Elijah on the steps of the cabin, playing the flute in the moonlight, the notes leaping one over the other. For that was the tune he heard.

He followed the music to an intersection, a tavern on one corner: diners and drunks stumbling through its doors. On the other corner stood a theatre, ablaze with candlelight, its entrance swirling with silks and satins, glorious bosoms in low-slung bodices, bow ties and black hats. A group of females threw lewd remarks at passing gentlemen, offering their bodies for service. Not ten steps from them a black man played the flute, a hat at his feet collecting coins. John and he acknowledged each other with a nod and a smile. Then John took his own flute from his bag and joined him, their music soaring in joyous, duelling harmony.

'Name's Charles.' The musician put out his hand to shake. 'Like the king.' He shrugged and looked down at his bare feet. 'Different circumstances,' he said with a slow smile.

'John. John Randall.' John took the man's hand.

'What brings you here?' asked Charles.

'Just off the ship. Need a place to sleep.'

'I'd offer you my place. But even the rats complain about it.' Charles jerked his head at the tavern. 'Got coin?'

'Some.'

'If no luck there. Two others 'round the corner.'

John nodded. 'I'll be off then.'

'Be seeing you. I'm here each night.' Charles returned to his music, but John could feel the man's eyes on his back as he walked away. It felt good to have a friend.

A lighter John entered the tavern and ordered himself a beer. But his enquiries of board received a tired shake of the head.

'You won't find none round here, son.' A tavern keeper, round of face and belly said. 'This town is full. Burst right apart it is. People coming in from the country, for work, you see. Can't build houses fast enough. You might try Ancoats, further out, that-a-way.' He jerked his head in an easterly direction.

John trudged in the direction he had been instructed, but dead-end alleyways and crooked streets left him lost. The city changed its mood: the harassed day submitted to ominous darkness. Fewer people trod the roads. Those that did hastened their steps and crossed the street on seeing him. Others approached slowly, speculation evident in the shape of their shoulders and the tilt of their head. At such times, he took what little courage he had left and pulled himself tall, staring them in the eyes. They hurried on. He passed no inns and regretted not staying for a pie and second pint at the last for his belly grumbled and he missed the sound of laughter and good cheer. There was no going back. He sought to recall the name of the place he sought: *Ants?* It had long since slipped his mind. Only the tall walls of factories lined the streets. Ragged men and scrawny women and near naked children sheltered under their archways and in doorways and their eyes followed him and sent shivers down his spine. On occasion He would put a hand to the eagle that hung from his neck. It gave both comfort and courage.

He trudged on. Tripping over a stone, he toppled forward, reached out a hand to brace himself against a wall and dropped the roses he still clutched. They landed in a puddle, muddied and crushed. He made to move on but stopped. He retrieved one, less bruised than others, broke the stem and put the flower in his breast pocket, a jaunty token of hope he didn't feel. Unsure of which way he had come for he thought he may have turned around, he sought refuge in a narrow-covered walkway. Leaning against the wall he rubbed first one foot and then the other, for they were bruised and frozen, and his head throbbed. Glancing up and out from his refuge, across the tops of houses, he sought the relief of a skyline, only to find it splintered by chimneys: some belching smoke, others still under construction.

Like a rat in a hole.

'Odsucks! You're a damned swindler is what you are!'

'I won! Ha! Fair and square!'

The voices came from the walkway behind.

Curious, he walked towards them, no longer noticing the reek of stale urine and fresh shit. Through a courtyard, stacked with barrels, both broken and whole, a door cracked open. The light from chandeliers spilt from the room beyond to flicker like fairies in the puddles on the ground.

John peered into the room. The smoke of cigars curled into the air and mingled there with the tune from a piano being played merrily in the corner. Gentlemen in extravagant silks bent over women in ... barely nothing, John thought, grinning at the breasts on display. A fellow lounged in a chaise, a woman across his knees, her skirts pulled up and over her head, as he buried his face in her buttocks. Muffled squeals from beneath the billowing skirts and a tossing of feet spoke of her laughter. A harridan in black, her face pocked with sores, maintained a proprietary air. But it was the centrepiece in the room that captured John's eyes. He thought perhaps he shouldn't look, but he couldn't turn away.

A man cavorted, waving a hand of cards, pointing and laughing.

'I have it. I've won,' he cried, to the moans and curses of those around.

Some slapped his shoulder in desultory appreciation of his luck. Others turned their back, threw an arm around a woman and snuck away to seek second prize in some dark corner.

Beside the laughing, card wheeling man stood four others. Dressed in gaudy colours, turbans around their heads, they held a platter, large and round and bronzed. And on the platter, half kneeling, half sitting, posed a lass, fully naked but for a flower in her hair and the sheerest silk cloth that floated across her shoulders. It did nothing to hide the small breasts with their deep-brown nipples, nor did it conceal the reddish-gold pubic hair. Her skin, John reflected, was as fair as he had ever seen, so milky fresh he could taste the farm upon her. With a jerk, she raised her head and her unfocused eyes startled open to gaze around, puzzled at finding themselves held upon a platter. Her mouth dropped open and a hand snuck across her breast, protectively, and she closed her legs together. But the moment did not last long and with a gentle sigh her head fell forward again.

'I have her!' cried the card wheeling man. 'She's mine.'

Mesmerised, John nudged open the door, just a crack, so that he could see more clearly. Too late he felt the hands that gripped his arms and threw him head long into the courtyard. Kicks landed on his head and body. Two doors slammed. He lay in the mud, clearing his head. Cold and damp soaked through his clothes. His wilted rose lay crumpled in a puddle. A single raindrop announced a storm. Piano music, muted, not meant for his ears, drifted from behind heavy closed doors.

'For the love of Mary, this place ain't for the likes of you. What were ya thinkin'?' The words came from above him.

With a small groan he pushed himself to his elbows. He wiped the blood from his nose and, cautiously, for pain ran up his neck to explode in his head, turned in search of the voice. A pair of scuffed and broken boots had planted themselves in the mud beside him. The buckle of one flapped open uselessly. With an effort he raised his eyes. Skinny white ankles. The torn and filthy hem of a dress. Arms on hips. Scrawny chest. Thin, lank hair. A face, long and narrow, its features hidden in the dark.

'Best get you up then, hadn't we!' A skinny pair of arms bent down, making futile little tugs against the bulk of him.

John almost laughed at the ludicrous effort until with a curse he grabbed a hand that had found his money bag.

'Hey! Keep your feckin' hands off.'

'Was just goin' to look after it for ya, is all.' The voice rang bright and unrepentant.

John staggered to his feet. He towered over a tiny girl, her face remarkable for the rash of red sores that covered it. He turned away, lurching toward the main road.

'So, where ya headin' then?' she called from behind.

He walked on. Black shadows from black buildings bent over him.

'You wanna rump then? Bit of kipper? Threepenny upright?'

She followed at a trot. He heard the soft swish of her skirts as she struggled to keep up.

'What about a place to stay. Where' ya layin' ya head tonight?'

On the street probably, he worried but didn't say, wincing as he slipped in the mud.

'So, will ya tell me your name then?'

No reply. Although he shied a little as something scuttled across his path.

'I'll call ya Blackie, shall I?'

Now there's a surprise.

'They call me Aine.'

His foot tangled in a root, or a rope. He swore to himself.

'Irish. Came here three years ago, bound for service I was. Thought I'd be workin' in some grand house with some grand madam, pretty white apron an' all.'

She took his silence as disbelief.

'I was a fair lass, ya know. You believe me now. Pretty as a picture I was. All the folks said. Cow milk. Grew up on cow milk. 'Til they threw me daddy off his land. That's why I come 'ere. He could na keep me no more.'

In the dark, as he trudged along, that one prattling voice kept the shadows away. He slowed that he might not lose it.

'Didn't end up in no mansion. Found myself up on a platter instead. To be sure it were jes' like that one there you saw. There I was, pure as the bloody Virgin Mary, swingin' around on a feckin' platter. That same ol' bawd ya saw ... she got me that very same moment I stepped into town. Said she would set me up. Took me home, gave me a feed. Next moment, I was up on a bloody platter with men makin' their bids. And when she were done with me and I got the pox... Threw me out. So much garbage.'

John stopped and turned to her, seeking to determine some truth in her tale. Chasing along behind, she smashed against him, her foot sliding in the mud. She would have fallen had he not put out an arm to steady her.

'Now see what ya gone done. Ruined me best boots, you have.' She burst into laughter at the expression on his face. 'So, ya want some tail or not?'

'You've got the clap!' he burst out.

'To be sure. But sure as I got a little sister at home too. You can do her afta.'

John gaped. Gobsmacked.

'Jesus man! You gotta know that you do it with a kid and it rids ya of the clap. Everybody knows that.'

John trudged on, but hoped she would follow for her voice, silly as it was, seemed like a warm blanket to him, and though his feet ached and his hands were raw with cold, he felt lonely for the banter of those he had left and that hurt the most.

You belong in a pack. Not meant to be a lone wolf, Ol' Ma muttered.

'So, Blackie, where ya off to then? Seems to me you not headin' anywheres.'

They had found themselves in a broad street, lined with huge warehouses. The rain had come and wind tore at his jacket. He pulled it over his ears.

'I need a boarding house.' He broke his silence at last.

'None round 'ere. Only get yourself mugged roun' ere. Ya should come and stay at my place'

'You tried to rob me.'

'Yeah. Prob'ly try again too.' She grinned and he could see she might have been pretty once. 'Look, everyone's gonna try and rob ya. That don't mean nothing. Keep ya bag close. But at least ya have a place to stay the night. Find someplace betta tomorra, ya don't like it.'

He followed her.

Chapter Twenty-One

It took but a short time for John and Aine to wind their way back through the maze of warrens to the town centre, past the theatre area and to the hovel that Aine shared with four others and John realised he had spent his day wandering in circles, snared in Manchester's web of lanes and alleyways. He glimpsed Charles, still playing tunes at his spot on the corner. They locked eyes for a moment before Aine grabbed the cuff of his jacket and hurried him on. She led him down a lane, narrow and dark; he put his hands out, using the slimy brick walls to guide him, treading so as not to slip or trip in the sucking mud. It smelt worse than mud. Four crooked buildings backed onto a courtyard. A brick privy stood in the corner, its sewerage overflowing to pool in a sludgy mess and trickle in rivulets across the yard and down the lane from where he'd come. A rusted pipe hung from a wall, dripping water into an open barrel. John could hear the pitter as the drops hit the surface and echoed around the tub. It reminded him of a drumbeat, calling for battle. No light made it into the courtyard, not from stars or moon, not from candle or lantern. John was as blind as a newborn puppy. Aine lifted the latch of a splintered wooden door and bent to enter.

Get away from there, boy! Now. Run. Ol' Ma urged, her voice as clear as though she sat at his ear.

But John was cold and tired. Aine had promised shelter and hot tea. Naught else mattered. He followed her.

They entered a smoke-filled, dingy room. Two men sat at a table, a near empty bottle of gin between them. A pallet lay on bare wooden floorboards, black and grimy from the grease of the city. A kettle hung from a tripod above an open fire. It hissed and spit over angry flames. Aine dug in a pocket under her skirts and pulled out a few coins, putting them on the table in front of a short, thick man. Dressed in a grubby singlet, his black hair grew so coarse across his body he had the appearance of a squat spider sitting in the centre of his web.

''E's me friend,' said Aine, jerking her head towards a wary, but weary, John. 'He's stayin' 'ere the night. This 'ere's Sid,' she told John. 'An' that there, 'e's Barney.' She nodded toward the man sitting across the table and John recalled the alligators he had seen in the swamps of Carolina with black eyes, soulless as the gates of hell. He reminded himself of the speed with which those brutes could strike.

'Aine.' A small girl threw herself from the shadows of the corner and into Aine's arms. John hadn't noticed her before. 'I put the kettle on for yer, but that was ages ago. Why are you so late?'

'An' this ugly little mite,' Aine picked up the child and swung her around, 'This 'ere's me little sister, Claire.' She lavished great kisses upon her head and whispered something into her ear.

'An' that there is Dooley,' said the child in a quiet voice, pointing to a large and oafish looking boy, with whom she had been playing string games. 'E's simple.'

Sid regarded Aine, a long and weighty look, his thoughts unreadable. 'Best get the tea for your man then,' he said, in a hearty voice that yet seemed hollow to John's ears. With the benefit of a toothless smile he continued, 'Can't give ya much, but ya welcome to what we got. Sit yourself down, why don't ya.'

John sunk down to sit cross-legged with his back against the brick wall, facing the room, and the door. *A cup of tea. And then I'll be off.* He tried to focus. His head swam. After the biting cold outside, the warm room had left him limp and weak. He wanted nought more than to curl up and close his eyes. Through habit he fondled his eagle. Aine murmured something he could not hear to Sid. Sid smiled. The lazy-lidded, reptilian eyes of the man called Barney marked his every move.

'So, what brings you to hereabouts?' asked the hearty-hollow-voiced Sid.

'Let go from the army.' John yawned, then blinked his eyes to freshen them and keep them from closing.

'Well, before ya fall asleep there, ya best give us your money bag. We'll keep it safe for ya, won't we Barney? Can't trust no-ones aroun' 'ere.'

All eyes fixed upon John. Predators all. At a nod from Sid, Dooley, a gormless smile on his pudgy face, approached John, his hand out for the money bag. It seemed to John as if the walls closed in, the web against which he had struggled all day pulled tight. Sid and Barney moved to stand above him.

John threw himself forward, tackling Sid around the knees and knocking him down. Using the table for leverage he heaved himself up. The table collapsed under his weight. His eagle screamed as the two others threw themselves upon him.

John broke free, flinging himself toward the door. Barney hurled forward, blocking his escape. He threw an arm around John's neck, swinging from him like a monkey in a tree. Dooley danced around in the centre of the room, clapping and scream-ing. 'Grab him by his baubles, Barney. Bring 'im down.'

For an instant John saw the scene through the eyes of his eagle. The table lay overturned, one leg busted off, the bottle of gin shattered on the floor, its contents soaking into bare wooden boards. The kettle spluttered its anger. Aine had backed into a corner, her face confused with fear and hope, eyes wild, one hand over her mouth, the other wrapped around Claire who had buried her face in her sister's chest. Sid struggled to his feet and threw himself at John, seizing him around the waist. Unable to hold the weight of both men and struggling to breathe from Barney's grip on his neck, John toppled to the floor.

He only glimpsed Aine as she inched nearer the leg of the broken table and bent to take it in both hands. She rushed towards him, her club raised above her head. *Fucking bitch. Should have known not to trust her.* But it was not his head she aimed for. She threw all her meagre weight behind a blow to Sid's skull. He crashed to the ground and she paused to look at him as if both surprised and pleased by her handiwork, then charged at Barney, swinging her weapon and whooping like a banshee. 'Run, Claire. Run,' she screamed at her sister.

Even as the child reached the door, it burst open and two men hurtled inside. One grabbed John, hauling him to his feet, and with one hand gripping his arm and the other on his back, half shoved, half pulled him through the door into the courtyard. John recognised the other as Charles, the flute player. Charles threw himself on top of Barney and drove his fist into the other's face.

It took but a short time for the two black intruders to clear the room, leaving Dooley standing alone, his back to a corner, his hands on his ears, and swaying back and forth, 'Sid. You done killed Sid.'

Chapter Twenty-Two

John rolled over and a spasm shot through his neck. He recalled Dooley swinging from it as though it were a maypole. With a groan he opened his eyes. Aine hunkered beside him, a plate of watery porridge in her hand. He glared at her, puzzled by this pesky girl and convinced that his life would be more peaceful were she not in it, but he took the porridge and ate it greedily.

He found himself in a small dark room, doors and windows shuttered against the cold. Charles lay on the floor beside him: a lump of gusty snores under a thin blanket.

Though, thought John, even asleep, there is something steady about the man.

John had been too tired and sore to talk at length last night but he had learnt that Charles had been a sailor with the British Navy, one of thousands let go at the end of the war.

'No coin. No job,' he had said, 'but I've got my flute, got my wits and got my arm. More than some.'

And John had felt strangely comforted, certain the man could pull himself free from the muck of the Manchester slums to make something of himself. And if he could...

Another man, the one who had shoved him from the room last night, huddled before a fireplace. It gave off little warmth, and the hard clay floor on which John slept and the rough slab walls were cold and damp. Broken bricks had blocked the chimney, trapping the smoke in the room. It hovered around the shoulders of his rescuer like shades from hell and John crossed himself with a prayer. The fellow hummed and crooned soft songs, the same that Ol' Ma had sung about lonesome roads and broad, deep rivers and though it was interrupted by his coughing and an occasional hopeless flapping of the arms, John relaxed. He dozed again until someone opened a door and a sudden breeze chilled the room. John heard a stream of piss hit water. He guessed the door led onto the canal. He had seen it yesterday, a sluggish muddy run of squalid water that caught the refuse from the surrounding slums. The waste from slaughterhouses and tanneries, dye houses and paper factories fed into the canal to mingle with the rotting corpses of dogs and cats and rats and people.

With sudden panic, John sought for his money belt. It no longer rested beneath his breeches. He pushed himself up.

'Don't fret yourself. I got it. Picked it off the floor last night. Thought ya might want it.' Aine still hovered beside him. She gestured towards her bodice. 'Eh, that's no gentleman you are then.' She laughed, shifting back, as he made a grab at the purse snuggled between her breasts. 'Now how abouts you take this.' She handed him some tea, lukewarm. 'An' I can get ya your coin.' And with a flourish and a teasing look that infuriated John, she dug beneath her bodice and returned his purse to him. 'Now, Claire has a notion to thankin' ya. For saving us an' all.'

John could hear children outside racing around the court-yard, their feet splashing through puddles, the thud of a stone thrown against the wall. Their voices sounded clearly in the room:

'There it be. Get it.'

'Missed it. Over there.'

'Aargh. It ran across me foot.'

'Claire. Get yerself in 'ere.' Aine's cry cut through their chase.

'Thank me?' John could think of no kindness he had done.

'Sure an' all. Got us out of that pit o' hell, didn't ya?' Aine seemed to believe John knew what she was talking about.

He remained blank.

'That evil bastard Sid held Claire while I went to work. Made sure I came back, didn't' he. Took me coin. I knew you were the one, soon's I saw ya. Strong fucker aren't ya? Not so bright I reckon!' She laughed. 'Knew ya could take 'em. Knew 'e'd be half outa it from the gin if I took long 'nuff. Knew 'e'd na wait to grab hold o' that money you got cashed in there. Sure as hell, I knew ya could take 'em.' She sat back, pleased with herself. 'Think I killed 'im. Yeah. Reckon I did. Good on me!' And she grinned again.

John did not grin back. This lunatic girl seemed to filch both his tongue and his wits. Claire came and sat next to him.

'I'll leave yers then,' said Aine, getting up.

The child smiled, blue eyes huge in the pale, tiny, heart-shaped face. She placed one timid hand beneath the blanket moving to seize John's member.

'For the life o' sweet Jesus,' he moaned. 'No. Get away.'

'Aine said you'd holler like a billy goat but enjoy it jes' the same. Steady now. I'm jes goin' to suck ya. Naught more.' Her voice came muffled for she already had her head beneath the blanket, but he leapt up, swiping her tiny hands from him as if they were fire.

'No, Claire!'

Wind-driven sleet stung John's face and his frozen fingers fumbled over the notes of music. At least he wore woollen gloves, bought second-hand. The tips had been cut to allow for the size of his fingers, but he gave thanks for them and the thick black coat he now wore. One for him and one for Charles. A shawl and new shoes for Aine. A dress, blue as the sky for Claire. And some mattresses. All that and a meal at the tavern for them had seen the end of his coin. His stomach rumbled at the memory. *Done add that night to me box. It were a great night.* John had eaten chops, and though the meat was charred and dry, the fat had dribbled down his cheeks, and he howled in laughter at Aine's description of that night. Charles chose cheese, roasted and half melted at the fire. 'Am I dead then, and gone to heaven?' he said over and over. Aine and Claire shared a rabbit stew, but John noticed that Aine fed Claire two spoons to her one.

'Soon as I saw you with that little witch, I knew you was in trouble.' Charles told John, making eyes at Aine, who bowed her head graciously as if acknowledging a compliment. Charles had stopped only to grab his friend, Michael, for help. He knew where Aine lived and who she lived with.

'Where is Michael?' asked John. 'Why's he not with us tonight?'

'Taken off to London. 'E said to wish you well.'

John shrugged, disappointed not to have seen more of the man, then glared at Aine. 'And may I ask why ya chose me for your freakin' little plan?'

'Sweet, when I saw ya lyin' in the puddle at the bawdy house, those big eyes of yours, all confused and hurt, I knew you were a sucker. And, well ... look at ya.' She touched his arm, allowing it to linger on his muscle and earning herself a scowl. 'Ahh, fer sure, you are a beauty,' she sighed.

He had spent his first week in Manchester shivering in the ranks of men that shuffled in the cold outside the factories, hoping for work. Some called out the names of their old regiments, 'Fourth Regiment', 'Forty-seventh Regiment', 'Sixty-third' hoping to wake some gratitude for service. John deemed this foolish. They don't thank soldiers who lose a war. He watched as women and children were pulled out of line, chosen ahead of him.

''Cause they're small,' said a burly man behind him. 'The mills need small fingers.'

John nodded respectfully as builders or leather workers or tin makers in need of a worker for the day prowled the queue, looked him up and down, appraised his size and demeanour. *They'll be inspectin' me teeth and feelin' me balls next.* One stopped in front of him and asked him his skills.

'I can shoot a musket,' he had blurted, but the man had already turned his back and moved further up the line. 'An' play a flute,' John muttered to the departing figure. *And fuck your wife!*

Charles suggested they play their flutes together, for their combined harmonies made magic and attracted crowds. 'Won't be for long,' he said. 'We'll come up with a plan. Get ourselves a business.'

In the meantime, theatregoers organised their evening to arrive a little early that they might enjoy their soulful, haunting tunes so different from the English ballads. Not tonight. Few people strode the streets this black night. Those who did raced past seeking shelter, huddled within their jackets, and loathe to pull a hand from the warmth of a pocket to throw a coin. He and Charles would crawl into bed hungry tonight unless Aine made some pennies.

A laugh from the harlots outside the theatre interrupted his thoughts. Aine was prancing around, mimicking a lady as she hustled into the theatre, head averted from the rambunctious group of women.

John grinned. *Foolish fuckin' woman.* As if she heard his thoughts, she turned towards him and gave him a finger. He winked in return and she grinned. His eyes searched for Claire and found her in the middle of the crowd. He knew her tiny hand sought out the pockets of distracted men. *At least someone might eat tonight.*

He turned toward Charles, who like him had backed against the wall out of the wind. As always when with his friend, John recalled a stallion he had once seen preparing for battle. Intelligent eyes looked upon chaos, remaining calm and steady but alert and tensed for action. Only the scars around his wrists told a story, for Charles never talked about his past.

'He too keeps his pain in a box, tightly sealed. It's best that way,' thought John. Instead they schemed their futures.

'I can make good strong ropes. Just need a bit to set me up.' Charles was optimistic.

'I can shoot. Be a gamekeeper maybe,' John mused.

But for now, they cursed the sleet and its icy bite. John wished for snow. It would cover the filth of the streets and lie like a blanket over leaking slate rooves and skeletal trees. The world would be new and clean and fresh and he would make his own tracks and they would take him where he wanted to go. *Master of my own path.* He smiled and again wondered if he would ever see his friend Johnston again.

And when the snow cleared ... But he stopped. There would be no fresh growth. No green crops. When the snow cleared in Manchester, the same sucking mud would still cling to his boots.

Chapter Twenty-Three

April 1885.

A body dangled from a rope, legs and feet twitching. Peering over the heads of the crowd, John could not drag his eyes away from those dancing feet. He shivered and put a hand to his own neck, the feel of the noose upon it.

Hangings took place on market days so they might attract a livelier audience. Today, the square was full of farmers and traders and families. A child, snot trailing from his nose, clung to his father's back. Two maids squabbled on a box and jostled each other for space. At a nudge, one slipped and squealed, falling into the throng, which grumbled and shoved her out of the way. Today's death delighted the mob. Until the end, the condemned man had trusted in a reprieve. He had peered around, a tentative smile on his lips, ready to thank the official who would acquit him. Only when the noose slithered around his neck and pulled tight did he realise his mistake. His mouth opened and formed a vacant 'O'. The crowd howled with glee.

When the cart pulled away, the thief stepped gently into the open space beneath him. That moment of suspense, that drop into hell, drew cheers from the mob. The fall. The jolt. The crack. But his neck had been stubborn. It hadn't snapped. His face turned red and then blue. His eyes popped. His tongue engorged and protruded from his mouth. Still twitching. The throng absorbed every detail. Falling quiet. Enthralled. Twenty minutes dragged by and still he did not die.

John startled at a clanking of beads just behind him and he turned, only to catch a glimpse of red and black twisting through the crowd. It was his imagination of course. Eligua could not have followed him here. But feeling uneasy, he detached himself and strolled away. He did not know the hanging man yet felt a bond to him. He had been a soldier. Fought in the Americas. Lost his arm there. Or at least that is what he had cried out to the joyous crowd. He had been a thief, but a desperate winter had made John skilled in pilfering as well.

That little devil Aine had taught him well. She had taught him how to spot a gentleman with a watch or a wallet stowed carelessly. A quick shove and muttered apologies gave time for Claire's nimble fingers to do their work. His own, Aine had glared at him, were too big and clumsy, and the very sight of him caused men to put a cautious hand to their pocket.

'Sure, as you don't have the makin's of a true artist. Yer only talent is to knock into people.' She had shaken her head mournfully.

So, he skidded close to hanging every day. It could as well be him hopping from that cart. The courts were hard on black men. It was a well-known fact. Superstitiously, he fondled his eagle totem for protection. Even the streets he walked echoed the gloom, for a shroud hung over the town. Alleyways and brick walls, shop fronts and factories alike lay buried under heavy cloud.

Ahh, he shrugged away his disquiet, *today is not a day for ill thoughts.*

As he turned a corner towards the markets at New Cross, slivers of blue shattered the Manchester sky spilling streams of light into dark lanes and warrens. Dejected passages danced for just a while before the shadows reclaimed them. John threw his head back and basked a moment in unexpected sunshine and the promise of a bright day. The hanging was forgotten and he crooned as he walked. 'Early one morning, just as the sun was rising.'

The evening before, while John and Charles played outside the theatre, a young woman returning home had paused, enjoying their tunes, encouraging them to play more. To impress her and regain her full attention, her swaggering and drunken escort had thrown a silver coin into their hat. Enough to buy a trout, John guessed, or a turbot, some bread and cheese too. Or an ale at the tavern across the way. His stomach growled for his adopted family had eaten little over the past week. A wander in the markets was better with coin in the pocket, he mused.

As he walked the familiar streets, he nodded to acquaintances, occasionally shaking hands or putting an arm around a shoulder in greeting. He nearly tripped over a ball that appeared underfoot. Stooping to retrieve it, he chased the child who had dropped it and who ran screaming in terrified delight to bury his head in the lap of a harridan, sitting on a bench outside her home. 'You attacking me with balls, Billy? I'll get cha.' John swooped up the toddler in a tickle. 'And how is the most charming maid in Manchester?' he asked the old woman

'Oh, be away with you, John. You and your sweet talk.' But she could not help the smile that cracked her sour old face. And what is that you have there? A rose? Someone won your heart today?'

'Eh, 'tis nothin'.' He unsuccessfully hid the flower behind his back. With a wave he wandered on.

It was not just his eagerness for fish, battered and fried, that had John smiling today, but the girl who sold the fish. Indeed, as John settled down to sleep at night, she wandered with him in the rose garden of the cottage of his dreams.

As he turned a bend and into the market, he stole into a corner so that he might watch her awhile. Unlike others, she did not call out her wares, but sat on a small stool beside her barrow, quiet patience on her face. Around her the markets clanged and clattered. A woman bartered for a fowl, her voice loud as she harassed the timid man with the weak chest who minded the stall. Two children crashed into a portly gentleman slow to move out of their way, and to their shouts of dismay a stolen egg smashed on the ground before them. A butcher fought to hang the carcass of a pig, too heavy to handle alone, so that it seemed he and the pig were doing a jig. A young girl offered candles, sweet smelling as a field of lavender, she claimed. And in the midst of this, Moira – *such a beautiful name* – sat in a space of peace and calm.

While John watched, a shaft of sun broke through the cloud to find her. In its light she glowed bright against the background of the market.

She has stolen all the colour from this grey town, he mused, with a wry glance to the sky, for he figured he heard Calvin's hooting laughter at this. Moira's hair shone with autumn lights, russet reds and chocolate browns. Her eyes reminded him of the swimming holes they had found in Carolina: still, green luminous pools. But he loved her mouth the most, for it spread wide and welcoming when she saw him, just him.

She surely is a beauty. Ol' Ma approved.

Some weeks had passed since he first caught her glances toward him. He had winked, teasing her. He knew his dark skin and height stood him apart, as did his strong build, and he enjoyed the attention. The army had taught him to carry himself tall, and he would not lose that lesson. *A slave will bend*, he reasoned, *but a man must stand straight*. In this town where wretched men hunched under clouds and bowed against poverty, he stood out like a beacon.

Moira had flushed at his notice, shy at spying upon him. They had talked since. She had asked questions of his life and seemed entranced by his stories. She had pried open his box, the one in which he kept his pain. And though it were just a crack, and he were ready to slam it shut at a notice, he allowed Calvin into the light.

'Calvin and I, we used to hunt in them woods. Weren't a rabbit safe from our slingshots. We both had a good eye. Reckon those varmints should have saved themselves the trouble of all that chasin' around and just handed themselves over to us, skinned and roasted and on a servin' dish, ready to eat.'

'Do you miss him? Calvin, I mean?'

His eyes had clouded at the question and she reached out her hand to his.

'You need to talk about these things, John. In truth, you must trust me.'

He had taken her hand and held it. Like a pearl, he marvelled, shiny and creamy against his dark skin.

They talked of other things too. He wanted children and they would have everything he never had.

He abandoned his corner to approach and, as he knew she would, she smiled her wide-open smile. She was the reason he had landed in this miserable place. *It is good.*

And Ol' Ma smiled.

'John, I have news. Old Art complains he gets too old. He can't manage his barrow anymore. He wants to sell. You could buy it.' She looked at him, pleading.

'I've no money. How could I?' He laughed to cover his embarrassment.

'Find some. My father says you're but a nobody. He scolds me for being too free with my smiles. You must find a job.'

'I've my flute,' he smiled, 'and a rose.' He handed her the flower with a flourish.

She shoved it away, so that it dropped to the ground. 'I can't marry someone who begs on street corners ... no matter how sweet a sound you make.' She turned from him. 'You want children, but you cannot even provide for yourself. Now go. I'll not talk further until you find yourself a barrow.'

As John hesitated, Moira turned her attention to a customer. He moved towards her, but with a flicker of one delicate hand, she drove him away. Those who owned barrows, or money to buy from them, bustled through the square, talking, bartering, making deals and coming to agreements. Without realising, they trampled his rose underfoot.

John and Charles talked that night, but no matter how they turned the problem, they could buy no cart.

Spring crawled in. The days stretched longer into the evening, relaxing from winter's grip. But clouds still loitered along the skyline. John could not shake his gloom. He woke each day heavy and listless. He shunned the market and the dreams that lay dashed there.

'It's useless,' he complained to Charles. 'This town has turned its back on us.'

'It is if you lie in bed all day,' said Charles.

'For the Lawd's sake. Will you move!' Aine hit him with a broom. 'Yer in my way.'

'Leave me be.' John pulled his blanket to cover his ears and turned over on his mattress. He hadn't stirred all morning and it was now afternoon. He planned on staying there. He had made a cave of the miserable room.

'No, I won't. One lousy rejection from a stuck-up snob and you fall apart. What a heap o' piss yer are. Pull yerself together.'

'Up yer get, John. We both need some air.' Charles pulled back the blanket and kicked John gently. 'Leave 'er to clean up a bit.'

Aine stuck out her tongue at them as they left.

They wended their way through the city down near the rail tracks.

'We could try London,' Charles said. 'Hunt up Michael. Maybe he has done well?'

John slowed his pace, placing a restraining arm across his friend. A man ahead, strolling with an air that owned the world, had sneezed. He had halted, not minding whose way he blocked and in pulling out a big red handkerchief from a pouch within his waistcoat, dislodged a watch chain. That precious barrow-sized prize, now dangled from his pocket.

Following his gaze, Charles shook his head. 'No, John. 'Tis too open here. Too many eyes.'

'I want my barrow.' John glared at his friend. 'Wait back if you're afraid.'

Charles moved first. He shoved the man, jostling him into an alcove where he lay claim to the red handkerchief and four and a half pence. The chain only needed a final nudge to fall to the ground, dropping so easily it might have been complicit in the crime.

The gentleman let out a howl, stumbling after Charles, and screaming for a sympathetic soul. With his attention on the red handkerchief that was racing down the road, he had no mind for John, who had come up behind to claim the chain that lay on the ground.

It was a simple thing for John to pick up his downfall. In the time it took to raise a hope, the chain and Moira rested in the palm of his hand. He lifted it to his lips and kissed it and then threw it back again. It wasn't gold, as he had hoped, or silver as he had supposed, but steel and worth not a penny. He turned just as arms apprehended him.

'Seize the other. They work together,' a voice called.

'You have my chain,' the gentleman blustered.

Ahead, Charles ran straight into the welcoming embrace of a policeman.

Chapter Twenty-Four

April 1785

Aine hung back in the gloom of the courtroom, Claire by her side. With no smart words on her tongue and no smile to remind anyone that she had once been pretty, Aine looked what she was, a harlot; wretched and diseased, with a year, maybe two, left to live. For this moment, Aine did not worry for herself, not even for Claire who would be left alone to work the streets without her. Her eyes were wet with tears for her friends. She put a fist in her mouth so that she would not cry aloud and chewed on her knuckles until they bled.

John and Charles stood together before the court. Hands and feet manacled. Heads bowed before an impatient judge. An image of a hanging man with twitching feet danced in John's skull and he couldn't shake it free. Like dead leaves, the words of the court rustled around him. He sought to catch them but couldn't pin one down. They fluttered just out of reach.

I am not ready to die yet, Ol' Ma.

Ol' Ma did not answer, so deep was her own fear and grief for him.

The judge yawned and passed sentence.

A wind of words blew through the court, so fierce that John felt both blind and deaf.

A thick arm took hold of him, to drag him from the court. But his feet refused to budge, so that he stumbled and fell, crashing to the floor.

'Playing tricks are we, ya black bastard. We'll see about that.'

'Am I to hang?' John whispered, as kicks battered his body.

Stand tall. You are a man. Show them you are a man. Ol' Ma's rage cut through the fog of his mind. With great will he stood. He lifted back his shoulders. He lifted his chin, and his eyes. Beside him Charles did likewise. They hobbled from the courthouse, kings in chains. *Am I to hang?*

Chapter Twenty-Five

July 1785

The Jurors for our Lord the King upon their Oath present: That John Randell late of Manchester... by Force and Arms feloniously did steal take and carry away one Steel Watch Chain of the value of One penny of the Goods and Chattles of Joseph Wardle.

Tryed & Guilty to be Transported to some parts beyond the seas for seven years next.

Indictment Roll for April Session, 1785 (Ref: QJ1/1/159) Lancashire Records Office, Quarter sessions Records England

The step off the shore and down into the boat was too big. The guards had refused to remove his shackles. 'Might do a runner.' So, he fell into the dingy, bruising his shin on the frame, and knocking his head. The world spun alarmingly and he thought he might pass out. Striving to right himself and find a seat, the dingy rocked and nearly upturned.

'Watch yerself, yer fool.'

'Jesus, man, you nearly put us all in the drink.'

He could smell the hulk, even from the land, but as the oars moved in and out of the muddy water and he approached the decaying carcass of the wreck that would be his prison, its shadow loomed over him and he gagged at the stench of rotting wood and excrement. He looked back at the shoreline, distorted and blurred in the early morning mist, lost to him, and he panicked that he might never return, for surely he was crossing the river of death and going to hell. I will be swallowed alive and perish in the belly of that beast. He struggled to stand – jump into the river if need be. He wondered if sharks lived there. Callous hands held him down. From behind him, someone laughed. His captors had seen it all before.

Not those sharks yer need to worry about, Ol' Ma whispered. *It's the ones you'll be livin' with yer need to fear. Become a shark, John. Make them fear you or you will not survive.*

He struggled up the rope ladder from the rowboat to the deck of the ship. The irons bit into his ankles. The gaolers below whacked his legs with their batons. The ones above struck his shoulders and head. On the deck, men stripped him of his coat and gloves, those he had bought that second day in Manchester when he had planned a free life. They were his, bought with his own money, and though they were filthy and worn, he ached to watch the gaolers squabble over them. One made to grab his eagle, but John growled and shoved him away. Even in chains he could do damage. The gaoler backed away. They washed him in a tub of cold and fetid water, drawn straight from the river and joked that they had no clothes of his size, finding him britches only. Then they shoved him through a hatch and down into darkness below decks. They threw him into a cell: a steel-barred cage, crammed with the damned in the bowels of the boat.

With his legs shackled, John crashed to the ground. He lay in the straw. It scratched, but his head still swam and he didn't want to move so he dragged up a forearm to cushion his face and twisted to rest more comfortably. The movement caused a wave of nausea and he vomited before collapsing exhausted into his own acid bile. He felt for his eagle and lifted it to his lips. It seemed to still the tumbling world and with a sigh he raised himself to an arm and looked around.

A narrow passage led down the length of the deck. Four cages clung to it. Dull light from a heavy hanging sky ventured through the hatch in the roof of the deck but shied away from exploring the cells. Those dungeons hid in shadow. John could barely see the forms of men. They slumped against walls or the bars of their cage. Some shuffled in circles, around and around with nowhere to go.

'Charles?' He recalled his friend.

Charles leaned against the wall. He wore the standard breeches, a waistcoat, but no shirt. He looked up at the sound of his name. His eyes held their easy calm.

'Here, John,' he called.

And in the cold, damp hole at the bottom of the boat, John soothed at the sight of his friend. He closed his eyes and let his head fall back again.

⌐

'Easy, John, we're just bringing you over 'ere. You've been muttering in your sleep. Keeping everyone amused, you have.'

No light, not even moonlight crept through the hatches. He heard a scuffle and a young voice cried out, 'No. Please no.' But he couldn't see anything in this dark.

He shook away the arms that held him and crawled towards the corner Charles had chosen. 'Ah, Jesus fuckin' Christ!' He shook a hand, then scrubbed it with hay, to clean it of shit. 'Who the fuck! Why would anyone shit there?' He didn't expect an answer, just kept scrubbing the offensive hand of the watery filth in which he had placed it.

'Maybe best to stand and walk?' John could hear the laughter in Charles' voice.

'Maybe best to shut up,' he replied, pulling himself to his feet.

Still trying to wipe the smell from his hand with a fistful of straw, he looked at the two men, both African, who shared their corner.

'Caesar.' The largest of them, a head taller even than John, put out his hand in greeting, and then pulled it back again, making a show of placing it safely behind his back away from John's reach, a laugh on his face.

''Ere. Try over there. Water running down the planks. Probably all going to drown.' An earnest looking man pointed to a wet patch of the hull. 'Name's John Martin.' John saw that Martin's nails were long and filed into sharp points. He thought to do the same.

Two men shoved their way across the cell to stand before John, like fighters, legs apart, arms on hips. 'Thought we better introduce ourselves, polite like,' one said. His nose was flattened against his face and he spoke in choked tones, as if the words were reluctant to leave his mouth.

'John, meet the Dobson brothers,' said Caesar. 'Look like pigs, grunt like pigs and have their sty over the other side of the cell.'

The larger and stockier of the two put a restraining arm across his smaller brother. 'Just let your new boy know we have a deal. You don't mess with us. We won't mess with you.' They turned and walked from whence they had come, carving a path across the cell as men shuffled out of their way.

So, they are the sharks, thought John.

Later that night, after their meal, John watched as Charles used a nail to notch a single line in the boards above their head. 'To keep count,' he said.

'All this for a length of chain,' John grumbled. 'And she didn't even come to court.'

'They say we're going to Africa. I wonder what it's like?'

'I wonder why she didn't come to court? Do you figure she knew?'

As they both curled up to sleep, John closed his eyes in hopes that his dreams might find Moira in the cottage, but she did not come. The roses had shrivelled, their red velvet petals had turned dry and brown and crumpled to dust in his hands.

Three notches scored the wood. His world had become a shadowland of wraiths who moved with a clanking of chains and a rattling of bars. John sat in his corner and worried at a bite on his arm. He scratched at the lice in his head. Then he threw a piece of rotten wood, broken from the hull, at a rat that sniffed too close.

The ladder groaned with the weight of boots. A heavy tread on creaking planks. A baton rattled against the bars. Men stood and shuffled into line.

'Feeding time for you brutes. Come and get it.'

He didn't move. He was so hungry, he wanted to beat his way to the front of the line and kill any man who stood between him and his meal. He wanted to stuff his bread in his mouth and then fight, to the death, if need be, the others for theirs. Instead, he waited. This was the only moment of the day that held any meaning. He would make it last. He would enjoy the aching of his belly and the tightness in his chest. And then he would eat his bread, crumb by crumb, and drink his broth, one sip at a time, and then slowly, very slowly, he and Charles would make another mark. And that would be another day.

He watched as others lined up and received their rations. Some gobbled it down, right there where they got it, right in front of the gaoler. Weak fuckers, small fuckers. Soon-to-be-dead fuckers, he reckoned. They knew that if they waited too long, they would lose their biscuit. The sharks would have it.

Finally, he dragged himself up to stand last in line. The gaoler thrust into his hand a taste of broth in a wooden bowl. John did not look at the man, just the bowl. A piece of meat, ox cheek, he supposed, floated there, more sinew than meat. He would take it back to his corner, chew every bite, while those who had finished theirs looked at him with hungry eyes.

'And here's your biscuit. An' what's yer hurry. You don't want your beer then?'

The gaoler had a belly that hung over his belt. His sleeves were rolled to show forearms covered in coarse hair. The voice so gravelly, it held the chipping of hard rock and seemed to John to come straight from the quarry. John startled. He recognised that voice and raised his eyes from the bowl.

'Badgely?' he asked.

The man before him lifted his head from the job of ladling soup, a growl upon his tongue that died on seeing the black man.

'John? That you, my son? Ahh, for the sake of the blessed Mary. What's bought you 'ere to this miserable pit o' 'ell?'

John felt tears come to his eyes, so sweet did that sour voice sound to his ears.

¬

Thirty-three notches scored the wood. John scratched. He picked a scab and sucked the pus. He kicked at a rat. He waited for his biscuit and pease and beer.

Charles drowsed, his head on John's lap. John and John Martin had propped themselves against each other, neither able to sleep. Caesar sprawled in the corner, his snores exploding through the cell like thunder. Like trees grafted together, they had become as one and John wondered that he could be content, even when in hell. A moment for his box.

A whimpering from the far side of the room disturbed him. He could not see through the shadows, but knew it for the lad called Stinky, not more than seventeen. One who gobbled his food before it could be stolen from him.

'Does he ever shut up?' John asked John Martin.

'Only when he has a dick in his mouth.'

He stroked Charles' hair back from his face. *Must be deaf to sleep through Caesar's snores.* He regarded the larger man. Even sleeping he had a smile on his face, planning some jest. He moved through his days as if their prison were but a temporary inconvenience and not to be taken seriously.

'He truly from Madagascar?' he asked John Martin.

'That's what he says. Maybe he is. Maybe he ain't. Maybe that be where his ma came from. But that's the place he likes to call home.' This was almost a speech from John Martin, who was mean with his words, saving them as though they were gold coin. He and Caesar were as different as two men could be. He knew the world as a dangerous place, and prepared accordingly, growing the bark around him so tough that none could chip it; sending down his roots so strong that none could budge him. 'Guess we all need to think we belong someplace, not just some piece of trash blown from one port to another.'

'And you? Where you from?' John asked to keep the conversation going.

'Place called St Thomas. Tobacco plantations. Sugar fields. A few white men and a lot of black. I was lucky. Taken from the fields and put on the docks. Used to watch them ships comin' and goin' and wonder what the world was like out there.

'How'd you get away?'

'Didn't have no say in it. Navy boat came into port. They needed crew. Picked me up. End of the war, they pitched me back to land. Happened to be England.' He shook his head, slowly. 'Just a bit of jetsam really.'

⌐

Eighty-three notches scored the wood.

'Stinky. You got a visitor.' Badgely thumped down the ladder. His heavy tread announced him before he came into view. ''Ere John. A little somfing.' He passed the broken crust of a loaf through the bars, followed by some sausage. John clasped hands briefly with the gaoler. A nod of the head. He broke the feast into bits, handing the largest to Caesar, always the hungriest, and shared the rest with his friends. Fifty pairs of eyes followed its path.

Badgely stood next to a boy, not sixteen, with the same brown hair and doe-like eyes of Stinky. When the loaf was devoured, the eyes turned back towards the visitor. He flinched and looked as if he might turn and run. He swallowed hard and seemed not to know what to say or do. Then, he passed a parcel wrapped in brown paper through the bars to Stinky.

'Mum says she'll send some every week. She says she didn't know where you were till just now. She's sorry 'bout that.' The boy had exhausted his courage. This time he did turn and run. Badgely followed him up the ladder. Six or seven scavenging convicts surrounded Stinky and tore the parcel from his grasp, scrabbling over the cheese and bread and smoked fish that fell to the floor and got kicked around in the straw before a bearded old man, deceptively nimble, secured it under his foot and popped it into his mouth. Neither John nor his friends took part in the scavenge. From where they stood, they could see only shadows, a thrashing and tumble of bodies and limbs, and hear only Stinky's wails.

John left his corner. His friends followed. They shoved through the mass of men, occasionally and strategically treading on a wrist or an ankle that lay in their way. They found Stinky curled up in a ball, on wet straw that stunk of shit. His shoulders shook and they could see he was crying. He had been relegated to the place near the slop bucket. It overflowed with excrement and piss, so that men now shit around it rather than in. John had watched as some had chosen to urinate on Stinky. He understood the despair that drove them to it, but he never did.

'Up you get.' John nudged Stinky's leg. 'We have a deal for you.'

Stinky pulled himself tighter into a ball, preparing for some new outrage upon him. He looked up at John, his face covered with snot and tears, his eyes swollen. 'Please, I can't do that no more. Please don't.'

'Oh Jesus friggin' Christ. I sure as hell don't want yer. Never fancied boys meself. You, Caesar?'

Caesar shrugged, as if considering, but at a look from John, smiled and shook his head.

'Nah, we just inviting you to come share our little corner of the world. Keep you nice and safe like.'

Stinky stared at them, waiting for the joke to reveal itself.

'And of course,' John continued, 'we make sure that no one else takes a fancy to that parcel of yours. We'll keep that nice and safe too. Long as your parcels keep coming, we'll look after yer. You good and dandy with that?'

'You ain't taking him or his parcels anyplace. He's our boy.' The Dobson brothers pushed through to stand between Stinky and John.

John put out his hand to haul Stinky up. 'Looks like you need a new boy... and a new parcel.' He flashed a smile at them.

'You're a dead man, Randall.'

Ninety-seven notches scored the wood.

'John, someone to visit you.' Badgely's gravelled voice called his attention. He was smiling. Badgely's smile, with his broken teeth, looked out of place upon his face and rarely visited there.

But, decided John, rousing himself, it's better than his frown.

Behind Badgely stood a small man. John squinted into the dark, and broke into a laugh when he recognised the upright stance and the large nose of sergeant Barker. He reached through the cell bars to grasp his arm. 'By my gods it is good to see you.'

'Ahh, John, my son. I came when I could.' – the sergeant paused. He fumbled with his words – 'I'm sorry to find you here.'

'And your wife with the rosy cheeks. She is well?' John ignored the intimacy.

'You remember?'

'I never forget. I'm not like you, old man.'

'I've brought you some apples and cheese and ham from the farm. Badgely said you suffered poorly here. They'll help a little and I'll visit when I can. Oh, and a pot of whisky. Didn't think it could do no harm. And a coat and some blankets. It'll get cold soon.'

John averted his gaze to hide his sudden and inexplicable need to cry. Seemed he no longer knew how to respond to a simple kindness. Instead, he looked at his feet. Thick callouses had split, the dead skin showing chalky white against the black. Ghost feet.

'You'll be fine, John. Ha, you'll sail away to Africa and become a prince. You are the son of warriors. Isn't that what you used to say?'

When the sergeant left, John handed the blanket to Charles. He broke the cheese into small pieces and distributed them to Charles and Caesar and John Martin. Then he passed the whisky around. 'One swig only. We'll make it last.' The apples and ham they would keep until tomorrow.

'Tell us one of Ol' Ma's stories.'

Those stories had been shared throughout the cell and gathered an audience whenever they were told. John sprawled next to Charles, his back cushioned by the coat. Caesar and Martin gathered near him. He took another swig of whisky, and called Ol' Ma forth. He put his head on her lap. He breathed in the sweet muskiness of her, the sweat of her work, the herbs she hung around her neck.

'In the beginning,' he started, 'our people in Africa dwelt in caves far below the ground. They suffered the dark and damp as we do now.'

'Did they eat mouldy biscuits too?' Charles interrupted.

'Shush. This is my tale – but I never did ask Ol' Ma what they ate. Perhaps the rats.' John kicked at one that crept close to his toes. 'One day,' he returned to his story, 'a small boy – Ol' Ma always said he were just like me and had gone wandering where he shouldn't – Anyways, this small boy, he let out a mighty cry. A giant worm had come a-tunnelling and left a great hole. A fearful light seeped down into the shadowy world in which they lived. Most of the people threw themselves back deeper into the shadows, so afeared they were. But seven men, five women, and a leopard crept up toward the surface of the earth. And in my heart, I know the small boy went too, for surely I would have.'

'What's a leopard?' The question came from another who had crept close to hear the story.

'A bobcat, but bigger and fiercer and stronger. An African bobcat.'

'What's a bobcat?' an English voice interrupted.

'A cat. A big, fierce cat ... that gets mad at stupid questions!' The others laughed as John lightly cuffed the shoulder of the enquirer. He continued. 'When those seven people followed the tunnel to the surface of the world and broke free of the dark caves, they threw themselves down in a heap, screaming and crying, so bright and terrible did it seem to them. But one among them, Adu Ogyinae did look about him and marvel. He stroked his black skin, warmed by the sun. He admired the leaves as they glistened on the branches of the trees. He opened his arms wide and fell to his knees to thank the gods for this boon.' John paused for a moment for he recalled how Ol' Ma always admonished at this point: Never forget to thank the gods, boy.

He continued the story. 'Adu Ogyinae, he calmed the others, resting an arm over their shaking shoulders, murmuring hope into their ears. "Look at what a wondrous place we have found," he said to them. And so it was that the African people came out of the ground to find their place in the world.' He stopped. Charles had closed his eyes and was sleeping.

'And we'll escape this hole, to a wondrous place,' John whispered to himself.

He rolled onto his side, and in the gloom, he imagined sunlight shining through the leaves.

'You know we'll die in Africa. Should be praying we never get there.'

John had not noticed Woodham settle himself beside him. A little younger and a lot smaller and a white boy to boot, Woodham had allied himself to the black men in the cell. They allowed it. 'He's a smart one, that one. Knows which way is up, 'e does.' John Martin, who had known him in Newgate Prison, had said.

'And you would know?' John replied to Woodham. 'Been there, have you?'

'As a matter of fact, I have. Sent there on the 'Dey Keyser', year or so back. They just dumped us. No food. No water. No tents. Some didn't even have clothes on their back. People dying on the rocks in the sun. This sun, it shrivelled people right up. They all died.'

John pondered this a while. He picked at a scab. 'How'd you get back?'

'Hitched a ride. Sure as hell don't have no inclination to go there again.'

⌐

Two hundred and twenty-eight notches. 'Ahh, my bones ache,' John complained to Charles. He shivered in the corner and wondered where the rats had gone. Black clouds covered the world above. He wondered if everything in the world outside had died. He would like that.

Charles didn't listen. His friend tossed this way and that, muttering nonsense.

'Stinky. Bring me that fella's coat.' John pulled Charles' head onto his lap.

Stinky moved to oblige, yanking the coat from a man with grey stubble on his chin and a wife who waited for him to come home. She had visited once, was fair of face, and John believed that the stubble-chinned man did not deserve her.

At mealtime, Badgely obliged with double beer. Soaking a shirt, John tried to squeeze the liquid through his friend's cracked lips.

He bent low to Charles' ear. 'Charles. Wake up. Drink for me. What's this rash upon you?' He put his hand to his own forehead, wiping away the sweat. 'How can it be so hot in here?'

He lay down next to Charles. In the gloom he opened his memory box and he and Calvin were wrestling together in the woods beside the church, laughing as they tumbled together into the grass where they lay watching the sunlight shine through the leaves.

Though days had passed, no new notches were scratched.

Two hundred and forty one notches.

'We thought you were gone.' Badgely handed John his bowl, rich with meat. Two biscuits, not even mouldy. 'You were sick with fever, long time.'

'Charles?'

Badgely shrugged.

John had a vision of them dragging Charles's body up the ladder. Was he still warm when they did it? Did they throw him overboard, into the river? The bowl slipped from his grasp. He crawled into the corner where he curled himself into a ball.

Caesar dropped down beside him.

John pulled himself tighter. In his fevered mind, his mother cackled, sounding more like a witch than she had done in life. *I told you. I warned you.*

He fingered his eagle, felt its wings spread, prepared to fly away. A touch stalled his flight.

Caesar put an arm around his shoulder. 'We're brothers. You're stuck with me.'

'Brothers,' John Martin echoed, plopping himself down on his other side.

John's head fell into his hands and he cried.

Seeing him bleed, the sharks gathered to feed.

Two hundred and eighty-nine notches. John fingered the charm. He ruffled its feathers and traced the line of its wings as they spread in blessed relief. The talons curled beneath his touch and in his mind he heard it screech and fly away. He lost himself, gliding the currents of his memories, with Calvin and Elijah and Ol' Ma, soaring through time and space. He sailed over a vast land of red earth where rivers undulated like snakes across the soil. He wondered at it, for it sang an ancient song.

'No, no. Get away. John, help me!' Stinky's voice interrupted his dreaming. Through bleary eyes John could just see the boy. A Dobson brother held his arms behind him, while another punched him in the gut.

'You want him, Randall? Best come and get him.' The elder of the two bent to retrieve a parcel, just delivered, they had wrested from Stinky's arms. 'We keep this.'

John pulled himself to his feet, still blurry from his dreams. Beside him, Caesar staggered up. The fever had a hold of him, and he wavered.

'Nah, I got to settle this.' John gestured him back.

John Martin came to his side and palmed him a sharpened blade. With a shrug, John stuck it in his belt. Bodies parted before him as he hobbled over to where Stinky and the Dobson brothers stood.

'One on one,' he said. 'Which of you slimy buggers has the balls to fight?'

The elder, Rob, stepped forward. 'I reckon you're mine.'

They circled. Crouched low. Rob lunged at him. John barely dodged away in time but avoided his opponent who fell into the watching crowd, only to be pushed back. John used the moment to punch him first in the belly, and then an uppercut to the chin, sending his opponent to the floor. It felt good. He had wanted to fight since he had come down here. He wanted to kill. Climbing on top of him, John pushed a knee into the other's back. Forcing his arm behind him, he jerked, pulling the joint from its socket.

With a howl of rage, Jack, the younger of the two brothers, threw himself upon John, and plunged a knife into his back, but it bent without doing damage. John rolled away. Jack tumbled to the ground beside him. Pulling his own blade from his belt, John grabbed the younger brother around the neck, and slit his throat.

Still lying on the ground, unable to raise himself on his dislocated shoulder, Rob let out a howl and struggled to reach his brother, crawling along the ground. The convicts who had scrambled to watch the fight now scattered as far away as they could. John pulled himself to his feet to walk back to his corner.

Now you gone done it. Ol' Ma sounded frightened. *For sure you'll hang now.*

Good. But 'til then, I'm top shark and ain't no one going to bother me.

No gaolers came down. They must have heard the noise, but it was not until lunchtime that Badgely appeared.

'He's done killed me brother!' Rob screamed, pointing at John who sat in his corner. 'He attacked me. I need a surgeon.'

Badgely looked around the cell where forty men avoided his gaze. He glanced at John who met his question with a shrug. He scratched the back of his neck, and sucked in his cheeks, and made small explosive noises with his mouth.

'You'll get your surgeon,' he finally replied to Rob, who knelt beside the body of his brother, alone in the middle of the cell. 'That's when you get your tongue straight. Your brother fell on his own knife, I don't doubt it. Anyone here says different then?' He gazed around the cell. No one looked at him. 'You saying me lad John there's dangerous? Nah! He's gentle as a little pussycat... Lest you get him riled.' He put a finger to the scar on his mouth. 'You remember that pussycat you had, John?'

Four hundred and fifty notches. A rat slunk across the beam above John's head. He didn't have the strength to throw anything at it. He watched as Caesar flicked the rat with a bit of cloth. It fell onto a sleeping Stinky who woke with a scream, 'It bit me. It bit me.' And indeed, it had, for blood streamed from Stinky's ear. Caesar laughed and flopped himself down next to John.

You reckon we gonna die here?' John asked. He wondered how old he was. Twenty-two? Twenty-three? Too young.

Convicts were being herded across England towards Portsmouth. Some travelled chained to wagons and carts along pot-holed tracks and country roads. John sat bound and shackled on a rowboat. He hunched his shoulders against the wind and pushed his hands between his legs for warmth. His clothes gave little protection on this bitter winter day. Caesar huddled on the wooden bench beside him, his arms wrapped around his body. The oars of the dinghy dipped in and out of the river in a steady, unrelenting rhythm, but it was easy work. The force of the tide carried them. They glided towards Woolwich. There he would be loaded, with cattle, sheep, goats, pigs and chickens and nearly 200 other convicts, onto the former merchant ship, the Alexander. They would be transported to Portsmouth where the fleet gathered. They had not told him where he was going. He knew only he had escaped that malignant hulk, the Ceres.

Heavy fog hung over London town obscuring landmarks, blanketing the sounds of early morning. As the boat moved along the river, the city slipped into the grey as if it had never been. He peered upriver, trying to discern their course, but that too lay in fog, and provided no clue as to what waited ahead. A scrap of paper, caught up in a gust, scuttled across the surface of the water before falling into the small boat. *Blown by the wind. I have as much choice as that bit of paper. I can do naught but sit and go with it.*

He squinted up at the sky, no longer contained behind a grated hatch, and through eyes that blinked and watered in the glare. *Too big. Too bright. Did I ever walk fearlessly beneath you?* He thought of those first Africans who had scuttled back to their dark cave. *No, I will be Adu Ogyinae.* With that, he looked around as if to take claim of the world again.

'Do yer ...' The words failed, afraid to voice themselves. John cleared his throat and tried again. 'Do yer think there might be roses, this place we're goin'?'

Chapter Twenty-Six

February 1787

'Any dead down 'ere?' A bored voice echoed through the shadows. John had heard voices like that after battle, when the fight had been lost and he'd clambered over rocks and rubble and the broken bodies of men. He listened to the heavy steps of the marines as they climbed down the ladder in search of corpses.

He had been rowed down river to Woolwich where, like so much coal, he had been bundled into the holds of the Alexander, a merchant vessel, and sailed to Portsmouth. The ship waited now at the docks, its human cargo of two hundred souls stowed and chained below decks: six convicts to a cabin of nine-foot square, eighteen inches of bed space to each. A metal-studded bulwark across the middle of the ship ensured no convicts escaped or air passed through.

He shivered in his berth, rocking to generate warmth to frozen limbs. Above him, he could hear the creaking of ropes and thud of crates being loaded onto the deck. The hooves of animals clipped across wooden boards. Shouts and curses mingled with the squawks of seagulls.

'Any dead?' The voice bellowed again.

John stirred. 'Over here.'

Thankfully Young Stinky had died last night.

Six of them shared a berth, transported together from the Ceres. John and Caesar with Stinky in the middle, John Martin and two others, Orford and Woodham at the end.

'Knock it orf!' Caesar had screamed, as Stinky had moaned, banging his fists at a pus-filled ear. Maggots crawled from it and down his face. It was a relief when he lapsed into fever, though he tossed and turned and still cried out. He had startled them all by sitting up, shaking them alert.

'Ain't right,' he said. 'Jest ain't right.' He looked at them with sad and serious eyes. 'I never hurt nobody. Never in me 'ole life. I swear you this on my dyin' breath.' He shook his head. 'Jes want to see me mam again. That's all I want.'

Then he fell back; his wide-open eyes still protested the injustice. The five cell mates rolled the body off their berth onto the floor, relishing the extra room.

'If we don't tell no one, we can get his food,' Caesar suggested. 'They won't knows unless we tell 'em. Take days for the body to turn in this bleedin' cold.'

John shrugged. So be it.

But he had sickened at the sight of the rats swarming over the corpse. Didn't seem just.

And so, despite the elbow that Caesar had shoved into his ribs, he had cried out to the marines. The door of the cell squealed open, metal complaining against metal. John watched as two men detached themselves from the shadows. They peered down at young Stinky. One of the marines kicked the corpse. Six, seven rats scuttled into the rafters.

'Yep. Dead,' he announced.

'Sure?'

The first marine landed a kick to the head. It fell aside revealing a devoured cheek, a chewed tongue. A black shape scurried away.

'Yep. Sure.'

They laid a hammock on the ground. Grabbing arms and legs they swung Stinky like a carcass of meat, dumping him upon the canvas where they sewed him up, nice and tight.

'Up we go,' the first marine said as they lugged him out of the cell.

John followed the bangs and bumps of their progress up the ladder and across the upper deck. Seems Stinky protested his treatment for he took the opportunity to catch himself in every cranny. Finally, a dull splash.

'Is that a friggin' body floating by my cabin?' a voice bellowed.

John looked at Caesar. 'Maggots, rats and now the fish? Bloody feedin' the world, he is.'

13th May 1787, Portsmouth

John, Caesar, John Martin, Orford and Woodham lay still, scarcely breathing on their bunk. Running feet pounded the decks above them. Cries of command rang through the ship. A chorus of sailors responded in union: 'Haul away!' Cables creaked as anchors tore free from their seabeds. The flapping of canvas- unfurled and caught in the wind.

John felt the smack of the swell against the hull; the sudden drop as the ship crested a wave. The voyage had begun.

A voice broke the silence. 'Are we on our way? To Africa?'

'No, some new place. A long ways off.'

'But my wife ...'

'My children ...'

'You won't ne'er see 'em again.'

John fondled the smooth and solid wood of his eagle and wondered if he were the only convict who did not grieve the loss of England. It had never been his home. Had he ever had a home? Perhaps he might find one in this new place. And he settled himself to dreams of forests and rivers and children who ran free.

It is good, Ol Ma whispered as he lay shackled in the cell.

¬

A sailor knelt at John's feet, grunting as he worked. Thin, greasy strands of hair fell from a balding crown and thick-set, rounded shoulders bent to their task. A short way from them stood a marine, watching curiously, although his musket sat ready in his hands. A line of convicts fidgeted, waiting their turn.

They gathered on the deck of the Alexander. They had been sailing for a week, cleared the Channel and met the open sea. The wind blew clean and salty, filling the sails and the sea sparkled with a thousand gems. Though John's eyes watered at the unaccustomed glare, they had lit up too as he was brought from the hold. It was his first time on deck and he sought to catch the small details of the moment so he may put them in his box for when he returned below.

'That's you done, then.' The man at John's feet sat back on his haunches. He held up the manacles he had unfastened from John's ankles, then chucked them into a barrel behind him.

John stared at his feet.

'Could row those tootsies 'cross the Channel, yer could. Big as boats they are,' the marine ventured.

John ignored the comment. He had worn irons for two years. The manacles had cut into his flesh, rubbing on bone and causing agony with every move. Badgely had ordered them to be loosened when they languished on the Ceres, but his ankles still festered with sores. He tested a leg, stretching it out before him, to the side, behind. His muscles complained at the unfamiliar movement; he grimaced through his grin.

No more chains. Never again. He would kill before submitting to shackles once more.

'Move along with yer then.' The marine jerked his head toward a spiked wooden wall that stretched the width of the deck.

John limped away to the enclosure, his steps still restricted. Behind him Dobson, further down the line of convicts, moved up a place. John felt his eyes on his back and the hairs prickled on the nape of his neck.

¬

Shortland perched on a small wooden bench, a notebook on his lap, a pen in his hand. The navy agent had established himself in a sheltered nook on the quarter deck of the Alexander where two by two, the convicts were led out to meet with him. He was engaged in gathering information on the skills, qualifications and limitations of the convicts, the better to organise them for the work ahead. He scowled at the long list of limitations.

The sea was a steely blue and a heavy swell set the Alexander rolling from side to side. Confined below decks because of the weather, the convicts hurled up their supper and their guts and cursed the very mothers who had borne them, but Shortland counted thirty years of naval experience, and other than a hand that reached out to steady his ink bottle or secure the wig that sat upon his head, he was unperturbed by the motion. His attention rested in building a colony.

Two Africans stood before him. He appraised the first: matted black hair grew in tails to his shoulders. The man held his arms across his chest as though to hide the scabs that covered his body. His ribs showed clear. He shuffled from foot to foot, his shoulders hunched, his attention on the papers in Shortland's hand.

From the hulks, no doubt. At least he appears to be healing somewhat. Captain Phillip has been wise. Fresh meat and vegetable. And exercise. I am no doctor, but it will help. He sighed, not attempting to hide his thoughts. *But how are we to build a colony with these wretches!*

As if in answer, the convict frowned, straightened his back, and lifted his head. He raised his eyes to hold Shortland's gaze. Head and shoulders taller than the other convicts, the black man stood steady, despite the pitching deck. His hands hung loose at his side. Shortland had seen a panther once, at an amusement park. He thought of that now.

'Your name is Randall. John Randall?' Shortland confirmed. 'Have you ever worked?'

Randall looked at his hands, cracked and bony, and after a pause nodded. As Shortland scribbled his observations, he recalled how the panther had slashed the hand of a child, stretched through the bars.

Shortland sighed. 'What were you doing before you went to prison?'

'Played the flute for coin.'

'Ah! So, you have musical abilities.'

The man shrugged.

'You were in the army.' It was a statement. 'Did you fire a musket?'

Randall looked out over the ocean, and Shortland wondered what he was recollecting.

'He can hit a bird from sixty yards. Best shot they had,' said his friend, who stood beside him.

Shortland said nothing. His gaze moved between the two men. He wrote again in his little book. Dismissing John with a nod, Shortland turned to Caesar. 'And what skills do you have?'

Over dinner that night, after reviewing his notes from the day, Shortland had a word with his son, Thomas George, who sailed as second mate on the Alexander.

'Keep an eye on the fellow Randall for me. Discern, if you can, the mettle of the man.'

¬

'Why'd you look at me like that? Could have sworn you were goin' to slug me.' Caesar had found John pacing the exercise yard, easing muscles too long restricted. Convicts crowded the confined space. At the far end, Dobson huddled in a corner with three others, seemingly agitated, for he shook his head angrily and then threw a glance at John. A fifth man stood guard, protecting the group from any foolish enough to come so close they might overhear.

John turned his attention to his friend. 'Is there a brain in that skull of yours? They won't welcome a convict who can handle arms.'

Caesar winced, then, with a grin, said, 'Thought you might bite him when he asked if you had ever worked. What did he think? You sat on your throne and had servants bring you tea?'

John didn't reply. He recalled tottering beside Ol' Ma on the farm. They both pulled weeds though he were little more than a toddler. He imagined her strong fingers around his own chubby ones, still dimpled with childhood, showing him how to pull the roots without breaking the stalk. *You gotta get it all out. Don't want to make more work for later.*

He threw a glance at Dobson.

¬

The tiny fleet of eleven ships forged on. Most convicts endured. They marked hours by the movement of the sun, months by the waxing and the waning of the moon. Changing stars in night skies told of their advance into new territories. They crossed imaginary lines in equatorial waters.

John stood on deck stealing some small shade from the barricade and staring out at the seamless painted sea. A white and soulless sun beat down. Water rations had been cut again and he wiped a woollen tongue over cracked lips and thought how cool the ocean would be against his skin.

Three men slunk up beside him, Dobson among them. They crowded him against the balustrade. John hated Dobson, but Powers, the first of them, made his skin crawl. With his thin brown hair stuck to his forehead, and his face shiny with sweat, he reminded John of the eels he had caught in the rivers back home. The man had tried to escape in Tenerife and landed in irons for his effort. Undaunted, he shared another plan.

'Some sailors are on our side. We can't fail. We've got weapons. The ship will be ours before it reaches the Cape,' Powers whispered.

'Good luck to you.' John kept his voice light. Only his foot jigged slightly as it remembered the fetters upon it.

'With us or against us, John.'

John recalled that one man had already fallen overboard. The three men crowded him, forcing him back so that the metal rivets of the barricade pressed into his flesh. He shoved them back.

'Told yer this was a bad idea. Should get rid of 'im now, while we can, while his mates aren't around.' Dobson glared at John, his small piggy eyes screwed tight with malice.

John ignored him. 'How can you be sure of weapons?' he asked Powers.

'We already have the iron bars. 'Spectin' some knives.' Powers stood so close John could smell his breath.

'And I get a blade?' He shot Dobson a look and grinned. 'I'm good with blades.'

Dobson made to fall upon him but was pulled back by his friends.

Powers ignored the interruption. 'In time. I'll keep 'em safe for a bit.'

'Won't join without Caesar. And John Martin.'

'Sure. Reckon they could be useful.'

'Guess I'm in then.' John thrust Powers from him, smiled deliberately at Dobson and headed back down below decks.

From the rigging where he worked, Thomas George took note.

'So, what did yer tell 'em?' Caesar whispered, though he had no need. The ship never ceased its creaking, and its grumbles joined with that of the convicts.

'Said we were in.' John flopped down, all energy drained now he had come below. The hot and heavy air stuck in his throat like wet felt and it seemed, he was always tired. His gums were inflamed and he fiddled with a loose tooth. 'While Dobson lives, he's gonna be a threat,' he continued after a while. 'He's a weed we gotta pull. Don't know how yet, but reckon if we stay in tight with 'em, we'll find a way.'

'Could snitch? Get 'em to search the cells. Find the weapons.' Caesar suggested, without conviction.

'Find ourselves with a knife in our back.' John stopped and raised a hand, craning his ear to listen. A sobbing from a cell at the far end of the passage had risen above the usual groans. He threw a questioning look at Caesar. 'Is that the boy? He crying again?'

'He ain't a boy. He's older than you.'

Gilly, the boy, the man, the man-boy with his flat face and protruding tongue had latched onto John, much to the latter's confusion. He would appear from around a corner, patting at John's chest with puffy hands, his face alight with joy. Embarrassed, John initially tried to disentangle himself, but now suffered in silence. He hadn't seen the man lately though. Heard only his sobbing.

With a sigh, John stood up. Caesar rolled his eyes, but followed.

'I'm hungry!' Gilly wailed, when they found him, rocking back and forth, cross-legged on the floor of his cell.

'We're all hungry Gilly.' Two months without fresh food and bodies were breaking down. Scurvy attacked sailors and convicts alike, riddled bones and tissue.

'But they took me rations. All of 'em,' Gilly complained, his arms spread wide to make a point. 'I ain't got none.' He raised a tear-stained face and desolate eyes.

John scrunched his eyes shut and shook his head. 'Gawd, as if we need this.' Then with a sigh, he patted Gilly's head. 'S'orite, Gilly. We'll sort it.'

Caesar sunk his face in his hands in mock despair. 'You planning to take on the whole bloody ship, John?'

They both jumped as Thomas George sauntered in. 'You right Gilly?' He looked at the two black men who stood over the crying man.

¬

The moon waned.

Thirteen guns sounded a salute to Rio as they sailed into port. The convicts feasted on fresh oranges and pineapples. The scurvy went into hiding.

The fleet sailed. Cape Town lay ahead.

John and Powers leant on the ship's railing, gazing out to sea. Dobson glowered behind them, warning off intruders.

'Not long now, Randall,' Powers growled. 'Not going to let me down, are you?' He looked out to the surging ocean. 'Hate to see you have an accident, like.'

'When do we get the knives,' John asked. He watched as an albatross landed heavily on the spar atop the mast. *I could get that, if I had a musket.*

Bad luck to shoot an albatross. Ol' Ma sounded stern.

'You'll get 'em when you get 'em.' Powers too, squinted up at the bird.

A blast rang out as a rifle exploded. A sailor cheered as the albatross toppled to the deck.

¬

The moon waxed.

Hunched against the barrier of the exercise yard, an arm wrapped around a pillar on the rolling, plunging boat, John spied the man he had been waiting for. The boy. The man-boy.

Ain't fair getting the child involved in this. Ol' Ma breathed over his shoulder.

Can't always be nice, Ol' Ma.

He had shared the idea with Caesar and John Martin. They hadn't liked it. Too risky. But it was the only way.

He beckoned Gilly over.

Honest eyes stared up at John, not hiding their joy. He patted John's chest with puffy hands.

'Hello, Randall. How are you today?' He spoke as if he needed to think about each word before releasing it. 'I've been eatin' good. Since you stopped 'em takin' my rations.'

'Weren't fair what they was doin' to ya.' John moved the boy's hands away from his chest and hoped no one was looking. 'Here, hold on tight.' Most convicts had headed below to their cells, safe from the waves that crashed over the upper decks and threatened to sweep them into the ocean.

'They ain't eatin' so good. You knocked their teeth out!' Gilly laughed.

'Hey, Gilly. Gotta a secret for you. A real big secret. You mustn't tell anyone, ya hear?'

Two round eyes stared back. Gilly nodded slowly, his mouth open wide.

'An' specially. I hear my name mentioned and ...' John gazed at the ocean. The swell smashed against the hull of the ship sending spray running down their heads.

'Ah!' Gilly's puffy hand flew up to his mouth as if to stop John's name from escaping.

'It's just,' John continued, 'I want ya to stay clear of that fella Powers. Heard he's got weapons on 'im. Dobson too. Lookin' for trouble they is.'

Thomas George headed towards them, staggering on the pitching deck and gesturing for them to go below, out of the storm.

Whispers spread. John held his breath. *If that little prick mentions me –*

Rumours passed from cell to cell. An eavesdropping deck-hand heard two convicts mutter about knives and iron bars.

'Do yer think he kept yer name out of it?' Caesar asked.

'Soon find out.'

A whisper of mutiny found the ears of the captain of the Alexander.

'If he's mentioned you, I'll kill the little bugger meself.' Caesar wrung his hands together, as if in practice.

Armed soldiers stomped down the ladders and streamed into each cell, tore apart mattresses, and terrorised wide-eyed and trembling men. They discovered iron bars and blades. Marines removed Powers and Dobson and four others from the ship in shackles. John heard the clanking as they left. Gilly, too, was removed to another ship. For his own safety. John saw him go. The boy's head spun back and forth as he was led off. He caught sight of Randall.

'I didn't say your name, John. I didn't. I didn't tell no one.'

John turned abruptly from him, afraid lest others hear and make sense of what had happened. *I've pulled the weed out by the root, Ol' Ma.* She did not answer him.

He caught a last glimpse of Gilly, who looked at his one friend, his face an open book of despair. He did not know what he had done to make John turn away. He would not last long. The whispers would follow him. Loose tongues got cut out.

John did not notice Thomas George who had witnessed the scene.

The fleet arrived in Cape Town. A month later it set out on the last leg of its voyage.

The new moon.

Caesar spilt the bones from the pouch that hung around his neck into John's palm. He closed John's hands around them and wrapped his own around those of his friend.

The pair squatted together above deck in the exercise yard. The convicts had gathered there throughout the day, gawking at faint hills and sandstone cliffs that occasionally crept from the distant mist, only to fade away as the ship voyaged past. A heavy overhung sky did nothing to daunt their spirits. The occasional break in cloud lit up red sandstone cliffs, spilling them in blood. Some said this marked the end of their voyage. A day. Maybe two.

Reedy voices raised themselves to rousing cheers at each new headland. Bony shoulders shook in sobs of relief and elation; smiles spread across faces that had been too long set in misery. Fingers pointed at columns of smoke seen spiralling into the skies.

In their corner, John and Caesar huddled together.

'Blow on them and say it with me,' Caesar whispered.

John's hands shook at the touch of magic in his hand. He thought that if it were not for Caesar's hands, clasped around his own, he might not have contained it. Intent, he took a deep breath, exhaling fully and slowly onto the yellowed bones they held between them.

'I breathe my soul and the soul of my guiding spirit upon you,' they chanted in unison.

With a nod from Caesar, they tossed the bones onto the deck before them.

'So, let's have a look.' Caesar bent over them. His finger traced the lines between. He nodded to himself.

'Well?' John prodded.

'These here - they are your ancestral spirits. See where they lie!' Caesar pointed at two cubed bones.

John looked at his friend, waiting for an explanation.

'Plenty of tail, no doubt 'bout it. And children too.'

'Children?' John whispered, afraid of alerting the gods to this blessing, but pictured himself teaching a son to track and shoot.

He didn't notice Caesar's troubled look or the way he righted four bones that had fallen face down.

'Here. These ones are for coin. Lookey here.' Caesar pointed to another group of bones. 'You will be well breeched and true. The bones have fallen well for you, John.'

But he swooped them away before John could question him further.

Thomas George watched.

Chapter Twenty-Seven

29th January, 1788

John stumbled ashore. The ground swayed beneath his feet, tumbling him to his knees: a tiny figure on the brink of a vast and unknown world. With tremulous hands, he scooped a fistful of sand. He buried his face in it, scratching the grit against his cheeks. He breathed in the sharp, dry tang of leaf and soil, sea and salt and when he exhaled, he released the stench of years. Muscles held tense for too long relaxed. He stretched his arms to the sky and let the sand fall through his fingers, showering himself, so it caught in his hair and across his shoulders.

Blessed earth.

The commands of officers, the murmurings of convicts, the gentle thump of a boat as it grounded against the shore. The bumping of oars. A splash of feet in water. The fleet disembarked around him. He scraped up two more handfuls of sand, needing its touch, but for the first time raised his head to peer around.

Despite the early hour, the light burned John's eyes. Near blind and weeping, he sought the sky. Blood-red streaks stretched to the horizon.

I am Adu Ogyinae, released from the ground to a new world.

Lowering his gaze, he took in his near surroundings. Trees grew to the ocean's edge, their limbs extended at awkward angles, as if interrupted in a wild frenzy of dance. They had shed their bark. Strips lay like discarded clothing, leaving the trunks vulnerable as flesh. The drone of cicadas hummed; the earth throbbed with life. He wished the trees had not stopped their dance and pictured himself with them, stamping his feet, clapping his hands, whooping and hollering and shouting to the world.

Disgusted with the stench of his body, he clambered to his feet – his limbs heavy and stiff – and hobbled to the shore, falling into the water. The salt stung his sores, but again and again he dived. He scrubbed scabs from his skin, rubbing until it burned, and washed the grit from his eyes. He raked his fingers through his hair, untangling knots and scratching until his skull screamed. And he scraped the lice from the body hair under his arms and scoured his groin. His body tingled as if receiving life. Cleansed and feeling born anew, he paddled back to the beach. He had his balance now and didn't fall.

Do you feel the gods, John? Ol' Ma whispered. John paused to hear her more clearly, shutting his eyes that he might see her face, and feel her touch against his cheek. *Ancient gods. They don't hide behind smoke and clouds and chimney towers.*

'Randall. Stop your larkin'. Get those tents up.' A marine pointed toward a pile of canvas.

⌐

John bent over the tent peg, worried that it wouldn't hold strong in the sandy soil.

As good as it gets, I figure. He straightened his back, rolling his shoulders to ease the aches. Hauling the heavy canvas tents had strained his reserves. He cast a look at the shaded woods beyond the camp and wondered if he dare escape for a rest.

'On the life of sweet baby Jesus, I need water.' Caesar hunkered beside him, sweat pouring from his body. The two had laboured together all day, whistling tunes to lighten their load.

John's attention was caught by a group of women, sauntering past with baskets to collect oysters from the rocks. He stared, his mouth open and then flushed and backed away near falling over a guy rope. They howled in laughter. The women were only now being unloaded from the other ships. He couldn't remember when he had last seen one.

Luckily the screams of a bull interrupted them. Deckhands struggled to lower the beast from a ship. Its legs pounded the air as it swung on ropes to the dinghy below while sailors bellowed advice and warning. A splash as a man fell from the small boat, knocked by the animal's thrashing feet. The vessel rocked from side to side as it made for shore and John held his breath, a grin on his face, hoping it might keel over. All over the bay, men had paused their work to see what would happen. As the boat neared land, the animal bolted, eyes rolling, foam frothing from its mouth, scattering crowds of panicked men. A cheer rose from the onlookers.

'Catch it!' an officer cried, diving for cover as it dashed past him.

'Eh, lookee 'ere,' John called to Caesar, pointing to a pint-sized man, a smuggler from Devon. He tottered beneath a sack of grain. He let out a curse when the rotten hessian split, spilling its contents, and a hoard of black rats sprang free, racing into the woods.

'This stuff is bloody spoiled,' he grumbled. 'Seawater got to it.'

As if wanting to join the fun, a rooster flapped its wings and tore from the grasp of a pickpocket from London, who screamed at the flurry of feathers and tripped over a tent line.

'Hope there's someplace hereabouts we can buy lunch,' Caesar laughed, 'Ours seems to be getting away.'

The steady thwack of an axe marked the newcomers' assault on the dancing trees.

'Over there!' John pointed. Three shadows within the bush slipped away even as he spoke. 'Did you see that?' He wondered if in fact he had seen anything or whether it had just been a trick of his eyes.

'Be seeing ghosts next. Ain't no one there.' Caesar was focused on rubbing his feet, muttering as to which part of him ached the most: his arms, back, feet or belly. He decided it was his belly. He could never fill his belly.

'Found you, By Gum!'

An arm hooked around John's neck, struggling to push him to the ground. With a yelp, John slipped out from under it, throwing himself at his assailant's legs to knock him off balance. Caesar sprang to his aid.

'Easy, John. Lord, you are finely-tuned.' The erect and red-coated figure of a lieutenant skipped back, putting out his hands to forestall the assault. He resembled a delighted Puck, with his wide curling and mischievous mouth and blue elven eyes. 'Even in New York, you were of formidable stature. But look at you, now. Ah, John, it is jolly good to see you.'

John scrambled to his feet. Images of New York, the tavern, the Holy Grounds flashed through his thoughts. 'George? Lieutenant Johnston?' he laughed and rushed to embrace his friend, before he remembered his position and backed off. He recalled their last night and the bravado of the toast they had made. *Master of my own path.*

He looked away, hot with shame and wishing that the ground could swallow him. *What a fool I was.* He was nothing more than the failure his master had predicted. All for a barrow and a heartless girl. He took a deep breath as instinct and habit pulled his shutters down; pride and defiance pulled his shoulders back. When he turned to face his former friend, he had in place the easy smile but his eyes were cold. 'You're a long way from New York. It's good to see you, Lieutenant.'

'And you, John.' But the lieutenant responded with a more formal tone, seemingly wary of the man before him.

Convict and officer faced each other. Neither said a word. John felt his control slipping, nodded and began to turn away.

'It seems we have both travelled a long way,' the lieutenant's voice stopped him.

Some more comfortably than others. But John kept his smile, pleasant as you please. 'Is there something I can help you with?' he asked. 'Your luggage, perhaps? Erect your tent? He wanted to place a wall between himself and this man who knew him too well; who knew he had failed; who could remind him of dreams that had been crushed in a marketplace. He noted the veil that slipped across the face of his former friend.

'My thanks but I am perfectly capable. I wished only to extend my greetings,' he paused, 'and issue a warning. John, Shortland has been using your name. He has eyes on you. Be careful.'

'Who's Shortland? What does he want with me?'

'I'm not sure. Yet. But he is an influential man.'

'Lieutenant Johnston. The governor requires you, sir.' A marine presented himself, red and clammy of face; anxious eyes betrayed the search he had made.

'Must go. Seems I am frightfully important around these parts. Aide de Camp. Who could imagine!' With a comical grimace that reminded John of a long ago friend and which made his heart ache, Lieutenant Johnston moved to leave but stopped and turned to speak once more.

'And John, neither of us are the boys we were. But this land does not need boys. And there will be opportunities here. I just know it. Feel it in the bones, you know.' A hint of a smile, but he continued in sober tones. 'We will both need allies. People we trust. Think on it.'

'Who's he?' Caesar looked after the disappearing figure of the officer.

'No one. Who's Shortland?'

'That officer with the long legs and the mouth full of questions. You remember. You played the tragic when I told him you could shoot.'

John winced.

'You think it's trouble?'

'What do you think!'

'We could leave. Just slip into them woods. No one would know in this mess.'

John's eyes roamed the thick bush.

'We can find them that live 'ere. Maybe there's a town nearby. Someplace we can disappear.'

'To a town?' John laughed.

'Yes! It'd be easy to run.'

'Did you see any towns all those days we travelled along the coast?'

But even as he teased his friend, he felt the tingles run down his back and looked around.

What does Shortland want of me?

He fondled his eagle.

Wednesday 6th February 1778

John wrestled with a canvas. The wind flicked it free of his grasp. He glanced to the sky where a thick black wall of cloud rolled in towards them. Dark night followed. Branches groaned and the leaves whispered among themselves. Birds, white and yellow, red and green, pink and grey, screeched and took to the air, in flocks so large they clouded the sky. John flinched as thunder cracked above his head and he tore towards the shelter of the trees.

Officers and marines raced to their tents as the first drops of rain bruised the sand. Shouts and a tussle as a canvas, unsecured, tore free and blew off to tangle in some trees. The cattle shuffled in their pens, lowing as they nuzzled each other. The convicts sheltered where they could, beneath trees and in caves, their grumbles lost beneath the howling of the wind, and the battering of the rain. Lightning forked from the sky to strike a giant tree. With a booming crack the trunk split in two and smashed to the ground, shattering the shed they had worked so hard to build and crushing the sheep that had sheltered there.

John and Caesar cowered in the hollow of a rock face.

'This wind could blow us back to England!' Caesar yelled above the noise.

John did not reply. He clenched his eagle, putting it to his mouth, sending prayers to the gods of this land. *They are come to test us.*

Eventually, the wind calmed and the rain settled into a relentless, rhythmic downpour. With a shrug, John stepped from their shelter. *We cannot cringe forever. This place will devour the weak.*

'You just a little lassie, clinging against the rock? Scared of a bit of water?' he taunted Caesar – 'We're soaked anyway' – and jumped into a puddle, splashing Caesar before sprinting away, only to slip on the soggy ground. Caesar followed and wrestled him in the mud.

Others joined them, stealing free of the confines of the trees. Like small animals scenting the scene, they squinted around, ready to dart back again. In minutes the rain drenched them. John threw a handful of mud at the man closest to him. His victim laughed, tearing off his shirt and making a show of rinsing it. Three women shrieked and then hooted. Without shame, they stood pointing at themselves, their nipples and belly and crotch showing clear through their simple and sodden shifts. Two men threw themselves upon them, grappling them to the ground. Nearby, a woman shook out her hair, letting it fall loose on her shoulders before throwing it forward over her face, letting water stream down the back of her neck. John drew in a breath, stilled by the image: the fragility of that neck. He would put his mouth to her flesh; to taste her; to drink from her skin. He would wrap his hands in her hair.

A pipe sounded, breaking the moment. A circle of convicts, their arms linked, began singing.

'Mush, mush, mush, turaliaddy! Sing, mush, mush, mush, turalia!'

The people started to dance. They danced with the rain pounding down and running over their heads and shoulders and down their chests. Skinny arms waved to the music, and skinny legs splashed in pools of water and pale, drawn faces began to glow with eyes alight, and voices rose, and they threw off the despair that had dogged their days, and abandoned all restraint. Stamping feet and thrashing leaves and creaking branches and the screech of the birds and the breaking of the waves on the shore joined as one deafening roar across the land. They slipped in mud, rolling and squealing and laughing until they were covered in sand and dirt and none could distinguish the people from the land.

John reached for his woman. He pulled her down upon him. He did not see her face or know her name. He only knew she felt soft and warm to his touch and responded with an ardour that matched his own. On the ground around him, other men and women fell upon each other, pulling off shirts and trousers, pushing up skirts. The earth rippled as they heaved in the mud.

John and his woman grappled through the night. If he were a drowning man, she was the debris on a heaving ocean and he grasped her to him, a union in an uncertain world. Through her, he relinquished his shame. In her, he was a man.

When the moon was high, the rain eased and then finally stopped. The clouds cleared, and the universe revealed itself. Stars blurred in a stream of light that spiralled across the sky. John lay on his back, lost. Beneath their power and beauty, he was aware only of his insignificance. He raised his arm uselessly toward the light. For a moment he yearned to be sucked into that swirling vortex: his body burned clean of its flesh, leaving only his spirit, pure and bright. Was Ol' Ma up there, watching down on him? A shower of shooting stars burst across the sky. As he always did, he wondered if the gods had dropped some souls by mistake. Perhaps even now they looked down, searching the skies to retrieve them. Perhaps they spied upon him, lying in the wet grass near the shore.

Do you see me here? I pray, grant me a boon. Let this land accept me. Let it take me to its bosom.

And he thought of a house by a river and a bonny wife and a garden with roses and a small toddling child clutching his hand and laughing up at him. Perhaps all was not lost.

Chapter Twenty-Eight

Two figures lay on a pile of leaves, limbs entwined. The newly ascended sun filtered through the branches, splattering them in a patchwork of light and shade. Mottled and muddied, their shapes undefined, they seemed to grow out of the earth.

John stretched and blinked as he woke and turned to the body beside him, trying to connect the scrawny stature, scraggy hair, the snuffling that escaped the wide-open mouth, with his images of the storm: brazen eyes and raucous singing, flashing feet and flesh and tongue, breast and buttock.

What's her name? Mary, Margaret, Rose or Rebecca? The light did her no favours as it crawled across every wrinkle and worry in her face. Indeed, she looked as splintered and worn as any piece of driftwood, washed onto the shore.

Her eyes opened and found his. She rolled towards him, pulling him down upon her, but they were interrupted by a drum roll.

Lined up, counted off, sat down, the convicts were called to order in the clearing that ran down to the beach, a plot of earth, felled of its trees, and trampled by a thousand feet. John sat cross-legged among them, John Martin to his left. Caesar had claimed a tree stump to his right. John had barely slept the night before and his head buzzed and his eyes felt hot and dry. He breathed deeply to clear his mind and looked around.

Having spent its force, the storm had slunk away, leaving a trail of grey clouds sulking across a blue sky. A wind from the south had driven off the steamy heat. The morning smelt fresh, despite the leaves and branches, torn cloth and canvas, frayed ropes and broken barrels that littered the cove.

He glanced at the tents he had pitched. They held strong, despite his fears, though he wondered why he cared.

Near the shoreline in a commotion of shouts and commands, the marines readied themselves for parade. Men in red uniform secured buttons and spat on leather shoes to bring out the shine. Band members hoisted drums, balancing the weight on their hips; John could almost feel their bulk and had a moment's yearning for a former life, and a friend long lost. He looked away.

The flagpole stood directly before him, stark and lonely amid the confusion. It did not seem worthy of the task before it, of holding the weight of the British Empire and the dreams of a new colony. A simple triangle of wood had been erected beside it.

Like a henchman, thought John, and nudged Caesar to point it out.

The triangle claimed the attention of all. The convicts might turn away but with a snap it dragged them back, as if their gaze were chained. A sudden blast of wind blew a rag to tangle upon it.

'Eh, that's my shirt,' cried a startled voice, and those close to the hollow-chested man who owned it erupted into jeers and laughter, a little too loud.

The shirt flattened itself against the frame like a body, its arms flung wide. John painted his own form there, stripped and whipped to the bone; the leather binding his wrists; the lash of the cat on his back. The convicts had fallen into silence. That triangle of wood, not five-foot high, cast its shadow over them all.

John shut his eyes. He nodded off to the drone of flies and the murmurings of men, only to be jolted awake by a poke from Caesar or the bite of an ant. He caught a glimpse of Esther. He had fixed her name now.

'Esther. Esther Harwood from London,' she had snapped when he asked her this morning. 'I told ya before!'

Huddled with the women convicts, she smiled and waggled her fingers at him, pointing him out to a buxom woman beside her. John turned away, not meeting her eyes. *It were only a night.*

A hush, like a gentle breeze, moved through the crowd. Commander Phillip strode out alone, ahead and apart from the small group of officers who straggled after him. Achingly erect, as if he would snap rather than bend, he sought to make a commanding figure. Instead he reminded John of the flag pole, too flimsy for the weight he needed to carry. Nor did his wigged hair and shiny medals seem at home in this untamed world.

The marines hustled the convicts to their feet as three men stepped forward to the flagpole. They saluted their governor and secured and raised the standard. For a moment, the time it takes for a dying man to breathe his last breath, the flag seemed to snag, caught at half-mast. A tug, a little force and it freed itself to fly high and proud, a blood-red cross, fluttering above the land. With a rolling of drums and the shrill sounds of the fife, the band broke into a marching tune, parading around the ground, looping the convicts, as if with a noose. The marines followed, backs erect, eyes forward, every step, one of tight precision. John's fingers echoed the notes of the fife as he watched the regiments file by. He tried to identify the regiments by the colours they bore: navy, green, red banners that jarred against the muted hues of this place.

Beside him, Caesar spat his disgust.

A movement caught his eye and he saw that Esther had redoubled her efforts to attract his attention, waving with exaggerated gestures. He ignored her. But a young boy, crouched in front of him, his face still wearing the pimples of youth stared over towards the women, and blushed. The boy raised his hand to reply and received a scowl for his efforts.

The judge advocate, Captain Collins, stepped forward. He raised his hand. Music and marching stopped. The marines stood to attention. Eight hundred convicts, seven hundred marines and sea men, and a handful of their wives and children, craned forward. John nudged Caesar so that he might share his tree stump for a better view. Collins strode to a table erected beside the flagpole. It was a nondescript wooden bench but it held the weight of two red leather, sealed cases. He broke the seals of the Commission.

A flock of birds took flight, screeching and cackling to each other, wheeling in huge circles and drowning all words. Only when the birds had swooped away could Collins declare Phillip governor of the land and all who stood upon her.

Despite the breeze, the noonday sun beat down upon the convicts. John struggled briefly with the formal language of the Commission, the long list of powers. He nodded off again.

Caesar pinched him awake. Phillip was speaking.

'You are here to work. If you do not work, you will not eat.'

'Any person caught stealing the most trifling of stock will be punished with death.'

'I will show great approbation to those who work hard and prove themselves worthy.'

Angry murmurings rustled throughout the crowd of seated convicts.

'I work,' muttered Caesar, 'but seems they neglect the part where they feed me!'

The governor's tone became shrill, snapping across the crowd like the crack of a whip.

'Depraved individuals ... licentious behaviour ... Further scenes of debauchery and riot as of last night will not be tolerated. Those who are seen around the women's tents will be fired upon.'

John whispered to Caesar. 'He needs a maid. Someone to right his bad temper.'

'I wholeheartedly encourage any who are in a position to marry to do so with the greatest dispatch,' Phillip admonished.

John winced as Caesar gave him a sharp jab to the ribs and a nod to Esther. 'Oh, for the love of Jesus. Stop that!'

⌐

Sheltered by the trees and unseen by the white men, a group of natives watched the proceedings. Among them, Abaroo studied every move. He had heard the elders discussing the new arrivals. Ancestral ghosts. Enemies. Strangers passing by. He had been present when one red man had exploded his stick, firing it into the sky. Like others, Abaroo had cowered before finding his courage and rushing forward, spear raised. But the man had not intended to hurt. The visitors had given the women some stones. Abaroo himself had touched them. He had held one to the light, tasted it, and rubbed it between his fingers. A dozen hands stroked the trinkets, before losing interest and tossing them into the dirt.

Beside him, his friend Alkira observed the foreigners with the intensity of an artist. He mimicked their gestures, their straight legs, the sticks over the shoulder. Abaroo knew he would see the moves in the dancing tonight.

His son jumped up and down in rhythm with the music. When the music stopped, Abaroo strained to glean some understanding of the words that followed. He couldn't, of course. Not only were the words foreign to him but the concepts beneath the words had no meaning in his world.

⌐

John slipped from the harness around his chest and examined the raised welts it had left. *They think we're goddammed horses.* Sweat poured down his brow, his chest, his back. He wiped his lips.

John Martin sat on the stump of a tree, studying hands that were blistered raw. He had swung the axe all morning but too often it had bounced off the hard wood, jarring his arm. Now John and Caesar, and a team of other convicts, used leather straps to haul the fallen giant clear to the sawpit.

John spat out a fly that had ventured too far down his mouth. 'I need a drink.' Since the ceremony three days ago they had laboured from dawn to dusk, clearing land, building sheds and enclosures, hoeing soil for wheat and corn, potatoes and peas. But it seemed to John that every move forward resulted in disaster. Fences toppled over. Insects and birds devoured young shoots. Even their cows had run away. He swatted another fly.

'Randall, may I have a word.'

John winced and didn't respond immediately, but with an effort of will, he recalled an impassive expression to his face and turned towards the speaker. 'Lieutenant Johnston.'

'I suggest you find yourself a maid and marry immediately.' The lieutenant spoke with utter sincerity, betrayed only by a smile which he sought to hide by sneezing vigorously into a handkerchief.

John recoiled but recovered himself to face this man who would taunt him. Eyes narrowed, muscles tensed, he growled. 'You stretch your authority too far, Lieutenant.'

Lieutenant Johnston seemed unaware of the danger he was in. With his head to one side, he scrutinised John, enjoying himself.

'What is it you really want?' John asked at length.

'You may recall that Shortland has an interest in you. He sought my opinion.' He waited for a response. Getting none, he laughed. 'You really will not be baited, John? Must you deprive me of my fun! Well, I will tell you in a nutshell. Shortland needs a gamekeeper. One who will explore these lands, hunt for game, feed the settlement. But Shortland is a cautious man. He does not want to arm just any convict with a musket, lest that musket be turned upon himself, or me, for instance.' With a familiar show of the dramatic, he put a hand to his heart, in a parody of horror, but continued in a crisp, clear tone. 'Nor does he want to lose said musket – or the convict for that matter – to the bush in an escape for freedom. He concludes that he needs a married man. A settled man. To wit! You must take a wife.'

The words came to John from a great distance. He had not wanted to listen.

'Say that again,' he finally said.

Calling for patience from the heavens, the lieutenant re-peated his tale.

'And how can I be sure I'll get the position? What if I get stuck with a lass and no favour?'

'Because I have vouched for you,' George said simply. 'I have told him that I have seen you shoot...and that I would trust you with my life. And...'

John interrupted. 'You feel it in your bones!'

'Indeed. So...do you have a maid?'

John thought of his cottage with the rose garden. He tried to place Esther there, to see her at the gate, welcoming him home. He put an infant to her breast. He listened for her laughter. The cottage slammed its gate shut upon her and the roses withered. But he shrugged.

'I figure I do,' was what he said.

Chapter Twenty-Nine

A twig cracked underfoot, exploding like a rifle shot in the forest. He had hardly heard the creaks and the croaking, the tweets and chirps, the hums and buzzing until they stopped, and the silence was deafening. Even the trees appeared to hold their breath at this foreign tread upon the land.

'God's oath,' John cursed his clumsiness and wondered who and what else may have heard him.

He had followed a creek that led to a swampy pasture – lush, despite the dry heat – and though it lay a long way from camp he knew it would be worth his while.

John and Esther had signed the marriage contract before a trestle table in the shade of a tree, its bark rough and furrowed, its branches straggling and sparse. Spiky, red flowers obscured the few leaves. As he had made his mark, a sudden gust rustled the branches above and showered the couple with red blossom.

He allowed his thoughts to dwell on her. Despite her smile, there was an absence to her. Hollows under her eyes where once youth blossomed. Thin lips where laughter may have sheltered. Shadows in a face where once had been light. At first, he had hoped to make her whole again. He had glimpsed who she might once have been. At dusk, when they crept through the trees and fell upon each other she overflowed in her need to give herself to him. At these moments she burned brightly and unknown fires lit her shrouded eyes. And when they were sated and she clung to him, the brittle case in which she held herself seemed fragile as an eggshell. But that was before the marriage.

He sighed. At least now his days were his own and so were his nights. He roamed the forests, shooting kangaroo, ducks and geese, trapping possum and iguana, and collecting eggs and berries to bring back to the colony. Many a night he slept in a nest of leaves, his eyes on the stars. And as he breathed in the strange, sharp smells, or studied new constellations, he basked in having no chains on his legs, no orders to follow, no judgements made of him. He was in no hurry to return to camp, where his wife waited with a mouth full of complaints and eyes that would cut him down and feed him to the dogs.

He turned his attention to the task. Hidden in the scrub, his musket raised and ready, breath slow and controlled, he relaxed his body. The sounds of the forest returned. A mosquito landed on his leg. He rubbed, careful not to swat. Other than an occasional blink to rid them from his eyes, he ignored the flies that crawled around his face. A lizard, a meal for five men, scuttled up a nearby tree. He noted it. He would kill it later.

He heard them before he saw them. A rustle. A thump. A mob of kangaroos loped into his vision, come to graze. Five. Six. Seven. More. Balancing back on their tails, they looked around, darting eyes and twitching ears, alert to signs of danger.

Jittery fellows, John thought. *Ready to flee at the rustle of wind.* He enjoyed the moment before the kill: the anxiety bubbling in his belly, the knowledge that death danced just a trigger away and he held life in his sway. A baby popped up from the mother's pouch. A second group arrived, settling to nibble the grass. Two males sparred, prize boxers in a ring.

I'll struggle to get that large one home, John decided. *I'll take the mother with the joey. The baby, I can cook tonight.*

A second explosion shattered the peace. No twig this time. With two or three jumps the mob escaped the clearing and fled for the cover of the woods, but John's shot had been true. The fallen, still convulsing body of the mother remained, abandoned by her family. Her joey sheltered in her pouch.

Throwing his musket over his shoulder, John strolled out to claim his kill. He knelt beside her, feeling her neck for a pulse. A tremble ran through her. He pulled his knife and slit her throat to end her suffering. He put his hand down her pouch, yanking out the bundle that hid there and wrenched its neck.

Crouching beside the two corpses, he closed his eyes. *Thank you for your strength and sacrifice.*

He didn't hear them come up on him. He saw only a spear as it plunged into the soil before him, throwing him off balance as he scrambled back. Behind the spear, a pair of legs – black and sinewy, red dust caught in coarse hair – grew from the ground.

Eyes, long lashed, set deep and as black as his own, stared down upon him.

⌐

'I had taken their kill,' John was to retell later. He sat with Esther and John Martin, who jumped up to help Caesar when he limped in. 'They had their spears and their throwing stick, silent as thieves in the night they were. Not yards away from me. They had their eye on the big one, waiting. Just like me ... all of us waiting for that moment. Then –' John let out a roar and threw his arms out, causing Esther to squeal and jump back. 'My musket exploded and scared the beasts right away. They were right mad, they were. And I can't blame them neither. I figure I'd be mad if someone spoiled my hunt.'

'How do you know all this?' John Martin liked facts.

'We had a good old parley. They get their message across alright. They pointed to where they were hiding out. And how they had their weapons ready and then how they threw their arms up, terrified at the blast of the gun and they tumbled back only to see the game leaping away. There I was, bum on the ground, surrounded by three very unhappy fellas and their great big spears.'

'You had your musket? Should have shot the lot of 'em.' Caesar growled.

John and John Martin exchanged a glance. Forever hungry, Caesar was always angry and becoming increasingly unpredictable. They feared for what he might do. Nearly twice the size of everyone else, he carried the load of four men, hauling timber and sacks of gravel, digging holes and steadying beams, but only received the same rations as other, smaller men.

'What do you think. When did I have time to reload? And you know another thing? They weren't afraid of the musket. They knew it was empty.'

'So, what did you do?' Esther was all but twitching with fear and excitement.

'I put on my sorry face. Then I pointed to the 'roo and told them to take it. But then I pointed to the baby, smallest scrap of fur and bones you ever saw, and I pointed to my belly.'

'Did they give it to you?'

'They threw it at me like they were throwin' scraps to a dog.'

John didn't share the rest of the story, a private moment and precious.

With the dead animal slung across a back, the three natives had slipped into the shadows so fluidly they may have never been. John turned to retrace his steps, but the one he thought of as the leader had returned and stood, motionless, waiting for John to notice him. The two studied each other. Two black men from different worlds.

The stillness of the man unsettled John. No smile, no nod of the head, no gesture. The man offered no pretensions of hostility or warmth, of power or humility. His stance, thought John, was of one who did not question his place in the world and needed to make no compromise. Only his body carried the

marks of concession, of trading with gods and making deals
with the unknown. Ridges of scars bound his chest, his arms,
his back, marks of ritual that identified the man, that spoke
of courage and beauty, that separated him from the soil from
which he grew and bound him to it.

Under his gaze John felt clumsy and ungainly. He wondered
what picture he presented. He had been reborn in this country
and roaming free and being well fed had cleared his skin of
sores and returned muscle to his frame. Did the Indian consider the colour of John's skin? Did he deem him kin?

John thought not. Both carried the markings of their own
world, more powerful than any colour. The two stood without
words, each taking the measure of the other, two men alone in
a moment.

The Aboriginal reached out to touch the eagle that hung
around John's neck.

'Burumurring?' he asked. 'Burumurring,' he pointed to the
sky and made a fluttering movement with his hands.

Puzzled, John repeated the motion and only then did he
recognise it for what it was, the flight of an eagle.

Fondling his talisman, John repeated, 'Burumurring?'

The eyes of the two men joined. Both smiled; the bond of
an eagle forged between the two.

'Abaroo,' the Aboriginal tapped his chest.

John pointed to him, repeating, 'Abaroo.' Then thumped his
own chest, 'John.'

Abaroo repeated the name formally, 'John.'

Then Abaroo was gone.

John retraced his steps to the river from where he had come.
He located a cave, just a hollow that he had noted earlier in
the day where he could settle for the night. Four miles' walk
would lead him to Sydney Cove, but not at this hour. The sun
was sliding beneath the horizon, warming the sky but leaving

the forest behind him dead and black. He wondered where the Indians had camped, but could see no trace of them, no hint of smoke. His eyes followed the river, flowing red in the dying sun, towards the colony and traced its passage to where Esther would be sitting outside their shanty. He had secured the spiky limbs of a cabbage tree to a skeleton of branches, creating a shelter of sorts.

Their shack sat on the eastern side of the bay, huddled in a cluster of hundreds. Between these, tired and hot and hungry men collided with each other, and the air bristled with injury.

'You fell upon my woman. It were no accident.'

'My biscuit is gone. I saw you hovering here.'

In the dry, crackling heat, the earth sizzled and scorched the feet that dared touch it.

In the rain, the piss and shit ran through the camp, soaking their bedding, fouling their food.

In the shelter of the cave, he cooked the joey on the camp-fire before him, drooling at the smell of roasting meat. To distract himself he took out his flute but then dismissed the notion and laid it aside again, settling instead to the simple joy of listening to the night, the spitting of the fire, a splash from the river, the rustle of leaves, the hum of insects. Not so long ago he had nearly given up hope of hearing these sounds again. *It is good*, he whispered to Ol' Ma.

It is good, she whispered back.

I'll put this moment in my box.

She smiled, pleased with that.

Turning the stick that held the skin and bone of the joey, John thought about the trade he had made. Those natives had won the day, stealing from him the prize of his hunt. He hadn't been thinking clearly. He could not let that happen again. Friends or not, he could not stretch the lieutenant's patience. He needed to show himself proficient in his role. He must teach those Indians some rules. He fingered his eagle. Abaroo, the man had called himself. He wondered if they would meet again. *April 1788*

Chapter Thirty

The swell lifted him high and John glimpsed the infant settlement clinging to the coastline; a squalid and desperate place, he thought, as if one wind would blow it into the sea. He slipped into the trough between the waves before rising again to new and greater heights. As was his custom, he had come to the ocean after a hunt to dive under waves, letting the water break over him and recharge body and spirit in the crashing surf.

He had journeyed far yesterday, slept rough in the forest to catch the game at dawn and made an early kill, deliberately choosing the largest animal. It had been an arduous trip home; a slippery, uneven trail, the game heavy on his shoulders, its blood running down his chest and back, a feast for the flies. He had tripped once, crashing to his knees, the load tumbling on top of him. Sitting on the track, he had looked at the carcass of the animal and cursed. His head throbbed and he ached all over and he deliberated whether to just leave it there, but with a snarl he had hauled it back onto his shoulders and stumbled on. Only the thought of the starving settlement, of his friends, had kept him going. It were worth it though, he thought, as he struggled back into camp, for convicts and officers alike had cheered him, the only hunter to return with food that day, and he hadn't been able to hide his grin or keep the sparkle from his eyes. *A warrior after all*...And though he laughed at his whimsy, he had been proud to be a someone.

The lieutenant signalled him from the shore. With a wave, he duck-dived down, before paddling to the beach.

George slapped an arm around his back. 'Seems you've become quite the celebrity. Good job.' John grinned, not hiding the pleasure he got at his friend's approval.

The two walked on the beach. Each looked out to sea, that vast and empty expanse that stretched so far it got lost in the sky. John sometimes thought he might lose himself staring out at those oceans, so small did they make him feel; but he could not turn away. They waited for that moment they would see a tiny speck on the horizon, watch it grow large. They waited for a ship from England to bring them supplies.

'What do you see?' his friend asked.

John shrugged. 'Water.'

'Know what the governor sees? A harbour full of trade ships. And over there?' Johnston pointed at a rocky outcrop, 'Warehouses full of timber. A town with merchants and banks and factories. And there...that will be the main street, and over two hundred feet wide. And John, the man already plans for a new settlement, out west, where we went last month.'

John looked to where the lieutenant pointed. He nodded, seeing the place afresh. His friend was right. In a few short months the settlement had sunk its roots into the ground. Small houses of daub and wattle had begun to replace crude convict huts. The governor's house was nearly finished and a brick-built courthouse, bursting with notions of British justice, was well underway.

'Opportunities, John. The bones are telling me. Just wait and see.' George winked, an invitation to collusion.

'Lest we starve first,' John thought, for he woke each morning in a sweat, the worry of finding fresh game heavy on his shoulders. The colony could not feed itself. Rations had been cut. Scurvy was rife.

He looked at George, whose face was alight with enthusiasm, and relented. *I want to see it as you do. To ride with you on the crest of the wave.* He sent a prayer to his gods.

⌐

'Seen Caesar?' Padding up on the soft sand, John had surprised John Martin at the stream, filling a flask and splashing water over his face in an attempt to wash away the aches of the day. John Martin took his time in looking up, as if even that effort were too much, and John winced at the stark, dull tiredness in his eyes, the grey of his skin.

'Seen Caesar?' He asked again, not looking John Martin in the eyes. The eels he had hidden under his shirt for Caesar seemed to writhe against his belly, taunting his starving friend. And he had sated his own hunger with berries and nuts and some fern fronds his friend Abaroo had pointed out. He knew his body shone rich and healthy, still glistening from the sea. He tried to swallow the guilt. It wasn't right to be so well.

Can only do so much. He was suddenly and irrationally angry at John Martin.

It was only a 500-yard walk from the beach, but he had crossed into a different world. There were no opportunities here. No merchants. Just the struggle to survive. John looked back in the direction where the lieutenant had been. He knew where he wanted to belong, but it felt like a betrayal.

John Martin jerked his head. 'That away. Up to no good if you ask me. And why would you look at me like that?'

But John had already turned away.

He walked, absorbed in his own thoughts. *Damn him for his sorry face. I need to eat if I'm to hunt. I do what I can.* But the memory of his friend's eyes, their utter exhaustion, bore a hole into his skull, leaving him weak and depleted, both ashamed of his good fortune and desperate to protect it.

'Tilly. Sorry.' He nearly knocked over the girl who had stepped into his path. She stood before him looking up with wide brown eyes, and though he could not be sure that it were not she who had accosted him, he wanted to pick her up and pat her down and make her feel better. Everything about her was delicate, her eyes huge in a fine face, her arms lean. She reminded him of a fawn he had once seen in Carolina. Its vulnerability had been its protection because he hated to shoot it. He knew Tilly. People liked to take care of her.

'John Randall. And where are you going looking so fine?' She spoke softly, her eyes warm beneath their dark lashes and he leaned in to hear her the better. She beckoned him over and settled herself against a tree. With her arms behind her back, her breasts and neck exposed, she seemed more helpless than ever, and apparently intent on lingering. 'Perhaps,' she whispered, a smile playing on her lips, 'you are looking for oysters?'

He shook his head, a mock mournful look on his face. 'I'm a married man, Tilly.' He knew enough of London slang to know the type of oysters she inferred. 'And anyway, didn't I see you with a seaman? He might not like any…er…interference.'

'He has left me. And I got nothing from him but this silly blue ribbon.' She fiddled with the bow that tied back her hair. Pulling it free, she brandished it before him, a look of mock sorrow on her face.

John shied back, as if fearing she would use it to tether him.

She laughed and retied her hair. 'Well, if ever you change your mind…' She sighed dramatically. 'You're about the only one round these parts ain't got one foot in the grave.' She opened her eyes wide. 'So what's a girl supposed to do?'

John rolled his eyes in mock exasperation. But, with a mind of their own, they returned to linger on her bust, and her waist, and her hips, and he felt sure he would find a warmer haven there than with Esther.

'Should've bedded her that first night,' he thought. He waved, though, and walked away. *Damn me if I didn't pick the wrong girl.*

He found Caesar slumped against a trunk in a clearing at the further perimeters of the settlement, a smile on his face. He wore no shirt, for none fit him, and was slick with sweat; he appeared to shine in the slanting light of dusk.

John studied him. His friend looked like a god, a wild and unholy god, with his hair growing in wild dreads; his eyes huge in a skeletal face; his limbs sheared of fat, though lean with muscle. John knew the power in those arms and chest, the strength of that back, but hunger seemed to have sucked the sanity from his friend. John feared for him. He recalled John Martin's words. *Up to no good.*

He nudged Caesar's leg.

'Got somfink for yer,' and with a flash of insight, 'lest, of course, you've already eaten.' He pulled the eels from their hiding place under his shirt and dangled them before Caesar; a test, for the man had been known to seize them and stuff them into his mouth without cooking, so ravenous he was.

'My thanks.' Caesar grinned, gesturing for them to be thrown on the ground beside him, 'But I have eaten a meal fit for a king. No dessert, though. Do you know where I might find some pudding?'

John felt the bottom slip from his belly. 'What have you done, you mad bugger?'

The trees whispered in the growing darkness, their shadows leaning over the two men. Insects and animals who liked the night watched on, preparing to stalk their prey.

'Taken what is my right.' Caesar shrugged, deliberately off-hand, daring John to react.

The woods hummed with dark business. The world closed in upon him and John screwed his eyes shut, struggling to keep his panic at bay. 'You already done finished your rations. Eat the lot the day you got them.'

Caesar grinned. 'Finished *my* rations. Found some others.' He sounded triumphant.

'Jesus Christ, Caesar. You gonna get yourself hung. You know that.' For the second time that night, the world tipped off balance, leaving him floundering. 'I bring what I can for yer.' The words sounded lame in his own ears.

'Ain't enough. And if I hang? Hell! I'll dance on the gallows.'

John wanted to shake the man; to knock some sense into him. He wanted to wrap his arms around him and keep him safe. He looked around the clearing as if searching for inspiration.

Caesar pulled himself upright, his face serious. 'John, we gotta talk. Brother to brother. Please, sit with me.' He patted the ground next to him.

In that clear direct gaze, John recognised his friend at last. He hunkered down next to him, leaning against the same tree, close enough to touch, though facing in a different direction. He held his breath, waiting for what was to come.

'We've been friends a long time, you and I,' Caesar said. 'Never had a friend like you.'

John tensed. *All my friends die.* He pretended to laugh. 'Don't speak so loud. The gods will hear you and no good will come of it.'

'Could be right there. They gonna kill me. No matter what ways I turn it, I can't see no other end. I work like a mule for them all day, and then just like a feckin' mule sit by humble as you please and let 'em starve me to death...or I can steal.' He looked at John, 'Or I can run. I have a plan.'

'No. No running. There's no place to run. You'll die out there, sure as here.'

'Not if you're with me. Not if you bring that musket of yours and a bit of powder, some balls. We're a team, John, you and I.' His smile was of pure love. His voice as soft and warm as treacle.

John hung his head in his hands, rubbing his eyes with his palms.

The forest had reached fever pitch. It hummed and chirped and buzzed. The very ground seemed to vibrate with its energy.

'Your eye. My arm. An' we both got a head on our shoulders. And your Indian friend. He would help.' Caesar had turned to face him, grabbing him by the shoulder. 'They can't break us, not the two of us together. And...ain't never begged before. John, you can't let them kill me.'

Caesar was as sane as John had ever known him. He was neither laughing, nor jesting nor raging. John looked deep into the heart of the man who had stood by his side, unflinching, at every turn. He groaned, a rough scratchy sound, like the tearing of a heart.

'I can't run. I – just – can't.' John wrapped his arms around his body and pushed himself back into the trunk of a tree as if he could disappear into it.

'Bloody Esther. That witch would have you boiling in her pot, stirring it with her broom in the flick of an eye. Give her a hiding and send her on her way.' Caesar's voice had lightened.

'Not Esther.' John couldn't bring himself to say more. He could have talked about opportunities, but the word felt oily in his mouth. He shook his head from side to side, wishing that none of this was happening.

'We're brothers.' Caesar's eyes fixed on John, searching for some sign that he had misunderstood.

'Who'd you steal the rations from? I'll go talk to him. Give him the eels. Fair exchange. Caesar, let me fix this.'

Caesar turned to face John. 'I'm not goin' to let them starve me to death. Now off with yer. Go lie down with your lieutenant friend.'

John stared at the man he had shared a cell with; who had held him when he was sick. He wanted to reach out, but the distance between them was too far. He struggled to his feet, and with a shake of his head flung the eels to the ground, not caring what Caesar did with them.

He heard maniacal laughter from deep in the woods and though he knew it for a bird, he could not help but believe the gods were chuckling at the decisions they tossed before him.

⌐

'You took yer time getting here. Heard you come into camp a while back.' Esther raised hard eyes from the pot she was stirring. 'Too busy bein' a somebody to come see your wife?'

John didn't answer. He had no energy for her tonight. He ducked into the shelter to lie down. He thought of Tilly. He needed a woman. One who would cry out for him.

'So...where's some meat then? Did yer bring some?'

John rolled over to block out the voice. It pursued him. 'Well, yer must've kept something back.' Pause. 'Who'd you give it to?'

Her voice reminded him of the harsh and forlorn call of the crow. In the early days of their marriage, it had broken across his consciousness with such yearning that he had longed to fill its need. He, Caesar, and John Martin had joined forces to build their huts; makeshift contraptions they might have been, but sturdier than most, and good to keep Esther dry. It hadn't been enough. He brought back bits of driftwood, strange nuts and seeds from his wanderings, hoping to catch her interest in the love he felt for this land. She only sniffed and tossed them away. She whined that he left her for days on end, that he cared for his friends more than herself, that he stayed late around the campfire, playing the flute. Her voice still reminded him of a crow, but that of a chick whose squawks for nourishment could never be met.

'She is broken,' Ol' Ma had observed. 'She can't never be filled.'

She followed him now into their shelter, standing over him. He rolled away, turning his back to her, in no mood for her demands. 'You always hold sumfink back. Who'd you give it to? Who deserves it if not your wife?'

And now she's swooping down to peck out my eyes.

'For the love of Mary, woman. If you don't get out of here and give me some peace, I I'm going to thrash the living lights from you.'

A body swung from the branch of a tree. Face swollen, tongue protruding, it no longer resembled the man who had once inhabited it. The soiled pants attracted a swarm of flies, deafening in their delight. The judge advocate had ordered the corpse to be left as a warning to others, for the man had been greedy and stolen some food.

Caesar stood beneath the boy, tied by his wrists to the triangle. He was grinning. Only the bead of sweat that ran from his forehead betrayed him. He had escaped death – too valuable to hang – but none would call him lucky.

Further afield, a sullen circle of fidgeting, anxious convicts muttered to each other or looked at the ground, ordered to pay witness to the king's justice.

An officer pulled the cat of nine tails from its red bag and handed it to the sergeant. That man took the lash, a length of rope unravelled at the end into nine twisted and knotted 'tails'. He stoked those thongs, almost sensuously, untangling them.

John stared straight at Caesar. *Stubborn, obstinate fool. I could have stopped this had you let me.* But he knew that his friend would not be standing there if he, John, had agreed to run. And he would use his own back to protect the man, if he only could.

A single drumbeat. The sergeant raised his arm swinging the cat over his head. He lunged forward delivering the blow with the full weight of his body, his arm outstretched. The claws of the cat ripped into flesh. Caesar tottered, but remained upright. The grin still firmly fixed.

A sixth, seventh and eighth drumbeat. Snakes of blood slithered across a reddened and swollen back. Caesar stood tall, refusing to bow. John felt the ravage of the claws and arched his back as if it were his own that took the blow. He caught his scream so it lodged in his throat, a lump that might choke him.

Two hundred drumbeats. A convict pulled bits of pulp and skin from the knotted rope. Caesar hung from his thronged wrists, unable to stand. His head lolled forward, mouth open. Eyes rolled back in his head.

John told himself to breathe. His legs felt weak and he feared he would fall. His mind confused the lines of chained slaves, the crowd of cowed convicts. They became as one. His decision had never been clearer. There were slaves and masters and he would never again be a slave.

Two hundred and fifty drumbeats. Caesar hung senseless.

John helped carry his friend to the hospital. He swallowed his despair. He shoved it deep into the box that held the pulsating, putrid moments of his life and pulled down the shutters. He would not give them light to grow or air to breathe. He would not acknowledge them.

Chapter Thirty-One

August 1788

Tilly wiggled closer, spooning against him, but didn't wake. Even though the wind tore at their tent and sliced through every crack and crevice to torment them, and though the canvas flapped and howled in its struggle to tear free of its ropes, still, she clung to her dreams. John tightened his grasp, smiling at the snuffles that escaped her mouth. She made a comfy pillow against the cold. He wondered what bound her so tightly to sleep. Had she escaped to childhood, to green fields and apple trees? Did the juice of a ripe peach dribble from her lips? Did an English summer sun warm her skin? No, he decided. Dreams didn't hold her. She would keep her eyes clenched closed until forced to open them and face a belly gripped with hunger, and feet swollen from winter frost, and the mind-numbing work of crushing shells for bricks, and the drab misery of a settlement stinking of sewerage and washed by a river of mud. He pulled her closer and stroked a single strand of hair from her forehead and nuzzled the back of her neck. She sighed. A leaf had caught in her curls; green and orange, it rested like a jewel in dark tousled tresses. He untangled it, crushing it between his fingers, and breathed in the tangy, clean smell before tossing away the fragments. Their fragrance cleared his brain and he pushed aside the tent flap to peer outside.

Only a faint lightening of the sky and the wild clamouring of birds suggested it was nearly dawn. Still dark enough for him to make his escape. Tilly's tent sat in the women's section, strictly out of bounds for men. To be shot on sight, the edict said, should a man intrude in the women's area. *But they won't shoot me.*

With one last peck to the top of Tilly's head, John crawled from the tent. Stretching first, he rubbed his upper arms to get the blood moving and blew on his fingers to warm them, but otherwise made no move to leave. In truth, he was undecided of his direction.

John Martin, too, had been flogged. He had been cold and had lit a fire in his hut. John knew he should check on him. Make sure he had water. Clean him if need be. Give him some of the berries he had found and that Doctor White said would help. But that would risk running into Esther, and he quailed at seeing her thin-lipped, mean little mouth, and enduring her ugly rants on this of all mornings

'E'll be fine. Were only twenty-five lashes. Why'd he go light-ing fires anyway!

Ol' Ma remonstrated. *Not like you to be unkind. Needs to watch yerself.*

One side of the tent sagged where the pegs had loosened and he bent to tighten them.

He had enjoyed the night with Tilly. He knew she thought of him as a bear, ready to fall into her honey trap, but she opened her legs without prompting, and as a hunter she was no match for him.

He made his decision. He couldn't face Esther this morn-ing. He would find the lieutenant and help him ready for their expedition. John Martin would understand.

You so big for your britches, you ain't got time for a friend? Ol' Ma hissed.

Leave me be, ol' woman.

Would 'ave thought you needed yer friends, place like this.

John shrugged her away but images of John Martin stalled him, standing steady at his back, small and squat and stubborn, when John faced down the Dobson brothers on the Ceres. With a grimace and a muttered oath, he turned to find his friend and to tackle his wife.

Esther leant against a tree, a few paces beyond their hovel, her shawl wrapped tight, a scowl upon her face. *Does the damned woman never sleep?*

'So, when did you crawl in? Been ruttin' with the camp dogs,'ave ya?'

He pushed past her and ducked into John Martin's lean-to. His friend tossed about, fevered and irritable. He refused to let John bathe him, batting his hands away. When John forced some berries into his mouth, John Martin spat them out and spun his head away; a red trickle of juice drooled from cracked lips. John sunk his head into his hands. *I have no time for this. Oh fuck, Caesar. We need yer, man.* But the thought of his other friend only caused grief. Since his flogging, Caesar had pulled into himself, refusing to acknowledge John, severing their friendship as brutally as the lashing had severed his skin. *Ahh, fuck yer, Caesar. I miss you, my brother.*

'I gotta go,' he told Esther when he had done what he could. 'You make sure he's alive when I come back or I'll whip you to your bones. He needs water. Plenty of it. And wash this.' He threw the blanket at her.

He hadn't needed to talk so harshly, for Esther was good with the sick and often seen around camp washing linen or topping up fresh water. Seems she didn't need to build walls around herself when with the dying.

She snarled at him but picked up the blanket with a sniff. She took the empty wooden pail he had kicked towards her and turned toward the stream, making a point of cursing when her bare feet stepped upon a stone.

¬

'Hop in, John. Let the boys do their job. You'll have your work cut out when we get there.' Lieutenant Johnston grabbed John's sleeve and hauled him into the dinghy. Governor Phillip, the surgeon, John White, and Lieutenant Tench already clung precariously to the pitching vessel as two marines struggled to push them through the surf and into deeper water. Waves sought to upturn them, grabbing the bow and tossing it high to spill the men into the sea. The wind whistled around them. It seized the wig from Lieutenant Tench's head and would have lobbed it into the ocean had John not reached out to grab it, nearly pitching the tiny dinghy into the sea. It threw the men into a fit of laughing and shouting, like schoolboys on an outing.

'Good save, lad. Jolly well done.' Governor Phillip usually sat hunched into himself as if the very clouds pressed down upon his shoulders and threatened to grind him into the earth, but not today. He cheered and punched the air at John's effort. This was the third exploratory expedition. The third opportunity to escape the disease and hunger and bickering that gripped the colony.

With the southerly gale driving them forward, they caught sight of the headland they called Manly before noon. The governor had named it on their first exploratory expedition, in honour of the group of Indians they had found there. 'Such confidence. Such manly bearing,' he had said. Abaroo had been among them then, and as they now approached, John searched the foreground for sight of his friend. He never knew when or where to expect him. He would think himself alone in the bush, stalking an animal or cooking a meal, when Abaroo would appear. Sometimes he would seat himself, cross-legged before the fire, helping himself to the duck that sizzled among the embers. Once he had broken off a piece of John's damper, stuck it into his mouth and chewed before abruptly spitting it out, his face crumpled in disgust. Another time he had brought a plant of purple black berries and spiky leaves and flung them to the ground beside John, with a gesture to eat. He had frowned as John touched them tentatively with his tongue and took only the smallest nibble but laughed at the delight that spread across the man's face and urged him to take more. Abaroo had seeped the leaves in water to make a tea, patting his belly to suggest it was a medicine. John had taken it back to the colony and now he collected it regularly for the officers. He never accepted payment or barter, preferring instead to build a bank of goodwill.

The beach appeared empty as the dinghy ground into shallow waters. Grumbling about wet clothes and stiff limbs, the officers disembarked and waded to shore, leaving John and two other convicts to unload the tents and supplies. Frypans and cooking pots, axes and machetes, ground sheets and blankets, flasks of whisky and bags of flour were unloaded.

John checked the gunpowder. It stayed dry. The three game-keepers would have to carry it all, to clear the tracks, to hunt and cook, but they didn't grumble. They were free of the damned colony. They weren't cutting down trees with blunt axes or hauling them to the sawmill or being whipped because they were starving.

Wading onto shore and letting drop his last load, John paused to stretch his lower back and relax his shoulders. When he raised himself again, five Indians had rounded the coast in their bark boats. They did not approach. Abaroo was not among them.

'They avoid us these days,' the governor remarked. He glanced at John. 'Would you have better luck, do you think? Might they think you're one of them?'

'They are very certain that I am not one of them, Governor.' John said, wincing. He wondered if that was how the governor thought of him.

John slashed at the bush. Prickly and dry, it spat back at him, snarling his jacket and scratching his cheek. He flicked a hand to drive away the flies, but it made no difference. They continued to torment him, crawling into his eyes, his nose, his mouth and ears. For four days, the group had followed a trail made by the natives. John led the way, one foot after another, tiny and insignificant in the forest of giant gums that soared above them. Step by step, up steep crevices and rocky slopes, beneath the watch of the ancients. Gnarled and warped, the red gums grew from the depths of rock and snaked their roots around giant boulders. They stretched aching, arthritic limbs – that rocked and groaned in the wind – across the sky. They murmured of life before the beginning of time.

They trudged uphill now and he moved wearily, slowed by the weight of tents on his back, tired from hacking at fallen branches and hauling away hollowed logs that blocked the path.

The group didn't talk. The officers had chatted on the first day, relieved to be free from the colony. *Even the fish have disappeared. The convicts do not work, too weak from hunger. We must increase the penalty for theft of food. Six hundred lashes. Eight hundred lashes. It's not enough. Ignorant fools. They barter the shredding of a back for a slice of bread.* But each day, the officers grew quieter, the colony more distant. This suited John. Interested at first, he had stored their gossip for retelling back at camp. But their chatter had come to annoy him. Small jabs at his peace. He preferred communion with the trees, watching the light as it fell through the leaves, or breathing in their sweet, piney smell, or listening to the birds as they squabbled in the branches. And when he had sufficed of that, he lost himself in his memory box and forgot his blisters and his aching back.

'John, we are not all of your olympic strength.' It was Tench who complained. 'Some of us need to rest.'

Jolted from his thoughts, John laughed and stopped. To his left and above him, a platform of sandstone jutted out above the landscape. With a questioning look to Phillip, he motioned the others to rest. They sank to the ground.

'Oh, good God. Right on an ants' nest,' Johnston complained, leaping up again.

'I might never get up should I sit,' the good doctor moaned. 'My oath, I am tired.'

John struggled free of the tents on his back and indicated that he'd clamber up for a better view. Roots grew from and around the rocks, making it an easy climb.

Beneath him, the cliff sloped down to a bay, and he ached to dive into it from where he stood, hot and sticky, his mouth dry. A million promises seemed to sparkle within its clear blue depths. A bent finger of land protected wooded islands, small havens of green, from the mouth of a raging ocean. He recalled an oath he had made to Ol' Ma and his mother, and scoured the shoreline with his eyes, seeking the place to put a farm-house. Further up that river, maybe. Dreamily, he fingered his eagle as he cleared a patch of land between the giant eucalypt trees and imagined for himself a garden. With roses. 'Home,' he murmured. He had only to find a woman to suit it, for Esther surely wouldn't. Nor could he see Tilly there. The grind of survival had worn his dream thin and faded, a child's pencil sketch on scrap paper. But here it gleamed, rich in colour and conception, perfect in dimension, demanding to be claimed. He would be master here. Master Randall.

He recalled the last time he had seen the man who had thought he owned him. He had stood on the veranda of the farmhouse, puffed up like a peacock in his new clothes, flicking imaginary specks of dust from his shoulders and cracking his knuckles. He was off to war, and if war could be won by an arrogant belief in your own importance and a smug disregard for anyone else, then they were well armed. But the man had something John wanted. Some people were afraid of him. They all respected him. Even his mother had.

Standing on a rock overlooking a bay, John renewed his vow. His children would run free here among the trees and swim in those rivers. And he would make his mother proud. Regardless of what it took.

'Randall. What do you see?' the lieutenant shouted from below.

John hesitated.

'Randall. Can you hear me?'

John squeezed his eyes shut. He put the scene in his happy box and sealed it with an oath. He took one last look. Standing on the ledge, he brushed imaginary specks of dust from his shoulders, turned his back and clambered down.

'A fine harbour. We can make it by mid-afternoon to camp, should you be agreeable.'

¬

Spray splashed from beneath webbed feet. Wings flapped. A flock of ducks skidded to a halt on the surface of the bay with rowdy, joyous life. One. Two. Three … John shot. A dark stain spread across the water. He reloaded and fired again. Two birds would feed them tonight.

A restless mood gripped the party that evening. Tomorrow they would explore this area, but already they knew it would not provide the timber they needed – no firs or oak trees. Only the eucalypt that split and cracked and refused to float.

The group circled the fire. The cold on their backs pushed them close to its warmth, hands stretched out, feet pointed to the flames. The rags of convicts tangled with tailored garb.

John finished a story, a man's story told for men, when men behaved like boys. 'And I never knew before how fast I could run, until she, or should I say, he, showed his true nature.'

Beside him the lieutenant roared with laughter, slapping John on the back. 'I know you too well; you are making this up.'

'No, I have seen such myself,' argued Dr White.

John reached behind him to grasp a log he had stockpiled and threw it on the fire.

'You pre-empted me, Randall. I was about to suggest we needed that,' Phillip said.

John nodded and smiled, comfortable in the company, though each considered himself better than he. Only Johnston would have sympathy for his dreams. He glanced over. His friend winked as if in collusion.

'Ahh, it is good to be away from Sydney Cove,' Tench muttered, and then winced clearly regretting his statement, for though mildly meant, it flattened the mood with the delicacy of a cannon ball.

No one replied. The campfire flickered and dimmed under the weight of the new log.

Phillip tossed the scraps of his meal into the ashes. Gristle hung from the joint and shreds of flesh clung to the bone and no doubt the marrow was rich and juicy. John didn't seek to retrieve it. He too, had had his fill. But he pictured the colony. Men would have thrown punches for that bone: futile, weak little punches betrayed by starvation; they would have scratched and bitten for it with gums empty of teeth and nails soft and broken. They would have sucked the bone until it was dry of its juice and gleamed white, until it softened and splintered in their mouth. Then they would have sucked some more, because it lessened the hunger to do so. Even a stone held in the mouth could fool the brain. A little. Not much.

Grey clouds threatened their journey home. And grey ocean stole the warmth from body and heart. The laughter of the past weeks froze on their breath. Faces settled into the tight expressions demanded by the colony.

No one greeted them. As John strode through the rows of tents towards his own, eyes followed him. Narrow, resentful eyes; speculative eyes; beckoning eyes; weary eyes. Not until he deposited himself outside of John Martin's canvas did he find friendly eyes. Eyes clear of fever.

John found his friend sitting cross-legged outside his lean-to. He slumped to the ground beside him, coughing and waving his hand. The fire had been fed with damp wood and smoke drifted between and around them, making ghosts of them both in the dull evening light. John tossed his satchel over. It was full of scraps and bones, morsels he had saved from their meals. No words were shared. John Martin munched and sucked. He found a piece of duck breast, fleshy and full of grease. His hands shook as he pulled it apart and offered some to John, but he just shook his head, glad not to be so desperate.

Esther crawled from her tent to glare and demand her share. John growled at her, but she didn't retreat.

'I kept 'im alive, din't I?'

He had saved a bunch of duck feet for Tilly. She would boil them for broth and munch on the glutinous web as if it were the finest steak, but he pulled one from his satchel and flung it at Esther.

'That all?'

But John turned back to John Martin. He began telling of the harbour they had found. The governor had named it Pittwater. 'Ain't never seen no place so pretty. Made me ache just to look at it, I reckon -' But he found it hard – even to John Martin, lost in the smoke from the fire – to share his oath. 'One day,' was all he could find to say.

John Martin sucked at the eyes of a fish head and smacked his lips. 'That's good.' He waited and then added. 'Your place sounds nice.'

'You know, not so long from now, our time will be up. We'll be free men. We should think about that.'

'Calleghan reckons his time is nearly up. Mine too. They ain't got no records though. Left 'em all in England. Convenient, don't you think.'

Chapter Thirty-Two

October 1788

A boy, dressed in the uniform of a marine, stumbled towards him. He walked jerkily, each leg arguing with itself before stepping forward. Soft smooth cheeks, not yet ripe for shaving, a fleshy pink mouth, skinny little wrists and unblemished hands. John knew him as the son of an officer, no doubt accompanying his father to make a man of him.

Well, ain't you got a long way to go. John sat on a tree trunk outside the shack he supposedly shared with Esther, but where he rarely spent his nights.

'Randall, orders to report to the carpenter tomorrow morning.' The words tumbled out as if they had struggled to stay unspoken until they had been given a kick up the arse and out the mouth.

John glared back at him. 'Must have the wrong man. I hunt for Lieutenant Johnston.'

'I do not have the wrong man!' And John was sure that the boy officer had stamped a furious and fearful foot, though in fact he remained still. Looking like he might turn and run, he instead pulled himself taller and forced authority into his voice. 'You are to report for work with the carpenter tomorrow.'

Languidly, John pulled himself to his feet, preparing to stare down the child. He would find the lieutenant and get him to sort this out.

'Report or face the consequences. You have been instructed.' With dignity, the child turned and marched away, leaving John staring behind him. 'Go be buggered you little brat. I'm not haulin' logs for no carpenter.'

'Stuck a stick up your arse, ain't he?' Esther rarely looked happy, but leaning against a tree, clasping her torn and dirty shawl to her chest, her lank hair in knots around her face, she looked delighted enough to dance the jig.

The lieutenant did not sort it out. 'I'm sorry, John. You're about the only convict in this damn place fit enough to work. They need you.'

¬

John let drop a load of sawn timber. The skin across his back bled red and raw where he had shouldered the wood, and the old familiar hunger – thought forgotten – returned with vengeance and gnawed at his belly. 'Enough now, we're done. It's nearly one o'clock. Can tell from the sky.' He motioned for his companion, Tom, to sit.

Thomas Joseph was a ruddy-faced man, big on swagger but short on brains. He looked up to John with something like awe, even though he were the older. They found a spot where a slice of sunshine had nudged through the clouds, but it offered meagre warmth on this slack, grey day. As he looked around, it seemed to John that time had slowed. Two convicts, bare-chested and skinny as rakes took hold of a sack of rocks. They dragged it two paces, stopped and rested. And tried again. Two paces. Drained faces. Heavy breathing. Hunched shoulders. A red-coated marine leant against a tree, mouth open, eyes closed, lids fluttering in dream. A bearded man slumped against a shovel. A hammer missed a nail. *Our lives are draining away. I think soon we will all just stop.* Meanwhile the ancient trees groaned and creaked and looked down on them.

John and Thomas had trudged between the sawmill and the building site, lugging loads of timber back and forth for three days now. Timber to build huts to house officers. With his first steps, and on the first day, John had turned at the sound of each new voice, sure the lieutenant would stroll along, a laugh on his face, and protest that it was all a bad joke. He had formed arguments in his head. Arguments to put before the lieutenant, and the governor if need be. *No one can shoot like I can. The colony will starve without the meat I bring. Let me hunt. I will bring back twice what I have in the past.* No one heard them. And so he raged. He would tear down the building frames and the wilted gardens and the beaten tents and the sorry-looking shacks if just one more person tried to tell him what to do.

'Whatcha doin', Randall? I didn't tell you to stop.' The carpenter, Robertson Reid, strolled towards them, standing directly above the two convicts. John didn't look up. He took a gulp of water from the flask and handed it to Thomas. 'I want you up, NOW!' Reid repeated.

The clouds closed over the sun. John sat in shade, his fists clenched. He closed his eyes. He breathed deeply. 'You can want. My work is done.'

'Yeah,' repeated Thomas. He took the flask that John handed him.

A short distance away the two convicts released their sack and straightened their backs and watched. The red-coated marine opened an eye.

Reid tensed and leaned forward. Spittle flew from his mouth, but his words came slow and hard. 'Get up, boy, or I'll have the flesh flogged from your black arse.'

John pulled himself to his feet. 'I'm not your boy.' He walked down to the ocean's edge, plunged in and swam out to deep water.

Forty-eight, forty-nine. The cat swung. Specks of flesh and blood sprayed from the shredded back. Fifty. The cat hissed again. The crowd watched with shuttered eyes. On this, the last lash, the legs of the ruddy-faced, red-haired and not-too-bright youth crumpled beneath him, broken of their bravado. Dismissed, the unwilling spectators shuffled away.

On the outer edge of the crowd, John's gaze remained on the limp body of the whipped man.

See what you gone done. Ol' Ma sounded tired.

I didn't order him flogged.

Youse the one encouraged 'im to act all high and mighty.

What do you want of me? To let that limp dick talk to me like I was nothin'?

But he knew he had been careless of the man. For apparently no reason, he thought of Gilly, patting John's chest; honest eyes full of joy to have a friend. He had trusted John too. *I'm sorry Gilly. And I'm sorry, Tom. I should not have involved you.*

Charges against John had been dropped.

'You have friends, John,' the lieutenant told him, 'but take care. We may not always win your pardon.'

Still, John cherished a small triumph. It burned through his guilt like a flame through wax. The incident had confirmed his standing. He could not be touched. With a shrug of his shoulders, he cracked his knuckles and turned away, striding through the shambling, aimless crowd, his bearing erect. *A man must stand tall.* Tomorrow he would return to hunting.

Chapter Thirty-Three

April 1789

'Must be news soon.' John and John Martin talked, as they always did, of Caesar.

He had stolen a musket and a cooking pot and fled into the bush. John didn't blame him for running. Only weeks ago, Caesar had stolen some food again and John had stood in the courtroom and watched as his friend had been sentenced to life imprisonment, never to be free. John had marked the precise moment that the full implications of a life sentence had hit him. Caesar was turning away, smiling, and then stopped and seemed to stumble. It was like the felling of a great tree, and John thought for a moment he might bring the whole room down with him, but he had caught himself and stood erect again. And that, John thought, showed the measure of the man. There were none his equal, despite their entitlements, despite their resolve to bring him to heel.

John and John Martin hunkered down outside John's hut, garnering what warmth they could from a spluttering fire and though they had wrapped themselves in their bed covers, an icy gust still cut through their threaded garments to bite at ears and nose. John pulled his blanket tighter, though it made little difference. He shrugged. His face had hardened over the years since the two had met. Burned by the sun and carved by the wind, deep lines were etched around his eyes and mouth, and though he still smiled readily, his dark, nearly black eyes held secrets.

'They'll hang him this time.' John Martin spoke in his usual sure tones.

John's attention was caught by a tremor that seemed to run through the camp. A muttering and a grumble. As if on a wave, heads turned toward the brickyard, questions were thrown with a look and a gesture, bodies raised themselves from where they sheltered.

'Want to wait here while I go look?' John asked, but his friend was already struggling to his feet.

John elbowed himself through the crowd, finding a spot where he could look over heads. A circle of marines provided guard as Caesar was led, stumbling, through the camp, his arms bound before him, his hair a mat of twigs, his skin scratched and bleeding.

'Found him not far from here.'

'Near the brickfields.'

'Near dead from hunger.'

'Says he didn't even put up a fight. Glad to get back to this here little bit of paradise.'

A mostly silent crowd had gathered to watch; again, he stumbled. A youth, a bare stripling of a lad, went to his aid, but bowed beneath the weight of the man, so that both crumpled to the ground. It may have been comical, but no one laughed.

John elbowed his path forward. Reaching Caesar's side, he tucked his shoulder under his friend. 'I have you. I'm here.'

Caesar leant heavily upon him. He weighed less than the carcasses John carried on his back.

An older woman hobbled out, a jug of water and filthy rag in her hand. She wiped Caesar's lips, crusted from thirst, and they stopped while he drank.

Still the crowd kept silent, as though in prayer. John understood. For the barest slice of time, Caesar had held their dreams, borne their hopes of escape and survival on his back. They returned now, weak and broken.

No sun reached through the thick windows of the court-house. It felt as cold and dank and dark as a tomb and seemed to suck the life from all who entered.

They've certainly stolen the soul from him, John thought as Collins, the chief magistrate entered the room. John had witnessed the judgements the man had made: a thousand lashes, two thousand, too many for a man to survive. *King Canute, trying to hold back the tide!* For throughout the settlement, hunger pushed men to reckless measures. Even the soldiers stole food when they could.

Caesar stood in chains below the bench, wild and dishevelled, but not the cornered beast that Collins would like to see. He shook away hands that would hold him and held the magistrate's eyes. Man to man. It was Collins who looked away.

From his now familiar position in the back corner, the cold damp of the bricks sinking through his shirt to freeze his back, John could scarcely breathe, so nervous was he. He barely listened as the evidence was read, the verdict given. It could not be contested. As Collins raised his head to pass sentence, the room hushed. John held his breath. The rough bricks bit into his back. The eyes of those gathered darted from magistrate to felon, settling first on the man with the wig and the pen, such feeble tools to control a new world, before tearing themselves away to the giant in chains. John's heart beat so loudly and with such urgency, he thought that they might hear and send him out.

Collins declared that a flogging would have no effect on Caesar. He was right in that, John agreed. Nor did the magistrate believe that a hanging 'of a mere animal' would be sufficient deterrent to the settlement. 'You are afraid of making a martyr of him,' John thought.

Caesar was to be sent to an island in the harbour, where he was to work in chains, permitted though to grow his own vegetables.

¬

August 1789

'John, come quickly. Can't you hear me? Come quick.'

'John!' John Martin limped up to him on wobbly legs. 'Esther is sick. She's dying.'

John made a wry face. 'Not that one. Death'd choke on her tongue. More's the pity.' But he stopped at John Martin's expression. 'Ah fuck! Okay, I'll come.'

He had avoided Esther over the last few weeks, preferring the company of Tilly. He smiled, thinking about the pregnant Tilly. *I'm to be a father.* Despite himself, he beamed at a woman who stood on the beach, holding her babe against her chest, watching out to sea. She grinned back, but then frowned, as if she had surprised herself, and looked at him with a questioning gaze. No one smiled these days.

'What's wrong with her?' he asked when he finally pushed aside the flap that hung across the doorway of the hut he once shared with Esther. She tossed on the mattress, fever-ridden eyes gleaming in a wasted face. 'Has the doctor been?'

'He has. Nothin' to be done.' John Martin crouched beside her.

John had brought a jug of water with him and tried to ease some down her mouth, but she gagged it up with a rattling cough. He watched over her throughout the night, his hands fluttering uselessly, tucking in a blanket, wiping a strand of hair from her face. Finally, she quieted, and he took a moment to go for more water. When he returned her body was warm and her eyes open, but there was nothing of her left. He had missed the breath that marked the end of her angry, brittle life. His eyes darted around the shack to catch a glimpse of her departing spirit, half fearing it might strike him in a last act of spite. And then, not wanting to take any risks, he pushed aside the curtain over the doorway, ushering it out with a wave of his hands. He then crouched down by her sleeping mat to remember that first night when they had clung to each other and dared to hope. But it eluded him.

'Just don't feel nothin',' he said to John Martin, who stood beside him, looking down at the corpse.

'Hard to love a porcupine.'

'Heard she's dead.' Tilly greeted him with a smile and open arms, not even pretending distress. She had taken care with her appearance, her hands and face scrubbed clean, the blue ribbon in a bow around her hair. She looked up at him and giggled. John pulled her close, fondling the small round mound of her belly, *where my baby lies*. He pushed his hands under the waist of her skirt, to feel her the better. Her stomach felt warm and taut to his touch. His moved up to her breasts, already fuller, heavier in his palms. He nuzzled Tilly's neck.

'Has she been busy today?' he whispered.

'How do you know she's a 'she'? Might be a 'he'. A little man who grows up to be just like his dad.

'I want a little girl. Can spoil a little girl.' His hands became more urgent. He nibbled on her ear. 'Come, let's go into the tent.'

'Oh, John, I wanted to walk with you.' She twisted around to smile up at him.

John sighed. Tilly had taken to parading both him and her pregnancy around the camp, leaning heavily on his arm, patting his cheek, smiling sweetly when people asked to touch her stomach. He felt like a prize heifer. It had been a source of grief to Esther, who had taken to her hut and rarely come out.

'People like to see a woman with child. A sign of hope in this miserable place.' She continued.

'Let them make their own signs. Come, I've been on my feet all day.' With his arm around her waist and a kiss to her cheek, he bundled her into the tent.

It was one of the last tents remaining and though it was only a piece of canvas, stretched tight, already mouldy, and even torn in parts, the soft glow of its filtered light created its own world.

John rolled Tilly onto her front, pulling up her skirts, and mounted her from behind.

'John, no. Not now. After our walk maybe.' Tilly struggled beneath him but one fist held both her slender hands above her head.

He bent to kiss the back of her head and then released the rope that belted his own trousers. 'Ssh, my sweet. Just lie still.'

'Oh, John...' Tilly started.

He rolled off Tilly and pulled her close to him. He stroked her hair back from her face and eased her skirts back over her legs. She turned her back on him.

'What's wrong with you, woman?'

'I told you I didn't feel like it.'

'You didn't feel like it? You were a whore for gawd's sake. You didn't sell oysters. You sold whole rock beds. But now you don't feel like it?'

'John. I'm your woman.' She hesitated. 'Your wife.' But it sounded more of a question than a conviction.

John retrieved the blue ribbon that had become tangled beneath him. 'Here, let me tie it for you.' He smoothed her hair back behind her ears and took his time. 'See, now, let's go for a walk. Fair exchange, don't you think?'

'No. No, it's not.' Doe-like eyes had hardened and now glowed black as coal. 'I carry your child. Esther is dead. You need to marry me. *That* is fair exchange!'

She has a point, Ol' Ma said.

Only the barest light crept into the tent. It no longer felt like a new world. It was cramped and stuffy and smelt of mould. The convicts settled down early these nights, too tired, too hungry to gather and gossip. The sounds were those of a retreat as they tidied up their campsites, bid farewells to the day, and retired to what peace they could find in sleep. Alone, they faced their demons or searched for lost loves.

John heard the muted sounds of footsteps on the path outside, and a gasp as someone tripped over a guy rope, pulling it loose. The tent sagged.

'Too late anyways.' John broke the silence that had stretched between them. He was unsure of which exchange he was referring to. Everything just felt too late. 'I've gotta go. I'll fix that rope for you.'

Chapter Thirty-Four

December 1789

Stretched out in the grass in the still hot night, John couldn't sleep. No breeze stirred in the trees. No clicks or creaks or chirps or squeaks sounded from the forest. Insects and birds and tiny beasts held their peace. No doubt, like him, flattened by the heavy heat.

He had built a 'hide', fashioned after the humpies the Indians used, of branches and bark, leaning against a tree and close to a waterhole, with an expanse of native grasses. A mob of kangaroos would visit early, he felt sure. He had been lucky here before.

And though he hadn't wanted to leave the settlement, not today, he was glad to be out here, alone, where he felt truly at peace; away from prying eyes; released from judgement and expectation.

Tilly was close to giving birth. He pictured her waddling about the camp, a hand supporting her back, looking up at him through those thick lashes of hers. Sad. Accusing. He had never told her that he would not marry her. He had just *disentangled* himself. He could not picture her in his cottage among the roses. 'I can handle a bear in the woods,' he thought, 'but not that bright blue ribbon that would lead me around like a dog to heel.'

And as the long hot hours passed, John gazed up at the stars, as if seeking a portal to another time and place. Finally he spoke aloud, addressing his words to his mother, wherever she may be. 'The baby will carry my name and I will be a father. And you, a grandmother.' And he could not keep the pride from his voice. His baby would be born free. And if he had done naught else in his life, he had given that one true gift to his child.

'I have done that.' And his voice rang across the forest, triumphant, challenging her to hear him; to see him. But he could not bring himself to voice the thought that sat at the back of his throat and threatened to choke him. *Are you proud of me yet?*

And so he spent the rest of the night making promises to his child – it would be a girl, he was sure of it – a home to lay her head, forests to run in and rivers to swim. He would teach her to shoot, and, he thought of his father. He would teach her to carve and tell her of the man with sad eyes. It was after all, his father's dream too that they would be living.

As dawn tiptoed across the land and the stars faded from the sky, he prepared for the kill. He was lucky. He had known he would be.

The lieutenant was the first to greet him as he struggled into camp. 'The governor has declared that all food is to be shared equally, officers and convicts alike. You have done well, but we need a miracle of the five thousand.'

John shrugged. He wanted only to dump the beast at the commissary and throw himself into the ocean. George stopped him.

'Your friend, Caesar.'

John let the kangaroo slide from his back and turned to face the officer.

'He's escaped. Again. Tricked his guards into releasing him from his manacles. Stole a boat. Out there somewhere.'

John chuckled. He would have laughed out loud but for the stern look he received. 'What can I say?' he said to George, 'He is a bigger man than most.' To himself he whispered. 'Run far and fast, Caesar.' He turned to retrieve the 'roo.

The lieutenant scowled. 'Your friendship with that man does you no favours, John. He will be found, and I caution you to keep your distance. But John,' his voice was lighter, 'almost forgot. Seems we have a new baby in camp. Leave that,' he gestured to the animal, 'I'll get it sorted. You might want to visit your "friend"?'

February 1790

'Hey now, my lady love.' John took the baby he had named Frances in his arms, carefully supporting her head, laughing as tiny arms waved in the air and tried to grab him. He buried his face into her neck, smothering her with kisses. 'Yum, I'm going to eat you up, you taste so good.'

'And me? Don't I get a greeting?' Tilly's smile didn't hide her longing.

'Ah, you want me to eat you, too,' John teased. 'Here, and maybe here?' He flicked her breast and pinched her arse, but too quickly returned his attention to the babe. 'I'll take her for a while.'

Tilly offered him her hand. 'I'll come with you. I'll enjoy a stroll.' Her voice sounded brittle, the smile forced.

'You need to rest.' John had buried his head once more in the baby's belly, blowing raspberries.

'She needs my milk.' Tilly retrieved her hand from where it had been left hanging.

'I'll bring her back.'

Where once a pipe may have played and a chorus of song sounded from a clearing, an eerie silence hung over the camp. Where once the smells of cooking may have lingered in the air, or ash from fires caught in the wind, the smell of vomit and sickness forced him to place a protective hand over Frances's face. Men squatted beside their tents, vacant eyed. Women no longer flirted. The colony waited. *A ship must come soon.* Rations had been cut, and cut again. They lived on the last of the salted pork they had brought from England two years ago and a handful of rice so full of weevils it walked off the plate.

With Frances tucked to his chest, her head resting on his shoulder, John wandered through the colony. She was a black-eyed, smiling baby who gurgled her greetings, clasped fingers to stick in her mouth, and slapped joyously at faces with her chubby, dimpled hand. He, on the other hand, could have been a pirate. With his tangle of dreads tied by a string in a tail behind his head and his shirt unbuttoned, he might more easily be seen waving a cutlass than a babe. But the sight of him holding his daughter, gentled even hardened men, so bright did his eyes shine.

He nuzzled her neck, soft and warm. *Ah, little one. Only three months and you own me.* She raised a fist to clutch at his hair, babbling her agreement.

John Martin whittled at a piece of wood when they joined him but put it down to take Frances.

'What yer making?' John picked up the misshapen block, hid a rueful expression and returned it to its maker.

'One of those hoppy things.'

John skipped the carving just out of reach of Frances's hands. She squirmed towards it, laughing.

'Taking her for a walk down the beach. Mebbe we'll be the first to spot a ship. Want to come?' John leant to retrieve the babe and then laid her on her belly on the ground. She pushed herself up with her arms, and looked at the two of them, as if for praise at this clever, new feat.

'Ain't no boat comin'. Those men back in England with their fat bellies and their big cigars and their fancy clothes just sent us here, so long and good riddance and off you go to die.'

'I don't plan on dying.'

'See Caesar?'

John nodded. Caesar had soon ditched the boat, preferring land to sea and after six weeks, their friend had been carried into the camp on a stretcher, speared by Aboriginals and near dead. Despite the lieutenant's warnings, John had visited as often as he could: bathing his friend, spoon-feeding him, changing bandages.

'Think you should have a word to those friends of yours,' Caesar had said. 'Weren't very hospitable to a hungry man.'

Caesar had been excited to come upon a group at camp, had thought to trade on the colour of his skin, had called the name of John's friend, Abaroo. 'Reckoned I could tag along with 'em. Get 'em to show me about town.'

John smiled.

'Weren't very helpful at all.' His gestures had been met by angry words and warning spears.

He had better success the next time. He waved an empty musket toward the group, frightening them away and stealing their food. 'Thought I had a winning formula. Kept me goin' awhile. Pity they wised up.'

John held a beaker of water to Caesar's mouth. 'Drink.'

Caesar did. 'Guess they definitely gonna hang me now?'

John shrugged. 'Guess they will. Funny thing about British justice. They gotta get you fit and healthy first.'

April 1790

John eased himself in the shallows along the shore, washing off the day and the ache of failure, letting cool water ease his feet, hot and sore from hunting. He collapsed to his knees, embracing the surf as it broke against his chest, surged over his shoulders and down his back. His breathing calmed. His satchel lay on the sand. Two ducks. He had wasted the day chasing a kangaroo. The thought of returning with it to the starving colony had lent him strength, and he had loped through the bush, leaping logs, stung by brush, tripping over vines, legs burning with the effort. Finally, dizzy with fatigue, he had paused to catch his breath and lost the animal. He lingered now on the beach, unwilling to face the lieutenant. *A ship must come soon. England can't just abandon us.*

'Nothing?' asked the lieutenant, when finally John found him. The officer remained level-voiced, belying the lines around his eyes and the pallor in his face. Even his erect bearing stooped against the weight of anxiety.

John pulled the birds from his sack. 'Something.' He had hoped to find some eggs and berries to bring back for Frances, but it was not the season. Tilly's milk had dried up, and the baby threw up the rice and pork he fed her. He had thought to hide a duck, even the bones to make a broth, but knew he couldn't hide meat from the desperate eyes around him. A fisherman had been lashed last week for secreting some of his catch.

'Something,' agreed the lieutenant. 'Maybe not enough to feed two thousand souls. If we cut rations again, we have supplies for ten weeks. Maybe not even that.'

John glanced at the line of convicts and soldiers waiting for their weekly rations. 'And then?'

'I assume we'll die. A fine end to a noble career, don't you think?'

'Have we heard from Norfolk Island? Have they food to send us?'

A ship of convicts had been sent to an island in the north, thought to be good farming country. Caesar had been on it. Spared yet again from the noose.

'A cat with nine lives,' John Martin had said.

'Favoured by the gods,' John had thought. He hoped his friend had found a place where they put food in his belly; maybe, even, a woman in his bed.

He pulled his thoughts back to the present. 'Saw something else too. While I was out.' John swallowed. His eyes clouded and he looked towards the ocean, seeking the right words. There were no right words.

The lieutenant waited.

'Came upon a beach. Looked like a whole tribe of them Aboriginals. Men. Women. Kids. All dead. Maybe thirty, forty of 'em. Smallpox. Just rotting on the beach, they were.'

He took a deep breath to steady his voice. He had walked the beach of corpses, a scarf tied around his nose and mouth, looking for one who might be taller, longer-legged than the others. Looking for Abaroo. With a sinking heart and trembling hands, he had crouched to turn over a body. Above him an eagle glided the thermals, wings outstretched, feathers splayed.

'Damned thing. Fishermen have reported the same. Their bodies fill the coves and inlets. May we be cursed if this is our gift. Our great contribution to their humanity. But for the life of me, I don't understand. Two years and the pox hasn't shown its face in the colony. It would have made itself known before now. Doctor White thinks it might be the rats that came on the boats.'

John recalled the rats on that first day, crawling from crates to escape into the bush. They had multiplied, returning in hordes. A plague had tormented the colony, scampering through huts and shacks and tents and over hands and feet and sleeping bodies and into the stores where they ate the grain and fought over the last of the salted meat.

Without warning he leapt sideways and towards the line of waiting men in time to throw out a steadying arm and stop a convict from keeling over. He recognised him: Archie, a labourer from Dorset who had stolen some shoes and won seven years transportation. In the early days a group would gather while John played the flute and Archie sang. John had shut his eyes while the man's deep rich voice had carried him across oceans and into the green eyes of a girl who sold fish in the market. Each evening Archie had tormented his listeners with memories of men with 'hearts of oak' and an England that would conquer again. He had sung of bonnie lasses with rosy-red lips and coal-black hair, of black birds and thrushes that sang in the bushes, of green fields and white cliffs. *Everyone stopped to listen. Esther had cried. Poor Esther.*

Archie waited now for his food, shoeless, and shirtless too, swaying slightly. Sunken eyes. Hollow cheeked. Lips tinged blue. His breath came fast and shallow. It could not hold a tune now. He did not seem to notice John's arm under his shoulder, bearing the weight of him. Only as he held out his plate to receive the handful of pork and the cup of rice that would serve him for a week did his face brighten, and light flare in his eyes. Suddenly aware of John, he beat one hand feebly against the other's chest and hunched over his food, prepared to protect it. John stepped back. Archie turned to totter away, staggered and fell. He didn't throw out an arm to protect himself, or even his rations that splattered to the ground. He fell like a stone. Cursing himself for having released him, John bent to help, but raised his eyes to the lieutenant. 'Dead,' he mouthed with a shake of the head.

Convicts and officers alike scrambled in the dirt to retrieve the spilt rations.

⌐

John planted himself upon a headland and gazed out across the horizon, waiting with Frances in his arms. She no longer raged at the shrunken breasts of a despairing mother or slammed tiny fists against a bony chest. Her head wobbled too big upon her wasted body. Eyes too large and black did not light up when he took hold of her, nor did she gurgle and laugh at the faces he pulled. He unearthed treasures from his memory box to share with her: the oranges from Rio, Ol' Ma's rabbit stew, hoping the sound of his voice might lighten her –

and keep his own terrors at bay. She did not react. She knew them for the farce they were. Only when he gave her his eagle to suck did she brighten a little.

Please come. He begged the ships that maybe rode just around the headland. Or maybe never were. He wondered what the sky could tell. Had it watched as they smashed apart on coral? Had it hung silent as a hungry ocean swallowed the stores of meats and flour, tea and sugar, and pickled vegetables? Or observed it lost and frozen among snow and ice? Or plundered by pirates? *If you watch down upon us, please help.* He didn't know if he prayed to a weeping Jesus, bleeding on the cross, or the African gods with their tricks, or even the ancient trees of this new land. Their branches swayed in the breeze. They creaked and rustled, but they kept their secrets to themselves. His prayer fell from his lips so often, it should have been worn smooth of any meaning. Instead it grew more desperate, scratched with longing. He fingered his eagle.

Chapter Thirty-Five

3rd June 1790

Sydney Cove cowered at the end of a violent day. Grey dusk threw its cowl across the sky and hid the colours of a declining sun. A southerly wind poked icy fingers into cabins and shacks and dispirited canvas tents. Its breath, cold with despair, whined through cracks and crevices. Within their hovels, convicts and officers alike pulled a blanket tight and huddled down to endure another night. Tomorrow, they knew, they would wake hungrier than today, and closer to death.

¬

In his hut, Lieutenant Johnston penned a letter home, which he knew was possibly his last, for his supplies were running thin. A gust of wind whistled down the chimney and his fire spluttered. *I remain confident and in good spirits*, he wrote, for he could not allow honesty to besmirch his reputation. He pushed away the fear that no one would ever see the letter, that the ink would fade and the paper would crumble before a ship came to save them.

¬

John crooned a tune to Frances. He had just fed her soup, made from his own gruel. But she could not digest the pickled meat and heaved up the putrid mess, to be left shaking and emptier than before. She gazed up at him, her eyes large and black and trusting in a face wizened and old.

¬

High on a cliff at South Head, about three miles away, with views of both ocean and harbour, a signal was raised. It flapped as if it would tear itself free. After a moment's hesitation, though, it accepted its responsibility and held sure and strong.

A child saw it first. Heedless of the gale, though bare of both pants and shoes, he had been wading in the cold water, searching the rocks for crabs. 'A ship. A ship is coming. Mumma. Come quickly.' And though the wind screamed as if to shred the news into a million pieces and blow it back into the ocean, the report spread from mouth to mouth. It burst upon the settlement like a river in flood, and young boys and old women, convict and free, sick and walking and barely alive, rushed from their cabins and tents. They ran and crawled and hopped and limped to the shore for a sight of that flag flying steady. And then they threw their arms around the other, slapped shoulders, kissed babes and cheered. Dry, hoarse cheers. They dropped to their knees in prayer and gave thanks to their god. They shook hands and smiled great toothless grins, while tears rolled down their cheeks. A ship was coming.

John held Frances with trembling arms. The lieutenant jogged up beside him. 'Can you see it yet. Is it really coming?'

'Not yet. What if it's not ours? Maybe the French are back. Even the Spanish.' John hadn't realised how tight he held her, for Frances wriggled and squawked in his grip. 'Sorry, little one.'

'It will be ours. It must be.' Only an ink stain on his fingers remained of the lieutenant's angst so short a time ago. 'But I worry it can't navigate the harbour in this weather. To see it go down, this close – Ahh, over there. Look.'

A rowboat pushed out from shore, bucking and protesting in the surf. Governor Phillip and Lieutenant Tench rode within it, gesticulating to the oarsmen to hurry.

'They'll bring news soon enough.'

But will they bring food? John stroked Frances's pinched cheek. Every muscle in his body strained taut.

The Lady Juliana sailed through the heads the next morning at dawn. She flew English colours and, in large letters, the word *London* embossed her stern. She carried supplies of pickled meat, flour, rice, vegetables, and rum: enough to allow them to linger a month or two longer. Mother England had not forgotten them, and as if to prove that point, she carried letters from anxious mothers, loving sweethearts, wives and friends and business acquaintances. She also carried two hundred and twenty-seven female convicts. More mouths to feed.

John worked with a crew unloading casks and crates. He had received no letter. There were none to write to him. Did an auburn-haired girl who sold fish in the market ever think of him? Among the whirlwind of gossip, he worked in brooding silence.

'See how them officers are mooning around, holding letters to their heart. All love-sick, they are. Missing their mammies and their women back home.' Small, a convict who worked in the hospital, helped him roll a barrel onto shore.

'Ah for fuck's sake. If their missuses knew what went on round 'ere, they wouldn't let them back home. Them same officers all shacked up with a bit of arse, no worries.' Patrick, an Irish rebel, took the barrel from them.

John lifted and hauled and dragged while the words floated past and around. He turned his thoughts to Frances and her laughter at her first suck of an orange. The stores had been released.

'What's with you, John? You're quiet.'

'Makes no sense all this talk about home. They tossed us out like a bit of garbage. This is my place now.' John made a sweeping gesture that took in the harbour, the ragged camp and the soft blue mountains beyond. *Ain't got no other.*

Two weeks later and the colony lined the beaches to cheer in the third ship from the Second Fleet. Two days ago, the second ship had docked, The Justinian, fully laden with provisions. They waited now in a carnival mood, keen to witness what new gifts Mother England might have sent them.

'Maybe some boots,' John, with Frances hoisted across his shoulder, said to John Martin next to him. 'Wonder if they thought of boots? There's not a pair left in the camp. And babies' clothes. She has only shawls to warm her.' He folded the red rag of wool, worn and threadbare and that had once been Esther's, around Frances's feet.

A roar went up as The Surprize bound through the heads under full sail. John held Frances and waved her arms in the air. 'I told you they wouldn't forget us, my pretty.' She gurgled and pulled at his nose with her two hands. After only two weeks of full rations the life had returned to her eyes. John caught sight of Tilly, standing in the crowd. An officer had his arm across her shoulders, pulling her close, owning her. She kept a fixed smile on her face, but she had her eyes on John and the baby, and John could feel the hunger in them. He knew she wanted him still, but he only visited her tent to collect or deposit Frances, always in a hurry, a muttered apology and a loose endearment on his tongue but not on his face.

''Ere. Let me have her before you go rubbing the skin off her belly with that stubble of yours.' John Martin held out his arms for Frances. 'Come to your Uncle John, now. Oh, what's that stink!' John Martin twisted Frances, suspecting her of having shat, but for the length of the beach, the onlookers groaned in disgust, hid their faces in their wraps, or put a hand to their nose. Just offshore, The Surprize had dropped anchor and opened her hatches. The wind moaned. A solemn silence rippled along the beach. A soldier clasped his woman, just a little tighter. A mother hugged her babe, just a little firmer.

John reclaimed Frances, hiding her to his chest, not taking his eyes from the anchored ship.

A splash came across the bay.

'Can you see, John? What's that they are doing?' John Martin squinted trying to get a better look.

'I think it's a body. I think they're throwing bodies from the ship. Ah, Jesus. There they go again. More of them. Look, you can see them floating. They haven't weighted them. And see there.' John pointed towards the end of the beach, where sailors pushed a dinghy from shore. 'Seems the Reverend White is curious. He goes for an inspection.'

The colony watched from the beach as The Surprize unloaded her cargo. They held their breath as men and women were tossed from the deck either into the ocean or to the long boats waiting below.

'They handle them like bags of grain.' John's voice rose in disgust.

And then the people released a muttered roar of impotent rage. For floating corpses now filled the bay. The tide delivered them to the beach and the feet of the watching crowd. Rotting, stinking carcasses of abused Englishmen: people who had once laughed in taverns and shared a joke and a beer with friends or stayed up late into the night, talking over candlelight and making plans for their future.

'What happened on that voyage?' John didn't expect an answer, nor receive one.

As the flood of corpses hit the shore, a second rowboat took off from the beach.

'I think they go to put a stop to this,' John said. 'But look, the first of the rowboats has landed. Take Frances to Tilly for me? I'm going to help.'

Racing up the beach, John watched as sailors pulled the dinghy ashore. Bodies, naked and near naked, lay in the boat. Only a movement of a finger, or the rapid rising of a chest gave sign of life. Red skin, raw and inflamed. Bruised flesh. Joints swollen. Hip bones, sharp and grazed. Eyes blank and listless. John forced himself forward. Gently, as if taking a babe into his arms, he lifted a body and carried it, light as a feather, to place it on the beach. 'Mother of God, what have they done to you?'

It took all day to unload The Surprize. Some of the cargo of convicts were able to crawl on hands and knees. One or two could walk, with the aid of a shoulder. Most needed to be carried.

The following day The Neptune and The Scarborough anchored in the harbour, and the scenes were repeated.

The colony's hospital became overwhelmed and John and others worked day and night to erect tents, which had been brought on The Justinian to shelter these new immigrants, though he doubted that many could survive. He scratched himself. The new arrivals were covered in lice, thousands of lice, and he worried he would never be rid of them.

From the corner of his eye, he caught sight of the lieutenant in consultation with Governor Phillip, outside the governor's house. As his friend left, John hurried over.

'Never seen Phillip so angry. He would whip the captain and the crew for what they've done, had he the authority.' Lieutenant Johnston looked grim.

'Do we know what happened? Were they run short of food?'

'Oh, they had enough all right. They just decided not to waste it on convicts when they could sell it to us on arrival. They've brought crates full of supplies.'

'They deliberately starved them?' John shook his head.

'And stole their clothing and valuables. Those poor wretches were held below deck, chained for the entire length of the voyage. Chains so tight they couldn't twist or bend a leg. Some were chained to corpses rotting beside them.'

John swallowed. He recalled Stinky, lying dead on the cell floor, his cheeks devoured by rats. To be chained to that? He heaved. And again, compulsively, as his body fought to rid it-self of the image.

The lieutenant took a step back, a look of distaste on his face, but continued. 'The Reverend Johnson reported that the stench was so bad he couldn't visit the hold for more than a minute. But he doubts he will ever erase the sights from his mind.'

The two men watched as a woman stumbled ashore un-aided, throwing off the arm of a sailor who would help her. 'She has some life in her. The women seemed to have had the better of it,' John said.

The lieutenant pursed his lips. 'They had something to trade.'

John watched as the woman slumped to the ground, her arms wrapped around her legs, her head on her knees. Think-ing to comfort her, he moved forward, but startled by his pres-ence, she raised her head. He backed away, intimidated by the rage in her eyes. Blue eyes, he couldn't help but notice. Deep, blue eyes, though her hair was near dark as his own. A change in the light made him look up as black and heavy clouds parted to allow a patch of the bluest sky to stream through. *Her colours.*

'They can get away with this?' John returned to the lieuten-ant, his eyes still on the woman.

'Oh, the governor will send missives recommending they be charged. But how –? How do you describe –?' The lieutenant's hand fluttered across the scene. 'These boats carried over a thousand convicts when they left England. We have counted some seven hundred barely alive, and of those–?' He shrugged. 'My guess is that not even three hundred can lift themselves.'

Chapter Thirty-Six

John woke in the darkest hour, his favourite hour, before daylight stole across the skies and while the camp slept. In this moment the world belonged to him, for it had no shape and was his to mould.

The body next to him stirred. He froze, not wanting to wake her and have to share his time. With a grunt, she shifted and settled back to her dreaming. He liked Annie, if only for her guileless honesty.

'Don't go getting no ideas about settling down with me, John Randall. I want more than the likes of you,' she had said. And he would laugh as he watched her toss her blonde hair and flash her dimples and flutter the lashes of her lynx-like eyes at every officer. *A puma pretending to be a pussycat.* But he never voiced his thoughts. Instead, he stroked the line from her ear down her neck. 'No settling.' He allowed his finger to steal between her breasts, circle her nipple, teasing. 'Just a bit of loving is all.'

Her breathing, as she lay next to him, was undisturbed. Satisfied, he gave himself back to his thoughts, listening to the world. The wind continued to howl. *Good. Let it blow the stink from this place.* The new arrivals camped along the beach. Some lay on the sand, without the protection of canvas, some without clothes on their back. And though he and others had worked all day to wash and tend them, the stench of their voyage hung over the camp. Now they knew what England was capable of. Over the last few months, so close to death, their trust in the motherland was all that had sustained them. What now? John would go hunting today. He would follow the river and walk in his forests and be glad to be rid of the settlement.

He thought he heard the whimper of a baby, fragile among the whining of the wind and the crashing waves, and it seized his heart in a vice-like grip. If Frances was awake, he would take this moment to hold her. Tilly would be pleased with the chance to sleep longer. Extricating himself from Annie's side, he slithered from the tent.

¬

'So which star is it, yer think?' The voice came low and husky from the bushes.

'My pardon?' It had startled John.

'She done been born under a lucky star, ain't she. Loving father and all. So which one is it?'

John glanced up at the heavens but could think of nothing to say. Instead he kissed the curls on Frances's head, and held her closer. He had brought her to the beach to watch the sunrise. But rather than feel upset at the intrusion, he wanted the voice to continue. It reminded him of rich dark soil and the rustle of leaves in the wood. And of friendship, for it held the same Irish lilt of Aine. He peered around, seeking its owner, but she stayed hidden in the dark hour.

'Name's John,' he offered.

'Sure as I know your name. John Randall it is. And a fine one to keep away from. Hear you have a way with the ladies. Is that the truth of it?'

Silhouetted against the ocean, John wondered how he might look to her. He held himself a little taller. Long, lean legs, capable of running for miles to track game. Muscled belly. Rope-like strands of matted hair tied back from his face. He looked like the hunter he was. John turned to search the darkness, but with a rustle she left, a shadow in the dark. He did not catch the first rays of the sun as it spilled over the horizon. He was staring into the space she had left, feeling its emptiness.

That night, John did not go to Annie, though she strolled by to tease him, arched her back, waited to be stroked. He sat with John Martin, examining each face as it passed, trying to attach the voice that reminded him of rich damp earth. Too many new arrivals had breached the tight familiarity of the camp for him to recognise each one.

'You feel like a walk?' he asked. 'See how the new ones are settling?'

John Martin whittled a piece of wood into what he thought looked like a possum, its long tail curled around a branch. He held it high for John to see. 'What do you think?'

'You're real good at that now. Can almost see its big eyes sparkling.' John looked down to hide the lie.

'Hoped you might play some fiddle. Full moon. Full belly. Long while since we had a celebration.' John Martin shot his friend a suspicious look. 'Lest you had other plans?'

John shrugged. He pulled his flute from where he kept it tucked into his belt and ran his fingers over the wood, smooth from a thousand songs, the concert of his life. *As good a weapon as any. Let her come to me.*

A circle gathered as he began to play. Tilly claimed the space next to him, Frances in her arms, earning for herself a slant-eyed glare from Annie. A sailor, his arm held tight around a girl, a mere wisp of a child, led the singing with a fine voice. John Martin added his deep, rich, African sounds so John switched to the soulful songs of his youth and the crowd hushed and swayed and felt a longing in their hearts. Convicts, new and old, crept up to join the circle, some content just to belong and to listen, others humming or singing.

'Come away from here. You're to come with me.' The voice cut through the mood. In the moonlight, John noticed a sailor grab the arm of a woman who had seated herself to the back of the group. John had not seen her join them but recognised her as the one from The Neptune. He recalled those blue eyes, hidden now. He watched as she yanked her arm away, hissing something he could not hear. The sailor slapped her face, grabbed a fistful of hair and made to drag her away.

John stopped playing. Following the direction of his look, the crowd fell silent.

'I done tell yer. I don't belong to you. Now remove your arm and leave me in peace to enjoy this evening.' The voice had the depth of rich warm soil and rustled like the leaves in the trees.

'Don't go acting all high and mighty on me. Let me fuck you good and proper on the voyage.'

'And sure I'd fuck the devil himself if I get to stay alive. But I don't need to now. And you can go.'

'Filthy whore.' But under the eyes of the group, silent and accusing, the sailor lost his bluster. If he had a tail, he would have tucked it tidily between his legs. John accompanied his departure with the chorus of 'Over the Hills and Far Away', his eyes locked with those of the black-haired woman.

Chapter Thirty-Seven

July 1790

Mary Butler was her name and John hunted her. He used every trick he knew. In the mornings, he crept into Tilly's shack to secure Frances.

'Leave her, John. She's sleeping,' a sleep-blurred Tilly objected.

But John knew the appeal of a man holding a baby. He used his smiling, black-eyed, tousle-haired child as the bait to lure his prey. And each morning he strolled with her along the beach and waited for the sun to creep above the horizon and bring with it the hopes of a new day. And if Mary were there, he would bide his time, move gently, not say a word, allowing her to make the first move. *Like gentling a bird - or a wild dog.*

At night, he called her with his flute. He observed which tunes she liked and played them often, tailoring the night to her taste. He used his hunter's eyes to trail her as she slipped from the shadows of the outer circle to move closer to the fire and join in the singing. Despite the beauty of her voice, she could not hold a tune. But, he noticed, she sung with gusto, and though there were many times when she managed to destroy a melody, no one bothered to give her the eye. Perhaps because they knew she wouldn't care.

And when it was time for sleep, and the circle had broken, John loudly went back to his shack to sleep alone.

'I see what you're doing.' She walked beside him along the shore.

'I'm walking with my daughter.' John held Frances by her two hands, swinging her so that her feet tickled the water.

'Dada.' The child flailed her legs about and laughed as he swept her back to his hip, throwing her arms around his neck.

'You use the babe like a net to catch your prey.' Mary reached out to take Frances from him, but the little one hid her head in John's shoulder.

'Is it working?' laughed John.

Mary didn't answer. As the two walked the beach, John noticed that her strides kept pace with his, though he was a full foot taller.

'I thought the great John Randall would just take what he wanted,' she said finally.

John raised his eyebrows. *The 'great' John Randall?* 'Not if I want to keep it,' was all he said. But he smiled, the same smile that had charmed every woman since first used on Mistress Randall.

The sun rounded the earth, unfolding its light to serve another day. John bid his farewell. 'So, I'll see you tonight then? You'll come to destroy another of my tunes?'

She laughed at that. A free and open-hearted laugh that lodged in his brain and that he replayed throughout the day, aching for the moment he would hear it again.

That night, John felt her arrival at the campfire as if someone had reached out their hand and yanked his heart from his chest. Late, as was her habit, she hovered on the outskirts of the circle, and he waited for her to settle, but she did not do so immediately. She seemed unsure of where to place herself. The gathering was midway through a tune of 'Early One Morning'. They sang the chorus lustily.

> *Oh don't deceive me, Oh never leave me,*
> *How could you use, a poor maiden so?*

As it finished and people called out the songs they wanted to hear, she still hadn't sat down. John caught her eye. He shifted his seat and urged Annie, who had stolen the place next to him, to move over. Then he patted the cleared space and beckoned Mary to claim it. His fingers trembled, afraid she wouldn't. He imagined her raising a finger to him. *And why would I want to sit myself near a fraud like you?* But she trod daintily over sprawled limbs to sit cross-legged beside him, smiled, and shot a rueful glance in Annie's direction.

John played late that night. An old man jumped into the circle to dance a jig, wobbly legs bent and crooked but he still moved with a grace and vigour that had the crowd clapping and laughing, and then to uproar as a pretty young maid jumped in to join him, hips moving flirtatiously, hands beckoning.

They didn't seem to notice that John occasionally lost a note. He could not think where to place his fingers. He felt Mary's leg resting against his. The heat of her body. The beating of her pulse. Her hand grazed his knee and the flame of it tore through his belly to explode in his chest. His heart throbbed so loudly he wondered that people could not hear it above the sounds of the flute. He watched himself from above and marvelled how collected he appeared, how gaily he laughed, what great wit he showed, when all he could think of was the touch of her skin next to his and the aching need to hold her.

When the moon shone fully in the sky and he laid down his flute, when the old, dancing man had clasped John's shoulder in thanks, when the flirting girl had been claimed by a younger man and the circle of singers had slipped away, she stayed.

'So, you're here,' he said.

'I am.'

'In my net?' he grinned.

'Ha! You fool yourself. It was I who threw the net.'

¬

They lay together in his shack. Moonlight filtered through the branches and leaves he had used for roofing and danced upon her stomach so that she flickered silver. John looked at their two bodies, woven together with moonbeams. They had rolled together, consumed each other, immersed themselves in the other and now they lay quiet, their eyes still locked on the other. They nuzzled together, no longer hungry, but unable to stop. He would have liked to tell her things, so many things, but the words he wanted fumbled in his mouth, unused to being there.

He pictured her at the door of his cottage, an infant at her breast. She walked its gardens full of roses. The cottage opened itself to her and welcomed her in. A lump caught in his chest. He belonged with her and she with him. She felt like the home he had never had. His eyes burned hot and he worried that he might bawl like a baby and frighten her away. Instead he squeezed her tighter.

'Alright?' she asked.

'I've come a long way for you,' was all he could say.

Be careful, Boy. You know what happens to those we love. It was not Ol' Ma who whispered in his head.

He struggled to place the voice. *Since when do you offer advice?* He dismissed his mother. But, he thought of all those he had lost and he tightened his grip on Mary. *No, not you. You will stay with me.*

They talked through the night.

'Huh. I pinched a basket of beans from a man as mean and nasty as the devil himself,' Mary told the story of her conviction. 'Truth to say, it were not even me that took them. It were me friend.' Pause. 'But I didn't stop her. And fully intended to have some for myself,' she added, her face crinkled in a mischievous grimace.

She held her tongue for a long while after that. John waited. She would say more if not pushed.

'But this I got to say,' she finally took up her story again. 'I took for meself some feckin' beans. Little green beans, dry and wrinkled they were, past their time and not worth a squat. But that captain – he starved us. He took our food and made us whore to get it. Stole our goods and our lives. But do you see him now, walking through the camp proud as can be and looking down his nose at us? Where's the justice in that, I ask you?'

'They are sending me to Rose Hill.' The words burst from Mary the moment she snuck into John's shack. People had abandoned the singing early. Though the wind had died, the air snapped with cold. Fingers froze red, noses ran, eyes were swollen and throats sore. No one had a heart for singing. In the moonless night, John couldn't see her eyes, but knew they begged him. *Don't let them take me away from you.*

Rose Hill. The name felt prophetic. The governor intended a new settlement there and John had accompanied him on his explorations of the region. He had hunted at the head of the river and at the foot of the mist-hidden mountains. He had knelt and grabbed handfuls of rich dark earth, smelt its pungent sweetness and let it run through his fingers. So different from the sand and rocks of Sydney Cove. He had swum in the river and collected oysters and shot the game that seemed more plentiful than ever he had known. He had not seen any roses but still it echoed in his thoughts. *Rose Hill.*

'Listen up, will you,' Mary demanded. 'Are you away with the fairies? They are sending me to god knows where and you have nothing to say?'

'They can send you where they like.' He pulled her closer to him. 'Don't mean I won't follow.'

But though he spoke with conviction, though it felt right for him, the governor would need to approve his move. Did he have enough good will in his bank? 'We may need to get married,' he said aloud.

'Fer sure, I'll not marry you out of convenience. And not without a proper proposal either,' she flashed back.

'I thought I was a mere rabbit in your trap. Perhaps you should ask me?' He received a cuff across the back of the head for that.

'Watch what comes out of yer mouth, John Randall, or I might clean it up for you. A lady needs to be wooed when it comes to weddings.'

He pulled her to her feet then, and on that cold night, when the waves and the trees and the birds held their peace, and people huddled close for warmth in the shelter of their shacks, he led her through the tangle of huts, past the granary and the hospital, the jail and the courthouse, towards the beach. And while the sea lapped at the land, winning and then losing its grip on the earth, John fell to his knee. 'Will you marry me, Mary Butler?'

'That I will, John Randall.'

And John could only gaze up at her in awe and wonder, while the moon and stars, the ocean and ancient trees spiralled around them in celebration.

He tied a piece of string around her finger.

'So as I won't forget?' she asked.

'One day you will have gold.' And if it had taken hunger and chains to find this woman, so be it. He would do it all again, just to be here with her.

I wish you could know her Ol' Ma. You were right. It is good. It is all good.

When they had returned to their shack, and Mary had fallen asleep, John lay awake. He heard the patter of rain upon his roof and the steady drip-drip as it trickled through a crack. His mother's voice rattled around his head: *You will lose her. Spare yourself the hurt.* He moved a cramped arm from under Mary's head and curled on his side. And when it was nearly dawn he waited for the first calls of the birds, the crazy laughter of the kookaburra, the rowdy, raucous commotion of the cockatoos. And while he threw himself from side to side and rearranged his arms and back and legs, and swatted a fly that buzzed around his head, a single thought worried his brain: the governor would not give him permission to leave. But he had given her an oath of betrothal and he would not break it.

Governor Phillip was a different man when seated behind his desk. No hint remained of the explorer. It was the administrator who ruled here, a quill in his ink-stained hand, shoulders hunched forward, brow furrowed. And though he looked up as John entered the office for his appointment, it was a somewhat harried effort, his attention clearly on the papers before him.

So John spoke quickly. The request tumbled from his mouth in a near incoherent fashion.

Phillip interrupted him. 'You want to be assigned to Rose Hill? Is that what you are asking?'

John nodded, before remembering to speak. 'Yes, Governor. Sir.'

Phillip paused but a moment, his head cocked to one side before replying. 'Out of the question.'

'But —'

The governor interjected. 'You are needed here John.' And then as if seeing the anguish on John's face, he softened. 'Paradoxical, I know, to reward your efforts by declining this request. It is a difficult time for us all.'

John shook his head slightly, denying the words he heard, his mouth moving soundlessly while he sought some argument but the governor had already dismissed him. He stood, searching for some way to redress the situation. Then, with a muffled oath, he turned on his heel and left. *I will go to Rose Hill. He will not stop me.*

Ol' Ma sank her head in her hands. *Foolish, headstrong child.*

And as he made his way back to his shack, he thought he heard a giggle from the surrounding trees. He glared around, seeking the child with the red and black beads. Eligua never bode well.

None could see him in the deep shadows beneath the trees. John had waited patiently since returning to camp from the hunt, watching while the shadows grew long, and the first blush of sunset caressed the clouds.

Chapter Thirty-Eight

He watched now as the man he stalked left his office at government house, apparently heading home to the officer's quarters. He reminded John of a plump little pigeon, more suited to the tame English countryside than this savage land. He took a deep breath. *Pigeons are easily trapped, aren't they?*

John followed in parallel, waiting for that moment he might catch his prey alone. A heavy sack bumped on his back and he pulled it forward and hugged it to his side, lest even that small thump warn of his presence.

Only after they were well distant from the offices did John stroll from the shadows, assuming a casual air he did not feel; a broad smile on his face.

'Captain Nepean. A word if I may?'

Only a remnant of light remained from a sunken sun, and a bitter night was promised. But sweat trickled down John's back. He held the sack tightly to his chest, its contents cold against his skin.

The man he addressed paused, looked him up and down, but then continued his stride, clearly intolerant of any interruption from a convict.

John hastened to walk beside him. 'I've brought these for you. Berries for indigestion. And this.' He pulled out the goanna he had caught at some risk to himself, given the size of its claws. 'Thought you might be tired of kangaroo. It tastes good. Like chicken.'

Nepean studied John, looking up at him over a long thin nose, his small mouth pursed. 'And you are?' Spittle caught on plump red lips.

In the short time since major Nepean had arrived at the colony, the man had twisted a reputation for himself, complaining loudly about the food, his indigestion, the accommodation and the convicts. However, he was well connected in Mother England.

John had learnt this from lieutenant Johnston who had already argued with the major and was scornful that the governor had not taken his side. 'Phillip tries too hard to appease him. He is fearful of a bad report.'

'Name's John Randall. I hunt for the colony. Best they got.' John stuffed the goanna back into its sack, avoiding the long sharp claws.

Nepean nodded slowly, a gleam of speculation in his eye. 'And why do you come bearing gifts?'

'Heard you were to be stationed at Rose Hill? In charge of the NSW Corps?'

'And?' Nepean asked, and John had the feeling the man was taunting him. He knew what John wanted.

John thought carefully about his next words. He could not be seen to be scheming against the governor's wishes. And he did not trust this man.

'Well, a gentleman like you, just thought you'd have your own hunter, is all. The least you deserve.'

Nepean nodded, accepting his dues.

'And if you ask around,' John continued. 'You'll hear I'm the best.' He took a deep breath and let it out again.

He had said as much as he could. He had brought himself to the man's attention. Even this could see him accused of defiance. He looked over his shoulder concerned about prying eyes.

Nepean studied John, a hint of a smile on those plump red lips. 'Take it to my cook,' he gestured at the sack, and resumed his walk.

¬

Rain thudded on the bark roof of his hut, and the wind howled through the settlement, striking at the flimsy shelters with malicious glee. Inside, they snuggled cosy and warm, relishing the wild weather and its helpless fury. John had patched and plugged his original shack into a formidable structure, a sanctuary amid the chaos. A lantern gifted by the lieutenant flitted in the corner and spilt light and shadows to play upon the walls and dance across their faces, so that it seemed a magic place. They lay on a mattress of fresh grasses, facing each other, body wrapped around body, nose to nose.

'Tell me again.'

Her mouth moved against his when she spoke. Her breath tickled his nose so he felt forced to kiss her.

'They are sending the new man, Nepean, to govern at Rose Hill. I am to be his gamekeeper.'

'And,' Mary prompted.

'We are to marry.'

'And—'

He could feel her smile against his lips. 'We will make a home together — with a rose garden — and have children who are born free to run through the woods and swim in the river.' He spoke the words as a prayer. Well used and loved. But unsure if it would be answered. His mother hovered close, whispering her fears. *Have you not learnt yet, Boy? You will get hurt.*

Mary let out a sigh and rolled atop John, where she traced the lines of his face with a finger, resting it to rub at the furrow between his brows.

'What troubles you?' she said.

A gust of wind rattled the rooftop and John worried that it might have torn away some cover. In the distance they heard the crack of a branch and the thud as it fell to the ground.

He clasped both hands to Mary's face and ran his fingers through her hair. 'Promise me. This minute. You will never leave me.'

She laughed. 'You demand my marriage vows? Should we not save them for the wedding?' But seeing his face, she wrapped her arms around his head and lay down upon him, heart to heart. 'I will never leave you.'

They lay entwined. Their two hearts beat to one rhythm.

'Tell me more,' she murmured at last. 'About when we are released.'

'There are opportunities to be had,' he said. 'I can't know them yet. Just that they are there. And we will be somebodies. We will walk down the street and people will say, "There goes Master and Mistress Randall, and don't they look fine."'

She giggled.

'And those people might stop, and seek my opinion, for my thoughts will matter.'

'And will they stand with paper and pen to record your words?' Mary teased.

John tweaked her nose. 'You jest, but wait and see.'

'John? Why is it so important to you? I would be happy with a humble life.'

He pulled back to look at her. 'It will be for you. That you might —,' he fumbled, too embarrassed to finish. *be proud of me.*

He didn't share the image that had flicked into his mind; that of a little boy laying a hand on his mother's lap, waiting for it to be grasped. He couldn't describe the yearning need for a mother's approval.

'It's a long journey you plan, Master Randall.'

'The lieutenant has his plans well mapped. I will be his second.'

'And if the lieutenant returns to England?'

'He won't. I have it on his word.'

'You will be his second,' Mary looked into his eyes, 'and I will be yours. Standing right by your side.'

'Damn.' John wiped his face. A bead of rain had fallen upon his forehead. 'Thought I had it tight,' he said. 'Never can tell.'

They shifted to avoid the leak. It had found its way in and now trickled in a confident stream.

Once settled, Mary supported herself on her elbow and looked at him, her storm blue eyes near black in the night. 'You avoid the one, truly momentous issue.'

John shrugged, a question in his eyes.

'Frances. It will be hard to leave her.'

John frowned. 'I'm not leaving her.' He pushed a lock of hair from her eyes, as if that might make her see more clearly.

Mary set back, the better to study his face. 'But—'

'She comes with us. She's my daughter.'

'John. She's Tilly's daughter too. You can't tear a babe from its Marm.' Mary reached out a hand, seeking to soften her words.

'She comes with me.' He changed his tone. 'You love her. You'll make a good mother. None better.'

Mary shook her head. 'No. She has a mother.'

'And she has a father.'

'Who did not carry her in his belly for nine months. I'll not be a part of this.' She sat up, struggling out of his reach.

They glared at each other before John broke the impasse. He scrambled to his feet, grabbed her wrist, and wrenched her up to shove her out the door. 'Out.'

The storm had unleashed itself, falling as a curtain and drowning out words. They stood as two shadows in the flittering of the lantern.

She twisted towards him. 'You want to be a 'someone', John? Maybe you need to behave like a man.'

His open palm landed on her cheek with the full force of his fury.

She faltered, too stunned to cry out. She turned to go. She had taken a step when she caught herself and faced him again. Mary held herself tall, her head high. The storm beat down upon her. Rain soaked through her hair. It poured down her face. And her eyes thundered. 'I gave you my vow. I will never leave. But I did not promise my love. Or my respect.' She turned as briskly as any soldier and walked out into the storm.

John lost sight of her in the night.

⌐

The lieutenant released the cannon ball. 'The governor cannot support your request.' He frowned as he searched for the right words. 'Tilly has the favour of an officer. She is well settled and Frances is provided for. There is no cause to take the child from her mother.'

John held his ground in the face of this explosion. He held himself erect, his brain addled by the shock, before turning away. He needed to find a hole in which he could crumple. He shuffled toward the harbour where the wind had whipped the waves into a fury of spray and foam. Water dripped into his eyes, down his cheeks, off his chin. Seawater or tears? He could not tell.

He walked against the wind until he could breathe more easily and unclench his fists and allow himself to buckle, falling against the sea wall, where he stayed with his head buried in his hands.

Images of Stonington came to mind: the night he had fled; the eyes of his mother, Ol' Ma and Elijah when last he had seen them – filled with grief. And blessing. So, it would be.

Tomorrow he would say his goodbyes.

Ol' Ma nodded approvingly. *And Mary. You did wrong by her, John. Make amends.*

⌐

5th September 1790 Rose Hill

A carpet of yellow blossoms cushioned their feet. John tried to calm his breath, savouring the perfume of the flowers and the pulsing hum of bees. He would enjoy this moment. He would study every detail to keep in his box so that it might last forever. He must tell her of his box. He would bring out the joys of his life, one by one, and offer them to her: the laughter in Calvin's voice, Ol' Ma's arthritic fingers wrapped around his. He noted the bleached marks he had made on Mary's hand, pale and fragile in his grip, and relaxed his hold, but she returned his squeeze the tighter. He cupped his other hand over their entwined fingers to bring them to his mouth to kiss but stopped at her look. *Not in front of the reverend.* But the corners of her mouth tweaked and her blue eyes sparkled.

She had forgiven him for that night, but with a warning. 'Don't you ever raise your hand to me, John Randall. I will not have it and you will regret it.' But her pardon had been absolute and she had never mentioned the matter again.

John looked at the woman beside him. Yellow flowers had caught in their hair and on their arms. It covered them like gold dust, sparkling in the kind spring sunlight.

As he had done before, he stood in front of the Reverend Johnson, in the shade of a tree and beside the river. The man had a book open, its pages white and clear. John's signature, for he had learned it, and Mary's mark would be the first.

'And will you, John Randall, take Mary to be your wedded wife?'

John could scarcely hear the words above the rushing of the river, but he knew them well enough, and did not hesitate. 'I do.' And then to savour them more fully he repeated himself, slower and clearer this time, 'I do.'

Mary smiled at him, her face tilted towards his. Her hand trembled and he patted it.

'And do you, Mary Butler, take John Randall to be your wedded husband?'

'I do.'

Chapter Thirty-Nine

November 1792

Two men, once slaves, gazed across a valley of eucalypt trees. They surveyed the kingdom their bondage had bought: a coarse, dry wilderness. But in the slanting light of a late sun, the landscape quivered under the ruffle of a breeze, and grasses, shrubs and wildflowers shivered, their colours shifting under the passing shadows of flimsy cloud. John breathed it all in: the colours and shapes; the sounds and smells. He wanted to experience this moment in his toes and in his fingertips. He wanted to hold it forever. He placed a hand on his friend's shoulder. 'It's beautiful, isn't it?'

John Martin grunted, his face set in its usual grim lines. 'Take a lifetime to clear.'

'But it's ours. And we have a lifetime.'

John and John Martin had received their freedom in April, and the grant of land some months later. Their properties bordered each other.

'My land,' John spoke the words slowly. 'Master Randall,' he laughed and stood a little taller, pulling at his knuckles.

He imagined a line of people standing behind him, sons and daughters, grandsons and granddaughters. He fidgeted with his eagle and wondered if his master was still alive. *You said I would come to nothing. That I would hang from a tree. But I've shown you. I am someone.*

And he called out to his mother. *My children will run free. This is for you too.*

And then he called to Ol' Ma. *You were right, you crazy old woman. It's good. It's all good.*

Mary slumped against the cartwheel. John Martin had married a mere few months earlier and his wife, Ann, lay next to her. Doubt and weariness lined their drawn faces and hung in the droop of their shoulders.

A dark-skinned, black-haired baby toddled over to John. She tripped over her own feet and fell upon his leg to cling for support. He swept his daughter into his arms. Just sixteen months old and Lydia had usurped the hole that Frances had left, claiming him for her own.

John threw his arm wide. 'See, my beauty. This is your playground. You'll cool yourself in that creek, down there. And over there we'll have our orchards. And here our vegetables. And I'll buy chickens.' He paused, 'And you can have your own special chicken.' He whispered, 'And no one can take it.'

'You indulge her,' Mary complained, but smiling.

'Mine to indulge.'

'Should set up camp before it gets too dark.' John Martin stared at their hand cart, shaking his head at the job to be done. Hessian bags of seed sat atop the canvas tents, which themselves were piled upon a crudely stuffed mattress and some blankets. A barrel of pickled pork, another of water, a tub of peas, some bags of flour and rice were crammed in a corner. Four pigs squealed. Their feet tied, and thrown upon the top, they had been subdued for most of the journey, but now they demanded release. Hatchets and tomahawks, some spades and shovels were heaped upon the lot. Cooking pots hung from the side. A small pile of clothes wrapped in a shawl was squashed in a corner next to the cask of whisky, donated by Lieutenant Johnston 'to celebrate'. At the very top lay John's musket and powder. He and Nepean had come to an agreement and he would be well rewarded for any game he brought into town. John did not like Nepean, with his long nose and pinched lips, and his air of dissatisfaction with the world. However, he had his uses.

And, there was one other thing. John had released Lydia and strode over to lift it from the cart with reverence. It looked like little more than a stick in a sack of soil, but now he crouched down on one knee and presented it to Mary, a squire offering tribute to his queen.

Her face crumpled, unable to stop the tears. He had often talked about his cottage with the rose trees.

'Where will you plant it?' he asked. And his voice held such wonder and joy, that she burst anew into fresh tears and threw her arms around him.

Lieutenant Johnston had bought the rose bush for him from one of the trading ships, though how it had stayed alive through that long journey he could not say.

'The canvasses first.' John was all business again. But as she brushed past him, he pulled her to him. 'Aren't you happy, my love?'

'This place ...' She shivered. 'It's so big. So far from every-thing. We'll be murdered in our sleep, of that I'm sure.' His face clouded and she forced a brightness into her voice. 'But the roses are just what it needs.'

He kissed her. 'Then off with you. Your man needs to eat tonight. And tomorrow I'll start on building our home.' He jerked his head towards John and Ann. 'And see. We have fine neighbours. None better.'

December 1792

A blast of scorching wind smacked John in the face, air so hot and heavy it felt like he was breathing through a damp towel. He wiped the sweat from his forehead. At last the tree had fallen. Three days it had taken. Three days of unrelenting, backbreaking, blistering labour and every muscle in his body screamed and his arms and legs trembled with exhaustion.

'Come on, Lydia, let's go,' he called to the little girl who played with wood chips at his side. Smiling, she toddled ahead of him.

Surely it will get cooler soon. He scanned the hilltop. The westerly wind had seared the ground. The grasses had parched and died. The trees hung weak and listless. The vegetable garden he had crafted with such hope lay scorched and beaten. Only his crop of corn showed any hope, tiny green seedlings clinging to life. That and the single rose tree, and both through Mary's efforts. Up and down the hill from the creek she struggled, buckets of water across her back. Less than half an acre had been cleared, though he worked from dusk to dawn, breaking only to hunt. He tried to calculate how long before it lay spread before him, rows and rows of fields, orchards and wheat, but he gave up with a curse. *I'll be dead before it's finished.* And not for the first time he wondered what crazy dreams had possessed him, for surely he were right back where he started, working in the fields. *For Lydia.*

He saw Mary lean against the door jamb. She had worked with him all morning, hacking at the undergrowth, dragging the rubbish into piles. She looked like a rag wrung out. Like the garden he had so carefully nurtured, she wilted before his eyes.

He had, however, kept his promise. Though their cottage had only one room with a cooking area in a lean-to at the side, they had a table and benches on which to sit and a veranda to catch the cooler air. He had promised her a rocking chair.

Lydia's laughter caught his attention. High squeals of excitement. *What's she doing now?* The leaves and branches of the giant, vanquished tree obscured his vision. He leaned over to pick up the axe and followed his daughter. Pushing aside some branches he found her, bouncing from leg to leg, hands outstretched, swatting at something and chattering to herself.

'Lydia. No. Get back.'

'Worm, Daddy.'

A snake, its red belly glistening in the sun, its tail held fast to the ground by the trunk of the fallen tree, weaved before her, flirted with her, and struck at her flapping arms.

John threw the axe. A helpless, useless gesture against an impossible target. He threw himself upon a screaming, squirming child and rolled her away. The snake struck again. But jammed by the tree, it too was a helpless gesture.

Lydia bawled in shock and fury, but John held her tight to him, his shoulders heaving with sobs.

Mary ran from the house to kneel beside them and wrapped her arms around them both. The three rocked together, a single unit. 'She be fine, John. You saved her. Her daddy saved her.'

The snake reared and spat, a finger's breadth out of reach.

⌐

The high, whining buzz of a mosquito circled John's head. He tossed, unable to sleep in the stuffy hut, but too drowsy to move outside to the cooler air of the veranda. Instead, he swatted at the insect only to slap himself in the head when it got too near.

'John. For the love of Mary, will you settle down.' His wife stretched on the mattress beside him, her shift gathered around her thighs, her hair a tangle of curls across her face. She smelt of the smoke of their cooking fire and the sweat of her labour and the breast milk that had dribbled onto her chest.

John pulled her closer to him so that he might smell more of her. 'Are you awake?' he asked.

'Stupid question.' She pulled away. 'It's too hot. Leave me be.'

'I've been thinking about Lydia,' he said.

'And I, too.'

From where she lay beside them, Lydia snuffled and laughed.

'Does she never stop? Little Minx. Even in her sleep.'

'John. I think we need a rope. A good long one to secure around her leg. She moves too quickly now. I can't keep up with her. She could so easily wander away.'

'No child of mine will be tied.'

'But, John...'

'I'll have no argument.'

'But—'

John turned, his arm raised against her, but stopped himself short. Speaking slowly, enunciating each word he repeated, 'My children run free.'

John leaned back and gave a loud belch. John Martin and Ann had stopped by on their way back from Parramatta, bringing news and gossip both. The two families gathered now around the kitchen bench. Ann jiggled Lydia on her lap. The child looked up at her adoringly, sweet as an angel. 'Have you ever seen such long lashes?' Ann asked.

'Only on John,' Mary said. 'Shame, John, we have guests.' She scowled at him as he gave another satisfied belch, and then laughed as he grinned up at her, batting his long lashes.

Turning back to his guests, John handed Lydia a bone to suck and frowned as she tossed it to the floor. 'Saw them damned birds just drop from the sky,' he continued with the story he had been telling. 'Never seen anything like it. The ground littered with dead birds.'

'It's true, John Martin. I seen it with my own two eyes,' Mary said, picking the bone off the ground and returning it to Lydia.

John Martin stretched his back, groaning a little. 'Sure as I believe yer. They talking 'bout it down Parramatta. Reckon it were sunstroke.'

'Ain't there some story, 'bout a man who made wings for himself. Got too close to the sun he did and they melted. Maybe them birds just got too close to the sun,' Mary said.

'Then that man deserves what happened to him,' Ann replied. 'Who'd he think he was anyways, trying to be what he wasn't?'

'Man can be anything he wants.' John frowned.

'You hear about Smythe?' John Martin changed the topic.

'Sure as I saw him just last week,' Mary interrupted. 'Wobbling 'long the laneway, drunk as a skunk, he were. I called him in. Said he were in no shape to go nowhere but he abused the life from me and kept on wobbling down that there road.'

'Well, he ain't wobbling nowhere now.' John Martin looked grim. 'They found him hanging from a tree. Stiff and cold and blowing in the wind.' He shook his head. 'It's them new soldiers. They's the ones to blame.'

'The corps?' John looked up. The NSW Corps had come over on the Second Fleet, intended to keep order in the growing colony. Nepean was in charge of them.

'Them's the ones. They kept selling poor old Smythe rum, not that he had a dime to buy it. His wife begging them not to. Every bottle he took, they took a promissory note. Called it in just the other day. Took all his land. Threw the family off.'

'What will happen to them?' Mary had taken John's hand as if to stay it from the rum. She put it to her lips, kissing it.

'They'll have the pleasure of going on stores and dragging a cart for the honour of it.'

'Or sewing,' said Ann. They reckon they starting a factory at Parramatta sometimes.'

'And Crompton,' John Martin continued. 'He borrowed from them to sow his wheat crop. They let him work that land. Near worked himself to death he did. A good bloke. A hard-working man. You know what the heat is like. But he got that wheat growing pure and gold and ready for harvest and they call in their debt. Before he has time to sell. Threw him off his own land, wife and kids and all. They get the land and the harvest. Evil bastards.'

John knew Crompton. He had seen him in Parramatta not so long ago. Could tell the fella by his walk. Fast and springy, as if he just couldn't keep up with himself.

Lydia squealed for the bone she had once more tossed to the floor. John bent and picked it up, then cursed as she chucked it down again. 'Lydia, your father is not a patient man,' he said, bending for the bone a last time.

⌐

It's the end of the world. From the doorway of the hut, John clasped Lydia in one arm, the other around Mary. Three tiny figures caught in a land about to explode.

A blood-red sun blistered in the sky. Burned clouds towered to the heavens. A wall of smoke crept toward them. From one end of the world to the other, it circled them on every front and leached light and colour from the day. Ungodly night had arrived.

Across the valley, mobs of kangaroos loped through the trees and the air screamed as flocks of birds escaped to the skies, chased by a wind of smoke and ash.

John and his family had run, too. To the lane and back again. Through the woods and to the creek and back again. They hadn't known which way to run. Instead they scuttled from corner to corner of their world, mice racing from a cat. But this cat was too big to outrun. In the end, they stayed in the house. Surrounded by cleared land, it might be safe. For the under-growth in the valley was dry tinder waiting for a spark. The leaves of the huge trees trembled. One flying ember would set them alight.

'For the love of Jesus, have you ever seen anything like this?' Mary asked. 'Is that thunder, I hear? Could it be rain do you think? Might we be saved?'

Or cannon fire, thought John, as an explosion shattered the valley. And far away, a wall of flames breached the hill and leapt towards them. Fireballs spat into the sky, and he felt that same dry choking fear he felt each time he had faced battle. But it was worse this time. Lydia clung to him, trusting him. Mary leant into him, merged herself with him.

As sparks floated towards them, he saw the threat of staying in the house. The cleared land wouldn't help. One flying cinder and the dry wood of the roof would catch. They would burn alive.

He sprung to grab some hessian sacks, soaking them with water. 'Cover your face and to the gulley.' He grabbed Mary's wrist, but she stood mouth open as hell unfurled before her eyes. 'Mary. Move.' Lydia's screams added to the rumbling, booming uproar around them. John muffled them with hessian and, taking Mary's hand, hurtled down the hill.

'We'll be safe here,' he lied, as they sheltered in a cave, little more than a rocky hollow in the wall of the creek. From where they lay they couldn't see the flames, but the fire had exploded around them. The air shimmered with heat. The forest cracked and shattered. Their breath caught in the hot, smoky air. As fireballs blasted across the sky, John prayed for mercy. The opposite bank caught alight. He wrapped Mary and Lydia in wet hessian and made them lay down in the trickle of water. It ran warm.

There was no knowing how long they lay. The stream flowed by and over them, noisy in their ears. Mary whispered Hail Marys. Lydia snoozed. *As if she knows she can't fight this and sleep is her only escape*, thought John. He watched as the fire approached. He heard the tortured screams of the trees. Saw them writhe like demons in hell. Turned his head away as the flames leapt for the sky. He covered the bodies of his wife and child with his own and waited, trying not to think how it would feel as the flames claimed him. His hand found the eagle on his neck, and he allowed his thoughts to soar. Like the notes of his flute, like the ash on the wind, he drifted away. He missed the point where the fire stopped. It twisted to chase a course up a different hill. A change of wind. An easier path.

⌐

They lay in the cave in the creek without moving for a long time, their heartbeats loud in their ears, and the rasp of their breaths hard and fast. The trickle of water. Hail Mary Full of Grace. Lydia snored. The sound of the fire died. John unfurled himself to look around.

Black silence hung over the world. Nothing stirred. Nothing to be seen. Just the twisted stumps of burned-out trees, glowing red. No flies or mosquitos. No crickets or cicadas. No wasps or bees or dragonflies. No birds. No singing or tweeting or screeching or squawking. No rustling in the leaves or scuttling in the debris underfoot. Even the wind had died.

A second silence gripped them as they climbed the hill towards the place they had left, their home: unspoken prayers as they bargained with God that it remain safe. John thought of the broken shovel and blunted axe he had dropped at the doorstep, the half loaf of bread left on the bench, the pigs staked to a pole. His flute. *Please leave me my flute!* Even Lydia kept quiet, her eyes huge in a sooty face, snot dribbling from her nose.

When they crested the hill, the silence broke: Mary cried out and fell to her knees. Hail Mary.

The hut was where they had left it. The shovel and the axe were safe. The bread still sat on the bench. The flute lay on the mattress. The pigs were dead. Their skin scorched. The rose tree, too, had survived.

⌐

They woke next morning to a different world. A black world. The grass, what leaves remained on the trees, their bark, all black. With their foliage gone, the giant trees stood on the landscape like stubble. Some trees still burned. No raging fire, just burning down, giving up. The smell of smoke clung to everything. Mary set to work to salt the pork. Their pigs were pork now and John felt that he should do something too. Clear fallen trees. But he didn't. He used his back as an excuse, for it had scorched and blistered. The skin peeled from it, leaving wet scabs.

'You alright, John?'

'Just trying to work it out, is all. I ain't ever felt so small in all my life.' He fumbled his words, trying to get his thoughts straight. 'It can happen again and I can't do nothing about it.'

'John. Our home stands.' She paused. 'And we're alive. And sure, don't we have pork for dinner?' she smiled.

He leant his chin on her head, his arms around her. 'You remind me of Ol' Ma. She reckoned it was all good. No matter what happened, it was all good.'

She smiled. 'And you?'

'This isn't good.'

¬

Over the next week, John wandered the landscape. But he no longer saw orchards or swings or a haven for his children. He no longer felt master of the land. More a slave to it.

He watched neighbours shuffle past the house, shoulders bent, blank faces, their homes and crops burned. Mary offered them water and a bite to eat before they trudged on. John watched them enviously. They had their escape. *This is no life for us.* He turned towards the house where his wife stood on the veranda, beckoning him to dinner, her green shawl around her shoulders, cool and vibrant in the black landscape.

Chapter Forty

February 1793

'John, get yourself up here. We have ... visitors.' Mary needn't have yelled.

From down the creek, where he had been washing away the sweat of a day's work, enjoying cool water in his hair and running down his back, John had heard the rumble of wagons. He guessed who his visitors were. Two carts. A tinkle of bottles in the first. The beat of horses' hooves. The guffaws of brazen men. Too harsh. Too confident. Yes, he knew who they were. And though his body ached, he forced himself to a trot. He didn't want them alone with Mary.

'See you've harvested. Ready to sell.' Perched astride a brindle horse, its brown streaks muddy on a tawny coat, the leader smiled down at them. A thin smile, sharp little teeth. 'Good timing, it seems. We can take that from you.'

John glanced at the hessian sacks that held his corn. A meagre harvest. But he had grown it from virgin land cleared by his labour and it had survived drought and fire and searing heat. He had watched Mary totter back and forth from the creek, heavy buckets across her shoulders, to water it. And they had laughed and clapped when it had finally been bundled and ready to sell. Enough to trade for some chickens perhaps and a supply of eggs. Maybe they could even replace their pigs. Or some cloth for a dress. Mary said that Lydia was getting too big to run around buck naked.

'What will you trade?' Though he knew the answer.

The officer of the NSW Corps gestured to the bottles of rum in the cart. 'A chance for you to relax after a day's work, forget your worries.' He laughed. 'We got orders to buy up the harvest and take it to Sydney Town. Starving down there, they are. Those fires destroyed near everything. And the Abos stealing the rest.'

John's gaze travelled from his corn to the soldier on his streaky horse. And from the man's tired leather boot with a hole in the sole, up the leg in its grubby trousers, worn at the knee, and to the red coat, stained with grease, to the grinning face of the soldier.

'Nope.'

'No one else round here will take it off your hands.'

'Get off my land.'

'I would watch your manners if I were you. Load your corn and my men will help you unload the rum. And then...' But he didn't finish his sentence. The thin smile faded and the soldier's fists tightened on his reins.

John stepped forward to take hold of the horse's bridle. He did so not as a subservient farmer or former convict. More like a puma, released from its cage, fast and vicious. He took hold of the officer's leg, ready to pull him off the horse. And then ... he thought he might smash the smile from his face and bruise his hands on those sharp little teeth.

'John, careful,' Mary called.

The officer had raised his crop.

'Sir,' a foot soldier had raced forward. 'Sir, this is Nepean's man. A favourite.'

John saw the uncertainty on the officer's face. He watched as pride and doubt and fear fought over a decision. He waited as the man lowered the crop and with a snarl jerked the reins of the horse. The caravan rode away.

¬

John swung Lydia into the handcart, seating her on a sack of corn. The cart was packed with their harvest, ready to be taken to Sydney Town for trade. He planned to meet with John Martin at his friend's house so they could travel on together, leaving his family with Ann for company and protection.

'Now stay put while I help your mum.' Lydia gave him the smile of an angel. He shook his head, then bent to tease a glob-ule of white gunk from her hair. *Whoever would guess what a little minx you are.*

Mary had found her last night as she pasted the last of the flour in streaks all over her body. 'She looks like one of the natives,' John had said.

'She looks like a ghost,' said Mary. But regardless of how she looked, they had no damper this morning and his belly growled.

'Here, play with this a while.' John gave Lydia his flute. She would suck it and blow it and possibly use it to hit at stuff but it would keep her occupied. He kissed her forehead, then stood back to look at the sky. It was the innocent blue of early morning, but the air was muggy and he already felt damp and sticky.

'Think we're up for a storm,' he said to Mary as he ducked under the doorway into the house. She was sweeping the room, 'One last go over before we leave.' Dust motes played around her head, caught in a shaft of sunlight. A lock of hair had fallen across her face, clammy with sweat. 'You are so beautiful,' he said.

She gave him a look of mock horror. 'Should we wait awhiles before we go, do yer think? Don't need a rain bath today.'

'Let's get to John Martin's. Not even a cloud in the sky at the moment. It's just a feeling.' He looked at the sky – honest as it had ever been and unblemished with cloud. But he couldn't help the feeling that stirred in the pit of his belly, a snake uncoiling. He shook it off, took her in his arms and kissed her ear and down her neck. 'Second thoughts, no hurry. Really. No hurry.'

'John Randall, enough.' She took a clumsy swipe at him with the broom and he backed away, laughing.

'Anything else we need?' John looked around their home. The mattresses in the corner, threadbare blankets folded neatly on top. The bench, scoured clean, but stained with the marks of their living: a spilt glass of rum, Lydia's greasy fingerprints, the nick of a blade. Their wooden plates stacked neatly. The cooking pots on top.

'I don't like leaving the house empty. Who knows what we'll come back to?' Lydia too was scanning the room.

'Better than leaving you here alone. I don't trust them soldiers. I'll be happier if you took my musket.'

'Sure as I'm likely to shoot myself in the head. You know I can't handle that thing. Now, where's your tools. Have you put them someplace safe?'

He nodded, but she narrowed her eyes and he knew his face held the unconvincing smile of guilt.

'John. Go hide them. We can't afford to lose 'em,' she roused.

John went outside to hide the shovel and axe in the wood pile, though for the life of him he couldn't imagine anyone stealing them: the blade on the axe already loose, the shovel already rusted. He wondered if he could trade for better. *No, chickens.* He glanced at the hand cart, checking on Lydia. It stood still and quiet as death.

'Mary. Lydia with you?'

His wife came to the doorway, her hand shaded her eyes from the glare to look around. 'No. I thought...' He watched her face as she saw the empty cart. He watched as she gathered her skirts to run, tossed aside the hessian bags of corn. She turned and looked down the laneway, dashed a few steps, spun on her heel and raced in the other direction. She stopped and looked at him, her mouth slightly open, her eyes questioning, her face white and blank. In a moment it would be old, drawn with lines of fear and anger and pain. But her thoughts had not yet caught up with her.

John watched as a lever was thrown and the world stopped on its axis and called a halt to life, for there was no sound or movement. And then it shattered. Mary screamed, 'Find her.'

He, too, ran to the cart. He copied Mary's moves, looked one way and the other, raced one way and the other. Then he looked down the slope at the black and burned-out valley. Stumps of trees with miracle green shoots sprouting from the branches. Patches of green grass among the churned-up clay. This morning he had stood on the veranda, tea in hand, and wondered at the power of this world to recover. *But that is the way of the gods- to tease before they knocks you off your feet.*

He ran down the valley toward the gulley, the path most often trod, most likely for a not-yet-two-year-old, her feet still unsteady at times. He stooped to pick up his flute, tossed lightly away by a child, her interest snatched by ... a butterfly, a bird, a kangaroo? He saw a footprint, as light and fragile in the mud as the touch of his kiss on her cheek when she slept tight and he wanted to hug her close but feared to wake her. He ran now as fast as he ever had, skidding down the hill. Storms had followed the fire. The wet clay, slick beneath his feet, provided no traction. His feet slid out beneath him. The creek was full. His heart pounded in his ears. And so did Mary's voice. *John, we need to tether her. She moves too fast. I can't keep up with her.*

She'll be fine. I'm being foolish. She'll look up at me, a face of sweet innocence. And I will hug her to me and squeeze her tight.

For hundreds and thousands of years, the little creek had worn its path through the land, building steep banks of mud and rubble, stone boulders and tree roots. Rain and use had made the way slippery. He could hear the tumbling of water.

He saw the place she had fallen. Could see where her body had smoothed the clay and slid over the edge. He leapt down over the boulders.

She lay in the creek, face down. The water murmured to her as it passed, a gentle lullaby as if she slept. It splashed over her body, so that she sparkled, clean and fresh in the dappled light. It washed away the blood that trickled from her head.

John knelt in the stream and cradled her in his arms. He kissed her wound and stroked her hair. He rocked her. He groaned, and the sound was hauled from the depths of his being. His tears ran down his cheeks and into the creek.

Mary heard and came running. She crouched next to him and tried to take Lydia into her arms. He wouldn't let her. He clutched his little girl tighter.

Later that night, he stalked the valley in the moonlight, leaving Mary to the ministrations of John Martin and Ann. Mary hadn't blamed him. Not yet. But her voice was in his head. *She needs to be tethered, John.*

I killed her. My fault. It's all my fault.

It is good, Boy. Everything is good. Ol' Ma whispered to him. *You will see.*

He halted at that. Not believing what she had said. *You stupid, ignorant old woman. Nothing is good.*

I warned you, Boy. You are too foolish with your love. It always ends badly. Protect your heart. He recognised his mother's voice and knew, at last, that she spoke true.

Chapter Forty-One

March 1793

John loped along, a kangaroo slung over his shoulders. He had left at first light. Now, sunset kindled in the sky. Vivid reds slashed the horizon, reflected in the rolling clouds and in the puddles on the ground so that the whole world was smouldering.

He didn't mind that the 'roo was heavy and he was tired. He needed to punish his body until every muscle screamed and his head clouded with exhaustion. He relished the slash of the sword grass, razor sharp, across his thighs, and the blood that ran down his legs.

His throat constricted as he trotted over the rise to see the little cottage, smoke drifting from the chimney. Mary had started the evening meal. For days after Lydia's death, he woke each morning, surprised to find the house still standing; perplexed that old Jack Mould, with his arthritic legs, and his life well behind him, tottered by each day, untouched. Angry that the fat Widow Burn, with her empty, lonely chatter still knocked on their door. It made no sense to him that they lived and the world carried on. He looked now at his house and imagined Lydia racing towards him, sturdy little legs tripping through the grass, arms outstretched, ready to be swung high into the air before coming to rest on his hip, where she would lavish cuddles and kisses upon him and babble nonsense in his ear. But she wasn't there and the cold void she left was too much to bear.

Instead, he unloaded the 'roo into the handcart. He would take it straight to Parramatta. Nepean would be pleased. No matter if he had to travel in the dark. Maybe he could tire himself enough that he would sleep tonight without the dreams. He stretched, bending to release the tightness in his back, swinging his arms, releasing the muscles of his shoulders, delaying his entry into the house.

'You stayin' out there all night, then?' Mary had appeared in the doorway, a cut-out figure with no form or feature against the light inside. Her voice, too, sounded hollow.

John didn't answer, but put one leg before another, a stiff march into what had been their home, bracing himself to face her.

'Dinner's ready.' Mary slapped a bowl of broth on the bench-top, slopping it over the side, not bothering to find a cloth to wipe the mess. Instead she stood as if challenging him to complain.

'Not hungry. I'll find something in Parramatta. Nepean will have a plate for me.'

Her face blanched and for a moment he thought she might break. He pictured her bones just crumbling into white dust as she sunk to the floor and wanted to reach out and hold her together and make it all right again. The space between them was too vast. He didn't know how to cross it.

'You ain't ever here no more. Hunting every day. When you going to put in the new seed?'

John didn't answer, but he liked it that she was angry. He picked up a pail of water. He would wash off the dust before he started out, though he would be dirty again by the time he arrived.

'Where will you sleep tonight?'

John knew she was too proud to ask him straight if he slept with another woman. He knew she suspected it and that it burned her up inside. He would catch her puzzling over him, seeking some hint of the truth as if it were tattooed on his skin.

He shrugged and turned towards the door. He truly didn't know where he would rest. It would be with one of a number of women, none of whom had known Lydia or would offer shallow condolence or ask how he was faring, but who would let him release himself in her body and tell him what a fine and upright man he was.

'Don't walk away from me.' Mary's voice was shrill. 'You never listen. You've never listened.'

He stopped. There it was. What he had been waiting for all these weeks. He turned and looked at her. The evening heaved and rumbled around them: the shrill drumbeat of cicadas, the drone of mosquitos. But the space between them was still and silent. The last reflections of a violent dusk had faded. Everything was black.

John returned inside the house. 'Say it,' he said. 'Say it.' He knew the words. He dreamt of them throughout the night, woke to them each morning, ran to their beat each day.

'I told you! I told you to tether her. You wouldn't listen.' She raged now. Her face screwed in a mask of anger. Her whole body trembled, desperate to hit him. Instead, she pummelled the air, fists clenched and white at the knuckles, screaming at him. 'I told you!'

He wanted her to savage him, to pound him with her rage. It was her right. And so he made it easy for her. He hit her across the face, palm open, full force. He waited for her to hit him back. But she didn't. She just looked at him, dull bemusement on her face. So he hit her again. But she just stood there, her eyes black with loathing. And it shattered him and he needed to be rid of her and every memory she held. He flew at her, punching her in the gut and on the back. Kicking her to the ground. Blind and deaf, he didn't hear her screams or see her arms flailing in the air, useless against his blows, or her legs bent to protect her belly.

'Stop. John. Please. Stop.'

Her finger caught in his eye. He shook his head, and for a moment his thoughts cleared. He looked at her. And then he was crying. He pulled her to him, trying to wrap his arms around her, seeking to wrap hers around him. But they wouldn't hold. They fell from him like those of a rag doll. 'I'm sorry. I'm sorry.'

He was a man drowning. Only she could save him.

'Get away. Get off me.' She groaned, her voice muffled. She spat out blood. She pushed him away, wriggled to escape his hold, batted at his face, his eyes.

'No. No. I need you to love me.'

He pushed her back to the ground and pulled up her skirts. 'Love me,' he pleaded. She played dead as he forced himself into her.

A few yards away, a wooden kangaroo lay on the floor. Lydia had clenched it in her hands, sucked it, buried it and revived it. Mary stared at it now. She seemed not to hear his cries.

¬

John woke the next morning, sapped by his dreams. He had finally passed out on the veranda. Without the will to raise himself, he looked at the blackened landscape. His eyes held to the jagged remains of a burned-out tree, its trunk hollowed. No life would come again from that.

Ol' Ma hovered around. *All things pass, John.*

He struck her away.

Your heart still beats.

Does it? I can't feel it. I want no more of you. Leave me.

You cannot push me away.

I can.

The sun was high in the sky, hot and burning and committed to baking the earth and all upon it before he shifted himself. He walked into the house where flies buzzed around the spilt bowl of stew and the floor felt gritty and dirty under his feet. A slime of dust had settled over the benchtop and windowpanes. Mary lay curled on the mattress. He crouched beside her and turned her towards him. He saw the swollen eye, the cheek already purple, the split lip. He hoped he had not knocked out her tooth, ruined her beautiful smile.

An arm fluttered in the air, pushing him away.

He looked at her and couldn't breathe, a dreadful ache where his heart had once been. His shutters crashed into place. He fondled his eagle and flew away.

Chapter Forty-Two

August 1793, Sydney

'Well, then.' John sat atop the cart, the reins in his hands. Beside him, Mary pulled a shawl tightly around her, as if shielding herself within the threadbare fabric, the bulge of her belly barely visible. He knew it was there, the treacherous evidence of that night.

John Martin nodded. 'Well then.'

'You'll check on the place?'

A single nod. Definitive. The lines of John Martin's face were etched so deeply, they seemed carved from rock. He would be just as solid. John could rely on him.

The three stood within arms' reach of each other, but distant as stars in the night, each orbiting their own dark space.

With a brief smile and bob of the head, John flicked the reins. The cart jolted and lurched down the track. Neither he nor Mary looked back at the house, still swathed in shadow. They certainly didn't look at the small wooden cross, already worn and old. John didn't think he could leave if it would be left alone and untended.

They had chosen to leave early, in the cool of dawn. Only a faint red line on the horizon and the wild chortle of birds gave any indication of the day ahead. They hoped to reach Sydney Town with light to spare. John would make himself known to his new employer, Governor Grose; he was to be his personal hunter. Mary could organise the household.

They rode in silence. The crunching of the wheels against the gravel path, the steady clop of horseshoes, and the rhythmic swaying of the cart produced an almost hypnotic effect allowing each the peace of their own orbit.

They were within reach of Sydney when John felt her eyes upon him, the prickle of the hairs on the back of his neck. He kept his gaze on the path ahead, the potholes and fallen branches, the thick bush that crowded the track. He tried to keep his breath in check but his heart beat a little faster and the blood rose to his face.

'Stop the cart.' She spoke in a small voice, and he could tell she was nervous, but it was not a request.

He pulled on the reins. The cart crunched to a halt and he braced himself against what she had to say.

'For the sake of the child we need to make the best of this.'

'Yes.' It sounded too bare so he added, 'You're right.' His voice surprised him. It worked, but it didn't feel like his. It didn't sound as if it had travelled from a deep and hollow place. It didn't wail.

She touched her hand to his arm. He studied it and in some distant state he recalled that hand. It was powerful. It could reach down into the deepest ocean to find him. Perhaps it could also touch his heart, for he felt it now, thudding in his chest, screaming for release. He only needed...but he couldn't figure what he needed to do. Ol' Ma would know, but Ol' Ma didn't visit anymore. His mother owned him now. He had finally understood that his love could only bring pain and death.

A sprinkle of rain splattered on his forehead and he raised his eyes to the clouds, scanning the skies. Did the gods look down on them? He could not allow them insight into how much he loved this woman. And if he had to live his life like a shadow in her presence, then that were preferable to losing her altogether. He screwed his eyes tight closed and breathed in deeply.

'John?' She sounded worried, scared even.

He pulled away from the hand and turned towards her, his face crumpled.

'Truce?' she asked.

'Yeah.' He nodded and returned his face to the blank regard he now reserved for her. 'Sure.' He flicked the reins and the cart jerked forward, jolting her back.

She retrieved her hand.

From his vantage point on the hill, John surveyed Sydney Town, trying to reconcile the place with the tree-covered cove where he had crawled to shore, shaking his head in wonder of it. Cottages teetered along the coastline, facing the ocean as if pining for a glimpse of Merry England, their backs turned on the vast expanse of this new country. He had a fleeting impression that they might throw themselves into the sea in an effort to escape, were they not tethered to the land by a front path, a fence and a garden. Soldiers, traders, settlers and convicts scuttled like tiny beetles, breaking stone in the quarries, labouring in the saw pits, the smithy, the shipyards, the brick kilns and farms. Over the dull sounds of hammering and sawing, the rattle of carts, and the haggling of men, a scream caught his attention. Two men dragged a convict, his legs splayed behind him at odd angles, up the path to the new hospital. John recalled the canvas tent they had first used and wondered if Dr White still provided. He hadn't heard the name for a while.

This area has been planned well. His eyes followed the coast, past a granary and storehouses which squatted beside the Parade Ground and the Marine Barracks. *At least the food stores are well guarded.* And conveniently next door, a bakehouse. He recognised Lieutenant Johnston's house – it hadn't been finished when last he had been in Sydney – and the governor's quarters, a fine two storey building. Extensive gardens lead to the shore and a fine jetty. *So that he might be the first to receive the news from a visiting ship's captain, or supplies from the holds?* A flag fluttered in the offshore breeze, proclaiming the town for England.

Only the convict camps seemed the same: worn and patched canvas tents, lean-tos and shacks made from bark and branch and the pinched and haggard faces of those wretches as they pushed their barrows, pulled on saws, and threw sledgehammers to break the stones to build the town.

'They have a church now.' He pointed it out to Mary.

'Looks like an English town,' she said. 'I wonder where our house will be.'

'Figure we better find out.'

October 1793

As delicate a piece he had ever seen, but the locket weighed heavy in his palm. John smoothed a thumb over the image of a sweet-faced girl, her smile only just cracking the shyness in her eyes. He had received it from a sailor off the Mary Ann, a convict ship; stolen, he guessed, from one of the half-starved and near naked wretches who had stumbled ashore to do their time. He wondered who had owned it. He doubted the high-born beauty depicted in the image could have sunk so low. A lover, then. He imagined the court scene: the shock of sentencing, a young squire condemned to transportation. A weeping girl, the locket, 'Remember me.' John wondered if he had seen the man around town, whether he would recognise him by the slump of the shoulders and the nervous fingering of his neck, longing for what was no longer there.

'Best you lose your little trinket,' thought John. 'This is no place for sentiment.'

'Thought you might like it.' He grinned as he handed it to Lieutenant Johnston.

Though he hunted for the governor, it was Lieutenant Johnston who put the bread and butter – jam, too – on his table. Johnston would buy the entire stock of the ships that streamed into harbour, only to sell at four or five times the price. But it was unseemly for an officer to deal in trade, and so he used John to manage the deals.

John fingered his eagle. *It has brought me far. The lieutenant, too.*

Perched on the edge of a delicate carved chair, feeling too big and worried he might break it, he glanced around the room. A vase, richly enamelled in gold, stood in the corner. He imagined Mary's response were he to take something like that home. 'For the love of Jesus, why did you bring that here? You got rocks in yer head or sumthin?'

Lieutenant Johnston dangled the locket up to the window that he might see it more clearly. Flashes of light sparkled across the shaded room. 'I'll take it. What do you want for it?'

'Got some tea?' John asked. 'And maybe some of that cloth?' *Blue to match Mary's eyes.*

Johnston slipped the locket into his pocket and held out his hand to seal the deal. Business done. Not for the first time, John breathed a sigh of relief that he was no longer struggling on the property. Two convicts did that for him now, thanks to Governor Grose. They worked. He profited. Fair exchange.

His thoughts returned to Mary. They circled each other, two dancers caught in an endless minuet, mindful of how they held their bodies, wary of the space between them. Occasionally she breached their distance, for the sake of the baby. She would take his hand and place it on her belly to feel the life squirming within, but it had been conceived on the blackest night and had no right to exist and he would snatch his hand away lest it be scalded in the fires of hell.

Only at night while she slept could he release himself to her. Watching as her lids fluttered in some dream, he would wonder where she had taken herself and how he could follow and he longed to fold her into his arms and bury his head in her breast, but he dared not wake her and lose the moment. He had no doubt that she stayed with him for the sake of the child. She could no longer love him. He no longer loved himself.

A piece of paper fluttered off the desk. Buoyed by a breeze it sailed over an expanse of carpet to land at his feet. He picked it up to return to the lieutenant.

'Been keeping a journal?' he asked.

'Mmm.' The lieutenant turned a thoughtful gaze upon him. 'Tell me,' he said. 'How did you get to be here? Here to this colony, I mean.'

John frowned. His friend knew as well as he the crime he had committed. He shrugged. 'The gods, I guess.'

Have you ever thought it might be those farmers, the milk-maids, the gossips and churchgoers from the colonies? From America? They didn't want to pay their taxes and ten years later, you find yourself four thousand miles away, in this god-forsaken land, building a new colony for the British empire.'

John shook his head. 'I had nothin' to do with taxes.'

The lieutenant laughed. 'No. But their complaints caused a war. And Britain lost. And do you know how many soldiers and sailors were laid off after that? Thousands. No money to live on. No choice but to beg or steal. Is it no wonder the prisons burst at the seams and we couldn't ship 'em off to the American colonies like we did in the past. England needed a solution and so, here we are.'

John didn't know what he was supposed to say, so he said nothing.

'I find it curious. Those farmers had no idea that this place even existed, possibly still don't, but they over there and we here, are connected. Everything is connected. Don't you find that strange?'

John looked out the window, wondering if he should see strings in the sky, magic lines leading back to Stonington. Or perhaps the lieutenant was drunk.

⌐

December 1793

A dark figure in dark clothes filled the doorway of the new brick-built house. He shaded his eyes to see the better, for the sun beat down on hardened clay, and the yard seemed impossibly bright after the gloomy interior of the tavern. But he knew his friends would be out there. Neither would choose to be contained in shadows when there was fresh air to breathe.

He smiled. As suspected, Caesar and John Martin sat on logs in the cool of a low hanging tree. They didn't appear to be talking but had the settled appearance of friends with no need of words. Caesar slouched with his elbows on his knees, a sardonic smile on his face, enjoying the antics of the drunks, the traders, the womanisers and schemers. He would have them pinned and marked, John knew. John Martin held himself rigidly straight, his arms clasped around the tankard as if it might leap from his grasp.

John didn't rush to join them but allowed himself the simple pleasure of seeing them again. He had last seen Caesar when his friend was being prodded onto a boat for a voyage to Norfolk Island, pardoned from execution, but exiled to the new convict settlement there. How long ago was that? Maybe three years? *He has never even met Mary. He will never know Lydia.* John shook the thought away and resumed his study of Caesar, back again now – and still a convict. He wore neither shirt nor shoes, and the scars on his back, his wrists and ankles showed clear. But the man seemed indomitable. Even from this distance, John could see the mischief in his eyes.

Caesar caught sight of him and waved. John pulled himself to his full height, flicked his shoulders as if to rid them of dust, pulled his new, satin waistcoat tight and stepped out to greet them, only to be knocked sideways by a drunk barrelling through the door.

'Mind yer...' The man looked up, struggling to focus, 'Oh, pardon me, Master Randall. Sorry, very sorry.' He stumbled sideways.

It would have been easy to topple him. A cuff to the ear. A knee to the groin. But the man had shown respect. Patronage, coin and a willingness to use his fists to those who were less co-operative had brought John a long way in the few months he had been in Sydney Town. They called him Master Randall now, to his face. Black Randall behind his back.

'On your way,' was all he said.

He found Caesar bent low, his arms wrapped around his body, snorting with laughter. He struggled to his feet and clasped John around the shoulders, leaning heavily on him, tears in eyes.

'Ah, my brother. You never cease to amaze me. Who are you now? I can't make it out.' He broke into laughter again, fluttering his hands at the waistcoat, the tight-fitting trousers.

John had hoped to impress them, and expected an altogether different reaction, and so he frowned and stepped back but Caesar's laughter was too infectious and he began to chuckle too, falling into his friend's embrace. The two clasped each other, dancing in small circles, together again.

'John Martin.' John released himself to greet his other friend.

John Martin nodded, only the hint of a smile breaching the hard lines of his face, but his eyes were warm, and he held the handshake for longer than necessary.

John raised a hand to beckon the barmaid. 'My shout, I think.'

'And Norfolk?' John ventured when the drinks arrived.

Caesar frowned and shook his head. 'The English know how to torment a man.' His voice was deep, nearly a growl.

John said nothing, giving space for Caesar to continue in his own time.

'Strangely enough, it was good,' Caesar finally said. ''Till the end. I worked hard, but they gave me a plot of land to till and keep for my own. I eat well.' He grinned and looked away, his eyes distant. 'Got myself a wife. And...'

They waited while he gathered himself together. 'And the sweetest little girl that ever walked this earth.'

John's insides jerked, but he held his calm. 'They're here with you now?' he asked.

Caesar shook his head. 'Still at Norfolk. 'Bout to give birth to another babe.' He looked at John with tears in his eyes. 'What are they thinking! Pulling me away and leaving her alone. No one to care for her.'

They sat with Caesar's pain. No words. And then they talked about nothing. The changes in the town; the successful harvest; those that had died; those that lived still. The barmaid came and went again. The sun hung low and the shadows long. Across the yard, the drunks became louder and fights broke out, but none of it affected them, bound tight in their circle.

'Remember when we first landed?' John Martin thought to lighten the mood. 'Used to wonder where the taverns were.'

John nodded. 'Changed alright. A man can make someone of themselves now. Opportunities to be had.'

Caesar rested his head in his hands. He looked up now through reddened eyes, his voice slurred. 'That's what you think? Makin' something of yerself? Them fancy clothes. Yer la-di-da ways. I don't even know who you are anymore.' He flicked imaginary dust from his shoulders in mocking imitation of John. 'You'll never be one of them. You think they remember who fed them when we were all starving? You think they give a damn about you? Nah, you and me and John Martin here, we'll always be the nigger slave. And when you're down on your luck, they'll forget you ever drew breath.'

John sat back, too stunned to move at first, but then leapt to his feet, ready to grab Caesar by the shoulders and throw a fist at his chin, but John Martin was quicker. He had leapt between them, small and solid as a tree trunk. He shook his head.

With a curse, John left his friends.

John barely heard the noise of the streets – harsh laugh, a mother yelling at her children, the clucking of chickens – above the sound of his own rough breath. He stood on the threshold of his home, unsure as to whether he should enter.

He had been away for three days, hunting further and further afield, though Mary, pregnant and about to give birth, had begged him not to go. She had broken their silences and the awkward niceties that had become their life. 'I need you, John. I want you here when the baby is born.' He hadn't listened.

He took one faltering step into the room. Shadows moved softly against the wall. The smell of blood and shit hung in the air. He had missed the birth of his child. A woman, unknown to him, excused herself and pushed past, leaving him alone with his wife.

Mary lay on a bloodstained mattress, a wad of soiled cotton pushed up between her legs, her hair wet with sweat and stuck to her head. She raised her eyes to his. They sat deep in their sockets, a bruise of blue across the lids and above her top lip. A baby lay upon her lap, an infant girl. It could have been Lydia. But it wasn't. She had been wiped, but blood and mucous from the birth still soiled her hair, and she held her fists and feet clenched tight and her eyes shut, a scowl on her wrinkled, red face, ready to bawl her anger at this world. He didn't blame her. He felt sorry for her.

'Do you want to hold her?' Mary asked. She looked tiny and fragile. Breakable.

John shook his head too quickly and backed away. His arm steadied on the doorway. The room was hot and airless and he found himself breathing too fast. He wiped sweat from his forehead. He wanted to turn and run, but the sight of Mary on her mattress held him. 'What you going to call her?'

She frowned at that. 'You name her. What was your mother's name?'

'Not that. I don't care what you call her. But not that.'

He heard her sharp intake of breath, as if he had slapped her. The baby whimpered. Mary wrapped a shawl around her, covering her nakedness as if suddenly realising she needed protection. 'Then I'll call her after me own marm.'

John shrugged. 'Fine.' But he didn't ask what name that was.

She held his gaze. A moth flittered close to the lamp, its shadow huge. 'Fine. Her name is Mary. We call her Minnie.'

John nodded. 'I'll let you rest then.' He escaped from the room, back into the street, scurrying down the laneways. He brushed hard against a marine, walking with his lady. They turned and scowled. He heard the soft call of a street woman. He found himself on the edge at the harbour and threw himself down onto a patch of grass to catch his breath and look to the sky. Above him, the stars spiralled in dizzy abandon. Below him, they reflected in the water. They knocked the world off balance. He clutched at the eagle around his neck and floated away.

Chapter Forty-Three

February 1796

A half-hearted day, during which the sun had languished behind cloud, had slouched into a night of half-hearted drizzle. Within the cottage, John lounged with his back against the wall and played his flute, idly experimenting with different tunes. The room was warm, both from the lingering heat of the day and the company of friends, for John Martin and Ann had come to visit. They fussed over Minnie, who bounced on John Martin's knee and bestowed him with cow-eyed looks of adoration.

There was a time he might once have put the moment in his memory box, but he had long ago discarded it, for he no longer trusted the beauty in this world. It was always followed by sorrow.

'Minnie, leave John Martin alone. He doesn't need you crawlin' all over 'im,' John growled.

The toddler froze, her lower lip trembling.

'She's not botherin' me, John.' John Martin put a reassuring arm on the child.

John shook his head. 'You never cease to amaze me.'

John Martin had never had children of his own and doted on Minnie. The creeks and gulleys that shaped the landscape of his face would soften and melt; the unyielding back would bend to put an ear to her whisperings; hands which used an axe to sever trees, took on a life of their own, all soft cuddles and curves.

'For the love of Pete, give the babe a break, John. Maybe if yer gave her the time of day now and then she wouldn't go huntin' for a father's love.' Mary scolded him from where she stood near the benchtop, serving bowls of soup, thick with meat and vegetable. The smell of hot damper filled the room; a pad of butter wrapped in waxed paper sat beside it.

John pretended not to hear the barb. Only Minnie could raise his wife out of the posed indifference that now sheltered their aching hearts. In truth he liked it when she spat her words at him, and he would bait her, just to hear some truth in her voice.

'I like nights like this, don't you, John Martin?' He looked around the room, as if he hadn't seen it a thousand times. Skins, bundled in piles, softened the hard earthen floor and kept out the cold. Barrels of rum, ready for trade, lined the far wall. Jugs and bowls, mugs, colanders, knives and spoons jostled for space on one rough-sawn sideboard, while a second held trinkets and odd bits he had traded or might yet trade. A basket with wool and knitting needles sat beside it, and some scrap bits of cloth that Mary was sewing into a cover for their bed. Hooks suspended from the ceiling, held sugar and salt. Barrels of flour, tea and rice stood on the floor. Mary's shawls and pinafores, John's hats and jackets and various items of Minnie's clothing hung from hooks on the wall. John's guns, for he now had a few, leant against the wall, next to a twig broom. The family slept in the second room, on a bedframe with leather supports, and a mattress stuffed with wool. It kept them off the cold, damp ground. Compared to many, they were wealthy. Compared to the slave huts, they lived in luxury.

'Remember sleepin' under canvas, John Martin?' John asked. 'We aren't doin' so bad.'

John Martin offered a barely perceptibly nod. 'Seen Caesar?'

John nodded. His friend released the toddler, who scurried over to hide in her mother's skirts, and settled for the story he knew was coming.

Caesar had escaped into the bush again and had gathered around himself a group of outlaws.

John had been at home when the message came, carried by a nod, a whisper, a guarded look. And in the dark hours of early morning, when nothing but dogs and sad looking drunks were on the street, John had slipped out of town, apparently to go hunting, but carrying an extra musket and gunpowder, a bundle of flour, some cheese and rice, and a grin upon his face. Caesar had stirred the hornet's nest again.

He found the camp easily enough: two lookouts slumped against a tree, snoring in gentle melody; the embers of a fire; the shadowed forms of bodies still curled within their dreams, despite the efforts of the nudging day.

John crept up to the largest, and prodded Caesar with the tip of his musket. 'You know there's a bounty on your head? I could claim it easily enough.'

A lazy smile appeared upon his friend's face. He yawned loudly and blinked open his eyes, as if startled by the light. 'Ahh, John, knew you would come.'

'And what do you think you are doing, lighting a fire at night? I could see it from Sydney Town. You trying to get caught or what?'

Caesar let out another yawn and held out his hand for John to pull him to his feet, opened his arms wide and embraced his friend in a bear hug. 'What do you have for me?'

'And your lookouts would sleep through an army.' John unloaded his supplies. 'Biscuits from Mary. She sends her greetings.'

'Do they talk about me in town?'

John grinned. 'You're a legend. Responsible for every bit of skulduggery from Parramatta to Botany Bay. If some milk sours in the sun, they blame you for breathing on it. Threaten the very future of the colony, you do. You even killed that Aboriginal, Pemulwuy.' John shook his head in comic disapproval. 'You have been a busy man.'

Caesar's laughter boomed across the camp. He stretched and thumped his chest with both fists. 'I am free and alive,' he shouted. 'Just try to get me, you buggers.'

And in between his attempts to quieten his friend, John felt tears come to his eyes. Tears with no words, but of a love so deep, they came from the marrow of his bones. Tears of worship for a man who had refused to bow; and of fear, for he knew Caesar could not survive. And of rage, at a world that had brought them all here.

Caesar stopped his heroics and looked at his friend, shaking his head. 'You are a very complex person,' was all he said.

They sat in silence together. Someone had rekindled the fire and the smell of damper made their bellies grumble.

'They'll get you this time, you know.' John's voice was muffled, partly from the damper.

Caesar nodded. The smile unexpectedly absent. No laughter in his voice. 'But I die free. You of all people know what that means.'

John held his friend's eyes and nodded.

'We have chosen different ways, John. You and I. You seek to join them. I try to escape them. Each of us just trying to get from under 'em.' He pulled John to his feet and hugged him. 'But we are of one blood. And I thanks the gods who brought you to me.'

John watched his friend as he and the others moved out. He cleared the campsite, removing clues to their presence, and started the journey back home. He should have hunted, brought back game for the governor, but his heart was not in it. He just wanted to lay his head down and sleep.

He told all this to John Martin in a flat tone. His voice only caught as he described watching Caesar swagger away into the bush, the huge, muscled frame striped with scars, and his conviction that it was the last time he would ever see his friend. John Martin listened without interruption, nodding now and then to show he heard.

The banging at the door was not unexpected. But it was different. An unapologetic hammering that demanded to be answered. John supplied the taverns with the lieutenant's rum but a few times a night, lost-looking men and women would appear, heads down and shoulders slumped, a wedding ring or a carton of oysters, even their weekly rations clutched in their hands to barter or plead for what they couldn't buy with coin. 'Little else to lighten the load,' they would say. John would weigh their treasure against his family's need, or Johnston's interest, or its future trading value, and measure out a mug or a pint or even a gallon of rum. 'Fair trade,' he would say to seal the deal, though he tried not to look them in the eyes.

And if he needed to step over them the next morning, collapsed in a laneway, he would tell himself that it had been their choice. He had made a fair exchange. In the meantime, the townspeople called him Sir, or Master Randall, and stood aside to let him pass.

'Thought you hated the Rum Corps,' Mary had said once.

'I ain't the Rum Corps,' he had replied.

The knock sounded again. John jerked his head towards Minnie, for her to answer it.

A man stood in the doorway, his fist raised, caught in the act of his third knock. A black, wide-brimmed hat shadowed his face, and a black cape, pulled tight, gave him a bulky misshapen appearance. Minnie scampered away to hide between her mother's skirts.

'Jethrow.' John recognised the lieutenant's manservant. He pulled himself to his feet. He didn't want anyone standing over him. 'What can I do for you? Best get yourself in and out the rain.'

'Lieutenant sent me. Thought you'd want to know. They got that Caesar fellow. One of his own men shot him.'

She turned to him that night, pulling him to her, her arms around his head, her hands tangling in his hair, stroking his neck, his shoulders, his back, turning him to caress his face, the lines of his cheeks.

'I know you loved him,' she said. 'Let me hold you. Let me love you.'

He moaned in the agony of his longing for her, and all the pain of his shuttered self rose in his gullet, festering and fly-blown, so putrid that he gagged; a violent upheaval of grief and guilt. She jerked away, convinced that it were her that made him sick, and perhaps it was, for he could not look at her without reliving that night of violence. Nor could he forgive Minnie for her being.

Chapter Forty-Four

Sydney 5th June 1799

He almost fell over the convict woman who was on her knees scrubbing the floor as he crept up the grand hallway of Government House. He hadn't expected to see anyone at this time of night, but he knew her, for she was not averse to sharing some arse and tit for the taste of some rum. She would keep her quiet. He pinched her bum as he passed but didn't stop. He was no stranger to the building. The governor had his offices here, just down to the left. He was glad the convict woman was not too bright, or maybe just too tired to care. She didn't question what business he had so late. It was nearly 6 pm and all officials had retired for the evening.

Up the hallway, with its cracked plaster and peeling paint, through the dining room, where the warped floorboards creaked at every step, and into the kitchens. He had sweet-talked Cook into fresh biscuits and tea often enough. He knew the layout. The plates and cups and some good glasses, fine and delicate as eggshells, sat on the polished sideboard. He wanted them. He had seen the like at the lieutenant's house, pretty birds flying around the sides, and ever since had pictured them in Mary's hands, her fingers twined around the handle, her lips poised upon the rim.

He wondered if they might bring a smile to her face, some light to her eyes, for she looked so sad. They had fumbled their way through the last five years, refining their dance, stepping

316

close and twirling away. They shared the same bed, and sometimes their bodies, but not their hearts. John knew only how to buy her things, which he would casually and wordlessly toss on the bench. Sometimes they sat there for days: boots, with neat little heels and laced to the ankles; flowery shawls and silk lined bonnets – intermediaries that shouted, 'Look at me! I have become someone!' But in time, they were tossed into a corner, got dusty and dull and, he thought, left his wife looking more lost than ever.

He yanked his thoughts into the present and surveyed his plunder. He had intended to carry it in his satchel, but chose instead to stack the plates, with the cups balanced on top, and carry them in his arms, for fear of cracking them. Deciding not to risk another encounter with the cleaning woman, he opened the back door of the kitchen and scanned the grounds. Murky brown clouds hid a dying sun and the moon was not yet up. He worried about stumbling in the dark on the uneven ground, or knocking something over and alerting the guards, but it would be safer than returning through the house. Testing the ground with each step, his booty held before him, he made it halfway to the gate.

'Who goes there?' The voice came from behind him. A servant stood in the kitchen doorway, silhouetted by the light of a lamp. 'I can see you. What are you doing? Tell me now or I'll call the guards.'

John thought of dropping the plates and running, but a host of constables would be upon him within a moment.

'Hullo, there. That you, Keys? Just me. Randall.'

'What are you doing? Come into the light where I can see you.'

'Just gathering a few things for the lieutenant. He has a big meeting tomorrow. Didn't want him caught short. Embarrassed, like.' John didn't move. He might still be let go about his business, but he knew Keys to be a fussy old bugger.

'Come back here. Yer can't go just takin' things without per-mission an' all. Gotta sign 'em out. What if the governor needs them things tomorrow? What then?'

'Keep yer knickers on, will you? I'm coming. Try and do a good deed an' what do I get? You're a right old biddy, you are.'

'And you're too big for your boots, John Randall. You'll get yours one day. I tell you that for free. Now bring that stuff right back here where it belongs.'

John returned to the kitchen, thrust the stack of plates onto the bench. 'I'll be off, then. Probably see you in the morning. Sign your authorities and kiss your arse then.'

¬

'Just bad luck. I was almost away. That frigging Keys has to stick his nose in things.' John paced the floor of his home, a mug of rum in his hand. Though he talked to Mary, she didn't answer, her face a picture of aggravation. The kids, for they had two now, had slipped to the safety of outside. He kicked a bucket to send it tumbling across the floor. Mary scowled at him.

'Well. What you looking at?' he demanded.

'It don't matter, John. We don't need no glasses. We have all we need.'

'And now you're telling me what we need?' He glared at her. 'Now what you doing?'

'Going to bed. It's late. You shouldn't drink. You can't handle it. We need some sleep.'

'Told ya. Don't tell me what I need.' The empty mug struck a wall.

'Please, John. Every soul is asleep. Just come to bed.'

John turned to face her but stopped. 'You're right. Every-body's asleep. Haha. My clever wife.'

¬

Government House loomed over Sydney Town. No windows were lit by lamplight. No hum of conversation. Not even a fingernail of a moon poked through the cloud.

John stumbled, catching himself on the gate. Though he sold rum, he despised those who drank it, bartering their souls for the release it brought, and so, though he had not drunk much that night, he had little tolerance for it. 'Alright, Keys my man. We'll see which of us wins out this night.' He hiccupped and laughed at himself. 'Let's go, shall we.'

A pebble slid from beneath him, tumbling him to the ground, and he decided to stay there, crawling on all fours across the yard to the kitchen. For sure, Keys would have latched the door, but maybe he could pry a window open.

On reaching the building he stood, feeling his way around, leaning too heavily so that he almost fell when the door to the dining room opened beneath his weight. He giggled as he spilled into the house. He giggled again when he caught sight of his booty, restored to the sideboard, and imagined Keys' face when he found them missing again. He wished he could see it. In fact, yes, he would make sure he visited nice and early just so that he could catch that moment. He found himself crying with laughter, bent over and holding his belly.

From the dining room door, John peered out at the vast expanse of land he had to cross to make it to the gates and safety. It reminded him of a battlefield, that no man's land between two armies, where he could be shot by a sniper from behind a tree, or blown to pieces by a cannonball. He would see neither before they struck. The gentle buzz of the rum abandoned him, leaving him flat and hollow. The glasses he clasped to his chest weighed heavily in his arms, like fate; there could be no wild stories and excuses if he were caught with them again. They were not worth hanging from a tree, nor a flogging. They were definitely not worth a return to convict status and a life of smashing rocks, or hauling timber or working someone else's land, for that was the most likely event were he to be caught and the thing he feared most. He considered returning the glasses to their place in the cabinet where they could sit dusty, unused, unnoticed, and taunt him each time he visited. But his mind was made up. Fighting the urge to run, and surely call attention to himself, he stepped out to walk, head high and innocent as a baby, through the gardens and out to the track beyond.

'Who's that there?' It was not a sniper's bullet or cannon fire but the challenge of a constable, patrolling the grounds and barely yards away.

John broke into a run too late for he had barely made two steps before he thudded to the ground, pinned by the constable on top of him, and surrounded by a mess of broken glasses.

'Like to see you get out of this one, Randall.'

Chapter Forty-Five

9th June, 1799

The prison was not the wooden shack with its crooked door loosely barred by a plank that it had once been. Instead, John hunched on the hard, rock floor of a cell built from sandstone, with walls so thick they blocked all noise and light. He could not follow the passage of the moon across the sky, or watch the earth warm with the pink of sunrise. He couldn't hear the cries of the kids as they played ball in the street, or the slapping of the waves, or even the bragging of the cockatoos. Nor could he smell the earth after the rain, or the sea on a breeze. He rotted in a tomb, dark and still as death, with only his thoughts to bounce off the walls and leave him trembling with dread. The judge advocate wanted to make an example of him; the guards told him that when they opened the door each morning to hand him his bread and water and empty the bucket that held his piss and shit. He would be flogged and then hung or manacled and sent to work on Pinchgut Island. He would be put in the stocks to be jeered at by every convict with a chip on his shoulder, and every officer with a point to make. The guards offered their guesses and discussed his options in nonchalant, cheerful voices, making no attempt to either console or hurt. This upset John. He would have preferred some cruel taunts against which he could have flung himself. But their disregard left him empty, as vague and shapeless as a sponge. They didn't care because he was nothing to them, not worth the bother of offence. He guessed by their visits that he had wasted there for four days, and in that time, no one had called upon him. Not even a rat for company. And so, he spent his time with his head in his hands, occasionally punching the wall or even his own skull. He pulled himself to his feet and trailed around the three-square yards that was spared to him of this world. He leant his forehead on the coarse brick of his cell and brushed his cheeks against its cool surface, almost an embrace, before beginning his wandering again. His fingers caught on marks scratched into the stone where others had sought to leave some record that they too had been in this world. He wondered if Caesar had made one of those marks. He had been held here. But Caesar was dead now. His fingers traced the path where an X had been scored in the rock and decided this was Caesar's. He put his palm over it, forcing the sandy surface to shed its memories so he might feel his friend one last time. He wept for their broken lives.

⌐

John jerked his head away, blinded by light as his cell door creaked open.

'Up you get, then. It's your time. Let's see what the judge has to say about ya.' Two cheerfully indifferent guards blocked the doorway; fetters dangled from their hands. 'Let's get these on you, shall we?'

John staggered the short distance from the prison to the courthouse. The irons on his legs weighed heavier than he remembered; so dense they rooted his feet to the ground. If this were to be his life, he would plead for the gibbet.

The courthouse did not appear big enough to reflect the might of English law that held the colony to account and stamped the rule of the king on the days of convicts and settlers alike. Nor did its bland, squat walls and flat facade hint at the suffering that issued from there, or the frustration of a government that could not stop hungry men from stealing food or freedom, no matter how cruel the punishment. John let out a sigh of relief as he stumbled through its doors, for the cool darkness of the shaded room soothed his eyes, still weeping from the light. He blinked and wiped the tears away, pulled himself tall and straight, and attempted to rid his face of fear.

The judge advocate and the Reverend Richard Johnson sat on an elevated bench at the end of the room. John didn't recognise the judge's face, but the man looked at him with such malevolence, such palpable anger, that John found himself trying to recall when they might have crossed paths, and whether he had cheated him. He nodded to the reverend however, for he had always liked that earnest man.

John's offence was read out. A long and detailed account was then delivered by the judge of the recent history of theft from Government House. The judge advocate had the habit of stopping after every sentence and glaring at John as if he could not possibly believe his audacity. 'Incidents such as these are an attack on the government, are they not?'

Unsure if he was expected to answer, John said nothing.

'I asked you a question. An attack on the government?' The judge advocate gripped a gavel in his fist so tightly his knuckles showed white. John had the impression that it would be thrown at him if he did not agree, but it seemed like a trap.

'No Sir. Not on the government. On some china cups. And that were an accident. Didn't mean to break them, Sir.'

A guard sniggered and John winced. He hadn't intended to antagonise the magistrate.

'And an affront to our noble king. Is it not?' He continued as if he had not heard.

'But, Sir ... can't say the king had anything to do with it.' John looked around. 'I like the king.' He finished lamely.

'An example is required.'

John realised he had clenched his fists. He wondered if maybe he was being set up for a charge of mutiny. *Stand tall.* He raised his head, relaxing his arms and shoulders.

The judge advocate glared at him, eyes bulging. 'I have it here that you took it upon yourself to write to the governor of your sincere remorse.' He waved a piece of paper in the air.

'Ah, sorry, sir?' John looked at the paper that had appeared like magic. His eyes followed it, wanting to pounce on it, trying to discern what it could possibly mean.

'You wrote this letter?' the judge advocate asked, although he clearly guessed that John could not write and had no previous knowledge of any letter.

The eyes of everyone in the courtroom were on John. A band practised on the parade grounds. Through the windows, from under the doors, the notes of a marching tune stirred the air, 'Hearts of Oak'. It spoke of victory and freedom. John wanted to sing along. He wanted to stamp his feet to the tune and raise his arm in triumph. He didn't bother to keep the smile from his face. 'Err, Yes, sir. Yes. That I did. Deep remorse.'

'I have here a letter from the governor himself. Governor Hunter accepts your apology and requests that you be liberated. I bow to his wishes. You are free to go with no judgement to be held against you.'

As John left the courtroom, he paused in the doorway and wiped imaginary flecks of dust from the shoulders of his jacket, dragged his fingers through his hair, and with a grin and a murmured a prayer of thanks to his friend, the lieutenant, he stepped back into the world.

November 1799

'Thinks he's going to clean things up. Orders from the king. Says he is displeased with the rumours he's heard...the "abuses of the Corps".'

Lieutenant Johnston and John sat in the loungeroom with its soft, soft carpet and brocade curtains and the flickers of light from the heavy chandelier playing 'catch me' on the walls.

'We need to talk.' The voice of the lieutenant called him to attention.

Colonel William Patterson had arrived in town as senior military officer. It had been a week of parades and marching bands, of balls and tea parties, but even John could see that trouble brewed beneath the formalities.

'Governor Hunter won't upset the applecart. Knows which side his bread is buttered, but - ' Johnston leaned forward to offer John a drink.

He declined with a shake of his head and a rueful smile. 'Gets me into trouble.' He waited. He knew there was a point to this story.

A breeze blew in from the window, fluttering some papers on the table around which they sat. Johnston slapped a hand down to catch one as it flew off but missed and it fell to the floor. John bent to catch it but it sailed out of his reach.

'Leave it.' Johnston was laughing. 'Can't win 'em all.' He looked at John, his face now serious. 'I tell you, John. Patterson will have his eye on me...and theretofore, you! We must take care. I want you to trade for me from Parramatta, out of his line of sight. And keep your head down. I won't be able to intercede for you again.'

The paper had caught on the leg of a chair. John watched as it flapped against it before the wind grabbed it and blew it out the door. He sighed and then nodded at his friend. 'Might have that drink now.'

Chapter Forty-Six

Parramatta April 1800

'I ain't cooked yer eggs, 'cause I ain't got no eggs to cook,' Mary growled at him, her summer-sky blue eyes dark and clouded. Arms on hips and feet apart, she seemed bigger and scarier than her five-foot, one inch.

Somewhere in the recesses of his being, John felt a wave of pride at her spirit, but he didn't say it and his face didn't show it, and it broke on the rocks of their anger and was forgotten in an eye blink. 'Perhaps because you killed the bloody chook,' was all he said. She had served him porridge, rich with cream and sugar and a blob of butter floating on the top and he had thrown it against the wall, breaking the bowl and leaving the gruel to slide in a sticky, greasy mess onto the floor. It pooled there still, being demolished by ants.

'An' I done told yer. She was old. She weren't laying no eggs. Jest a dried-up old bag of bones and waste of space.'

'Who you talking about? You or the hen?' John snapped, hungry and mad at himself for now he had nothing to eat and he was pretty sure Mary wouldn't be cooking for him anytime soon.

The door slammed behind her as she fled the house, seven-year-old Minnie scuttling behind, hiding in the tails of her mother's skirts.

'And for the sake of all the gods, grow some balls,' he yelled at the little girl.

John Junior looked up from where he played jacks on the floor, *Now look what you have done,* written all over his face. He had sat quietly throughout the argument, tossing the stones in the air and swearing energetically as they rolled across the floor or behind his back and, for one frightening moment, onto his father's lap, but nowhere near his hand as they were meant.

'Wipe that look from your face,' John snarled. The boy stuck to him like a limpet though for the life of him John couldn't understand why. The children were Mary's business, but John Junior refused to learn that lesson. 'Skiddat.' He shuffled his son out the door with a gentle kick to his three-year-old backside. 'Go play with the other kids.'

The child trudged down the path and through the gardens, shoulders slumped in a dramatic show of misery. Occasionally he stopped to turn to his father with reproachful eyes, as if to make sure he hadn't changed his mind. John smiled. The boy reminded him so much of himself. Hadn't he rebuked Ol' Ma in just that same way?

He stood on the doorstep, surveying the scene. High overhead an eagle glided on the winds, a lonely speck. He fingered his talisman and, as always, thought of his mother. *Do you see me now? People respect me in this town.* It was a challenge.

His home was one of many that lined the main road that led from Government House to the river. Humble enough but neatly pegged out, with vegetable gardens and fruit trees and pleasant views of the surrounding hills, they housed the more affluent of the freed convict population. John no longer hunted, committing himself to trading for the officers. His children wore shoes and good clothes. They had flesh on their bones and slept warm under blankets. *More than anybody ever gave me.* He watched as John Junior joined some children playing hopscotch. The sounds of their rhyming trickled through the air:

One, two, buckle my shoe,

Three, four, close the door,
Five, six, pick up sticks.

A woman passed by, a wicker bag on her back, a knife dangling from her hand. 'Eels?' She caught John's eye. He shook his head. Not today. But he did signal the youth who followed behind her. He pushed a barrow of firewood, six pennies a load. John held out the coin. The fire had burned down. It might mollify Mary if he stoked it before she returned.

Not for the first time he wondered if he would ever find a way through the mess he had made of their lives. He knew he had deliberately caused the fight this morning. They had made love last night and he had fallen asleep, his limbs entwined with hers. But the remnants of old dreams had returned. He had wandered through a grey landscape; become entangled in webs; had called for Mary but she had abandoned him. *I warned you*, his mother had crowed.

Hunched in front of the fireplace, with his back to the door and his arms full of wood, he did not see the woman as she sauntered up the path. He blew on the embers to stir some flame.

'Mary not here, then?'

He jumped, turning to see Kit Murphy on the steps, a pretty girl with bouncy, brown hair and brown eyes that spoke of knowing the way of the world. 'Jes' you an' I. Best come in. No use standing in the doorway.'

Kit raised her eyebrows, gave him an arch look, and smiled as she sauntered in. She had arrived recently on a convict ship and worked at the women's camp down the road. Mary had taken her under her wing for a while but had soured of her of late, making excuses to leave the girl on the front step with the door slammed in her face. John thought he could guess the reason as the girl collapsed into a chair and pulled up her skirts to rub her feet and show some leg. She looked at him from beneath those bouncing curls. 'Got any liquor then?' she asked.

'Was going to invite you to sit yourself down. No need of that, I guess.' John lined up two mugs on the kitchen table, scrubbed clean by Mary, and poured two slugs of rum. He slid one across to her. 'Here, let me rub that for you.' He put his hand over hers and removed it from the foot, a delicate, if grubby, little morsel. He squeezed it between his two large hands, massaging the sole with his thumb.

'Thought you might have a pound of tea for me to take back to me quarters.' She made to move his hand from her foot.

John smiled. *Sounds like a fair exchange.* He kept rubbing. The sole of her foot and her heel were coarse in sharp contrast to the fragile white ankles. He moved his hands further up the leg. His argument with Mary seemed a long time ago.

'The tea?' she said. 'And you got another of these then?' She held out her empty mug. Her tongue flickered between her lips and she looked around the room, suddenly less sure of herself. As John released her to get the rum, she pulled down her skirts and planted her feet on the floor, sitting straighter. She had, he thought, almost managed to pull a cloak of propriety around those slender shoulders. *Teasing little bitch.*

He went to his chest to collect the tea and put it on the table. He looked at it and then at her.

Her eyes darted around the room, and though she didn't move she seemed to lean back away from him. 'Just want some tea, John. And a bit to drink. Nothing else. You can afford it, like.'

He handed her the liquor, but as she reached to take it, he caught her wrist and pulled her to her feet. With one arm around her waist, he lifted her chin with the other to kiss her. 'This what you want, then?' But he didn't listen to her muffled response.

He shuffled her against the wall, tearing her bodice to get at her breasts.

'No, John. Stop it. Please.'

'You been coming here looking for this a long time.' He wrestled the squirming girl to the floor, holding her wrists above her head with one hand. With the other he pulled up her skirts and struggled with the buttons of his own britches. She screamed. He slapped her. 'Shut up. You think you can play games with me?'

'What's happening in there?'

John glanced over his shoulder. He recognised the voice of his neighbour, a top-heavy man with a portly belly that hung over two spindly legs. He had flapping jowls and a flapping mouth, and a sanctimonious way of speaking that left John wanting to prick him to release all that hot air. He imagined him at the gate, head cocked, attentive, his hand raised to his ear, ready to hasten up the path and put the world to rights.

'Help me!'

The gate squeaked and the crunch of footsteps sounded on the path. John struggled off Kit, pulling his breeches up as he did so, and scurried out the back door. Her word against his.

⌐

The day had shaken off its morning chill and families had retired indoors for their midday meal before John returned to the house. Mary had made a pie and the smell of bacon and cabbage and potato wafted through the room. She threw him a puzzled look as he came in. 'Have you seen my pinafore? I'm sure I left it on the bench.'

John glanced at the bench where he had left the tea. And the rum. Gone.

'Little bitch,' he snarled, more to himself than to Mary. He had offered the trade fair and square and she hadn't delivered.

'Who? What bitch?'

'Your friend Kit Murphy is who. Damn me. That tea was worth four guineas.'

Mary looked at him, her eyes narrowed. 'You were here with Kit? Alone?'

'Don't look at me like that, woman. It does you no justice. She came visiting for you. I had business to do and left her here to wait. That's all.'

'She took my pinafore?'

'And the tea. And the rum.'

'What business did you have?'

John had expected this. He pulled out a pouch in which he kept some trading items and fiddled inside before finding a gold ring. 'I promised you this.' He held it to her.

Surprise and hope and something else flitted across Mary's face. John recognised it. She didn't believe him. But she wanted to, so much she would force herself to. He slumped to the bench, the strength gone from his legs, and sighed. His next words surprised him, as did the longing that accompanied them, for he thought he had long ago nailed down his heart and placed it in protection. 'I know I don't show it. But I do love you.' And for the second time that day he wished there were someway he could find his path back to the man she had once loved.

Mary gaped at him, thrown off balance. Her eyes filled with tears and she wiped them away, with short, jerky slaps. She turned from him, picked up a rag, still dirty with splattered porridge and cream, and began wiping the table clean until she regained her composure. 'Will you call the constable?' she asked eventually. 'She can't just come in here and steal our stuff.'

'Have to. No choice. Can't let her get away with it.'

Mary didn't seem to hear him. She was looking at the ring.

John Junior sat on the doorstep. His sister and the other kids had abandoned him. He was too little to play with them, they had said, and then raced up the street, too fast for him to follow, no matter how hard he forced his legs to go.

John hung back, gazing at his son, touched by the slump in his shoulders. *I will do better by you.* But for now, he had a task to manage.

John Junior's glum little face brightened when he saw his father.

'Fancy a walk?' John asked and grasped his son's hand to help him up. Clasped within his big one, it felt smooth and soft and innocent, not yet roughened or scarred.

The two wandered down to the river. John Junior delivered a long story with great gusto, plenty of facial expression and expansive gestures, most of which his father couldn't understand, although he got the gist: his sister had been very mean. They sat on the banks of the river. John Junior threw pebbles into the water.

'So, do you remember this morning, you were playing hopscotch in the street. Did you see Kit Murphy go into the house?' John started with a solid fact the boy could hang onto.

The child nodded. He found a flat stone and passed it to his father to skip across the water.

'And later on, your mother and I left the house and went visiting,' John told his son. He skipped the stone across the surface. One, two, three hops. Then found another. He handed it to his son, moulding his fingers around it.

The boy looked at him, his face crumpled in a frown, the beginnings of a 'no' upon his mouth. John continued. 'Yes, you're a big boy. You remember when your mother and I left to go visiting.' John Junior said nothing. 'Say, "Yes. I remember that my father and my mother left the house to go visiting,"' John urged.

Clear now on what was expected of him, John Junior mumbled some semblance of the words.

'So, Kit was alone in the house when your mother and I were out, wasn't she?' John urged.

The child thought for a moment, then nodded, with a questioning look.

'And because I know that you are a brave and smart boy, I expect you followed her, didn't you?'

The child paused, but he was getting the hang of this game. 'Brave boy.' He stretched up his arms, squeezed his fists and looked fierce.

'You saw Kitty go into Daddy's box and take some things, didn't you? You saw her steal the tea and a pinafore from the house.'

John Junior nodded.

'Tell me what you saw.'

'Kitty's bad.' The child clearly pictured the scene in every detail.

John ran through it again before they started back home, stopping only to buy a boiled lolly for the boy.

'John Randall got me drunk and ill-used me.' The members of the courtroom murmured as tears flowed down Kitty's face.

John had charged Kit with theft. Now he scowled at her on the stand. The whore looked like a choir girl and her words held the conviction of truth. Certainly, she appeared a more convincing witness than John Junior had been, for despite his earnest expression and the oft repeated 'Bad Kitty' it had been difficult to get a clear account of events from a three-year old who wanted the court to understand he was a brave boy.

John's neighbour took the stand next. 'Indeed, I ran up the path immediately I heard a cry for help.'

John thought the man reported the scene with a little too much relish, particularly when he described the breasts clearly exposed through her torn clothing. *That man probably hasn't seen a naked woman in his life.*

'The thighs of the accused were bruised, and scratches could be seen on her knees. Injuries consistent with forced sexual intercourse.' The evidence provided by D'Arcy Wentworth drew gasps from the crowd and John shook his head, a look of sorrow on his face that he might be painted in such a way.

John failed to convince anyone that Kitty had stolen the tea and his case against her was dismissed. She left the courtroom with an arrogant tilt of the head.

Could be worse, thought John. *Mary might have been in court and heard that evidence.*

The Rose Hill Package began its slow voyage back to Sydney Town. From the shores of the river, and in the shade of a giant eucalypt tree, John watched as the boat wound its way through the narrow channel. He would not be here next week to see it. He swung around at the sound of a splash. A fish had leapt from the water, pursued by a predator. *Good luck to you*, John thought, *but don't like your chances.* Though the river ran slow with barely a ripple to trouble its surface, he knew that sharks lurked beneath. He had seen it in flood too, turbulent, muddy waters that came from nowhere, and without notice, to wash away everything in its path.

The boat had brought him confirmation of the rumours. His friend, Lieutenant Johnston, had been arrested and sent to England for court martial. He was charged with dealing in spirits and had paid a sergeant of his company in rum, rather than coin – a common practice, but illegal, particularly when the cost of the rum was valued at over twice its true price. John shook his head, scarcely able to believe that they dared to touch his friend. He knew the lieutenant had taken every advantage of his position, had used every devious means available to become one of the wealthiest men in the colony. But irrepressible and loyal, he had taken John along for the ride.

It was, John understood, a clear message to the officers of the NSW Corps. There would be no more dealing in rum. No need for a middleman. His business was finished. He was too tired and too old to return to hunting and anyway, who would employ him?

He saw everything he had worked for, borne away on the tide of these changes. *'I am no better than that fish,'* he thought, *'and the sharks are coming.'* And for a moment he felt that he were drowning and struggled to catch his breath, his hands planted across his mouth.

It is good. Ol' Ma's voice was barely discernible. But gradually, he calmed.

Been in worse positions. I'll work it out.

He got up and trudged slowly back to the house, delaying his arrival, the moment they would pack to leave, and the end of the good times.

Chapter Forty-Seven

May 1800 Age 36

It felt like yesterday. And a hundred years ago. John stood on the same spot he had been when he surveyed his land for the first time. Then, he had wanted to start work immediately, cutting down trees, building their home, sowing the seeds for their future. He had pictured the sun catching the tips of the corn as it rustled in the breeze and had seen orchards growing down the hills and his wife nurse a child on her lap as she rocked in a chair on the veranda. He had planned roses to line the path. He had found death. Death and fire, drought and storm. Now when he surveyed his land, his eye followed the trail down to the creek and he saw Lydia's dead body. Mary's accusing eyes. His own guilt. He felt tired and wanted to lie down and sleep forever. Instead, he forced his eyes away and turned towards the house.

It looked sad. The convicts he had been given had long since gone, recalled to work for an officer of the Corps. Weeds grew up and around the windows and sniffed through the slats of the veranda. Timbers had loosened and hung like broken arms at odd angles and birds' nests lined the rafters, making a wiry and unruly fringe. The rose bush was nowhere to be seen.

John could hear the faint clip clop of the horses' hooves and the creaking of the wagon he had hired to transport his goods, as it disappeared around a bend and out of sight, breaking the last link to their town life. Their belongings were strewn

across the edge of the track and it surprised him how much
they had: chests of shawls; shirts and skirts; shoes and warm,
woollen socks; boxes of brushes and combs; pots and pans;
blankets and curtains. Their sideboards and a mirror, tables
and benches and the rocking chair were piled awkwardly and
exposed to the world, almost embarrassed by being outside
and privy to spying eyes. John had sold all he did not need
to buy seed and stock, tools and food supplies of tea and
sugar, rice, flour, cheese and preserves and already Mary was
trudging down the hill, two pails across her shoulders, intent
on getting water for tea. It was a job she would not entrust to
the children. He would light the fire and unpack the kettle and
help set up the lean-to they used as a kitchen.

'Bugger your soul to hell.'

John jumped at the expletive, unsure whether to cuff his
son or laugh. The boy had tied a rope around the neck of a goat
and was tugging it to lash to a tree but the goat had other ideas
and had dug in its hooves and refused to budge. Boy and goat
glared at each other, face to face, eye to eye, each stubborn.
Idly, John wondered who would win. He looked around for his
daughter and caught sight of her dragging a chest, near as big
as herself, up the steps to the house. 'Leave that there,' he
said to her. 'Your mam will need to sweep and wash the floors
before we bring our stuff in.' The child looked at the sky and he
knew she was thinking of the rain that softened the horizon. 'I
said to leave it.' He repeated.

A wooden cross, lopsided and rotten, the carved name now
faded. A pile of stones, infinitely small and pitted with weeds.
It was all that marked the grave. John crouched beside it, dog-
gedly pulling at the grasses. 'I'm sorry,' he muttered so quietly
it could scarce be heard. 'I shouldn't have left you here alone.'
He reached out and stroked a smooth round rock. 'I had to go.
I couldn't stay.'

'She is with the Lord, John. There is nothin' she don't understand.'

John jolted, slapped by the sound of Mary's voice, and raised his eyes reluctantly to hers. They never talked about Lydia. It led them to places they shouldn't go. She hadn't blamed him, not really, not after the first flush of pain. But he blamed himself and punished her for it, until the air between them bristled with their barbs, stung and cut and made them bleed.

She hunkered down beside him. 'Maybe - maybe we could start again?'

He glowered at her, waiting for the stick. 'Not now, Mary. Please. Not now.'

She put her hand to his shoulder and he caught a glint of the wedding ring on her finger. She never took it off.

He spun around, 'Can I jes' have a moment here alone? Is that too much to ask?'

Still she didn't move.

'Go!' he yelled at her, jerking away from under her touch.

He stayed by the grave, pulling at the weeds, trying to put it to rights, but he would need more time for they were strongly rooted and tangled in the rocks.

July 1800

It was a crisp, cold night. The family had worked hard at clearing the four acres of the invading bush and weed and they sparkled, frost-covered, under the light of a full moon. John sat on the veranda steps, fidgeting. He rubbed his knuckles and then ran his fingers through his hair before letting them wander to the eagle at his neck. He couldn't stay in the house to watch Mary dole out the pease in measured portions for their evening meal while the kids watched every move with hungry eyes, the flesh on their bones already wasting. He couldn't plant until spring and then they would have to wait for harvest, praying for good rain, though he put no faith in prayer. Until then the family had had to sign onto government stores to feed themselves and he knew that all eyes watched him, and all mouths whispered, 'Well, Black Randall has fallen a long way. Can't even support his family.' And it was true.

With a grunt of frustration he kicked at the cold hard ground which Mary and the children had worked until their fingers had bled. He thought of John Martin, who'd never given up and still worked his land but he and Ann looked older than their years and were poor as church mice. At least John hunted still and could supplement their meals when lucky, though the mobs of kangaroo that once sheltered in the valley had left for safer grounds.

Mary came out, a plate in her hand of pease and meat and the last of their potatoes. She handed it to him.

'Did you have some?' He didn't take it.

'Sure, I did. Not going to starve myself.' She urged it towards him.

'The kids have enough?'

'Enough.'

'Share this between them. They worked hard today.'

'No. Show me your hands.' She took them and turned them over to examine his palms, red raw and blistered. 'You worked harder.'

He jerked them from her grasp. 'Not hard enough. I'm no farmer.'

She seemed to fumble for words before giving up but slipped down to sit beside him.

They sat together on the steps under the cold blue gaze of the moon.

'Truth be, I hate this place.' It had been years since John had spoken his heart to Mary. The 'pretend man', he thought of himself, circling her with a smile and gifts, talking of necessities and practicalities but he had kept her at a distance with the stick of his indifference. She had changed since she wore his ring, as if the glinting gold had cleared the shadows from her eyes and she saw him clearly again. It seemed strange to have her there beside him.

'Heard Paterson is recruiting to the choir. Ready to take anyone was once a soldier, don't matter if he were convict or not.' Mary used the slang term the locals used for the Rum Corps. She had been chatting to the neighbours as they trod the path from Parramatta. She'd give them a cup of tea and the chance of a breather in return for the news and some company and the new lieutenant governor, William Paterson, and his reinvention of the Rum Corps was on everyone's lips.

'Not anyone. *Those of good character.* Not the sort who steal the plates from the governor's house. What was I thinkin'! An' he hates Johnston and I'm well an' truly under that cloud. No. Reckon we're stuck in this pit of hell.' John's foot scuffed at the dirt.

In the black, cloudless sky, a million stars glittered, the blinking eyes of uncaring gods.

'Gotta make a wish,' Mary said as a shooting star split the heavens with its trail of light.

John watched as it burned itself out but didn't reply.

Mary pushed forward, stumbling through his silence and the heavy blanket of his mood. 'I wish for things to be as they were. I want you back,' she said.

'Mary, go back inside.' He jerked his head towards the house.

'No. Not this time, John Randall. I'm not lettin' you push me away again. Not no more.'

'Why? Why do you bother?' He buried his face in his two hands, as if to hide her from his sight.

'You're my husband.'

'I'm not the man you married.'

'I know who you are. I know you to your core. I know you more than you know you. An' I want you back.'

She sat beside him in the darkness, refusing to budge. The sound of his breathing, heavy and fast, the sound of his fear, was all that broke their silence.

Don't do it, John. Ain't no good lovin' someone, his mother whispered to him in the dark. *They all get taken away.*

Mary refused to budge. Later that night, still together on the steps, her hand crept into his. It sat there awhile, untouched, but it was a powerful hand and its magic swept down into his hidden and shuttered spaces and found him there, quivering among the guilt and the fear, and led him out into the light.

He turned to look her fully in the face with open eyes, eyes not hooded by self- loathing.

In the moonlight, the blue of hers seemed deep and dark as the ocean. He sank into them, deeper and deeper, allowing the layers of his filth to float away and leave him polished clean. He shook his head in wonder. And as he surfaced he saw her for what she was, no longer hidden in the cloak of his guilt, but a woman who had promised to stand by him and had never left his side.

'Argh, forgive me.' With a grunt he grabbed the hand and held it to his mouth and buried his face in her neck as if he would drink of her life-giving powers. He wrapped his arms around her and they lay in the starlight. Mouths and hands and arms and legs sought for each other: touching, exploring, finding. They surged together, pressing deeper and deeper until they lay as one. And at peace.

Late that night, with Mary asleep beside him, he looked up at the stars.

It is good?

He started. He hadn't heard Ol' Ma's voice for so long. Tears threatened to spill.

You've been away a long time, he replied at last

No. Always here. It was you who got lost.

'Met that fella, Holt.' John Martin slid the knife down the belly of the 'roo and peeled back the skin. 'Seems orite.'

'He Cox's new manager?' John had only half an ear to the conversation. John Martin's wife, Ann, had miscarried again, and Mary had insisted that they visit so she could lend a hand and an ear. He had brought the beast to his friend for a fry-up that night. He hadn't been to the house for many years and was surveying the property, in awe of the work that had been done. John Martin had cleared the land around his hut as far as the eye could see and though it lay fallow through the winter, John thought it an impressive effort. To his knowledge, John Martin and he were the only original settlers left. The rest had lost their land to the Rum Corps and returned to working for the government, pulling carts, building homes for the officers, living off government stores and in government quarters, as measly a life as could be lived and not much better than a convict. *We have done well, he and I. I should be happy for my blessings.* But the thought of living out his days, breaking his back morning to night, in fear of fire and flood and drought, made him want to run. *There must be an easier way.*

'Sure is. Irish. Rebel.' John Martin's voice called him back. 'But seems to be doin' a good job for Cox. Reckon he'll be lookin' for some land himself soon. Get that impression.'

'Minnie, leave John Martin alone. Go worry your mam,' John chided his daughter who clung to his friend's leg. He watched her wander off – small, sullen steps – and then thought to check for John Jnr. The boy was sure to have found some trouble. Sure enough, he sat in the pigsty, covered in mud and looking cross, his lower lip sunk in a sulk, having been tossed by the animal he had tried to ride. John shook his head. He knew better than to laugh but couldn't help himself.

'I'm not funny,' the child growled, in unconscious parody of a long ago boy.

And John laughed louder.

Hearing him, Mary came from the house to see what was happening. She placed a hand on her husband's shoulder and lay a kiss on the top of his head. She didn't say the words, not in front of John Martin, but John knew what they were. *It is good to hear you laugh again.*

John Martin must have heard them too, for he nodded his head in agreement.

John returned to the conversation. 'You reckon Cox is on the up and up?' he asked John Martin, referring to their neighbour, newly arrived to the area and paymaster for the New South Wales Corps.

'Don't trust no one can't look me in the eye. An' his eye wanders right on by. Reckon it's busy hunting out new ways to make a quid.'

John digested this. A high-ranking man. Paymaster to the Corps. Not too fussy about the detail of things. There had to be something in this for him.

⌐

Heavy rain had given life to the creek so that it splashed gleefully against rocks and toppled over boulders, slapped at the banks and snatched up leaves and twigs, in a joyful dance downstream. It didn't care that over time it would smooth down the rocks, wear boulders into pebbles and erode the banks. And it didn't care that it had drowned a small child. John sat in the place where he had found Lydia and saw again her white face; the blue around her eyes and nose and mouth; the wide, blind stare. He watched as a twig caught in an eddy and spun round and round and round, before being shot out to join the other muck and rubbish in the pursuit to who knows where. He wondered idly how long it would be before it was submerged. Life did that.

He had come here to think, to place the arguments that spun around his mind into some order. He wanted to quit the land. There seemed to be no sound reason other than his dread at waking each morning, and his fear at going to sleep and knowing that another day, just the same, awaited him. Mary had said that the decision was his but reminded him that the land was the children's inheritance too, their safeguard against poverty. And what work would he do? The money from the land couldn't keep them for long, and he was getting too old for hunting. And what would happen if they sold it and ran into trouble? They would have lost their bolthole. The land is their security, she had said. Where is the security in drought or flood or fire? he had countered. The thoughts twirled around and around and around, like the twig in the eddy. He picked up a handful of soil and threw it into the creek. He had made his decision.

While we were in conversation a black man John Randall passed by the window. Mr. Cox asked me who he was and said, 'Go and learn what he wants.' Randall told me that he wished to dispose of his farm and would sell it cheap if I would promise to get him into the choir. I told him I was busy at the moment but would talk to him about the matter the next day. This man had been sportsman to Governor Grose. His farm was about a mile and three quarters from Mr. Cox's estate and I recommended Mr. Cox to purchase it. Mr. Cox looked at me for some time, as if hesitating, but at length, to my surprise, he said, 'Holt, if you like the farm, why not buy it for yourself? I am sure I can get him into the choir and it is time you should do something for yourself and your own family.'

The next day Randall came, and I went with him to view the farm; it was very well circumstanced and convenient for me, being so near Mr. Cox's estate, and as I had hoped to continue with that gentleman, I considered it very eligible, I asked the price. Randall said 60 pound and to engage him to get into the choir. I told him that was more than I could do at present, but I would give him 40 pound if I could get him into the choir and fifty if I could not do it and if he came with me so he should have my letter to Colonel Patterson. This black man was a well-made fellow, about six feet high and a good musician on the flute and tambour.'

Excerpt from the Memoirs of Joseph Holt (1759–1826)

Chapter Forty-Eight

December 1801.

Few heard the first notes of John's last solo piece. They crept across the room, soft and low, delicate as a teardrop.

Since being accepted into the band of the NSW Corps, and moving back to Sydney Town, John's days had been easy and his nights full of music.

The band had been playing in the officers' mess since the first shadows of dusk had stretched across the parade ground to consume the light and send another day whimpering into the night. They had played since the first officer had rolled up his sleeves and downed his first jug of rum with a sigh and a burp, wiped his mouth with the back of his hand, slammed the empty jug onto the counter and demanded another.

Now the mess jangled with voices raised in opinion, guffaws of laughter, grunts of outrage, deep tones of earnest conversation and the perspiring faces and red-rimmed eyes that signalled the end of another evening.

A quiet settled upon the crowd as they strained to hear the fragile melody. Subtly, John built on each note, making them stronger, stretching them longer, until the room echoed with a haunting sadness that tugged at the hearts of men exiled in an alien land. And now the music swelled with a violent aching pain and thundered with the rage of loss. One fierce note and it stopped, abruptly, and left men rocking gently on their chairs, yearning for more, each alone in their memories.

Aware of eyes upon him, John stood tall before he returned to his band members, falling into the bench space offered.

His new friend, Thomas slid a tankard of rum into John's hand. He would have been a handsome man were it not for the smallpox scars that marked his face. Like John he had fought for the king in America and, when the wars were over, had been tossed out to the streets with less than a few weeks' pay in his pocket. He had taken to stalking the highways, 'and re-lievin' gentlemen of their heavy wallets'. Only his war service had saved him from the hangman's gibbet.

John drank deeply. 'Better make this the last. Gotta be up for practice in six hours.'

'Need yer beauty sleep then? That ugly mug ain't doin' it for yer?' Thomas took another sip of his rum, relaxing back in his chair.

'Need my woman.' John thought of Mary. She would be tangled up in her sheets, the kids asleep on the floor or curled at her feet. He would cuddle up beside her and she would reach for him.

One, two, buckle my shoe
Three, four, lock the door,
Five, six, pick up sticks
Seven, eight, shut the gate.

'Aw, Johnnie. Give it back.'

John climbed the steep track that led to his house. Like most of the soldiers, he had his home in the area called 'The Rocks', where ramshackle huts and cottages crawled up the steep slope that overlooked the bay. They followed no pattern but nestled in every crack and corner, squeezed into every hollow and clung precariously to every outcrop. From where he perched, high above the town, John could imagine himself as an eagle looking down on the world. He could see the laneway in which the children played hopscotch, and where his young son raced away with the chalk they had been using as a marker, taunting them into a chase. The little rascal squeezed himself behind some barrels while five kids went flying by, knocking into the street vendors, pushing over barrows, cursing in high childish voices.

John widened his view. It was hard to recall the harbour as it once had been, those times when men and women with desperate eyes had gazed out to sea in the hopes of seeing a ship, their stomachs clenched in hunger. Now six ships, with the flags of six different countries, swayed on the gentle swell.

He grunted with some satisfaction when he recognised the Minorca, and already a dinghy had been dropped over its side to ferry passengers to shore. He fancied that the officer with the long legs and jaunty gait who even now was taking his seat was the lieutenant, for his friend Johnston was arriving today. He had been pardoned of any wrongdoing and had returned to take up his role as second-in-command. John had reason to feel pleased. He could start trading again and, maybe, start a business of his own. He caught sight of a street girl - she would pay coin for a little protection. The shopkeepers too. There was no end to what he could do with the lieutenant's good favour. A proper home for Mary. A girl to help her in the house.

His eye found his son again. The boy was struggling to pull up his sister who had tripped and fallen. *Whatever it takes. He'll have better than me.*

He took the last few steps into his house. It had none of the grandeur of his former cottage at Parramatta. Built against the rockface it was a single room only, and dark and damp. Mary raised her eyes to him from where she squatted, spewing over a bucket. She pushed back a lock of hair slick with sweat from her face and let out a small groan. 'Reckon I'm with child.'

John stopped in his tracks. Another child to keep safe. He sighed. Then it truly was time to get to work.

¬

July 1802

Rain stung his face, running down his cheeks like tears. He cursed as a stone slid from underfoot, throwing him off balance. *The imps from hell will be out on a night like this.* He clenched his right fist, reassured by the knuckle-duster that sat in his palm, alert to any movement, a shadow in a dark alley, someone desperate enough to endure the wind and wet for a few coins. And then he looked at the rose he carried in the other hand. And smiled.

He was glad he didn't need to negotiate the steep path where he had once lived. Only last month he had secured a room on the lower slopes in Cribbs Lane, and while the original tenant may have been reluctant to move, it had been necessary. Mary had had a troubled pregnancy and couldn't manoeuvre the climb.

He rounded the corner of the lane, pulling his jacket close as the wind near knocked him over, and felt a tight knot of worry as he saw the lamp alight in the window of his house, its reflection fluttering on the wet, black cobblestones. Mary should be asleep by now. The revelry at the officers' mess had lasted longer than usual, and he had stayed on talking and laughing, telling his stories, and putting off the moment when he would have to leave its warmth to struggle home.

The groan was low and guttural, wretched with pain. John threw himself through the door, stopping dead when he saw her writhing on the bed they shared. Two women knelt beside her. John recognised them as the neighbours who had offered to attend Mary during the birth. Sarah was the younger and she looked down as he barged in, studied the ground, fiddled with the hem of her dress. The other of the two – a stout, middle-aged woman known as Betty – looked up at him. She was as ugly a person as he had ever seen, and belonged, he thought, in the nightmares of a fairy story: the bad witch, complete with lank, grey hair, large nose, and unseemly warts.

But she always wore a smile that coaxed many a man into a happier mood. Not today.

''Bout time you turned up, but it's too late now.'

'Mary? The baby?'

'Baby's stuck. Facin' the wrong way. We can't get 'im out.'

'Then you're not doin' enuff. Cut it out if you have to but get it out of her.'

'She bin struggling nigh on twenty hours. Where were yer? She callin' you. Sent the kids out to find you. All I can say is if you have a Christian soul in that black body of yours, then you better start prayin', for only the God Almighty himself can help her now.'

Where was I? I wasn't nowhere. I was... He looked down at the rose he carried in his hand. He had taken it from George Johnston's garden. He always brought a rose back for Mary, to place upon the bench. He shook his head to clear it. He had met up with Lieutenant Johnston, Major Johnston now, shared drinks with him, spent time at his house. He hadn't come home last night. John fell to his knees, taking Mary's hand. It felt sticky and clammy, a heavy weight between his own two, not like her hand at all. He held it to his mouth and kissed it and put it to his cheek. He wanted those fingers to stroke his face as they used to, but they just hung, like those of a dead man. 'Mary, can you hear me? I'm here. I'm sorry, Mary. I didn't know you were due. I'm sorry.'

He thought he might have seen recognition in the half-closed eyes, but even at that moment, she let out another scream, arcing her body and throwing her head back.

'Nothin' you can do here but get in the way. Go get yerself drunk. Yer goin' to need it.'

John looked at the two women, women who dealt with this sort of thing, and though he shook his head as if to say no, and his eyes pleaded with them to let him stay, they shooed him away and he did as he was bid.

As he edged backwards towards the door, he stumbled over the cot he had made, just a box with rockers at the base. Mary had sewed a mattress and coverlet. A white gown, each tiny invisible stitch made with her hands, lay folded on top together with a baby shawl she had crocheted, staying up late at night, straining her eyes in the lamplight, while he played in the band and the kids slept. Each morning she held it up for him to see her progress, put it against his arm and made him feel how soft it was. He had nodded absently, 'Nice.'

He didn't go to find a tavern but sat on the doorstep with his back to the door, clasping the rose as if it alone could keep her alive. And though he strained to hear what went on inside, prayed for the cry of a newborn, the wind and the rain beat against the house and drowned all other sounds.

The squeals of a pig woke him from his drowse. Bleary eyed, he watched as the butcher threw the head into a barrel and then slashed the belly to let the guts fall out into the tray beneath. Rivulets of blood trickled down the lane, eddying in pools between the paving stones before soaking into the dirt. The pig was dead, but the screams didn't stop. Suddenly awake, he thrust open the door and rushed to Mary's side, knocking over the crib and treading the pretty, white baby gown, and the fine, lacy shawl into the muddy floor.

He caught Mary's last whimper as she lapsed into unconsciousness, her face as white as the baby clothes had been, her breath shallow and fast and ineffective, running a race she couldn't win.

Betty kneeled between Mary's legs, trying hopelessly to stem the flow of blood, ringing out red, sodden cloths into a bowl before reapplying the pressure, and though she made small soothing noises, the shake of her head, back and forth, said all that needed to be said.

Sarah held a bundle wrapped in a sheet, with the look of one who had received a gift she did not want and didn't know what to do. She gazed around for somewhere to put it, unwilling to lie it in the cradle that had been built to nurse the dreams of a newborn, or place it on the table next to the pots and pans. So, she held it in stiff, unwelcoming arms, supporting the neck as though it mattered.

Fearful of disturbing his wife, John did not sit on the mattress, but knelt beside it as if in prayer, his head bowed. Time stopped and the world and their room dissolved. Just he and she shared this space and he would have stayed like that for a thousand years, listening to the panicked beats of her heart, feeling the warmth of her hand in his, but he heard her last silent breath. He knew the moment she left, when the soul abandoned the body and all that remained was the corpse that had held her. The rose fell from his fingers. He searched the room, praying that she might see him. *I love you. Please hear me.* And the weight of all those times when he had left the words unsaid, when she had reached for him to be turned away, choked in his chest, so heavy he could not breathe. *Oh god, Mary, I can't live without you. Don't leave me, please.* But only her carcass remained.

'May she rest in peace,' Betty whispered. 'We'll give you a moment, John.' The woman struggled to her feet and nodded at Sarah that she should leave. The younger woman held the bundle up, questioning.

'Give him to his father. He needs his time to grieve.'

But John had already stood and brushed past the two of them to make his escape, convinced he would shatter from the howling in his brain.

Chapter Forty-Nine

1802

John buried Mary with her unnamed infant beneath grey skies and a drizzling rain. He was glad of the weather, for in this hazy netherworld of dim shapes and blunted edges, nothing seemed real or solid, and he could pretend he walked in a dream, and just as he pulled his jacket tight to protect himself from the cold, so too did he keep his heart battened down. Only when he threw the first sod of soil into the grave and heard the hollow plop as it fell upon the coffin, did it tear apart; and he thought he might not be able to bear it, that it would be better if he could be buried with her. He stifled the scream that threatened to shatter him and kept his face blank but gripped his son's hand with such pressure that the boy screwed up his face and looked up at his father. 'Ow.'

From the shadows, Ol' Ma sought to comfort him. She whispered to him, but he wasn't ready to listen. He knew the words she spoke. Knew the words she wanted from him.

Not now, Ol' Ma. Not yet.

'Poor little blighters. All alone. Who will care for them now?'

'Maybe ... the Orphans' School?'

'Why can't their father look after them?'

'Him? That man ain't got no heart. Heard he didn't even mourn his wife. Just up and left the moment she passed.'

'That's the truth of it.' The last speaker was Sarah. 'He just left me holdin' that dead babe. Sure as I didn't know what to do with it. He walked out, fine as you please. Aw,' – she paused, her eyes moistened with the memory – 'it was so sad. That pretty robe she had made for the christening? He just trod it underfoot. Betty had to wash it for the burial an' all.'

'Heart as black as his skin.'

The three women threw glances to the place where John lounged against the wall, John Martin at his side. The women may have thought they were being discreet, but their lust for the gossip had given their whispers a higher pitch and agitated their gestures. To John's eyes they looked like a bunch of squawking hens pecking over the remains of yesterday's meal. He raised his middle finger at them, pleased to see that they clucked harder and faster, horrified and delighted by this new outrage – fuel for scandal for days to come.

'Really?' John Martin shook his head. 'You had to do that?'

John shrugged and took another swig of rum.

'To Major Johnston!' He raised his glass. Though Major Johnston had been held under house arrest since his return nearly eight months ago, he had supplied barrels of rum and platters of chicken and pork for the wake.

'To Major Johnston!' Members of John's battalion cheered the most popular officer in the NSW Corps.

'So? What will you do with the children?' John Martin asked. His casual tone failed to hide a vested interest.

John cocked his head, curious. 'Why do you ask?'

'Ann is barren. We have the farm. I have a job with the constabulary. We could look after 'em for you.' John Martin faltered, failing to sound nonchalant.

John heard the room fall quiet, every ear veered in his direction, every breath held lest it muffle the reply, eyes turned studiously away. He nodded, the gesture of a man who understood the question, found it of interest and was considering it, but had not yet agreed. He scanned the crowd for his children.

John Junior had climbed onto the bench and sat cross-legged, surrounded by discarded tankards of rum, most empty, but not all, by the look on the boy's face. One by one, he was picking them up to drain of their last dregs. *Just turned five*, thought John, *and already more than I can handle*. He wondered whether he should give the child a hiding or simply send him to bed, but even as he considered the matter, the boy gave a shudder and heaved up the contents of his belly. That and tomorrow's headache would be better than a beating, so bed it was. Shaking his head, John walked over to the bench where he was greeted by a small boy with sorry eyes and a woebegone expression. As John bent to pick him up, the boy wrapped his arms around John's neck and lay his head on his shoulder. John paused, savouring the weight of the child's body on his. He dropped a kiss on the boy's head, screwing up his nose at the stink of puke. He stopped to ladle some water from the pail and carried the boy to the pile of bedding in the corner of the room. Minnie was already there, hunched against the wall, her eyes red and swollen, her mother's shawl tangled in her hands and held against her face. With a nudge of his foot, John moved her over so he could lay down his son, already asleep on his shoulder and snoring loud as any drunk. 'Welcome to your first hangover,' John muttered as he pulled the blankets around him.

Minnie looked up at him, her dark eyes wary.

He hated that look. It made him want to kick her. 'What are you doing with that?' he motioned at the shawl. 'It's not yours.'

She cringed further into the wall, clutching the shawl tighter, her face crumpled in a mixture of defiance and despair. Tears gathered in the corner of her eyes. For a second John thought he might pick her up and wring her neck. Instead, he wrenched the shawl from her hold and stuffed it carelessly into his belt.

But with the warmth of John Junior's small body still on his skin, and the memory of those trusting eyes turned upon him, he returned to John Martin. 'No one's taking my kids.'

Chapter Fifty

He paused in his walk, fingers moving to the beat of the music that played in his head, fixed on getting the tune right. He had woken with it running around his brain, a haunting melody, it captured the winds howling across empty plains. But it was one that soothed him, and he had been fine-tuning it all day. It filled the lonely spaces of his mind. His right hand clutched a sack to his chest. He scarcely noticed the people who swerved around him until one portly gentleman poked him with his cane, 'You're blocking the lane.'

John looked up and held his eyes. Entitlement drained from the other's face. Flustered, the gentleman moved aside.

John's smile was one of contempt as he pushed through the piece of putrid material that hung in the doorway of the butcher shop and failed to keep the flies away.

With a quizzical look at the sack in John's arm, the butcher nudged a scrawny chicken across the counter to him. 'What's in the sack.'

'Nought to do with you.' John picked up the chicken with two fingers and dangled it by its feet, frowning. 'What am I supposed to do with this?' he asked, pinching the flaccid skin.

'It's all I got, John. Truth to tell, I coulda sold it many a times today. But I knew you'd be in. Kept it back for yer, I did.' A stout man, with strong, hairy arms and big fists, the butcher could throw a pig over his shoulder with no problem but couldn't hold John's gaze. He wiped his hands on the blood-streaked apron. He picked up the broom to sweep the gore-soaked sawdust into the street and put it down again. A black, frustrated cloud of flies buzzed around his ankles.

Business was difficult in the rowdy, dangerous streets of The Rocks where neighbours turned a blind eye to muggings, or couldn't say who set a wagon on fire, or walked past at a trot, their mouths closed tight, eyes averted when a street gang crowded into a shop and cleaned it out. John had made the most of the opportunity, and the price of a chicken or a leg of lamb or a string of sausages kept the butcher safe. And if John were seen walking the streets, whistling and carrying a large box of peaches, or slabs of cheese, or wearing fine boots that maybe he couldn't afford on his salary as a private in the corps, then no one asked questions. The Rum Corps looked after their own. And John's friend, Major George Johnston, was acting commander-in-chief of the corps.

'Ain't good enough. Can't feed my kids on this.' John swung the chicken in the face of the butcher. Its head wobbled obscenely, catching the man on the chin. 'You must have over-looked somethin'.'

The butcher glanced towards the bin. John caught the look.

'Ah! There it is. Fancy forgetting that.' He grinned, reaching to claim his prize.

'Um. Yeah. Well, no. That's for my wife. She's coming any minute now. Got held up or else it would be already in the cooking pot.' He appealed to John, forcing a smile. 'You know what she's like. Give me hell if I ain't kept nothin' for her.'

'Here. Give her this.' John let the unfortunate chicken fall to the floor to roll in the sawdust. The flies swooped upon it. He patted the butcher on the shoulder. Smiling, and with a perky little wave, he strolled out, carrying two plump birds and one sack.

John knew the man hated him. And accepted it. He had fought for his place in Sydney Town. He was a man to be reckoned with. *Can you see me now, Mother? Is this what you wanted?* But if she heard him, there were no words of approval.

And if he was plagued with dreams at night, abandoned in the empty wastelands, in a battle ground of craters and dead men and unable to find a way home; if he called out for Calvin or Mary and they didn't come. Then, that was just fair exchange.

¬

He made his next call. He found Nellie, the seamstress, supervising her girls in the courtyard behind her house. In truth, he visited here more often than business demanded. In the soft light, the girls made a pretty picture, surrounded by folds of glistening fabric, bright ribbons and bows. A pin tucked into a mouth, a strand of lace draped carelessly over a shoulder, gleaming hair gathered neatly into caps. They talked quietly together as they sewed, a gentle hum in harmony with the spring day, part of the chorus of insects and birds and rustling leaves. The streets of Sydney Town might not have existed.

They were the lucky ones: rescued by Nellie the moment they arrived on the convict transports, taught a skill, provided accommodation and food, if not a wage. They glanced up at the newcomer as he came in, and quickly down again, as could be expected from demure young mistresses. John gave an appreciative whistle and winked as one of the needlewoman defied decorum and raised mischievous eyes to him. Nellie was scrutinising the neckline of a brocaded dress of russets and blue while a young convict girl looked on anxiously. 'Take a break.' Nellie waved away her employee, making space for John.

He sat with the sack at his feet, and rubbed his neck, the tension already leaving his shoulders, a genuine smile on his face for the first time that day. He did not belong here. It was not his home. But he breathed easily in this gentle space.

He picked up the dress they had been working on. 'Beauti-ful,' he said, running his hands over the fabric. 'Reminds me of a sunset sky.'

'Didn't figure you as a poet, Randall.'

'Maybe you should get to know me better.' He wiggled his eyebrows.

Nellie laughed in spite of herself, a full deep-throated laugh. She had arrived in the colony as a convict and built herself a thriving business in this place of men. Her laugh had the confidence of a woman comfortable with herself. 'Alright then. What've you got?'

'Bolts of silk, colours like you never saw. Party season comin' up. Those ladies be wanting their pretty dresses.' He told her the price. Major Johnston had been stockpiling the cloth and determined that now was the moment to sell.

'Daylight robbery. Nothing's worth that.'

'Ah, but that's the catch, you see. Who puts the value on a robe? Ain't like it falls from heaven with the price neatly scribed upon it.' He raised his eyes to the sky, arms spread wide as if waiting for it.

Nellie shook her head, her mouth tight in exasperation.

'No, it's what people will pay,' John continued. 'And those pretty ladies you sew for? They will sell their own mother if they can swish around a ballroom in one of your gowns made of this silk.' Nellie looked doubtful. 'And truth to say. They won't be seen dead in a gown they already worn and where you getting new cloth from if it's not from my friend, the Major?'

Nellie sighed. 'You're killin' me, Randall. But tell me true now. You goin' to sell direct to the officers?'

John nodded. 'Could be. But I'll give you the better deal. You know I always look after you, Nellie. You can sell it on to them cheaper than they can buy it themselves and make a tidy profit in the meantime.'

The woman nodded. 'I need cottons, too. Got some linen?'

They discussed prices and made a time when she could come and look for herself and confirm the order. Pleased with his work, John picked up the sack he had been carrying. 'One more thing.'

Earlier that day he had rescued it from the banks of a river, where it had snagged on some bushes. He had heard the mewing from within, had realised what it contained and had told himself to walk on by. Not his business. But he might at least un-tie the neck of the sack and release them. He could do that. Three kittens had crawled out. Three others lay dead inside. A tiny black blur of fur raced blindly towards the river and he reached out to turn it to safety. It spat at him. Outraged and scared and prepared to fight for his life, baring its tiny claws. *Like a little puma, you are.*

He had stood to walk away but swore softly as the kitten yet again raced toward the river, not knowing where home or sanctuary lay. Shaking his head, John had retrieved the sack and the three kittens.

One he had given to the lieutenant. He pulled the black one out now, his little puma, holding it by the nape of its neck. It mewed, its eyes huge in a skeleton face.

'You need a ratter?' he asked Nellie.

She looked at the tiny furball, now planted against his chest, and snuggling down under his chin. John stroked it clumsily, for his hand was bigger than the kitten.

'Couldn't just abandon it,' he said to a question that hadn't been asked. 'Think it could find a nice home here, company for you.' He sounded almost envious.

'You could keep it.' Her voice was soft.

He had the kitten on his lap now and was tickling its tummy. 'Nah, I'm not good at looking after things. They have a habit of dying on me.' He spoke lightly as if it were a joke.

Nellie shook her head. 'I'll look after it.' Her voice cracked. Then, as if pulling herself together, 'And you can put away them sad eyes, too.'

With a nod and a smile, John got up to leave. He hunched his shoulders as if preparing to face a storm and then he grinned. He glanced at the girl with the 'come hither' eyes and gestured in the direction of the public house. She would be finished work in an hour or so.

'And you, Nellie?' John turned to the older woman, 'When will you come and enjoy a drink with me? Or...' He winked.

Nellie rolled her eyes. 'Not if you were the last man on God's good earth.' But she was teasing the kitten with a ball of wool and her eyes stayed on him as he walked out, the sack with the remaining cat in his arm.

¬

He stopped in the doorway of the pub, letting his eyes adjust to the light, his ears to the noise and coughing at the smoke. He spotted Thomas and threaded through the crowds to reach him. A path opened before him. Some offered a greeting, too hearty, but many looked away or stepped back.

'You look like the cat.-.who didn't get the cream.' John laughed as he looked at the sack. 'Thinking of which, wonder if I can get some cream here.'

Thomas shook his head, confused. Even if he had seen the cat in the sack, he may not have understood. He was not a bright man. And if John suspected that the man's only interest in him was to bask in his notoriety or exploit his connections, then this suited him. It was, perhaps, why John associated with him. He wanted no demands, not for real friendship.

John waved an arm for a jug. 'My shout. What's up then?'

'Been on guard duty all week. You wouldn't understand.' Thomas turned sulky eyes on him. 'You wear the uniform, play in the band, but ain't ever seen you rostered for anything.' He frowned, then spat out his problem. 'They got me scheduled for Norfolk Island. I can't go. Wife won't have it. Can you talk to someone for me?' There was no need to name the 'someone'.

John didn't like asking favours for others; didn't want George to think he was taking advantage. 'Maybe.' He dug down into his sack. 'If you take this.' He thrust the kitten at a bemused Thomas. 'Gift for your wife, like?' He lay a hand on George's outreached arm. 'Gotta treat it right, though.'

It relieved him to be rid of the last of them. He had feared taking it home, seeing the joy in Johnnie's eyes, having to deal with the heartbreak when the little mite ran beneath the wheels of a cart, or got attacked by a dog, or simply diseased and died.

John broke into a smile as a young girl with that look in her eyes appeared in the doorway. In the dark room, crowded with men, loud with argument and talk, and where most of the other women were on the game, she looked unexpectedly shy. 'Now, if you'll excuse me.' He waved her over.

Chapter Fifty-One

September 1806

'Mares and sows. Mares and sows being served at the docks.' The bell ringer wandered through the streets, sounding his bell, singing his song and leaving chaos in his wake. Rich men, poor men, fat men and thin downed their tools, shut up their shops, broke ranks and ran for the docks. A new transport of female convicts was being unloaded. There were ten men to every woman in the colony, and those men notched the days in anticipation of these arrivals. And though the women would be sorted to work in the convict factories, they were not provided accommodation. This was the moment, when they arrived without homes or husbands, dazed and afraid and unsteady on their legs, when they could be snatched up and taken to wife.

John lounged at the barracks. He had found a warm spot in the spring sunshine, protected from the breeze, and had stripped off his jacket to bask like a lizard, listening to the idle chat of the soldiers around him. He had woken at the commotion and shut his eyes again. He hated these events. They reminded him too much of the slave sales. He had never seen a convict woman have her mouth forced open and her teeth inspected, be made to bend down to be prodded or poked, but it was, in his opinion, much the same. Men still walked up the lines, made crude comments about the size of her hips, or the flatness of her breasts, and jostled each other at the thought of getting laid while the women shivered in frightened, confused horror. No, he would stay here and relish the peace. Besides, he found plenty of women to bed; married or single, pretty or not, it didn't matter. He got what he needed and didn't want more.

'Come with me. Help me look.' Thomas had lost his wife to the flu a few months ago and was keen to find another.

'Can understand why you might want my help,' John yawned and stretched, 'ugly bugger that you are. But not today.'

But Thomas grabbed his wrist and hauled him to his feet. 'You may find someone.'

'I sincerely hope not.' And it was the truest thing he had ever said. No one would ever again reach into his heart. Nor did he allow the memories of Mary to leak from his box. To do so would knock him to his knees, drowning beneath a tsunami of pain.

They joined the shoving, shouting crowd at the docks to amble along the lines of women who huddled together in groups of two or three, their belongings wrapped in a shawl, clutched to their chest. Some gathered their last shred of courage to hold as a shield and met the stares of the men with blank, defiant faces. Others returned the curses, tit for tat, and others still had donned a smiling mask, seeking to please.

'Could bed her.' A skinny runt stood in front of a short, acne-faced woman, his legs apart, a trader discussing his cattle. 'But wouldn't want to wake up with her.'

'Now that's what I like, a bit of rump.'

John turned to Thomas, 'I've had enough. See you back at the barracks.' He had reached the far edges of the crowd when he noticed a small, skinny girl, her arms clasped around her chest, standing by herself, separated from the protection of the herd. Straggly, mousey hair fell over her face, but as she raised her head to look longingly after her friend who walked away with an officer, John caught sight of two dove-grey eyes, black-rimmed and long-lashed. She caught his gaze and dropped her eyes to the ground again. *I can still see you,* he didn't say.

'I reckon you can come with me, love!' A barrel-chested man stood inches before her, a toothless grin on his face.

She stepped back, one skinny hand raised against him, a sparrow fluttering in the face of a bear. He grabbed her wrist.

'No need to be shy. Ain't like you got nowheres else to go.' With his trousers held up by a piece of cord and his feet bare, he looked like what he was, a local bully-boy who took whatever work he could find, regardless of what it entailed. He and John had scuffled more than once, fighting over the same prize. She twisted from his grip.

'You be nice to me and I'll be nice to you.' He had her elbow now, gripping it tightly, and moved to drag her away.

She crumpled in the dust, feet splayed out in front of her, pulling against him.

'I don't think she's accepted your offer, Warton.' John stepped forward. *Fine filly like that don't belong to a mule like him.*

'What's it your business.' Warton kicked the girl.

'Rules are rules. Can't force someone to go with you.' John caught sight of Thomas and signalled him over. A small group gathered around, prepared for some entertainment. John didn't want to fight. He had a suspicion that the younger man would get the better of him, and his reputation was only as good as his last fight.

'Leave her alone,' he repeated as Thomas sidled up, staying a step behind.

With a curse, Warton let the girl drop. 'Be seein' you sometime, Randall.' He strode away.

John frowned down at the pitiful scrap that lay in the dirt. He didn't need or want her, but with a sigh, he offered his hand to haul her up. She took it, eyes huge in a tiny face, reminding him of the kittens.

Ah! *The kittens.*

'I think I know a place for you,' he said finally.

Nellie growled at John when he landed the girl on her door-step. 'Can't keep takin' all your scraps, Randall. You gotta stop pickin' things up off the street.' She looked the girl up and down. 'And what's yer name then?'

'Fanny.' Calmer in the presence of the older woman and re-assured by the other girls who sat in the sun, sewing and chatting quietly to themselves, she raised her head to look directly at Nellie. 'And I can sew. Me marm taught me.'

'No promises.' Nellie dismissed John.

January 1807

John perched on a stool inside McKay's pub, wiping froth from Fanny's mouth, his fingers lingering and tracing the lines of her lips, which was hard because she kept laughing and spluttering beer down her chin. Fanny wasn't Mary. She was nothing like Mary. But she had refused to go away. She had a will of steel, and a backbone of iron. At first, he had bellowed at her, his face purple with anger. 'I have no place for the likes of you, or anyone for that matter.' She had stood before him, head hung low, tears pooling in her eyes, but she hadn't turned from him. She had followed him home like an unwanted kitten, had helped with the meal, made John Junior take a wash and shown young Mary how to repair her mother's shawl, and then taken herself back to Nellie's.

She's a resourceful little thing, Ol' Ma had said, thoughtfully. *And you stay out of it.*

Eventually, Fanny had moved in, but when she had told him she was with child, he had sighed, 'I'm not goin' to marry you. And the kid ain't taking my name.' Then he took her by the shoulders, looking her in the eyes. 'I told you before. I can't love you. Ain't got any love left.' He spoke as gently as he could. 'I'll see you don't want for anything though. I won't abandon you.'

Fanny remained silent for a long time, gazing into his eyes. 'But you do, John. You do love me. You're just not man enough to admit it.'

He growled in exasperation and made to turn away, but she stopped him.

'And he will have your name, John Randall. But I ain't getting married. Can't get married without a priest, and ain't no priests gonna marry you.' Her chin had jutted out in that stubborn way she had and he knew there would be no changing her mind. 'Anyways' – she looked at him – 'are you even a Christian? All I ever hear is you talking about those black gods of yours from Africa.'

He had shrugged.

'Gotta moment, John?'

John Martin stood before him, a parcel in his arms, possibly a leg of pork from the farm. John grinned, acknowledging the gift, but then cocked his head to one side. 'What's up?' John Martin, a solid tree trunk of a man who had stood beside him in every crisis, an unflappable man who absorbed every blow, shifted his weight from foot to foot, as if the world had become unbalanced.

He had seen a lot of his friend this past year. Ever since John Martin's wife Ann had died, John Martin had become a frequent visitor, arriving without notice, happy to lounge around the house talking to the children for a few hours before setting out on the long journey back to Parramatta. *Lonely*, thought John. It seemed a cruel fate that Ann had died just as the farm had begun to turn a profit and John Martin had become almost affluent. He even employed workers to help him now.

His friend mouthed something that couldn't be heard in the confined space, crowded with drunken revellers. With a jerk of his head, he gestured for John to follow him outside.

John followed, blinking in the daylight after the smoky darkness of the tavern.

A young girl joined them, a slight child with a look of glowering defiance on her face, and stubborn eyes that refused to back down from his.

'What are you doin' here?' he asked his daughter. 'Ain't you got work to do at home?'

She didn't reply, just jutted out her chin a little further. He thought maybe she had been taking lessons from Fanny. He almost laughed, surprised, and pleased, to see the fight in her. 'What's this, then?'

John Martin licked his lips, taking his time, hunting for the right words. He took a deep breath. 'Minnie's coming with me. Live at the farm, like.'

John choked on the mouthful of beer he had been sipping. He stared first at one and then the other, shaking his head as if he had been struck. How old was the girl now? Did she even have breasts? 'She's only fourteen' he objected. 'An' you're older than me.'

Chapter Fifty-Two

November 1807

'That there's Black Randall.'

John liked the sound of these words and heard them often as he stalked the laneways of 'The Rocks', where he lived. He liked the slightly hushed voice in which they were uttered. There was respect in those words.

And so he nodded at the three urchins who had turned to stare at him. Crouched in a circle, they made a small, tight, band of trouble. One held a rat, battered and bloody, tied by a string to a stick. They had been taking turns to swing it through the air against a wall.

'Afternoon, Master Randall,' the bravest of the three called out. 'Got somfink fer us?'

'Boys,' John acknowledged, flipping them a brass coin.

He walked on, eyes ranging ahead, searching the shadows for signs of trouble, but turned eventually into Cribbs lane. It was the room he had shared with Mary. It was where he still lived. His neighbour, Betty, the same who had been at Mary's death, was sweeping her front step with strong, vigorous strokes of the broom, as if she would sweep her way to China. She shot him a sour look and retreated inside before he passed.

The strong, gamey whiff of rabbit stew pulled him up short and he smiled. Fanny had hinted at a surprise this evening. He would die before giving her the satisfaction of saying so, but her stews were better than those of Ol' Ma, flavoured with strange herbs she traded at the market and often a good slug of beer. His stomach growled as he ducked under the doorway, and into the small room.

The roses snagged him first. Rich, red blooms sat in a jug on a white cloth on the bench. He shook his head. New yellow curtains fluttered in the windows.

In the shadows at the far end, Mary – her back towards him, her hair tucked up in a neat little cap – crooned a tune to the babe in her arms. She swayed, ever so gently, settling the child to sleep.

John stumbled sideways, reaching out to the bench for balance and knocking the jug to the ground. It shattered. Petals and thorns and shafts of clay lay in a muddy puddle on the earthen floor. For a moment he wondered if it had all been a night mare. And now he were awake. Mary had never died. She was here with him.

'Oh!' It was Fanny who swung around, the baby at her breast. 'What happened?' With her head cocked on one side, a question in her eyes, she came to greet him. Handing him the baby she stooped down to retrieve the flowers.

'Are you feeling alright?' Grey eyes, Fanny's eyes, not Mary's, regarded him. 'Do you like them?' Her hand swung round at the new curtains. She stood and, self-consciously and a little awkwardly, twirled to show the dress she had remodelled – Mary's dress – to fit herself.

John still leant against the bench. He scarcely heard the words over the heavy beating of his heart, the rushing of blood in his ears. He swallowed as he tried to organise this topsy turvy world into some rational shape.

'I thought to make it more of a home. It doesn't feel like home.' Mary stumbled on. She stood and brushed her hands against the dress. 'I thought you liked roses.'

He fled.

John stumbled home, a bottle in his hand. Fanny sat on the doorstep, her bodice open, feeding the baby. The same place John had sat on the night of Mary's death. She said nothing but made space for him next to her.

He slumped down, taking a swig of liquor. 'This isn't my home. You're not Mary,' he said, as if it were an explanation.

'No. I'm Fanny.' Her clear grey eyes regarded him. 'And it's about time you took a good long look at me.'

John let his head fall into his hands, rubbing his eyes, his cheeks.

'And something else,' she continued. 'You're right. This isn't a home, but it's about time you made it one. You need to belong somewhere.'

He had no words for her. He felt so weighed down, shackled to a chest of pain and fear and grief, that he wondered he could even breathe. He didn't even know who he was any more. Old words drifted back to him. *Master of my own fate.* That's a joke.

'What is it you want, John? I'm tired of tip-toeing round you.'

He looked at her and then let his head slump into his hands. 'I don't know. I don't know what I want. I just want to stop feelin' like this.'

Something Ol' Ma had said, so long ago, when he was just a boy, nibbled at his mind. *A man can be free and roam the world but still wear chains.*

Chapter Fifty-Three

12 January 1808 Aged 44

Sydney Town heaved under the blazing heat. Citizens sheltered in groups, muttering and cursing and throwing suspicious glances across their shoulders. Some looked skyward for signs of the storm. It was coming. There was no stopping it. They waited for the change; for the wind that would drive up from the south; for the clouds to open; for the rains that would settle the dust and wash them clean; for release from the simmering tension.

The governor, Bligh, was implementing his plans for a new Sydney Town. He tore down the homes of soldiers and shopkeepers. They cluttered his dreams for parkland and gardens. Homes that provided shelter and comfort to a family, that marked a legacy of a hard-won life – they all came tumbling down. No one knew who would be the next to be tossed onto the streets.

And so, John prowled the rows and alleyways. He watched and listened. Occasionally, he thought he caught sight of Eligua, racing around a corner or somersaulting from a barrow, throwing him a gleeful grin, or perhaps it was just his imagination. Only one thing was certain. His world was at a crossroads. The town was like tinder-wood. Ready to explode into flames. And when it did? He wondered where he might land; what he might find.

Yerself maybe? Lost him a long while ago.

He wasn't surprised to hear the voice of Ol' Ma. He had been thinking of her often, longing for her guidance. He smiled.

'Is it really broken?'

'No.' Johnston's arm hung in a sling, held close to his chest. 'But tell me of the mood in town.'

They sat in Johnston's lounge room and John marvelled at the calm. The scent of dried flowers, the swish of silk as Esther entered the room with tea, the sound of children playing on manicured lawns – there was no indication of the shadows that crept towards them.

'All hell has broken loose. They're calling for you.'

In an effort to quell opposition, Governor Bligh had over-stepped his mark. He had arrested John Macarthur, a wealthy landowner and voice of the people. And in a show of defiance, the courts had released him. Now, led by Macarthur, the people bayed for Bligh's blood.

'Damned if this isn't a fine mess. Bligh has sent for my aid. If I support him my own officers might turn against me. Should I side with them, I'll be leading a rebellion and committing treason against the king. Here, pass my tea, will you?' Johnston ran his one free hand through his hair

'And the arm?'

'An excuse to bury my head in the sand. Stay at home and do nothing.'

John snorted, spilling his tea, trying not to laugh and failing.

After a moment, George chuckled too. He shrugged. 'Worth a try.'

They tensed at the rumbling of a carriage up the drive-way, quick footsteps on the path, the opening of the door, and the voice of John Harris, a senior officer, demanding to see Johnston urgently.

With a nod to his friend, John excused himself. 'I'll leave you to your business.'

'God's curse,' was the only reply he got.

But as John headed out, he knew what happened to those who stuck their head in the sand. Got their bum shot off. And he felt an aching need to protect his friend – with his own body if need be – but he couldn't think of a single thing to do.

John never learnt what words Harris used to stir Major Johnston from his flower-scented room, with its pretty china cups and the laughter of children drifting through the open windows, but that same night he watched as his friend rode into town, his arm still in a sling. He heard the cheers of the soldiers, drunk on Macarthur's wine, shipped from Cape Town and distributed freely. He watched as they waved their rifles in the air, stamped their feet and called for an end to tyranny.

And still he watched as merchants and bankers, the chief constable, the gaoler, reporters and craftsmen gathered around Major Johnston, their voices raised, calling for his action. They called for rebellion. He read the curse on his friend's lips.

As the contingent retired indoors, a hush fell on the town. The citizens of Sydney waited. They could have held their breath, so quickly did events move.

'Johnston proclaims himself Lieutenant Governor.'

'Call to arms. We march on Bligh.'

That night, bonfires were lit. Flames soared into the sky. Immense shadows – grotesquely misshapen – cavorted across the town.

And John joined in the celebrations; he cheered and danced and played in the band; he drank free wine and clapped his neighbours on their shoulders. But it felt to him more like a wake.

They had found Bligh hiding under the bed. He had been arrested, and John's friend George Johnston was now acting Governor. And a traitor to England.

A log exploded, sending sparks into the sky. They flashed brightly and died. He thought of his friend and imagined Johnston's head on the block – the fall of the blade, the head rolling away, its lifeless eyes staring up at him.

1809

Cloud and mist swallowed the tiny boat. From his position on the heads, John had watched while the ship got smaller and fainter and then disappeared. Still, he could not move. His friend, Lieutenant Governor Johnston, was on that vessel, heading towards England and court martial for his part in the Rum Rebellion and the imprisonment of Governor Bligh. John would have sent up a prayer, imploring the gods to keep him safe, but he knew the gods did not listen. He tucked up the collar of his jacket and walked home. *Fuck the gods.*

The Rocks had battened down against the storm. Deserted streets and empty shops. Doors fastened tight. Just the squeal of wind as it whistled around corners, the flap of a discarded sack caught on a fence, the drip of water off the eaves. He gave the front door an extra heave to open it, knowing it swelled and stuck in wet weather.

The warmth of the room hit him as he entered. A fire smouldered in the hearth against the back wall, and smoke from the wet wood clung to the ceiling, mingling with the smell of lamb stew, potatoes and carrots and celery. His son, Johnnie, only just thirteen, had found work on the trawlers that traded up and down the coast and would be leaving tomorrow. He crawled now around the floor, his bum in the air, barking like a dog to the screaming delight of the baby Thomas – for Fanny had borne a second child – who struck out with harmless fists.

His eldest son reminded John of a young deer: long, lanky legs that seemed too big for him; curly hair, soft, not tight like his own that fell in knots around his face; and he hated the child for sneaking into his heart, only to leave. He had warned him against working on the boats.

'It's alright for you,' Johnnie had pouted, 'You've travelled. You've seen the world.'

'Yeah, well why don't you go see America. That could be fun for yer,' John had said before storming away. He had never talked of slavery.

And now the boy was leaving him. 'What are you? A bitch or a dog?' John asked. ''Cause they like bitches on those boats. Young skinny ones like you.'

His son jerked back on his haunches.

It was Mary's face that turned to him, her eyes, so hurt he wished he could reach out and pull back his words. The boy truly was beautiful.

He reminds me of you, Ol' Ma whispered.

I was a slave when I was his age. Master controlled every-thing I did.

And now? There was the hint of challenge in her words. *You be just like the master. If that ain't control, I don't know what is.*

Fanny leant against a wall, her hand on her hip, some sewing discarded on the floor beside her rocking chair. 'John, it's his last night. Why spoil things!'

'Just sayin'.' John swallowed and tried again. 'Not the sharks in the ocean you need to worry about. It's the ones on the boat. And if they see you bleed, there will be a feedin' frenzy. Stand tall and don't let them see you bleed.' He looked away and then back again before adding, 'Worried about you, is all.'

Fanny smiled. So did Ol' Ma.

Fanny changed the subject. 'I sent word to Minnie and John Martin. Asked them to come tonight. Bring the baby.'

Minnie had given birth to a boy, twelve months ago now. John had still not seen him. He cocked an eye in question.

Fanny shook her head. 'No.'

'Good. Can't get used to him rootin' my daughter.'

¬

31 December 1809

He should have been in uniform and playing with his band. He could hear them from the parade ground, beating out a tune that was too cheerful, too lively, but he had called in sick and instead lounged on this street corner, too weary for words, and watched as the 73rd Regiment marched past. The new troops had arrived from England and now marched through the town to the parade grounds where they would take official control. Disciplined, he thought, as he studied them. Not one soldier turned a curious eye to glance sideways at the town or the people who booed and cheered as they felt fit. They must be curious, though, about this country they had been sent to tame, the rebels they had been sent to quell. But they marched with single purpose, with the authority of England and the Crown. They would put to rights this far-flung colony, and every beat of their drum felt like a nail in his coffin. He heard but couldn't see as arms were presented, and the NSW Corps, his personal haven, was dissolved.

¬

The tavern jostled with the men of the 73rd Regiment.

'Whatcha gonna do?' John asked Thomas. 'Transfer to the 73rd?'

Thomas shook his head. 'Joinin' the constabulary. You?'

John looked down at his belly, at the beginning of a paunch. He was still a good-looking man, and fit for his age, but closer to fifty than forty. He rolled his eyes. 'Can you see me running up and down a parade ground?'

He held his tankard in two hands, gazing at the froth on his beer, lost in thought. *Its good. Isn't that what Ol' Ma says?* And though he had no job, and no influential friends, he felt somehow excited about the future.

'Well?' Thomas prompted. 'Whatcha going to do?'

John shrugged. 'I'd like to get out of this town. Always happiest in the bush, when I'm hunting. Saw this place once. Pittwater. Little finger of land, curving around a bay. Like it's calling me.' He shrugged.

'There's nothing out there.' Thomas looked confused. 'No farm land. Nothing. You can't survive out there on your own.'

'I can.'

'You even have money for a boat? To get supplies? How you going to earn a quid? What's Fanny gonna think?'

John shrugged again. Fanny wasn't going to like it.

Chapter Fifty-Four

January 1810

The butcher chattered with the customers, his voice too brittle, his movements a little jerky. He pretended to ignore John standing in the corner, but, sure enough, he fumbled the coins he was handed, dropping them to the floor.

John bent, picked up the silver pieces and handed them to him with a smile. 'Almost makes me feel like a paying customer.'

'What can I do for you, Randall?' The butcher slid the coins into his box and finally raised his eyes to John, fleetingly, before they fell down again.

John looked at him, considering. His package usually waited for him, wrapped and ready. He reached out, snatched a fly from the air, and dropped it dead onto the counter. 'The usual.' He did not take his eyes from the butcher who squirmed under the scrutiny, but stood his ground.

'Ain't got nothin' for yer. Not less you pay like everyone else.' The words exploded from the butcher's mouth as if shot from a cannon, reverberating around the tiny shop.

John had expected this moment but he kept his face blank, his eyes cold. He had no wage, no goods to sell. He had only his reputation and now it seemed even that had worn thin. 'Like to explain yerself?' was all he asked.

'They cleanin' up this place. Constables looking out for us.'

John held the man's eye, then straightened up and grabbed a duck that hung from the ceiling. 'Consider it a parting gift.' He flourished it in the air and left the shop, tearing the curtain from the doorway as his farewell gesture.

It's good? He asked Ol' Ma, although his voice held no conviction.

He had talked to Fanny about Pittwater. She hadn't liked it.

'You promised,' she had said, cradling the baby. 'You promised to look after us. How you going to do that in the middle of nowhere?'

And so, he had stayed in Sydney Town, doing his rounds, but without his job and without his protection. Ever decreasing circles. Around and around.

¬

August 1811

The brothel had none of the luxury of those he had once seen in England. No piano music trickled through the walls, just the grunting and groaning of women at work, and men at pleasure, of blustering flirtations and obliging giggles. John raised a glass to the whore who sat across from him. 'Get me another before I go, will you.'

Time and again he had broached the idea of leaving town, but Fanny had put her foot down. She was not running off into the bush to be killed by savages or mauled by wild animals or starve to death. She was not taking her boys to follow some wild dream of his. He would just have to find a job like every other man.

He had been lucky to find work as a policeman, patrolling the streets from Surry Hills to The Rocks, keeping the streets safe – ensuring the brothels did not sell spirits and shopkeepers were protected. It offered opportunities for a thinking man.

And if at times he wondered who he was or thought of that dancing bear he had once seen, going around and around on his chain, he could think of no other way to be.

Only in his quiet moments did he allow himself to dream of a finger of land that beckoned to him, and a bay that sparkled with a million promises.

'You leaving early tonight, John?'

'Bit of business.'

'Thought we were your business.'

He smiled. 'Love my job.'

He usually spent his shifts at one brothel or another, and though he did not avail himself of the girls – Fanny would kill him – it was as good a way as any other to earn a quid.

The cold hit him as he stepped into the alley, enough to keep people inside and close to their fires. Only rats and roaches would be creeping along the streets tonight. He didn't want any idle onlookers, no lovers walking hand in hand, or brawling drunks or gangs of youths out looking for a lark. No, he needed this malevolent wind and the moon hidden behind the clouds. He scuttled down George Street towards the harbour and its warehouses stocked with iron and steel, timber and coal, which he was paid to guard.

When he reached his meeting point, he sheltered in a laneway, pulled out a pocket watch he had purloined from a drunk, and squinted to make out the time in the dark. Still early. He settled himself down with the rodents and roaches to wait.

He heard them coming, the muffled sound of horses' hooves wrapped in cloth, the rattle of a wagon, hushed whispers, a cough and a rebuke.

'Over here.' He stepped from his shelter, shivering as the wind hit him anew. 'Got the money?'

It was coal they were after. Unmarked and easy to trade, it had been shipped from Newcastle to be stored until sold. John had already broken open the bolt with his machete and would stand guard while they loaded the wagon. Tomorrow it would be for sale on the streets, a hundred small boys employed to push their barrows, a hundred housewives filling their sacks, gossiping about the bargain. Tomorrow he would have meat in his stew, and new jumpers for the boys, and coal in his hearth.

It was still dark when he finally snuck back into his home. Fanny lay curled up in bed; her snores from a stuffed-up nose were rhythmic and even.

The fire had died down, but there were enough embers to relight it if he piled the coal just right. It would make her day a little easier if she woke to a warm room, and, a thought struck him, water already boiling in the pot. He filled the kettle, hung it above the fire and snuggled down next to her.

'John.' Fanny's voice came from a long way away, taking its time to break through his dreams.

'John, it's me, Thomas. You gotta get up, man.' A different voice, louder and more urgent.

John sat up. He scratched his head, rubbed bleary eyes, blinked and tried to wake. 'What do yer want?' He squinted to make out the form in the doorway.

Thomas was in his police uniform, a look of excitement in his eyes. 'I'm sorry, mate. Come to bring you in. You're in shit trouble.' He shook his head as if he were truly regretful, but couldn't pull it off. He was enjoying himself.

The two walked through streets, jostled by Saturday morning crowds, and screwing up their noses at the refuse of a Friday night.

'Don't think they're going to charge you. Don't think they'll do that. Just your name keeps coming up. Black Randall this, Black Randall that.'

They arrived at the courthouse that served as the police station and where the magistrate who employed them could be found. Stomping up the worn steps, moving from the light into familiar darkness, John felt the echoes of previous visits. His stomach churned, and he took a deep breath. *Ahh fuck. Should have been more careful.* But, he argued, his pay barely covered his rent and he had a family of four to feed. He swallowed. *Just been doing what I can.*

They waited on a bench in a dark corner of the room while court was held, and then they waited some more while the magistrate had his lunch, and then retired to his office. They watched important men go in and out, shuffling papers, conversing in deep and serious tones, not deigning to give them a glance. As the minutes and hours ticked by, John felt the weight of his insignificance. His temper flared. 'Tell him he can come get me when he's ready,' he growled at Thomas, and stood to go, but it was a feeble attempt to assert himself, and he sat again once his friend put a steadying hand upon his arm.

The workday was all but over and the streets outside growing dark before they were called in to see the magistrate. With a nod, he dismissed Thomas.

John forced himself to stand tall, his hands clasped behind his back, his face impassive, while the magistrate fumbled through some papers. 'I don't see any value in dragging this out, Randall. You have held a sacred role that requires men of honesty and integrity. They are qualities you lack. It seems, however that you do have the fortunate knack of engendering loyalty in those you mix with, and so I do not have the evidence I need to convict you.' He looked up. 'When I do, you will be charged as the felon I believe you are. Is that understood?'

John nodded. He wasn't to be charged.

'As it is I am relieving you of your office henceforth. You are dismissed.'

He took the long way home. He knew Fanny would be waiting for news but he needed his heart to stop pounding, his fingers to stop trembling. No pay, no rent, no food. No coal or firewood. He shivered. It was dastardly cold. He needed a plan to present to Fanny so that he didn't have to watch the colour fade from her face. He went through the list of everyone he knew, those who might have something for him: those who could be bullied, who owed him, or who liked him.

Chapter Fifty-Five

1814

How long since I been here? Had money to buy myself a rum? Shout my mates a beer?

John scowled as he shoved through the crowded tavern, ignoring the curses and spilling drinks as he passed. None stepped aside obligingly or shook hands or greeted him with a hearty clap on the back.

A glance at his bare feet and the patched shirt, told its own story. He drew himself up taller, held his head higher and steeled his eyes against any ill-considered remarks about his fall from grace.

The man he sought sat alone at a bench in a far corner, claiming a respectful space in the jostling, noisy crowd. John headed toward him and, at a nod, sat down.

'Ahh. Randall, good of you to come. What's your preference, rum or wine?' Campbell signalled the barmaid. John liked the man, had traded with him in happier days and knew him as a merchant who dealt fairly. He had an open, honest face. Large heavy-set eyes took the world seriously and right now they looked at John with earnest consideration. His mouth, generous in both size and demeanour, did not ask that humiliating question, 'How are you?' but paid John the respect of coming straight to the point. 'I understand your farm is for sale? What are your plans?'

After he had been dismissed from the constabulary, John had borrowed and begged to buy a plot of land, not far from his original grant. He had bent his back to the task but failed to make repayments. Everything was to be auctioned, every stick of furniture, every pot and pan. His family would soon be destitute. He had no plans.

John squirmed. The room felt too hot and stuffy and suddenly he needed some fresh air. 'Not sure my plans are your business.' He put a hand to his eagle, seeking support in the familiar movement, but unable to control the despair of his thoughts. *Ain't got much more to my name than when I was five and got fewer dreams.* He stood to leave.

Campbell raised a restraining arm, thanked the barmaid who had returned with two tankards of rum and pushed one towards John. 'You're right, of course. I apologise. What I really want to know is if you are in a position to work for me. You're a bit of a legend, you know. Weren't you with Governor Phillip when he first explored Pittwater?'

John pulled his bench closer to that of Campbell, and nodded for him to continue, trying not to let his desperation show. They talked. The barmaid refilled their jugs, served both rum and wine and, when it got darker, large bowls of broth and crusty bread. They became more animated and leaned in closer across the table, their foreheads almost touching. Occasionally John laughed, throwing back his head, his face lit up with some old memory, or he pounded the table to make a point.

When he left the pub, it was with a wobble in his step. He rehearsed the words he would use to tell Fanny that he was dragging her to the middle of nowhere. *It's not like the last time. I'm to manage his property. This is something I can do. A house. A good wage. Monthly provisions. You'll love this place, the most beautiful place in the world. The boys can swim in the river.*

¬

John dragged Fanny up the rock by one hand, while she shrieked and laughed, and tottered and slipped. 'Stop it, John. Let me be.' But finally, she stood sure-footed beside him.

Today had been their first opportunity to explore after settling into their new home, and he had brought Fanny to this spot, perhaps the very same rocky crest from where he had first looked down at Pittwater.

The view was unchanged: the broad expanse of water, three rivers, that wonderful finger of land, beckoning him. He breathed in, savouring the air, warm and alive with the smells of the forest, and leant his back against the ancient tree. He knew these trees as gods, guardians of the earth. And in the noisy silence of the woods, amid the lazy creaking of branches and rustle of foliage, he hoped they were welcoming him home.

'It's beautiful,' Fanny whispered.

They stood in dappled light beneath a canopy of leaves. He stroked her hair. He had always thought it a mousey brown, but caught in the sun, it gleamed as if threaded with gold.

She is right. I have never truly looked at her.

And he touched a hand to her chin, raising it that he might see her more clearly. She laughed and then quieted, returning his gaze, grey eyes steady. *She trusts me.* It was a baffling thought – it had been a long time since he had trusted himself. *And she loves me.* And unexpectedly, his eyes burned hot and he blinked away the tears that had come unbidden. *And I do love her.*

A grumbling, like thunder scratched at the edge of his awareness. Impending doom prickled his thoughts. Like a startled deer, caught in the lights of those clear all seeing eyes, he froze, his heart pounding in furious, startled panic.

With a strangled sob, he drew himself tall and stood against his mother. *I'm not you. I won't live like you.* She had owned him since Mary's death. But it was time now. Time to be free.

He had known it was coming. Had been preparing for it. He had just needed the right place.

A ray of light struggled through the canopy of leaves. John raised his face to it, feeling the warmth on his face. His breathing slowed. *And anyway. You did love me. You were just too scared to show it.*

He smiled down at Fanny who was looking at him, a question on her face.

And now, he thought, *it's time to be master of my own fate. Not Master Randall's nor the Lieutenant's. Time to be me.*

He raised his hands to trace the gold in Fanny's hair. He followed the lines of her cheek, down to her mouth. 'I do love you.' This time he said it out loud. For her to hear. And let the gods hear it too.

'I know.'

I'll look after you. Always.'

'You always have.'

John nodded. A lump in his throat. From the moment he had first come here, nearly twenty-five years ago, this place had called him. It had taken so long.

'You're different here.' Fanny broke the silence.

He lay a kiss on her head.

It's good?

John smiled at Ol' Ma's voice.

'John, you alright? What's the matter?' Fanny was looking at him, a puzzled look on her face.

John raised his eyes, his fingers playing with the carving he wore around his neck. 'I'm good.' And smiled.

They returned home at dusk, caught in a spring shower. John stopped to breathe in the smell of the earth, rich and pungently alive, before stepping inside the door. 'The ground smells better after rain,' he said to no one in particular.

He turned as something clattered to the ground. His flute rolled along the wooden floor; his son, George, was pretending not to have heard it, and not to have dropped it in his haste to hide it. He looked up at his father and turned away quickly as if bracing himself for a clout across the head.

'I told you not to touch that!' John barked and the child stiffened. *The apple doesn't fall far from the tree*, people said when father and son were together and for a moment John could see himself: long-limbed, graceful features and eyes that burned with resentment. *And wipe that look from your eyes.* The words came from across the years.

Time for miracles, Ol' Ma whispered.

John held the boy's eyes, struggling to actually see him. They had been Fanny's responsibility and mouths to feed, and he wondered that it had taken so long for him to truly see him.

'He's been teaching himself to play.' Fanny had come to his side, picked up the flute and handed it to him. 'Haven't you noticed how carefully he watches you when you play?'

John frowned. He heard the notes of Elijah's music and felt the scratch of his whiskers on his chin. 'How old are you? Eight?' he asked his son.

The boy nodded. 'Thomas is six.' He gestured to his younger brother with the formality of introducing a stranger. Then, as if he didn't know what else to say, 'Eliza's one.' The baby made herself known by banging on a pot, 'Mumumum.'

John nodded. 'I was five when I learnt to play. I can teach you if you like.' He pointed towards the front step. 'It's better in the moonlight.' He smiled.

John settled George into his lap, placed the child's fingers on the flute, his own arms wrapped around him, and guided him in the way of the music. Small, tentative notes whispered through the forest, while the ancient trees murmured around them. *But they will get stronger*, thought John.

January 1816

Rain drummed on the corrugated iron roof. A leak dripped into a bucket positioned beneath with a steady plop. A single lamp flickered in the breeze from the open door but its light was warm and yellow and comfortable. The family lounged on the mattresses in a room still stifling from the heat of the day. They had eaten early and might have slept, for John had taken the boys fishing and they had walked far and were tired, but there was magic in being sheltered on a wild night in a wilderness and it kept them awake.

'Tell us a story, John.' Fanny had pulled George's head onto her lap and was scouring his scalp for lice. She couldn't know how the image resonated back in time, to other nights in another country. John could feel the fingers stalking through his own hair.

'You won't hear nothin' over the rain.'

'We can draw close.' She smiled at him and shuffled the boys into a circle.

'Ol' Ma loved the one about an African chief and his friend Adisa. Always tellin' me that one, she was.'

'Go on.' Fanny scratched at her son's head, a gentle, soothing touch that had his eyelids fluttering, fighting sleep. He wanted to hear the story.

'This friend, Adisa, he used to say that everything was good. Didn't matter what happened. All good.'

'Did bad things ever happen?' George asked.

'They did.'

'Then why did he say it was good?' Thomas screwed up his face.

'Taken me a while to work out that one myself.' John sat silent, watching Fanny at her work, enjoying the scepticism on the faces of the boys. 'Are you going to let me tell the story or not?'

Epilogue

Dear John,

I have lost you.

I read that your boys both drowned, off the beach at Manly. I wonder how much loss one man can absorb. You have had too much.

We hear nothing about you after that. I picture you disappearing into the forest, like a wraith. And then you are no more.

Fanny returns in 1822. Homeless and destitute she is unable to support her two black-haired, dark-skinned daughters and is forced to place them into an orphanage, just for a short time. I assume that this was the year of your death.

As I write this last letter, I am in a shed, much the same as you might have built, in the middle of a forest and listening to the night settle itself. The same galaxy of stars looks down upon me. As you may have, I send them my dreams.

This is my healing place, where I can be the most me I can be. This is where I have come to mourn you.

I hope your gods healed you, that they softened the callous of your heart and that you found yourself. I hope you were kind to Fanny and a good father to your girls.

I wish I could include that in your story and restore the young John. I honour you for your resilience and the strength of your spirit. I have loved you and I celebrate you. But you have wreaked havoc on me. I am burnt from grasping those coals.

And now I grieve for you.

Jo

An Apology: A letter to John

Dear John,

Dawn is breaking. Moments ago, a single bird fractured the quiet with a haunting melody. She sang alone for a while before others joined her in a rousing chorus of songs and cries, twitters, chirps and tweets that announced the dawn in glorious and chaotic harmony. You would have heard this in your time. It wouldn't have changed.

I do that a lot: collect the 'dawn chorus' of your life, those events we might genuinely share. But that is fabrication. We don't share them. It is an impossible task to know how you may have responded to even the simplest, purest event. I can't know.

After seven years of research, knowing, or thinking I know, every battle you fought, the women you married, where you lived, how tall you were, what crimes you committed, what crimes you were accused of, I have enough material to draw a stick figure. And maybe not even that. For even as I write, new information is found, conjectures are made. How did you escape to England? Who really was the mother of Frances? Some say she was an Indigenous woman. And we have no information on Fanny. They say that she, too, might have been Indigenous.

I wish we could talk, but we can't.

And so, I make things up. With the best of motives, with the most accurate information, with as much authenticity and moral integrity I can find, I weave a tale of lies.

I thought to honour you. Yours was an extraordinary life and needs to be told. I am so very grateful to you for the risks you took, the choices you made. Your survival is mine. Your genes are mine. I truly want to thank you.

So, it worries me that I take your name. I take the bones of your life. I take these and dress them with stories and characters, motives and perceptions I think are reasonable, given the circumstances. However, I have hijacked your identity in the process.

I hope you forgive me. I hope I have your blessing.

Yours Sincerely,

Jo

Acknowledgements

I wish to acknowledge the people of the Eora nation, and the 29 clan groups that exist within the Sydney region. They are the traditional owners of this land. The day the First Fleet, with John Randall, my great (x6) grandfather on board as an unwilling passenger, sailed through the heads to settle a colony, was a day of invasion, whether they understood that or not.

Black Randall makes some, but limited, reference to the Indigenous people of this land. Theirs is not my story to tell. However, much as I celebrate John's resilience and love this country, the place I call home, I recognise and mourn the impact of that day and the horrors that followed.

I began researching my family history and John Randall's life in the 1990s, finding and seizing small nuggets of information to add to my hoard. Cassandra Pybus's extraordinary work, *The Unknown Story of Australia's First Black Settlers* first pulled things together for me

I have spent hours, days, weeks and years burrowing down rabbit holes to ensure authenticity to this manuscript. I wish to acknowledge the various historical societies for their generous support: the New York Historical Society, the Charlestown Historical Society, Manchester Historical Society. Also, the many books, fiction and non-fiction, that allowed me to enter John's world, and my researcher in England. A list of these sources, is provided at the end

However, much as I enjoyed this aspect of the writing, my purpose was not to break historical ground, but to 'find' John. I needed to stick a toe in the muck of his experiences, explore the roots of his resilience, the costs of his survival. I wanted to move from the cerebral knowledge of his life to the experience of it.

I thought I could write. I couldn't. Seems that business reports do not segue into a creative writing career. I was also terrified. Simply opening a laptop sent my brain into paralysis.

So, I took myself off to the University of the Sunshine Coast to complete a Master of Professional Practice (Creative Writing) and loved every moment of it. I am deeply grateful to Dr Shelley Davidow and Dr Paul Williams for their extraordinary patience, commitment, and encouragement. I'm mildly surprised neither are raging alcoholics, for I'm sure there were moments that tested their sobriety.

Our final projects were assessed by Dr Melanie Myers, award-winning author of *Meet Me at Lennons*. I found myself looking forward to her critique. Tough and uncompromising, she was also unfailingly instructive and encouraging. I was in awe of her.

On graduation, I knew I was not ready to fly, and so, in a state of high anxiety, I approached her for mentoring. That was four years ago, and I am indebted to her skill and wisdom, and grateful to call her friend. Other than me, there is no one who has been more invested in ensuring *Black Randall* does justice to the man. Nor can I count the number of times she has yanked me out of a hole of despair. I don't think she signed on for that.

Melanie suggested that I contact author and editor Angela Meyer, for a manuscript assessment. I am very grateful for Angela's guidance and encouragement. Again, her generosity and support was so much more than I could ever have expected.

Finally, I need to thank my beta writers, those friends and fellow budding authors who read my chapters, made suggestions, shared my tears, and kept me going over the years. In no order, Lee, Melinda, Richard.

Inspirations:

Black Founders, Cassandra Pybus

1788, Watkins Tench

1788 The brutal truth of the First Fleet, David Hill

The First Fleet, Robert Mundle

The Colony, A history of early Sydney, Grace Karsk

On slavery

The Underground Railroad, Colson Whitehead

The Book of Negroes, Lawrence Hill

Incidents in the Life of a Slave Girl, Harriet Jacobs

Narrative of the Life of Frederick Douglass, by Frederick Douglass

Beloved, Toni Morrison

The War of Independence

The Glorious Cause, Jeff Shara

My Brother Sam is Dead, James Lincoln Collier, Christopher Collier

Civil War Drummer Boy, John Lincoln Clem

New York, Edward Rutherford

Manchester

The Manchester Man, Mrs G Linnaeus Banks

Jo Braithwaite is the great (x6) granddaughter of John Randall, a slave of African heritage, born in Connecticut in 1763, who was also on the First Fleet to Australia. Her family lived in Carlingford Sydney, a suburb once known as Dixieland, where many convicts of African descent settled, and where John Randall was granted land on his release. In fact Jo was married within metres of where he stood surveying his land, thinking of the descendants who would be free because of his actions.

She has an MA Professional Practice (Creative Writing) Program at the University of the Sunshine Coast and an MA in Behavioural Psychology (Macquarie University).

An excerpt of Black Randall was published in the international magazine for emerging authors, Embark Literary Magazine.